Magic City Murder Déjà Vu

By R. Earl Muir

Magic City Murder

Déjà Vu

By R. Earl Muir

First Edition

First Printing, 2019

Book Design by Robert Patterson

Cover Design by REBOB Art

Cover Photograph by Larry O. Gay

Final Cover Design and Production by Natasha Walsh

Proofreading and Editing by Dr. Jesse R. Hale, PhD

ISBIN: 978-0-9600383-0-5

Shades Creek Press, LLC

Printed in United States of America

Magic City Murder

Déjà Vu

By R. Earl Muir

Shades Creek Press, LLC
www.shadescreekpress.com

ACKNOWLEDGEMENTS

This is a work of fiction, but many of the historical facts and persons depicted are real and were accurately represented to the best of my knowledge and ability. The historical accounts depicted in this book would not have been possible except for the countless reporters, newspapers and court records that were meticulously saved and stored by the Birmingham Public Library and others.

My research was made much easier by BHAMWIKI and to those that create and maintain the content of that great site, I am forever grateful.

Also, as mentioned in the book, valuable resources for historical content were found in two books. First, ***The Hawes Horror***, by Goldsmith B. West, 1888, Birmingham, Alabama and secondly, ***The Birmingham Horrors***, by W. Stanley Hoole, 1980, Huntsville, Alabama: the Strode Publishers.

I am also indebted to a number of people who served to help as proofreaders, editors and provided guidance in this project including my wife, Pam and friends, Ethel Morgan Smith, Randy Hale, Evan Owen and Mike Perez.

Their encouragement and advice was both needed and uplifting through the process and I could never adequately express my gratitude.

Finally, I would be remiss if I didn't acknowledge the great City of Birmingham. Its history is complex and compelling and I cannot imagine living anywhere else in the world.

DEDICATION

This book is dedicated to three women that are responsible for my ability to write it and my love for history and telling stories.

First, my mother Ruth Parker Patterson, who always encouraged my imagination and taught me that all people are important. Her sacrifices set me on a path for a great life.

Secondly, Ms. Suzanne Boles Burnett, who as a young college graduate in her first year as a teacher at Hueytown High School, inspired and encouraged a goofy sophomore by simply telling me that my writing was good. She introduced me to creative writing and showed me the power of the written word to both entertain and inform. Although I only spent one year there, her guidance and encouragement took root and flourished decades later and I will be forever grateful.

And finally, my beautiful and devoted wife, Pamela Muir Patterson, who has been by my side since second grade. As I continue to explore what I want to be when I grow up, she is always with me. Encouraging and guiding me. Never afraid to step out with me into the unknown. Always serving as moderator, advisor, mentor, encourager and defender depending on my situation. Words can never express what her inspiration and partnership have meant and continue to mean to

Chapter 1

Friday December 4, 2017 Birmingham, Alabama

When the phone rang, Fay Findlay was already awake and running through her to-do list in her mind while waiting for the alarm to sound. It was Friday and her alarm was set for 6 AM.

As her iPhone sounded, she looked her iWatch in its charger on the bedside table – 5:42. The phone would only ring at that time for work, which meant that any plans for the weekend would likely be wrecked.

Fay Findlay was a Lieutenant with Birmingham Police Department and headed the Special Crimes Unit (SCU), a small squad of five detectives, including her, that worked all major crimes in the city, and when the caseload permitted, the unit worked cold cases – mainly homicides.

Birmingham, Alabama is the largest city in the state with a population of about 250,000 although the metro area, which included more than 40 other municipalities and unincorporated areas, is about 1.3 million.

Fay picked up her ringing phone from the bedside table and the name on the screen verified what she already knew -- It was work. The display read **Nate Parker**. Fay hit the answer button, "What's up, Nate?

"Sorry to wake you up early boss, but we have a potential case and I wanted to alert you ASAP," Detective Sergeant Nate Parker answered.

Fay sat up in the bed, "Potential? What the hell does that mean?"

Parker took a deep breath and tried to explain, "Well, we have a body and I got called out and for the same reason I got called, I thought you should know. CSI is still mapping the scene and shooting photos, but Daniels was the homicide detective on call so he was the first detective on the scene."

Parker was pacing the edge of scene as he watched the Crime Scene Investigation Team work. "Like me, he has sat in on your Investigation Classes more than once so as soon as he got to the scene and saw what he had, he called me," he added.

Fay headed to the bathroom feeling both confused and intrigued. "Okay, do we have multiple victims or what? And what does my class have to do with it?"

Parker continued to explain, "No, there is only one body as far as we know. It is a little girl, probably 8 -10 years old. The body is floating in East Lake," hesitating for another brief moment, Parker took a deep breath, "and it's December 4th."

Fay was reaching into the shower to turn it on when she heard those words. Startled, she almost dropped the phone and then leaned against the bathroom counter, "Holy Shit!"

Parker was relieved to get it out, "Yeah, I know your philosophy about 'no such thing as a coincidence', so I called… which is the same reason Daniels called me. He said he got here and started making his notes and it hit him as recorded the date."

Fay regained her composure as her mind raced, "I'll be headed there in a minute. Is the M.E. there yet?"

Parker was relieved that his boss was okay with his call, "Yep, they are waiting for CSI to finish with the photos, which it looks like they are, so they'll be removing the body in a minute."

Parker noticed the team seemed to be wrapping up and the coroner was donning new gloves. "Dan Jacobs is the M.E. here. He went out with CSI in the boat to take a look. He said, his best guess is that she's been dead for less than 16 hours maybe. No signs of other injuries, but of course, he can't tell much until they get her out."

Fay was gathering clothes from the closet, "Okay. I'm jumping in the shower now. I will be there in 30 minutes."

As the hot water ran over her, Fay's mind couldn't help but run through the story that was the opening of her *Intro to Investigation* class that she taught both at the BPD Academy and the expanded version she taught for University of Alabama at Birmingham Criminal Justice students.

The Hawes Murders were one the first major cases to confront the Birmingham Police Department when the city was only 17 years old. It was both intriguing and complex and because of the nature of the crime, it garnered national attention. While technically it was a closed case, it was still intriguing and debated more than a hundred years later.

Chapter 2

Tuesday, December 4, 1888 Birmingham, Alabama

Just after 11 in the morning on that chilly day, Officers Jack Pinkerton and Robert Carlisle of the Birmingham Police Department were dispatched to East Lake where a body had been discovered floating in the lake.

East Lake was a recreational area and new community about 7 miles east of the city. Birmingham, incorporated as a city just 17 years ago, was a city growing and expanding rapidly. Founded along the rail lines in central Alabama near what had formerly been known as Jones Valley and the town of Elyton. Just three decades ago the area was totally occupied by large farms and plantations. The discovery of all the needed ingredients for steel – coal and iron ore, along with other natural resources such as water and an abundance of limestone, made the area perfect for fueling the industrial age and the nation's need for steel. The railways solidified the assurance that Birmingham would become a large city in short time.

Planners and developers laid out the city streets in a grid centered by the main rail lines. As ore mines developed along the ridges of Red Mountain, and coal mines to the south and west, the valley to the north become the new city of Birmingham.

The area developed so quickly that often deeds to property were bought and sold on the courthouse steps, sometimes trading multiple times in a single day and escalating in price with each transaction. The city was dubbed the Magic City for its seemingly overnight growth.

As the city grew, all sorts of businesses developed to support the mining and steel industry along with other businesses to service the ever-increasing population. Workers flocked to the new city. Immigrants and farm workers alike made there way to the Magic City in hopes of a better life with good steady jobs. As the workers came so did businesses to support the population influx. Along with legitimate businesses also came saloons, whorehouses, gamblers and swindlers.

City planners not only laid out a very well planned city center, they also developed areas for that growing work force to live and enjoy recreation. On the southern edge of the city the Lakeview area contained a large man-made lake with an island in the middle. Just beyond the lake on the hill was a large hotel and casino. Along the lake were pavilions and boat docks where city residents and visitors could rent boats and enjoy the outdoors.

Nearby was a ballpark where baseball games were a regular occurrence with teams from various communities in and around the city. In 1873 it also served as the site of the very first football game between teams from the University of Alabama and Auburn University (then known as the Agricultural and Mechanical College of Alabama). The rivalry game between the state's two largest schools was contested in the city for decades earning the name, the Iron Bowl.

About seven miles east of the city was East Lake. This man-made lake, about 30 acres in size, also had pavilions and boating docks. The area surrounding the recreational park was developing as modest suburban community, dubbed Eastlake, for those who preferred being away from the bustle of the city.

Both East Lake and Lakeview were served by the trolley system that provided public transportation within the city and to surrounding areas. Spur lines that ran out of the city to these recreational enclaves were referred to as dummy lines since the routes ended at their destination. Initially, trolleys were pulled by mules along the tracks and later steam engines were used and eventually electric streetcars.

When Officers Pinkerton and Carlisle arrived at the east end of East Lake they saw a small crowd of 40-50 people, mostly women, had gathered in one of the pavilions.

The officers were immediately met by Coroner Alfred Babbitt. "Good Morning, Officers! The body is here," pointing toward the gathered crowd at the pavilion. As the trio made their way through the crowd the officers saw the small, lifeless body of a small girl laid out on one of the picnic tables. The girl was pale white with light brown curly hair. She was dressed in a neat blue dress with a plaid flannel underskirt. Black socks and black button shoes adorned her feet. She was about four feet tall, slim in stature and appeared to be about 10 years old.

Babbitt continued, "Two young boys discovered the body floating over there," pointing to the eastern edge of the lake. "They were in a boat and saw the body and got close enough to see what it was. They were quiet frightened and hurried to shore to tell the adults."

"I was summoned and arrived just as those two fellows were arriving at shore with the body," Babbitt continued pointing two gentlemen standing nearby. "I have taken a preliminary look and don't see any obvious signs of injury. She appears to have drowned. I've sent for Dr. Cunningham to meet me at the office."

"Do we know who she is?" Carlisle interrupted.

Babbitt removed his hat and answered, "That is the odd thing. All these people have taken a look and no one seems to recognize the child. Most of these ladies live in the neighborhood and have children but no one can place the girl."

"Perhaps she is one the news girls from town?" Pinkerton interjected.

"They usually stay in town. I've never seen any of those hooligans out here. I suppose it is possible though," Carlisle replied.

"Mr. Miller is here for the body. He will take the child to his place for further examination and preparation. Once she is ready, we will notify the newspapers so that they can write something for the morning and see if we can identify who she belongs to," Babbitt said.

The lifeless body of the child was carefully removed by the undertakers of Messrs. Lockwood and Miller and placed in the curtained wagon.

Upon arrival at the mortuary office, Dr. Cunningham performed the initial examination of the child and then summoned Dr. H.S. Duncan to assist.

Chapter 3

Wednesday, December 5, 1888

The morning papers announced the gruesome discovery of the dead child found floating in East Lake. The *Birmingham Daily Herald* wrote, "There may develop something today. If it does not, then foul play must have been brought to bear, or else the child has run away from home outside of the city. The case is indeed a sad and complicated one."

The newspaper also reported that the body of the child would be available for viewing at Lockwood and Miller's in hopes of someone being able to identify the child. No one had reported a child missing.

From the early morning, a steady stream of people processed by the body, each one stopping to take a long and careful look at the child. Some wept for the child, while others showed no emotion as they gazed at the lifeless child before them.

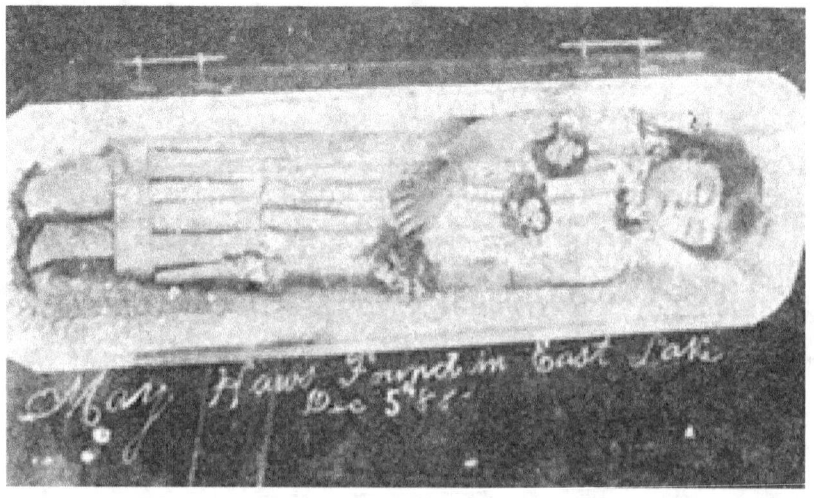

The crowd was occupied by a variety of citizens of all ages, colors and economic standings. Some didn't recognize the child. Others claimed that while she looked very familiar, although they couldn't quiet place where they had seen her. As the lunch hour passed, more than a thousand people had viewed the body but no one had yet identified the little girl.

Finally, around 2 in the afternoon a local butcher, Mr. W.O. Franklin, filed through and immediately recognized the girl. He told the Coroner, "I know the girl well. Her name is May. May Hawes. She is the daughter of Richard Hawes. He is a locomotive engineer at Georgia-Pacific. They live over near the ballpark in Lakeview."

"Do you remember when you last saw the girl?" Babbitt asked.

"Yes, she came to my shop Saturday for some meat" Franklin answered. "She told me that her father was leaving that evening for Meridian, Mississippi and that she along her mother and brother and sister was to join him in a few days."

The butcher explained that a neighbor had told him the family's house was cleared out on Monday so he assumed they had moved to Mississippi as the child described. "The child was very keen and mature for her age. She did a lot to care for her younger sister and brother."

With the child now tentatively identified, Officers Carlisle and Pinkerton, along with Sheriff Deputy W.L. Truss went to the neighborhood adjacent to the ballpark and spoke with neighbors of the Hawes family. Several neighbors and others familiar to the family confirmed the identity of the child. However, the story about the family moving to Mississippi was not as certain.

The Hawes modest cottage was indeed void of any furnishings. There were a few belongings strewn about but nothing that gave the officers reason to suspect a crime or anything other than a family that had moved out. The officers gathered information about the family and heard several conflicting accounts of where they were going and when, but no one remembered seeing any of them since the weekend.

Officers learned that the father, Richard or Dick Hawes, worked as a locomotive engineer with the Georgia-Pacific Railway and was often gone for days at a time. The wife and mother was Emma Hawes. The couple had three children - Mamie, also known as May, who was about 10. Her sister, Irene, about age 7, and brother Willie, about age 5.

As the officers compared notes, the stories they gathered ranged widely, from the wife and children leaving for a trip to Atlanta, Georgia, while another had them heading to visit relatives in the Midwest, either Missouri or Illinois. Another account said the girls were being placed in a convent in Mobile and only the boy and his mother were moving. Others said that the couple was divorced and that Mr. Hawes had moved to a boarding house on 2nd Avenue last month. Another common theme with almost all the accounts was that, either married or divorced, the Hawes marriage was not a happy one.

The neighbors reported that fighting could often be heard coming from the house and May often took the other children from the house to the ballpark when things were volatile. It also seemed to be common knowledge that Mrs. Hawes had a drinking problem, often appearing intoxicated.

At the end of the day, while a lot of information had been gathered, the officers were no closer to finding out what happened to May Hawes nor how she ended up in East Lake. Plus, there was also no information as to where any of the other family members were.

There were many leads to follow but in 1888, that was a slow process. Not only were there no computer networks and Internet resources, telephones were not even common. The seven-mile trek from downtown to East Lake took almost an hour on the trolley, and much longer if one walked or arrived by horse.

That evening, Coroner Babbitt convened the Coroner's Jury in his office at the rear of Lockwood and Miller Undertakers, located at 1822 2nd Avenue North. The facts and evidence gathered by the police was presented along with the testimony of various individuals connected to the case and the Hawes family. As the jury convened, police and deputies continued to gather evidence, track down leads and search for the missing family.

Dr. Cunningham was the first to testify. He stated that he had performed the autopsy and failed to find any evidence of violence on the body, saying, "It is my opinion that the child died from drowning."

Dr. H. S. Duncan testified that he knew the deceased as the child of Mrs. Emma Hawes who lived near the baseball park. "I was once called to the home to attend to Mrs. Dawes who appeared to be recovering from a protracted case of debauch. The little girl seem to be her only nurse," the Doctor said.

Eliza Johnson, a black woman, testified she was familiar with the family having furnished them with meals for a time. Her testimony confirmed that she recognized the deceased as the oldest child, May Hawes. She further testified that it was common knowledge that Mrs. Hawes was a hard drinker and was often impaired.

Mr. Charles S. Chapman testified that the Hawes family had purchased a sewing machine from him on installment. First, Mr. Chapman testified that he recognized the deceased as May Hawes. He went on to explain his most recent calling to the family. "On Monday (December 3) I went the Hawes house to collect payment. I saw May there but none of the rest of the family. Fanny Bryant, who is often there doing chores was also there and told me that neither Mr.

nor Mrs. Hawes were there. She told me that Mr. Hawes was staying in the city at a boarding house." Chapman pulled a paper from his vest pocket and read, "at 2313 2nd Avenue. She also told me that she heard Mrs. Hawes and the other two children had gone to Atlanta, but that I should check with Mr. Hawes about that. I spoke with some of the neighbors outside and they informed me that the furniture had been removed from the Hawes house on Saturday. Mr. Hawes had reported to them that it was headed to the auctioneer. The neighbors also informed me that Mr. and Mrs. Hawes were divorced, but when Mrs. Hawes made arrangements for the sewing machine she informed me that she was married to Richard Hawes."

Chapman continued, "I went to the boarding house on 2nd Avenue that evening and found Mr. Hawes and the sewing machine. Mr. Hawes signed a lease for it and paid $5.00 in cash."

The Coroner then asked Chapman if he knew the whereabouts of Mr. or Mrs. Hawes at the present time. "No Sir, I don't know for sure. I assume that Mrs. Hawes was in Atlanta as Fanny told me. I also heard that Mr. Hawes was to be married in Columbus, Mississippi on this day, but I have no idea of whether that is true."

The small office was packed with those called to testify and others that were simple curious to find out more about the case. Several reporters were seated at the front and took notes with each testimony. The room was full to capacity and others stood outside the door trying to hear and get a look inside at the proceedings.

Luther W. Randall was called and he identified the corpse as that of the child, May Hawes. He further testified, "Dick Hawes told Riley, my Brother-in-Law, that Mrs. Hawes had gone to Indiana. He said he gave her $500 but he still had money in the bank. He said that he had sent his two girls to a convent and that his boy was still here with him."

"And when did Mr. Hawes make these statements to your brother-in-law?" asked the Coroner.

"That would have been last Thursday (November 30)," answered Randall.

Fanny Bryant, a mixed-race woman, who often cooked and cleaned for the Hawes family was next to testify. The Coroner asked the witness, "Fanny, tell us how you know the Hawes family."

Bryant appeared nervous but quietly answered, "I know Mrs. Hawes, but not her husband. I live near there and washed for her and waited on her."

"And when did you last see Mrs. Hawes?" The Coroner asked.

"Well, that would be on last Saturday. She was packing things up Friday and Saturday. She said to me, 'Now you be sure and come back tomorrow, Fanny and help finish'."

"And did you return on Sunday?" the Coroner inquired.

"Yes Sir, I did. I went over there about 9 o'clock in the morning but she wasn't there. The little girl and the daddy were in the house. The little girl told me her mama had gone off. She said she got mad about her Papa sending Willie off to Atlanta and said she was gonna go get him back."

Coroner Babbitt pressed on, "The girl to which you refer, would that be the dead child here?"

Bryant lowered her eyes and spoke softly, "Yes, sir. Miss Mamie. They called her May."

"She came over to my house later on Sunday afternoon and I carried her back home," Bryant continued. "When I took her home, Mr. Hawes asked me to come back and help them finish packing the pictures and things. He told me that his wife, Emma would probably return soon."

"Did you go back to help?" Babbitt asked.

"Yes sir. I was there about seven Monday morning. Him and May was the only ones there. He said he was gonna take May to his place at the boarding house. Then he asked May what she gonna do when he brung in his girl and asked her if she would call her Mama. May said she would call her Mama. Mr. Hawes then told her it would be a little while before she saw her. He said, 'I am gong to send you to a school.' Mr. Hawes asked me how much I would charge him to work for him and his girl. He said he gonna be bringing his girl to the boarding house to live."

The Coroner was taking notes on occasion and then continued his questions, "So, did you help Mr. Hawes at his new place?"

"Yes Sir. I helped him fix up his room." Bryant answered.

"And this was at the boarding house on Second Avenue?" The Coroner inquired.

"Yes Sir," she answered.

"And when was the last time you saw either Mr. Hawes or the child?" Babbitt asked.

"It would have been on Monday. She stayed with me at my house and her Daddy picked her that night just after dark. I sewed buttons on her shoes and plaited her hair. Mr. Hawes said he was taking her to Montgomery to put her in a convent. They were taking a train at 3 AM Tuesday morning."

The Coroner asked about the shoes she had sewed the buttons on and asked to describe what the child was wearing. Bryant's description matched what the child was wearing when her body was discovered in the lake.

The Coroner then asked if she had seen either of them since that night. "No Sir, I ain't seen them since. Mr. Hawes said he wouldn't be back until the 12th when he would come back with his new bride," she answered.

The Coroner took more notes and thumbed back through the notes then asked, "When did you last see Mrs. Hawes?"

Bryant seemed to think for a few seconds and then said, "That was Saturday evening."

"Did you ever know Mrs. Hawes to consume alcoholic drink or appear drunken?" The Coroner asked.

With a slight hesitation, Bryant continued, "Yes sir, she drank whiskey a good bit."

"What else can you tell us about Mrs. Hawes?" Babbitt asked.

"Well, she was a fine looking woman, I'd say. She was about 25 or 26 years old... and I already told you, she drank a bit," Bryant answered.

"Did Mr. or Mrs. Hawes ever tell you anything about their relationship or marriage?" He asked.

Bryant thought for a moment before answering, "She once said they been married ten years and one time a while back, when they had been fighting, she said she might go to her Aunt up in New York. Mamie told me that her Papa had offered Mrs. Hawes a ticket to New York if she would go and that her Mama said she was going."

"And did Mr. Hawes ever say anything?" He asked.

"Well he said the other night that he supposed that his wife heard he had got a divorce is the reason she had left," she answered.

Coroner Babbitt then inquired, "How long have you known the Hawes, Fanny?"

Bryant seemed relieved to get an easy question, "I've been doing chores and looking out for them about 3 or 4 years, I guess."

"Do you live near their house?" He asked.

"No Sir, but I work for some other folks by the ball park there. I live in Avondale over by the rolling mill," she answered.

"Do you own a house there with your husband?" The Coroner asked.

"I pay my rent to Mr. Edwards for my place. It's on 32nd Street between Avenue E and F. My husband,

James Bryant, he got run over by train seven years ago. I been on my own ever since," she said proudly.

It was getting late and the Coroner returned to his notes and flipped through the pages for a minute or two before speaking. "Fanny you have told us a lot today, but I am concerned about what you may not have told us. From your own accounts you were the last to see the dead child and most likely her father. For that, I am requiring a $1,000 bail to ensure your continued presence in these proceedings. If you cannot post the bail, you will be held in the county jail."

Rumblings from others present felt that the Coroner's actions were both surprising and severe. The inquest adjourned. It was 9 o'clock in the evening.

At about that same time, the local newspaper – the *Age-Herald*, who had two reporters attending the Coroner's Inquest, received special telegram dispatch from a courier that read as follows:

Columbus, Mississippi, December 5 --- Mr. R. R. Hawes, one of the most popular employees of the Georgia Pacific Railway, and Miss Mayes Story, daughter of Mr. J.D. Story, of this place, were married this evening at 3 o'clock at the residence of the bride's father, the Rev. J. W. Price officiating. They left at once to visit relatives in Augusta, Georgia, and a bridal tour through the East. There were no cards and only a few friends were present.

Within minutes of reading the telegram reporters were asking authorities if they were aware of Hawes whereabouts and passed along this new information.

The police, of course, had already deduced that May Hawes was likely with her father on Monday night and that her body was found the following morning, so Richard Hawes was certainly a person of interest. His absence after Monday night and the various myriad of tales that he had told in the preceding weeks gave credence to his being the number one suspect unless an ironclad alibi could be produced.

Officer Pinkerton had attended the Coroner's Inquiry, taking notes of each witness, while Officer Carlisle contacted police departments in Atlanta, Meridian and New York following leads on the whereabouts of the Hawes family and anything that may be point to the location of any of the family members. The two men had just been comparing notes and wrapping up their day when the news of the telegram came. They immediately headed for the train station where they learned that the train that Hawes was reportedly a passenger on was scheduled to pass through Birmingham at 9:40 PM, only 20 minutes away. Pinkerton remained at the station while Carlisle hurried away to obtain a warrant.

Chapter 4

Wednesday, December 5, 1888

At 9:37 PM, Carlisle returned to the train station accompanied by Deputy Sherriff Truss. “I didn’t think you would ever make it back in time,” exclaimed Pinkerton.

Carlisle smiled, “I was very lucky. I literally ran into Judge Owens and Truss leaving the courthouse as I approached. The Judge had already heard about the testimony today, so he didn’t hesitate to issue the warrant.” And just then the inbound train came into view.

The Officers moved toward the platform. “The train is scheduled for a brief stop only, so we will need to board immediately and locate him,” Pinkerton said.

As the train slowed to a crawl, all three policemen hopped aboard the platform of the first car startling the conductor standing just inside awaiting to disembark. Pinkerton showed the warrant and asked if Hawes were on board.

"Will there be trouble?" The conductor asked,

"We have no reason to think so," Pinkerton replied quickly.

"Second car, on the right," the conductor said pointing to the rear of the train.

The three officers strode through the car exiting the rear just as the train came to a complete stop. As the trio entered the next car, they recognized Hawes sitting in the third row on the right, adjacent to a young woman they assumed was his new bride.

As planned, Carlisle approach the man touching him on the shoulder and asked in a low voice, "Are you Mr. Richard Hawes of Birmingham?"

Hawes, nodded and said, "Yes."

"Sir I have a warrant for your arrest for the murder of your child, and must take you into custody." Carlisle said, again in a very low voice.

Hawes showed neither alarm nor resistance in his expression. As a matter fact, the officers described his reaction as calm and emotionless. His bride seemed unaware of the interaction. Hawes simply nodded to the officer and turned to his bride, and gesturing to another gentleman seated across from the couple, "Dear, there has been a misunderstanding that I must go with these gentlemen to explain. This may take all night, so please go with my friends until I can make arrangements to come for you."

The young woman, dressed in a fine dress and hat, appeared to be surprised at his request but said nothing and simply nodded. Hawes then arose from his seat and followed Deputy Truss to the door with Pinkerton and Carlisle following close behind him. Hawes asked no questions nor made any statements as they exited the train to find a dozen or so newspaper reporters waiting on the platform.

Hawes was neatly dressed in black suit with a light brown overcoat. He wore a crisp white shirt and white satin necktie, somewhat confirming his marriage ceremony reported earlier in the day. Hawes's demeanor did not change even when confronted by the small crowd that awaited them on the train platform. He did not seem the least bit surprised. Carlisle watched Hawes as they made their way from the train. He hadn't expected a confrontation with his suspect but he also hadn't expected this total lack of emotion. He didn't express any concern upon the news that his child had been murdered. He didn't even inquire as to which child. Carlisle reasoned that only a man who had committed the crime and already knew these facts could be so apathetic.

As reporters shouted a barrage of questions regarding the crime, Hawes seemed to totally ignore them. A reporter from the *Age-Herald* continued to ask Hawes if he had murdered his child, he simply said, "I am innocent," and continued walking with the officers.

When a reporter ask about his dead child lying in the undertaker's parlor not far away, Hawes neither asked to see the child nor even asked which child had been killed.

When they arrived at the jail, another group of curious citizens and reporters were gathered and were joined by those that were following from the train station. The *Age-Herald* reporter once again was front and center, "Sir, would you like to make a statement before they take you in?"

Hawes paused and looked to the officers at his side, "No, I have nothing to say," he said in a calm and steady voice. "I will answer any question put to me."

"You know, sir, I suppose, the charge on which you were arrested?" The reported said.

Hawes stood firmly and looked the growing crowd and said, "Yes, for murder, I believe. It is stated that I have killed one of my children."

"It was your daughter Mamie," The reporter retorted.

Hawes sighed and took a deep breath, "May, you mean, I suppose. She is the one," he stated rather matter-of-factly. The crowd then began a barrage of questions, not waiting for an answer but just shouting one question after another. After a brief moment, Hawes raised his hand slightly and began to speak again. The crowd hushed.

In a deliberate and calm voice, Hawes made the following statement answering the questions, "I saw May last, I think, on Saturday at the house on 32nd Street near the ballpark."

The group again shouted questions and Hawes seemed to only answer one at a time. "I brought my boy to the car that evening and sent him to Atlanta with my brother, who is taking care of him," he answered.

"How long were you away?" one reporter shouted and another added, "Where were your wife and dughters?"

"I was away from the house about two hours and when I returned I found that the mother of my children and my two girls were gone," Hawes said solemnly.

"So, you live with your family on 32nd Street?" a reporter asked.

"The woman was once my wife, but I was divorced from her in October last, and have not lived with her since. She has taken care of our children and I have provided her with money. I have been on the road most of the time since. When I came to town, I would stop at the hotels and sometimes went out to see the children," Hawes answered without any emotion as he stood flanked by the Police Officers.

"How often did you call on your family," a reporter asked.

"I would frequently see her and always spoke to her. She is the mother of the three children and I am their father," he answered.

"How long were you married," another asked.

"We have been married nine years," he answered.

"How old is daughter?" another reporter asked.

"May is eight years old on the 31st of next month," he said.

The Age-Herald reporter asked, "What did you do when you came home to find your wife and daughters gone, sir?"

Hawes paused for only a second before answering, "I searched for the children on Saturday night and Sunday, and concluded that she had left town with them."

"When did you leave town?" Came a question from the rear of the growing crowd.

"I left the city for Columbus yesterday morning at seven o'clock," Hawes answered quickly.

“Were you with your daughter Monday night?” another reporter asked.

“No,” was Hawes simple reply.

Then where were you?” the reporter asked.

“I stopped at the Florence Hotel Monday night,” Hawes answered. “I think I returned around twelve. I sat around the office with a friend of mine named Wylie for a couple of hours before I retired. I spent the first part of the night with my brother at the depot. He left for Atlanta during the night.”

When a reporter who attended the inquest asked if Hawes knew a woman named Bryant, Hawes answered, “No”.

“Her first name is Fanny,” the reporter followed.

“Yes,” Hawes replied, “She does do washing for my family.”

The reporter was now on a roll, “When did you last see her?”

“I saw her on Saturday morning,” Hawes answered.

“But you didn’t see her on Monday?” the reporter continued.

Hawes did not hesitate, “No. I am sure of that.”

“How long have you worked for the railroad?” Another reporter asked.

“I have been connected to the Georgia-Pacific Railroad for four years,” he answered.

“You were no longer residing at the house on 32nd Street with your family?” Asked the reporter who had earlier inquired about his residency.

“I moved my affairs into Mrs. Fuller’s boarding house on 2nd Avenue last Saturday,” Hawes answered.

"It has been reported that you have told people that you had given your wife the sum of $500 for her to leave and stay with relatives?" Inquired a reporter from the back.

"Yes, I told my brother that I had given my divorced wife $500 to go to her aunt in Paris, Illinois," Hawes answered.

"How long were you married to Emma and when did you divorce?" Asked a report late in joining the crowd.

"I married my first wife in Atlanta nine years ago, on the 8th day of July. We ran away and married," Hawes explained. "She was about 18 years old. I was married to her twice - the first time in Payne's Chapel by a Methodist Minister, and the second time by a Priest in the Catholic Church in Atlanta, she being a Catholic." He continued, "I got a divorce from my wife in Atlanta last October. I don't remember what court. My plea was infidelity on her part. I filed the suit two years ago, but according to Georgia law a couple must wait two years before the decree can be granted. The decree of the divorce court gave me custody of the children."

"It has been reported that you had sent your daughters off to a school or convent?" a reporter asked.

"I was going to take the girls off to school in Mobile on Sunday last. I made all arrangements through Father O'Reilly, of this place, and was to leave them there until they were grown, paying only $25 per month for the two."

"Did you have custody of the children in the divorce?" Another asked.

Hawes simply replied, "Yes."

"Why were you granted custody? Was it your wife's drinking?" The reported followed.

"Yes, the mother of the children drank to excess. That is one reason I left her," Hawes answered solemnly. "She used to send May all over town after liquor."

"Did the mother of your children know of your plans for divorce?" another asked.

"Yes, my divorced wife knew that I was going to marry and knew the date," Hawes said. "She had known it for months."

"How long have you lived in Birmingham?" A reporter asked seeming to struggle to ask a question that had not yet been asked.

"I came to this city from Atlanta about a year since. I brought my wife and children with me," Hawes answered.

"You said you filed for divorce two years ago?" Asked the reporter who seemed to be stuck on the marriage issue.

"My suit for divorce had been filed, but we decided to live together until the decree had been issued. I paid her rent and other expenses."

"Sir, if you care for your children, why did you not continue to search for them?" Asked the reporter who had earlier inquired of his whereabouts on Monday.

"I love all my children and I gave up the search for them on Sunday because I had to leave to fill my engagement in Mississippi." Hawes replied,

"Did you employ or ask others to continue the search?" The reporter asked in an indigent tone.

Hawes hesitated, looked down at his feet and then answered softly, "No, I did not have anyone to look for them."

"Sir, did you visit East Lake last weekend?" Shouted a reporter from the back of the growing crowd.

"No, I have not been at East Lake since Fisk jumped from the balloon." His reference was to an entertainer who jumped from a hot air balloon over East Lake last August.

“You stated you married ten years ago, can you tell us more about your marriage and your wife?” Asked the reporter who was hell bent to get more information regarding the relationship between Hawes and his wife.

“My divorced wife’s name was Emma Pettis. She was about 18 years old when I married her, and our first child, May was born in about twelve months.”

“When and where did you last see your daughter May?” Asked the reporter show continued his line of questions on Hawes whereabouts on Monday.

“The last time I saw May she was home in bed.” He answered

“Your accounts are different from others interviewed including those in your employ. What do you say to that?” The reporter asked pointedly.

“The woman, Fanny, claimed that I owed her a balance on washing, but I did not think so and refused to pay her," he offered although Bryant had not been identified as the source of the information.

The night air was getting colder and the police officers patience ended as they waved to the crowd and grabbed Hawes by the arm and then led him into the jailhouse leaving reporters on the outside.

Richard R. Hawes

Chapter 5

Friday December 4, 2017

Fay Findlay emerged from the shower removing the shower cap that kept her shoulder length hair dry and sped up her ability to get out to the scene. She stepped into the walk-in closet and slipped on her panties and bra and then into the slacks and blue blouse she had pulled while on the phone earlier. She slipped them on and grabbed a pair of gray flats from the shelf and a gray jacket with a soft abstract print.

Nice clothes were one of the few luxuries Findlay allowed for herself. Her style was nowhere near flashy or trendy, but definitely stylish. Even when pressed for time like today, she always was dressed to impress. Even though she would soon be sixty years old, her fit body, smooth skin and thick, blonde hair would be the envy of many women twenty years younger. She paused for a quick look in the seven-foot tall framed mirror leaned against the brick wall just inside the closet door. Everything was intact and she was ready to meet the world.

Fay Findlay's downtown loft was spacious as downtown lofts go, just over 2,000 square feet. Located in the historic loft district, which is a six-block area of converted office buildings, warehouses and factories that once lined Morris, 1st and 2nd Avenues North. Lofts in the district ranged from units as small as 800 square feet to those of more than 5,000 square feet that occupied an entire floor of the building. The Findlay loft was on the top floor of a three story brick building erected in 1905 and had seen many lives through the century, from warehouse to furniture store, among other things until it was converted to lofts about ten years ago. The developers had kept as much of the historic charms of the structure as possible including maple floors that were still beautiful despite their scars of more than a hundred years of use. All of the exterior walls, as well as some interior ones, were exposed brick. The lobby of the building was only opened to the residents of the 21 lofts **the Rat** filled the building. It was not large but was well appointed with art adorning the brick walls and a comfortable seating area in the center that could easily grace the cover of any home décor magazine. A wall of antique brass mailboxes was tucked around the corner next to the elevator doors. The developers had acquired them from a local antiques dealer that had rescued them when one the largest hotels in Birmingham was demolished in 1974 to make way for a 49-story office tower that would be the new headquarters for a bank. The 13-story, 425-room, Tutwiler Hotel was one of the last of these grand historic buildings to meet that fate.

After the magnificent Terminal Station, that was often compared to the Grand Central and Penn Stations in New York for it's elaborate architecture, was demolished in 1969 by a developer who wanted the space for a proposed new Federal Building that never came to fruition, there was a major outcry from the public to preserve historic downtown buildings. Five years later when the wrecking ball hit the Tutwiler, it was the last straw and tough laws and restrictions made destroying older buildings much more difficult and much less profitable for developers. Unfortunately, many of the buildings sat empty and decaying for decades as a result, but at least they were saved from demolition. The cost of updating the buildings for current codes was cost prohibitive until a new tax incentive was passed in 2004 for historic building renovations. Even in decay, they did survive. The new tax incentives spurred a lot of redevelopment downtown that is still underway today.

Fay Findlay was fortunate and bought her loft before the downtown redevelopment hit its stride. As a result, her loft was now worth more than twice what she paid, but she would never sell. To her it was home. Birmingham was her home and being able to see the city skyline up close from her large windows along 2nd Avenue was something she could never imagine parting with.

Just a little more than two blocks away stood the iconic City Federal Building with its red neon sign spelling out its name from the rooftop on each side of the building. The 27-story building was the tallest building in the south when it was completed in 1913 as the headquarters for the Jefferson County Savings Bank Building. It remained the tallest building in the city until the completion of the AmSouth-Sonat Tower in 1969. The City Federal dominated the view from Fay's front windows as the taller, newer buildings provided a backdrop for the iconic building. Unfortunately, the bank ran into financial trouble two years after the building was erected, some say due in part to building the skyscraper. The bank closed in 1915 and the building was renamed the Comer Building after the

Governor B. B. Comer. The penthouse served as headquarters for the Birmingham Press Club and the 11th floor served as the National Headquarters for the Women's Missionary Union that had relocated from Maryland to Birmingham to occupy the new towering structure.

In 1962, the building underwent a major renovation for the City Federal Savings & Loan, which occupied the majority of the building. The penthouse became the studios for the Rock and Roll radio station, WSGN 610. The towering red letters of CITY FEDERAL were erected to the rooftop extending the already 325 feet tall building even taller. The neon sign was visible across the city despite the smoky haze that always enveloped downtown from the nearby steel factories. The smog was ever present until the clean air laws were enacted in the 1980's.

The neo-classical City Federal building is now home to 85 condominiums, and many of Fay's friends make their home there. The rooftop sign remains lit and much of the interior embellishments remain, including the ornate barrel ceiling in the lobby and the brass door elevators that now take resident up to their homes. The ground floor is home to a nationally renowned restaurant and the former bank's three walk-in vaults have been preserved as wine cellars and tasting rooms.

Beyond the City Federal was the handful of new skyscrapers that anchored Birmingham's Financial District. Fay loved to sit and look at the skyline view from her loft. Something about the view brought a sense of peace to her, even when life was tense. Her work often brought her the worst of humanity, but something about this city that she had called home all of her life seemed to provide hope for a brighter day.

Perhaps it was seeing her city emerge and be recognized as a world leader in human rights after its ugly past during the civil rights struggles of the 1960's. Fay has vivid memories of the demonstrations she witnessed as a little girl on downtown shopping trips with her mother. While, like most white parents of that era, she was shielded as much as possible from the happenings of the day, she had a keen sense of the history, melding her memories with the history she studied about her city and that era. During her childhood, there was little talk of what was unfolding in the city and throughout the nation. She was not really aware until years later that her hometown had been the epicenter of change that had been a long time in coming and was still emerging today.

Even though Fay was proud of the changes that had come during her lifetime, she knew that there was still much work to be done. Her yearning to be a part of that change is what eventually led her to become only the third female to be hired as a Birmingham Police officer in 1980. She was finishing her junior year of college at UAB when she applied for the Civil Service exam. She entered the Police Academy the day after her graduation.

Even though Fay was a top student she knew early on that she would not fit in to the stereotype assigned to most working women of her generation. Most of her high school friends went to college to find a husband and settle into a life of motherhood and suburban housewives like their mothers and grandmothers before them. Those that did seek careers settled on the established "women professions" of schoolteacher or nurse. While Fay admired both professions, she knew that neither would ever work for her. She wasn't sure what she wanted to do as she entered college but she knew there had to be more. Until her junior year she was working toward a degree in American Literature and had no real plan for how she would make a living when she graduated but there had to be something. She had an incredible work ethic thanks to her hard working parents, which was the reason she was always a top student. It did not come easy. She worked hard and studied hard just as she had witnessed her parents do, scraping out a decent living even though it wasn't easy.

Her father served as an Army Air-Force pilot in World War II. Like most of "The Greatest Generation", he never wanted to talk much about the War or his service. It wasn't until after her parent's death that Fay discovered all of the medals her father had earned along with all his flight logs and other mementos from that time. When the War ended, he went to work at Hayes Aircraft in Birmingham. The company spent the next two decades converting and refurbishing Armed Forces aircraft for civilian use.

Fay's mother also worked hard her entire life. Upon graduating from Jones Valley High School in Birmingham, she also joined the war effort going to work at U.S. Steel inspecting sheets of tin in the Tin Mill. With most of the able-bodied men called to serve, almost the entire USS workforce was comprised of women. They were the "Rosie the Riveters" working in plants all across America. When the war ended, she remained with the company as a clerk.

While the returning men took back their jobs in the factories, she worked in a small shed in the corner of the factory sorting orders, maintaining payroll records and any other paperwork that was needed. She remained there for 42 years before retiring.

In her junior year, Fay was looking for interesting classes to fill her fall schedule and chose "Introduction to Criminal Justice." She found the instructor, a retired FBI agent, to be beyond boring as an instructor, but she found the subject matter both complex and compelling. She had never really known anyone in law enforcement or affiliated with the criminal justice system. The class intrigued her to explore more and by the end of the next semester, she had declared her major as Criminal Justice, along with Psychology. She reasoned that with this double major, surely she could find a job upon graduation that would allow her to support herself, something her father constantly preached to her. For the first time in her college career, she found herself eager for class and soon began volunteering for projects outside of class including internships at the Birmingham Police Department and the local office of the Southern Poverty Law Center offices.

While those two entities were often at opposite sides of controversy that was exactly what Fay Findlay thrived on. Her Dad had always instilled in her that there were always two sides to a story and sometimes both were the truth. "You just have to separate the truth from all the bullshit that people tend to add on" he would often say. Sometimes both sides were right in their own way and sometimes both were wrong because they could not recognize the truth because of their own agendas.

By the time Fay was a senior she came to the realization that her aging father was wise beyond his 9th grade education. As a matter of fact, he was the wisest person she had ever known. His common sense approach to life had gotten him through a rough early life that began with the death of his parents when he was barely a year old. It served him well through the war and as he settled back into civilian life.

He was raised by his grandparents along with their ten other children. While they provided a home and a sound upbringing, those times were rough for everyone, especially a young man trying to make his way during the Great Depression. He dropped out of school to work in the ore mines when he was only sixteen and then went to War with every other able bodied man. He was in his mid forties when he met Fay's mom and after a disastrous first marriage when he was barely out of his teens. He thought he would never cross that bridge again, but he met this woman who was happy with whom she was. A woman who had her made her own way and at age 35 was happy with her own life without a husband. A woman, who much like him, worked hard and enjoyed life. They both loved music and loved to dance and that brought them together after an introduction by a mutual friend. After a whirlwind courtship they married. Neither planned a family at this late stage of life. In the fifties, women in their late thirties having their first baby was almost unheard of, but nine months and sixteen days after their wedding day, Margaret Fay Findlay was born.

Fay was unexpected but no less adored by both parents. Since both worked, she stayed with a baby sitter during the day. Mary Newcomb was a retired LPN that was a friend of a family member and was a perfect fit for the unexpected child. Mary lived in the Elyton Village housing project near the famed Legion Field in west Birmingham and Pam's mom dropped her there on her way to work each morning.

Legion Field started life in 1927 with a seating capacity of 21,000. Almost immediately, discussions of expansion began and seating was soon increased to 25,000. Over the years, the stadium was used for football games of Birmingham-Southern and Howard College (now Samford University) along with numerous high school games. Expansions became the norm until the stadium reached it's peak capacity of over 80,000 in the 1980's. From the 1950's through the 1970's the stadium was an icon of the growth of college football and Birmingham was widely know as "The Football Capitol of the South." During this period, the University of Alabama football team traveled to Birmingham from Tuscaloosa to play their home games at Legion Field except for their Homecoming game, which was played on campus at the much smaller Denny Field. The annual rivalry game between the University of Alabama and Auburn University was always played at Legion Field and was soon touted as the "Iron Bowl" in recognition of the city's history of the steel industry.

Fay has fond memories of Miss Newcomb and her time spent with her. Bus rides downtown for trips to the library and for shopping. Sitting in her apartment and listening to her read all the books they selected at the library and later reading herself. Playing in the nearby park and other activities that can only be truly relished when we reach adulthood and look back. Her relationship continued with Miss Newcomb until her death during Fay's freshman year of college.

In later years, as her Mom left for work when she left for school and didn't get home until dinnertime, Fay spent much of her time with her father. Working the day shift, he was gone when she got up for school but he was done in time to pick her from school every day. Most days they would go home, do homework together and then get dinner ready, but on Wednesdays, they went to the library to return books from the previous week and check out more. Fay has been a voracious reader since those early days.

Her father was a very patient man and his life as a doting father of a frail little tow-headed girl, was so distant from the rough and tumble veteran he had been before her birth. When she reached adulthood, he often told her that she saved his life. He said his detrimental lifestyle took a hard right turn when he met her mother, but that it made a full one-eighty when she came along. Everyone that knew him "before and after Fay" echoed that sentiment. He taught her a lot about life and his wisdom emerges in some form or fashion every single day of her life.

When she announced to her parents that she was going to be a police officer, her mother was furious and tried all she could to change her mind. "It's too dangerous," she claimed. Her father, who no doubt harbored those same fears, was full of pride and encouragement. "You will be the best damn cop this city has ever seen," was his comment as he gave her a big hug. That memory is one that often flashes in Fay's mind, especially when her job gets tough. Soon after she began her career, her father was beset with Alzheimer's and died before her first promotion after only three years on the job. Her mom retired and spent her remaining years caring for him, which took a toll on her own health and she died four years later. Fay was devastated by each loss, and as an only child, she threw herself into her work and completing her education.

She was promoted to Detective after three years on the job and assigned to property crimes and then homicide where she excelled and quickly became one of the top detectives in the unit. She was promoted to Detective Sergeant after only six years, becoming the first female to hold the rank in the department. Five years later, the Special Crime Unit was created to deal with high profile crimes that were growing in the city. Fay was promoted to Lieutenant and named to head the new unit.

The SCU soon gained national recognition for their work even though Birmingham P.D. is a rather small department with only 800 total officers. Detectives from much larger departments traveled to Birmingham to observe and learn the tactics used and developed by Fay Findlay and her team.

The team was ever changing as Detectives achieved the honor of being assigned to SCU. All are handpicked by Findlay. Average tenure is about 6 years, as being a SCU team member is good for one's resume. Some have been promoted out of the unit to lead their own units and others have been recruited to higher positions in other police departments. Two alumni serve as Chief of Police in other departments, one is a Captain and three are Lieutenants in the BPD. Several others have taken high-ranking positions with state or federal agencies. Her current team was her most well rounded and longest tenured. They have been together for a little over four years.

As Fay pulled her car into the lot at Eastlake, the crowd of onlookers was growing. One local TV crew was set up and filming. Another was getting set up and a third was pulling into the lot just ahead of her. As she got out of the car she saw Nate Parker heading her way with an eager TV reporter on his heels. The young woman was towing her cameraman along who was struggling to keep up with the camera o his shoulder. Nate gave her a stern glance as he picked up his pace rounding the front of Fay's car. Before he could say a word, a microphone was in Fay's face. "Since the Special Crime Unit is here does this mean this murder is the work of a serial murderer or something else?" blurted the reporter.

Fay thought she looked as though she was barely out of college and had spent way too much time getting her red hair to curl just perfectly around her face. Nate was now pissed and started to send her on her way, but Fay just nodded in his direction and he stopped in his tracks just beside the reporter. With all the calm and seriousness she could muster, Fay looked directly into the reporter's eyes and said, "So you know that this scene is a murder scene? That is rather odd since we have just launched an investigation. Since you seem to know so much, that we obviously don't, I would consider you a prime suspect. Can you give Detective Parker here your name... he will have a lot of questions for you. Nate, perhaps you could have one of the uniforms take her downtown and we can question her there."

Even through all the make-up, Nate Parker could see the blood drain from the fledgling reporters face. Fay noticed the wry smile from the veteran cameraman who was trying to not let it show.

"Uh, Uh... I don't know anything, I promise," the reporter stammered. "I just saw the body and I recognized you so I assumed..."

Fay walked passed her without another look. Nate smiled and leaned into the woman's ear and whispered loudly, "Ask your cameraman what happens when we assume."

Nate then fell in behind Fay as they headed back to the scene.

"What do we have so far?" Fay asked.

"They just got the body out and the M.E. did a quick survey of the body here before they transported. She is zipped up and in the van now" Nate reported as they continued to walk toward the scene marked with yellow tape.

"He said there were no visible marks that he could see. The little girl was dressed in a dress and patent leather shoes – kinda like church clothes I would say." Nate continued. "M.E. didn't see anything extraordinary. No stains. No marks. Only odd thing – she was dressed like that and had a frilly under skirt thing on..."

Fay interrupted, "A slip?"

Parker looked puzzled, "Yeah, I guess... I didn't have sisters so I don't know what you call it, but the odd thing was the M.E. said she didn't have on underpants."

Fay froze in her tracks and spun to face Parker.

"Yes, I know," he responded deadpanned. "When the M.E. told us, both Daniels and I gasped out loud. He had no idea why. We had to explain that May Hawes was found in a similar condition in this lake over a hundred years ago. He had no idea what we were talking about. I told him we would explain later, but it would take a while."

Fay regained her composure and asked, "How long before they can start the autopsy?"

"They are going to prioritize her, so he said he would get it done today," Nate answered. "Probably be tonight, but he said he would get it done. He looked her over good and said it looks like a drowning, but of course, he won't go on the record until he gets her on the table."

Fay walked over to edge of the lake. "Any clue who she is?" she asked although she knew it was too early.

"Well, you know the few white folks that still live in the neighborhood are way too old to have young kids, although she could be a grandkid or something, I suppose. The car that works this beat knows the neighborhood, so they are checking now. He said there were only four white families that he knew of."

Eastlake was no different than most Birmingham neighborhoods. In the late sixties and early nineteen-seventies, white families fled the city to the suburbs in what is commonly known as "White Flight." Once school integration became the norm, white families fearing their property values would decline or fearing having black neighbors or simply fear in general, left the city for the suburbs. Once thriving neighborhoods deteriorated in many areas. Not because black families were bad neighbors or didn't keep up their homes, but rather because the flight was so fast and widespread, many areas were left with vacant houses and blight ensued.

Eastlake was such a neighborhood. Most of the homes were beautiful craftsman and Tudor homes with manicured lawns. When white flight first began, East Lake Park featured the lake and a tennis complex operated by the Birmingham Park and Recreation Department. It was a beautiful urban neighborhood. By the nineteen-nineties, the neighborhood, because of the large park, had become a haven for gangs and other thugs. The neighborhood itself was trying to hang on but that is hard to do when you have drug dealers hanging out in the park and gang bangers having shootouts in the streets. The neighborhood is going to suffer and it did. The tennis center closed when during a junior tennis tournament filled with promising players from across the South, a gang shootout occurred along the street in front of the complex and into the park. By the time police arrived, all the culprits had disappeared including 3 young men that later ended up in the ER of UAB Hospital suffering gunshot wounds. Needless to say, that was the last tournament at the complex and the facility was soon shuttered by the city leading to further decay of the neighborhood. Like most neighborhoods in transition, there are always a sprinkling of homeowners who tough it out, some out of stubbornness and others simply because they cannot afford to go anywhere else. Usually these are older residents living on a fixed income who become recluses in their homes because they are afraid to emerge.

Eastlake was now seeing a transition back to life as young families were buying homes and restoring them to their previous grandeur. Police presence and programs were keeping the crime at bay or at least had moved it out, but the neighborhood was still far from what it once was. The park was also rebounding. Although the tennis complex was still closed, the city had invested in keeping the lake looking nice and installed several new docks and stocked the lake with fish. Several charities hosted fishing tournaments for inner-city kids there on weekends several times per year.

"So, if she wasn't from the neighborhood, where the hell did she come from?" Fay wondered aloud. "And dressed up like that... it makes no sense."

Nate spoke up, “I totally agree. I hate to bring it up but...” he hesitated as Fay turned to look at him. “What do you think about the Hawes tie-in, Boss? It is kinda creepy, don’t you think?”

Fay tilted her head slightly, “Sure, it’s creepy, but it is still too early yet to go down that road,” Fay responded. “Let’s get back to the office and fill the others in,” she said as they headed back toward the cars.

“I will go by Starbucks,” Nate said. “I am thinking the office Kuerig will not do this morning,” he joked.

“See you there,” Fay responded. “I will take care of giving the press a no comment since I see they’re still waiting. The Public Information team should be here in a minute,” she said.

Nate laughed, “Don’t make that girl cry again, okay?” She waived him off and smiled.

Fay walked toward the press who had been shooting the scene and patiently waiting. Most were familiar with dealing with the Special Crimes Unit and knew that information would come, but only when Fay Findlay was ready and only if they acted in a professional manner. Most of the information would flow through the department's Public Information Team that would be on the scene soon. The fledgling reporter had learned a lesson this morning and had, no doubt, been filled in by her colleagues afterward. She waited with them but was much more reserved and less enthusiastic now.

"You all know the drill. I don't have a lot of information for you and probably won't have anything really until tomorrow, if then. Let me know when you are ready and I will give you what I do have for broadcast."

The cameramen all made adjustments and readied their cameras as the reporters handed their microphones to one reporter who held them in a cluster and stood just out of the shot beside Findlay.

"Is this okay?" she asked.

A unison nod was the response and with that, Fay began, "This morning a body was discovered by a city public works employee in the east end of Eastlake. The body appears to be that of a Caucasian female approximately 10 years old. The child has not yet been identified and our investigation is just getting started. We have not yet determined if this was a result of foul play or simply an accident. We will be able to determine that as our investigation continues. I would ask that if anyone knows of any missing child that has not yet been reported or a child that is unaccounted for, that they contact the Birmingham Police Department."

Fay paused for a few seconds and waited for the camera operators to stop. "One question each," she said matter-of-factly, "then I have to get to the office and I will let you know when we have anything worth telling."

One by one, each reporter asked a question that she had just answered, but this gave each one the opportunity to appear on-air asking the question and making for good local news. The fledgling reporter was learning a lot today. Even though she had been doing this for more than a year after graduating college, she was new to the Birmingham market and she was getting an education today.

"The PI Team will be here soon and any developments going forward will be passed through them. Thank you all," Fay concluded. Dealing with media was one of the things that Fay Findlay detested when she first started as a detective. She had no patience and every reporter seemed to get more stupid with each question. It wasn't until her third year in homicide that she learned that the media could be her friend and could help her. She had a case with a Jane Doe victim and no matter how much physical evidence you have, if you don't know who your victim is, getting a conviction or even naming a suspect can prove most difficult. Fay finally utilized the press to identify the victim through the only real identification means available – two tattoos from Jane Doe's body. The local press kept following the story and it soon garnered national press and within a week the victim was identified as a hitchhiker transient from Arizona. Soon afterward, a suspect was identified and an arrest and conviction followed.

From that point on, Fay worked with the press, but just like her team, respect and decorum was required. Act professionally and you will be treated professionally. Otherwise, you won't get much, as the young reporter discovered today. Most of the local press had learned this and there was a mutual respect. They always got more information from Findlay and her team than other Detectives. They knew she would not hold back anything that didn't need to be held and she would release any information when she could. In turn, they didn't hound her or her detectives for information that would never come until she was ready.

In recent years, the department had formed the Public Information team with detectives and officers especially trained to deal with the press and disseminate information in a controlled manner. Fay was glad to have them.

As Findlay pulled into her space behind the Police Headquarters Building on 1st Avenue North, she put the car in park, unbuckled her seat belt and closed her eyes and leaned her head back against the headrest and took a deep breath. Miles Davis was playing through her iPod in the car.

She thought, "This could be as simple as a child that accidently slipped into the lake and drowned... not really a case at all", but her gut told her differently. Too many unanswered questions.

In that regard it was no different than any other case at this early stage. But the unanswered circumstances surrounding this one sent a chill up her spine. She didn't believe in coincidences anyway, but the similarities to this body and one from a case more than a hundred years old that was the recurring subject of many of her lectures, made certain that this was no coincidence. What it was exactly was yet to unfold, but Fay Findlay had a sinking feeling that it was not going to be good and she felt that this might not be the only victim.

With another deep breath, Findlay exited her car and reached in the backseat for her bag. For work, she carried a small fashionable backpack that doubled as both purse and briefcase. She swiped her ID at the door and waited until she heard the click. Normally she would take the stairs but today seemed like a good day to use the elevator. She stepped in and hit 4.

The doors opened on the third floor and Detective Sergeant Amy Boyd stepped in. Boyd was second in command of the SCU and handled most of the day-to-day operations and assignments.

"Good Morning, Sunshine" Findlay greeted her. Sunshine had become Boyd's nickname in her rookie year of patrol. Her ever-beaming smile and can-do attitude had caused her Shift Commander to address her with that moniker in roll call one morning and it stuck.

"Morning, Ma'am," she replied. "You okay? I mean I have seen you take the elevator like four times as long as I have known you."

"I'm fine," Fay smiled. "Just thinking and didn't want to risk injury doing too many thing at once."

Amy giggled at that explanation. "I was checking with both Homicide and Juvenile to see if they had anything that could help us on the case," she said.

Findlay looked at her iWatch for the time – 7:37. She always kept her iWatch face set with the image of the iconic Mickey Mouse, tapping his foot to the seconds and extending his gloved hands to point to the time. She felt that looking at Mickey for the time would always make her smile even when the job made everything seem serious.

"So you have already been briefed?" She asked.

Boyd's smile widened, "Not officially, but you know how news travels here. I talked to Nate on the phone after you guys wrapped at the scene... he's picking up coffee at Lucy's. The drive through at Starbuck's was too long. I don't know why he even tries. Lucy has way better coffee."

The doors opened to the 4th floor and the two women exited and made their way to the SCU offices. The SCU consisted of a glass enclosure of the front corner of the fourth floor. The top floor of the Police headquarters was divided by glass partitions that juxtaposed their modern appearance with the old building.

The SCU occupied a little more than a quarter of the floor. Large windows overlooking 1st Avenue North and the Southside of the city lined one wall. The other wall was exposed brick of the 90-year-old building and the remaining two walls were floor to ceiling glass. Mini-blinds were installed on the glass enclosure but were rarely used. Five desks were arranged through the space. Four large file cabinets lined the brick wall. Each desk was equipped with a flat screen monitor. Each detective was issued a Mac laptop and when working in the office could plug into the monitor for more screen space.

Four large screen monitors were suspended from the sixteen-foot ceiling along one glass wall. These were utilized as the team analyzed and discussed cases. Information could be displayed on the screens so that everyone could see.

Information displayed varied from photos of crime scenes or suspects to timelines to lab reports.

Two whiteboards were mounted to one glass wall. One was 4 feet tall and 4 feet wide. It was lined with a grid in black tape. It contained the case number and name of open cases along with the progress of each one. Currently there were four cold cases listed. The most recent was a double homicide from 3 years ago. The oldest was a drive-by shooting that occurred in 1983.

The second whiteboard was twice as long and was used to log anything being discussed by the team. It was usually occupied with information and time lines of the current case.

Generally, it was a place to log their brainstorming sessions that occurred often during an investigation. As new information was gathered it was added to the board. The team met daily, or more, to exchange information and discuss. Findlay had taken various methods she had been taught and had acquired from other veterans of the BPD, as well as other departments and agencies. Over time she had carefully honed and tweaked the process to what was used today.

Her system allowed each detective to do their work but allowed a means for everyone to review, critique, brainstorm and discuss it in a team environment. In these meetings, egos were left at the door. Everyone had the same goal – solve the case and bring justice. The open nature of the information allowed for unfettered collaboration. This system had led the team to an 88% case closure rate for the last ten years. Although this was almost double what is expected in most agencies, the SCU members were never satisfied. They all strived for 100%.

As Boyd and Findlay entered the office, Detectives Jerome Clark and Walt Ellison were at their desks. Clark was on the phone and busily taking notes. Ellison was scrolling through a blue screen of information on his computer screen. Two large flat screen monitors occupied his desk. He spun around in his chair as the women entered and greeted them, "Morning, Boss! Anything from downstairs, Amy?"

"Nothing now, but both homicide and juvie are digging to see if they can find anything that may be connected," Boyd answered.

Fay sat her bag down and took her chair and spun it around to face the room before taking a seat. "Well, I guess I can skip the part where I tell everyone about the case, since you are all already working it," she quipped.

Clark hung up the phone and turned around to face the group. "I've been on the phone with all four women's shelters... no children unaccounted for now, but two of them only allow 48 hour stays so they have a lot coming and going. I emailed a photo of the deceased to each shelter, so hopefully someone may recognize her."

And with that, Nate Parker appeared in the office carrying a tray of coffee cups and a bag. "Lucy was just putting out fresh beignets, so I couldn't resist," he said as he handed out the coffees and then passed the bag around the room before taking his seat.

Fay leaned forward in her chair and said, "Okay, so let's start at the top and see what we know... Nate, tell us about the scene and what you know so that we are all working in the same page."

Nate held up a finger while he swallowed his last beignet and took a drink from his coffee. "Sorry, but I didn't get breakfast! Okay, so George Daniels called me when he got to the scene. He was actually on call last night and was heading back home from a drive-by out in Ensley when he heard this call. He was heading home and was actually on I-59 passing Eastlake so he got off and went over before dispatch even called him. He arrived just as the patrol car did.

A couple of Public Works guys came in early to fix some lights on the walkway and pavilion. They said they came early while it was still dark so they could check to see if there were more lights out. They had been there working for about 45 minutes and when they got the lights working, one of them noticed something in the lake and they walked out on the dock to take a closer look and saw the girls hair floating and one hand on the surface. They called 911. Call came in at 5:14 AM," he said looking at his notebook.

"As I said, the beat car and Daniels arrived at the same time. CSI arrived about 15 minutes later and Jacobs from the M.E. office about 5 minutes after that." Parker continued, "CSI didn't see anything else floating and no obvious signs of anything out of the ordinary. They had someone walking the entire perimeter of the lake to see if they found anything or saw anything unusual. It is not a big lake but it isn't small either, so that will take some time. They also took water samples for the M.E.

When they got the body out, Lt. Guyer and I were present when the M.E. did the preliminary check of the body. No obvious wounds or signs of trauma. He looked in hers eyes and said it looked like cause of death was drowning, but emphasized that was off the record until he got her on the table and looked further. As I think everyone knows already, she was kinda dressed up... wearing a blue dress and socks and patent leather shoes... she had on a frilly slip under the dress but no panties. She had a blue ribbon in her hair. M.E. said she had been in the water no more than 8-10 hours, maybe less by just looking at the body. He could maybe pinpoint that more after the autopsy. So that would put her going in the water sometime after seven last night." Parker leaned back, "That is not much, but it is what we have for now."

"Any cameras in the park?" Boyd asked.

"There is a camera on each corner of the tennis building, but that has been shut down for a while according to the guys that work that beat," Nate responded. "So we don't know if they are operational. I put in a call in to the

Parks and Recreation Department and left a voice mail. I am pretty sure that like most of the park facilities, the cameras feed to a local server on premise and since that has been shut down, I am sure the cameras are inoperable."

Boyd pointed at the other two.

Clark spoke up, "I checked with all four of the women's shelters and they have no unaccounted children. First Hope, on 5th and the New Light only have temporary Emergency Shelters, so they have a 48-hour max on stays. As such, they have a lot of turnover, so they are checking. I sent a photo to all four in hopes that if the kid has been through someone will recognize her."

Ellison was the last to report, "I checked missing person and child abduction reports both locally and all the National sites... Nothing so far. Nothing close to the description in Alabama and so far nothing nationally but it will take some time. I also was searching through social media to see if there was any mention of anything and I got nothing other than an apparent custody situation south of Tuscaloosa last night... but it was a male age 3."

Boyd stood and walked to the large board. She picked up and a marker and began writing... ***Eastlake 12/04/2017 White Female Juvenile – Jane Doe.*** Underneath that she wrote ***~Body in Water ~ After 19:00 12/3. Body Found 05:14 12/4/17***. "That it?" She asked. The team was silent looking at one another.

Fay finally spoke, "Before we start brainstorming, I will address the elephant in the room... Amy is correct, this is certainly not much to start with, but we can't ignore the similarities of this victim and that of May Hawes. I think the similarities have been adequately described as creepy" Fay reasoned as she leaned forward in her chair. "In both cases, we have a deceased female juvenile found floating in the east end of East Lake. The bodies show no signs of obvious trauma. Both are well dressed and fully clothed except minus panties," she said.

Fay stood and began to pace slowly as she continued, "The bodies are discovered 129 years apart, so I think we can rule out the same culprit for both. Richard Hawes was convicted and hanged for the murder of his daughter May, but we know there are many theories that he may not have been guilty or may not have been solely responsible, but, unless we have a vampire or someone who is more than 129 years old, we have two different culprits here."

Her words were careful and she spoke to the team as she thought, "The obvious answer is a well-staged copycat, but if that is the case, and I am not saying it is... that raises even more questions: Why? What is the purpose? Local history buff psychopath? Why this case? Certainly there are more recent murders? If it is a copycat... does that mean there are more bodies? To complete the Hawes trio?"

Clark interjected, "If that turns out to be the case, we are dealing with one serious sick fuck that would kill two kids just fit is recreation scenario."

Parker agreed, "That is for damn sure!"

Following a brief quiet that seem to last for days, Amy Boyd broke the silence. "Boss, with what we have now do you see any other alternative?" she asked timidly. "I mean, I don't know that I have ever fully agreed with the "no such thing as coincidence thing" but I certainly don't see this as coincidence."

Fay stopped pacing and looked at Amy and shook her head and took her seat again. "No, Amy. I don't see another way. I hope we are wrong but my gut tells me this is the work of a sick fuck, as Jerome says. Perhaps we will get something from the autopsy or from CSI that will open another door, but until that happens let's go with this but keep your minds open..."

"Follow the evidence," was the response from the team in unison. They all chuckled.

"Are we trained well or what, Boss?" Nate joked.
"Yes you are," Fay responded.

Chapter 6

Thursday December 6, 1888 - 09:00

As scheduled, Coroner Babbitt called the second session of the inquest to order. This session was convened in a much larger room of the Lockwood & Miller Funeral Home due to the large crowd that had gathered.

A total of seven witnesses testified. First to testify, Mr. T. A. Grambling, a friend of Richard Hawes and an employee of Hochstadter's Restaurant. Grambling testified that Hawes, who had eaten lunch at the restaurant on Monday, had told him that his two daughters were in a convent in Atlanta and that he was going to Augusta to be married.

Mr. Thomas Hall was called and testified he had known Hawes for about a year and a half when the

Hawes family boarded at his house on 24th Street. He could never recall seeing the children and couldn't identify the deceased child.

Mrs. M. E. Black was next and testified that she knew May Hawes and had seen her and her little brother on Monday morning, playing on Avenue C, between 22nd and 23rd Streets.

Although the testimonies were somewhat mundane, the gathered crowd seemed to pay attention to each and every word from each witness.

Mrs. Fuller testified that when Hawes rented the room in her boarding house, a mulatto woman named Fannie Bryant came and made the arrangements for him. When she asked Fannie about Hawes, Fannie told her that everyone had sympathy for the man. She said that he had one child in a convent in Atlanta, but that Mrs. Hawes had taken the other child and gone to New York.

Beverly Johnson testified that she knew Richard Hawes well. She said, "Sometimes he used bad language toward his wife, especially when they were quarrelling." She continued, "I've heard him three or four times say that he would stomp the hell out of her. I never saw him strike her. She drank considerably."

Dell Pullins then testified that she once nursed Mrs. Hawes. "Sometimes, Mr. Hawes abused her and cursed her. When they quarreled she drank more than usual."

Mr. A. B. Jackson testified that he had seen May Hawes around noon on Monday with a "Bright Mulatto woman who told him that Mrs. Hawes had gone to Atlanta with the other two children."

At this juncture, Coroner Babbitt adjourned the jury for lunch and the spectators left the room. Reporters and law enforcement officers that were present remained and talked with one another about the testimonies presented. Rumors were circulating in the room and through the city about the case. One was that Fannie Bryant had become distraught in jail overnight and confessed, telling police where Mrs. Hawes body could be found. Another rumor was that Mrs. Hawes was seen on Wednesday night and was "playing dead" in order to see her husband hanged for the murders. Another rumor coincided with some of the testimony that she was in Atlanta. None of the rumors ever proved to be true and when Coroner Babbitt reconvened the jury for the afternoon session, the room was once again packed with curious spectators and reporters with several people forced to stand outside for lack of seats and room inside.

Deputy Sherriff, J. Bronger, was called to testify. He testified that he, Deputy Truss, Officers Carlisle and J. B. Robbins had searched Fannie Bryant's house and found "a piece of braided passementerie entangled with blonde hair." He showed it to the jurors and stated that the carpet in the house was strewn with hair of the same color. He reported that they had found a piece of oilcloth "with blood on diagonal corners, on the ends of which it seemed as though blood had dripped and ran after it fell." The Deputy also said that he had interviewed Fannie Bryant in the jail that morning and that she had admitted to washing bloodstains from a pillowcase from Mrs. Hawes bed. He said that Bryant identified the oilcloth, stating that Mrs. Hawes had told her, “that her husband had struck her on the head with a club.”

Mr. R. M. Brown, a conductor on the Highland Avenue and Belt Railroad, testified that May Hawes and Richard Hawes had boarded his coach at Lakeview at about six o’clock on the morning of Saturday, December 1st. “My attention was attracted to her by seeing Mr. Hawes take her up in his lap and carry her to the fire to warm her feet. My attention was also called to his caressing the girl because I knew her and wondered why he fondled her. I did not know that she was his daughter.”

Mr. W. E. Auger testified that he had known Hawes for a year and had seen him at Lakeview with his son Willie on Saturday night. Hawes told him that night that he was sending the boy to school in Atlanta.

Once again, Fannie Bryant was brought into the room as all eyes turned to her, knowing that she was now the key witness and was suspected by many as being either the culprit or an accomplice in the death of the child. Fannie testified that she had done washing for Mrs. Hawes on the previous Friday, November 30th. She stated that Mrs. Hawes had told her that she and her husband were selling their furniture and they were moving to a boarding house at 23rd Street and 2nd Avenue.

When she asked Mrs. Hawes about a place on her head, Bryant said "she pointed to a stick on the fireplace and said her husband had hit her with that." Bryant then explained that the blood on the pillowcase had come from the wound that was still oozing on Friday. "The oilcloth at my house was given to me by Mrs. Hawes. She gave me the carpet the same day. I never noticed any blood on the carpet. I never unrolled it since I took it," she said.

Fannie also testified that Hawes and his daughter, May, were home on Monday at which time he instructed her to take May to her house and keep her there until he came for her, because he was on his way to Montgomery. "He told May not to play with the Negros. He did not like Negroes and did not want them to come to his house," Bryant said.

The Coroner then handed Fannie the passementerie. She immediately recognized it as her own and said that the police must have taken it from her house. "The beads came from one of Miss Emma's dresses," Bryant said. "Miss Emma's hair, I think is darker than this. I got this out of a vase when I was packing up things on Monday."

Fannie continued her testimony telling the jury that she had seen Mrs. Hawes for the last time on Saturday Morning. "She was at her house. I delivered her clothes and she told me to come back the next day and help her move, but she said nothing about leaving town. I went back about nine on Sunday and Mr. Hawes and May were there... and May said her mother went away that morning." Fannie Bryant was direct and looked at the jurors as she continued, "I asked him what it meant and where his wife was. He told me she got mad cause he had sent Willie to Atlanta and that she was going to go there to bring the little boy back home."

Bryant testified that the Hawes house had two mattresses on the floor and it appeared they had been occupied. May said she had slept there with her father and that her mother had taken Irene with her. She then told the jury that Mr. Hawes had come to her house sometime just after dark on Monday. May had played in the yard all day with a little boy who lived across the street.

Fannie Bryant surprised the coroner and jurors as well as the officers in the room when she concluded her testimony by revealing two new names to the investigation: Sarah Lett and Albert Patterson, both Negroes and her close friends. “Sarah Lett lives behind Miss Worthington’s place on 30th Street,” Fannie said. “She was at my house when Mr. Hawes came for May on Monday night. My nephew, Albert Patterson, works at the Georgia-Pacific Shops. I think he saw Mr. Hawes and May leave my house. I know Sarah saw them together.”

Finally Bryant’s testimony ended and Maria Jones, Fannie’s next-door neighbor was called to testify. Jones testified that May had been at Fannie’s about three o’clock in the afternoon on Monday. When asked if she had seen the passementerie, she said that she had seen Mrs. Hawes wearing it on Saturday morning. She then added, at that time the

Hawes house was "all torn up" and she had picked up a lock of hair from the floor and laid it on the mantelpiece. "It was the same color as that in the passementerie. It was lying around on the floor in large bunches. May said it was her Mama's hair," Jones said.

Eliza Gordon, who also lived near Fannie, testified that Fannie had brought May down to her house Monday morning and that Mr. Hawes had come for her that night. As they were leaving, she said that Hawes told May to say goodbye to Fannie and they left in the direction of the East Lake dummy line. "I know it was Mr. Hawes. He had on a long black overcoat and black pants. He has a mustache and no beard," Gordon said.

Another neighbor, Paralee Gardner, told the jury that she lived two houses from Fannie Bryant and on Saturday morning she had gone to the Hawes house to collect some money. Mrs. Hawes told her that she didn't have any money. When she went back the next day, Mrs. Hawes offered to give her a table in lieu of the money but she refused. On Monday, she again returned to the Hawes house and knocked on the door several times before anyone answered. Mr. Hawes finally answered the door. As she entered the house, she said that she saw Fannie Bryant standing in the hallway. "I asked Fannie where Mrs. Hawes was, but she said nothing and Mr. Hawes said she didn't stay there," Gardner said. "He said she left last night and went to Atlanta. I found hair in the floor by the bed. May held it and plaited it." Gardner was very convincing as she looked at Babbitt and then to the jurors, "It was mighty like Mrs. Hawes hair. Several chucks of hair were lying on the floor. I have seen that passementerie on Mrs. Hawes dressing case. Mr. Hawes told May, when he put the last load of furniture on the hack, to go down to Fannie's and to stay there until he came back."

Eliza Gordon was recalled to the stand and testified that she had seen both Sarah Lett and Albert Patterson at Fannie's house on Monday and they had remained after Mr. Hawes and May had left. She further stated that Fannie had told her that Hawes told her that he was going to put May in a school in Montgomery and that "Mrs. Hawes was gone and would not bother him anymore."

Paralee Gardner was also recalled to the stand and stated that Fannie had told her that Albert Patterson was her husband and not her nephew.

A new witness, John D. Patterson, an engineer, testified that he had run a train over to Atlanta on Sunday morning, but that "Mrs. Hawes did not leave here Sunday morning on my train as has been claimed. I know her personally," he said.

Dr. H.S. Duncan was recalled to the stand. He testified that he knew Albert Patterson and that once Fannie Bryant had told him that he was her nephew. "Last October I employed Fannie Bryant to Mrs. Hawes bedside during her sickness. The greatest affection I have ever known existed between May Hawes and her mother. One of the Negro girls told me that May had come to their house a few nights before and told them that her mother was dead. They found though that she was only sick. Mrs. Hawes told me that May sat up day and night to tend her sickness. She said if it had not been for May she would have died. I thought so too. The affection between the two was wonderful. If anyone should say that the girl did not love her mother dearly, I should pronounce the statement false." Dr. Duncan's testimony ended the proceedings of the second session and upon adjournment, Coroner Babbitt announced that a third session would convene on the following morning, December 7th at nine o'clock.

While the jury and Coroner were hearing testimony, many new developments in the case were unfolding. A telegram published in the Birmingham *Age-Herald* detailed the surprise of the citizens of Columbus, Mississippi regarding the news from Birmingham. *"No little excitement was caused here today by the news of the arrest of Richard R. Hawes last night, charged with the murder of his child. A number of men who have known Mr. Hawes quite intimately for years believe him to be innocent of the crime. With the officials of the railroad, Mr. Hawes has always borne a splendid character as a sober and reliable business man."*

The article continued, *"The friends of the bride say that Mr. Hawes has not tried to keep his former marriage a secret. Mrs. Hawes is expected home tomorrow. The family have sympathy from the whole community who join them in hope and belief that Mr. Hawes will soon prove his innocence, and that the future of the newly married wife and husband will be all the brighter for the cloud that now hangs over them."*

The police, believing that Mrs. Hawes, like her daughter, may have been drowned in East Lake, secured permission from Robert Jemison, Sr., President of the East Lake Land Company, to drain the lake. Arrangements were hastily made to drain the lake as quickly as possible as officers continued to drag the lake for the bodies.

It was made known that Fannie Bryant had engaged a well-known attorney, William H. Wade, who immediately sought to have Bryant's $1,000 bond reduced, but Babbitt refused. Later, upon Wade's insistence, Judge Samuel E. Greene issued a writ of habeas corpus on December 10th that the bond be reduced, although Bryant could not post it and remained incarcerated.

It was reported that Richard Hawes brother, James, arrived in Birmingham to claim the body of May and return it to Atlanta for burial. James Hawes refused to talk to reporters but stated that he would testify before the

Coroner's Jury if requested. The *Age-Herald* described the man as "a gentlemanly man, very much embarrassed by the turn affairs have taken here."

Several Birmingham citizens had donated money in excess of a hundred dollars for the dead girl's burial expenses. The *Age-Herald* reported that this act "speaks well of the charity of Birmingham. It is sufficient for a decent burial."

The story had totally dominated the news in Birmingham and other cities across the South and rumors were circulating that various groups in the city were planning to lynch Richard Hawes for the heinous crime. Meanwhile, rumors continued regarding the whereabouts of Emma Hawes and her other daughter, Irene. The youngest child, Willie, was reported safe in Atlanta with the family of brother, James Hawes. The missing mother and daughter were the subject of rumor and gossip. Were they alive or dead? Rumors and theory abounded. Police had sent telegraphs to a number of cities throughout the country where testimony indicated the wife might have gone, but the police were convinced that Emma had also been killed and continued to search for her body and more evidence.

Chapter 7

Friday , December 7, 1888 09:00

Coroner Babbitt called the third session of the Coroner's Inquest to order, even as East Lake was draining and being dragged in hope of recovering the bodies of Emma and Irene Hawes. An even larger crowd than the previous day had began gathering outside the Coroner's office hours before the nine o'clock start time. Word had spread through the evening that the new bride of Richard Hawes, Mrs. Mayes Storey Hawes, would be appearing to testify today. Babbitt had foreseen the calamity that this would create and had ordered the hearing moved to the Commercial Hotel, where the young bride was staying. The jurors were escorted in one at a time rather than as a group to keep down the commotion as much as possible.

The new Mrs. Hawes was the first to testify and stated that her husband had told her several months ago that he was a divorced man with one child, a boy named Willie, who lived in Birmingham. She also said that he told her that his first wife now resided in Lockport, New York. He never mentioned having two other children.

She then produced a letter that she said she had received from her husband following his arrest. She read the letter aloud:

"My Darling Mayes,

What can I say to you for the terrible trouble I have got into? I know how independent you are and only blame myself for not telling you all. For God's sake do not think I am guilty of this terrible thing. Try and judge me as light as you can. I loved you so I was afraid to tell you about her (May). I knew you would not have to be troubled with her as she would be in a convent. Don't believe anything you see in the papers, as not one-half is true. Let me know what you are going to do to me, this eve. This terrible suspense is just killing me. I don't think I can stand it much longer. Oh, my darling, if you

knew you would not censure me too severe, for it will prove out all right.

Your broken-hearted and most miserable one. Richard.

P.S. You will see me this p.m. If I can get off."

Following Mrs. Hawes testimony, Babbitt adjourned the jury to reconvene back at his office. Once the jury was reconvened, Albert Patterson was called back to the stand, where he stated that Fannie Bryant was his uncle's wife and that he had seen her and a Negro woman named Sarah Lett on Monday night. Patterson testified that Fannie showed him the "the plunder and stuff which Mrs. Hawes had given her." He said that he did not see a child that evening. He further stated that on Wednesday night (December 5) he heard of May Hawes death. Earlier on Saturday, he had seen May and Willie in a grove of haw trees on 24th Street, between Avenues A and B. Following his long and sometimes rambling testimony, Patterson was also placed under a $1,000 bond and was committed to the county jail.

The next witness to testify was John Olson, of Avondale, a painter on the Georgia-Pacific Railroad. Olson testified that he had seen Hawes board the dummy line for East Lake at 24th Street on Monday night, accompanied by a girl wearing a red straw hat. He testified that Hawes was dressed in a dark suit and soft hat and carried an umbrella.

G.W. Warren, the prescription clerk at Nabors & Morrow's Drug Store, told the jury that he had seen Hawes in that store on Monday night and that Hawes had told him that he had been waiting on the East Lake dummy for nearly two hours.

James H. Hawes, of Atlanta was the last witness called. He testified that like his brother, he was an engineer with Georgia-Pacific, running between Atlanta and Birmingham. On Saturday night (December 1), he said his brother Richard, brought little Willie down to the train shed for him to take to Atlanta. They left around eleven o'clock and arrived in Atlanta at seven the next morning. He explained that the boy was now at his home in Atlanta. He continued that his brother had told him that the two girls, Irene and May, were going to be put into a convent and that he had given Mrs. Hawes $500 with which to go live with her aunt in New York. He said that on his next run to Birmingham, he had again met his brother, this time at Weil's clothing store, where Richard was buying an overcoat, underwear and a valise. He said nothing about the girls.

James then explained, "Dick and Emma did not live happily together. I had them both speak of domestic trouble before they left Atlanta three years ago," he said.

Answering questions regarding his brother, James offered, "Before they left, Emma sold the property they owned there. Richard was making about $150 to $200 a month. I know but little about his family affairs. I don't know of his having money accumulated."

Coroner Babbitt adjourned the jury for lunch. When they started again at three o'clock, Babbitt called the first witness, Reuben B. Butler, an employee of the Birmingham Electric Light Company, who confirmed with his testimony that Richard Hawes was on the East Lake Dummy car alone on

Monday night. Butler said that he and Hawes engaged in conversation and Hawes told him that a "young lady had been staying at his house very late in the evening and that he had accompanied her back to her home at East Lake." Butler described Hawes as wearing a "mixed gray suit, standing collar, black derby hat, wore no overcoat and carried a gold-headed umbrella."

Mr. J. T. Glover, a clerk in the law firm of Hewitt, Walker & Porter, testified next that three months prior Hawes had told him he wanted his firm to get a divorce for him. "Our letter book shows that Hawes wrote to his lawyers, Hoke & Burton Smith in Atlanta, to whom he claimed he had paid $25.00 as part compensation. He wanted to know if our firm could get a speedy divorce for him. Subsequently, he called at our office to know what the substance of the reply we had received was."

Sarah Lett was called back to the stand, but added little to the previous testimony by her friend, Fannie Bryant. She testified that she had been at Fannie's house on the night of Monday, December 3rd, and had seen Hawes and May leave. She stated that she knew Fannie's nephew, Albert Patterson, but only slightly.

Rachel Whitfield, who resides at the corner of 1st Avenue and 21st Street, testified that she knew the Hawes family. She reported, "Mr. Hawes would beat his wife and curse her. I have seen him do it. He once struck her on the head with his shoe, and slapped her. I have seen him beat her twice." When asked about Mrs. Hawes reputation as a hard drinker, she replied, "She drank beer sometimes." When asked if she knew the reason for the violence, she answered, "I did not know what he was beating her for. He called her names. I have heard him call her a damn slut and she said to him, 'If I am, you are the cause of it.'" The witness reported that on one occasion when Mrs. Hawes asked her husband for money to pay the house rent, he told her "that was none of her damned business." Whitfield continued, "She told me that he threw his money away and that is why the children were neglected, ragged and naked. He then pushed her to the floor and kicked her."

Matilda Johnson, who cooked at Mrs. Hill's boarding house, corroborated Whitfield's testimony saying, "I know of one fuss they had... I saw him slap her on the face."

Babbitt announced that the inquest would adjourn for the night and resume at nine o'clock in the morning. However, events would delay that until the afternoon.

Earlier that same day an *Age-Herald* reporter had accompanied Birmingham Police Officers, Swain and Robbins to re-examine the Hawes house. The reporter wrote about his observations: *The Hawes place is the central of three neatly constructed cottages surrounded by a picket fence. The place is devoid of any evidence of attempts at flower culture, the few straggling patches of weeds and grass serving to but partially hide the red clay soil. It was far from being an attractive home.*

The reporter went on to describe in great detail the six-room cottage that had been home to the Hawes family, stating that police found "every indication of a hasty departure by the resident inmates." He described how the rooms were strewn with "paper, trash and worn copies of two old books."

He stated that a Negro woman followed the three men into the house and pointed out an "*ugly looking club, four feet long and two inches thick*," that she indicated was used as a window stop but hinted that she knew it had also been used as a weapon on more than one occasion. The police officers found what they believed to be blood stains on the floor near the doors in the kitchen and hallway and another similar stain on the wall of the rear bedroom.

The search continued at the house of Fannie Bryant where they found nothing of interest. The reporter wrote, "*The main importance attached to this dwelling is the fact that, as was gleaned from several witnesses, here were the spent the last hours of little May Hawes, before being hurried in a dark night to a watery grave.*"

Word quickly spread that the Hawes house was again being searched and soon a crowd reported to be more than two thousand curiosity seekers gathered in the vicinity and soon entered the house. The litter that was strewn throughout was gathered up as souvenirs. The *Age-Herald* reporter later wrote,

"Never have we seen so rabid a mob of curiosity seekers, men and women alike were mad-mad."

By evening, the mood in the city was tense as police continued the search for the bodies of Emma and Irene Hawes, concluding that they two were likely murdered. Draining and dragging the lake at East Lake had provided no further evidence.

According to newspaper articles and accounts, rumors of groups bent on lynching Richard Hawes for the heinous crime were mounting. Several editorials were published in the local newspapers deploring even the consideration of mob violence, but it seemed to fall on deaf ears. It seemed that despite the editorials and pleas from city officials, lawyers and other respectable citizens, the hatred and rage against Richard Hawes was escalating.

Chapter 8

Saturday December 8, 1888 07:35

On a cool blustery day, a group of police officers led by Captain O. A. Pickard of the Birmingham Police Department again examined the Hawes residence on 32nd Street. Two reporters from the Birmingham *Age-Herald* accompanied the group of officers. With no bodies found in East Lake, the police had reasoned that the body of Emma Hawes, and likely the other child, would have been disposed of near the residence or the nearby baseball park, and as such they returned to search the house and premises again for any evidence or clues that may have been missed on previous searches.

Sherriff Truss and another group of officers were working on a theory that perhaps the killer disposed of the other bodies in a similar manner as the one discovered in East Lake. Looking at the city map it was apparent that the lake at Lakeview was less than a quarter mile from the Hawes residence. Police reckoned that Hawes could easily have made the short trip in a horse-drawn carriage or on the Highland Avenue & Belt Railroad that ran south from 30th Street curving around Lakeview Park via Highland Avenue.

After gaining permission from Elyton Land Company to drain the lake if necessary, the officers began initiating operations to drag the lake to search for bodies. Dragging the lake would prove to be a very cumbersome task as the depth of the lake varied greatly and in some spots was as deep as thirty feet. As the dragging operation commenced, the coroner continued his inquest.

Coroner Babbitt called the inquest to order just after noon. A long list of witnesses testified and their testimony added to the story of the details leading up to and during the days of December 1st through the 3rd.

Mr. H. F. Brown, a fellow engineer with the Georgia-Pacific Railroad testified that Richard Hawes had told him that he had divorced his wife and that he had just returned from Mobile, where he had placed his three children in a convent.

Mr. J. A. Fanning, conductor on the East Lake Dummy Line testified that he was on duty on the night of Monday, December 3rd and that he saw a man get on the rear car at 24th Street with a little girl and take a seat near the stove. He said that he had been escorted to the jail by a police officer and saw Hawes in jail and concluded that he was the man he saw board the car with the little girl. "His features were like the one I saw, and I believe him to be the same man I saw... and there were several other prisoners standing around and I picked Hawes out of the crowd," Fanning said.

Mr. C. R. Willis, a rent collector employed by John L. Worthington, the landlord and owner of the house occupied by the Hawes family, testified that in September he had gone to the Hawes residence only to find Mrs. Hawes in bed. "Her face very much swollen, eyes blue and blood shot. She said she wanted me to see her condition so that I wouldn't attach her furniture. She said one arm was broken and one rib. She said her husband knocked her down, jumped on her, and stomped her. I asked why he did it and she said she thought he was trying to get rid of her, that she had some property in Atlanta and he wanted her to dispose of it and she would not consent and would probably die before she would agree to it," Willis stated.

Mr. Willis's testimony was interrupted as a young boy ran into the room and excitedly announced that police had just pulled Mrs. Hawes body from the south end of Lakeview Lake. After restoring order, Coroner Babbitt called an immediate adjournment to the proceedings as reporters and observers scrambled from the room to head to Lakeview.

Emma Hawes

Chapter 9

Friday, December 4, 2017 -- SCU Office Birmingham, Alabama

"So, what is our action plan until we get more info?" Fay asked, standing again.

"CSI was going to send divers down at East Lake this afternoon just to make sure they didn't miss anything. Should I tell them to hit the lake at Highland too?" Nate asked.

"Okay, I was following this until just now," Jerome interrupted. "I have heard your lecture about the Hawes murders twice and thought I had the story down, but Highland Lake?"

Nate laughed, "Well I have heard the story a few more times than you, but I was talking about the lake at the

Highland Park Golf Course, not the fancy subdivision on Double Oak Mountain."

Nate laughed and continued to explain, "The wife and other daughter in the Hawes story were found in Lakeview Lake but that lake is gone for the most part. Most of what you know as Lakeview was underwater back in the day. It was similar to Eastlake, complete with hotel, casino and the works. The small lake on the golf course is all that is left. I thought it would be worth a look."

"See, Nate, I am still learning things!" Clark smiled as gave Nate a fist bump.

Fay had a pensive look on her face, "Yes, Nate, I think that would be a good idea... But, I don't want to make a spectacle of this. All we need is word getting out that we are looking for more bodies without any real evidence or reason to, then a news frenzy will start and we will never be able to contain it."

"Understood Boss," Nate answered as he stood. "They should be able to send two divers down to take a look, discretely... I'll coordinate it with Lt. Guyer. I don't think the lake is very deep. If anybody asks, I'll tell them they are looking for my putter that I threw in after I missed an easy putt!" Everyone laughed. As Nate walked toward the door, he said, "I'll keep you posted."

"Jerome and I will go canvas the shelters," Amy said. "You never know, someone may not be speaking up for one reason or another. Walt, you hold down the fort and keep checking the wire and social media to see if anything turns up. Do that computer magic you do and dig us up something. And, if you don't hear from the M.E. in the next two hours, bug them too."

"Got it!" Said Walt as he was already typing on the keyboard,

Amy paused, "Anything else, Boss?"

Fay was returning to her desk. "I'm going to do some profile digging to see if there are any other copycats of really old cases anywhere. Let's meet back up this afternoon and see what we have."

Chapter 10

December 4, 2017 16:37

The desk phone rang and startled Walt Ellison. He had been combing through missing persons photo files for almost two hours.

"Ellison, SCU," he answered.

"Walt, it's Dan Jacobs. We are done with the autopsy. Report is not quite ready, but I know you guys need all you can get as quick as you can," said the medical Examiner. Walt got Fay's attention and put the call on speaker. "Short story is we are not going to be much help. C.O.D. is not drowning," Jacobs announced. "We put her time of death somewhere between midnight and 2 AM so she wasn't a floater in the classic sense. She had never sank when she was found. We are still waiting on the toxicology but it appears she was chloroformed."

Walt interrupted, “Is that what killed her?”

“Won’t know that until we get the full tox report, but it certainly could be fatal, especially on a child. Tox report will verify how much concentration or if there are any other drugs present.”

Walt looked back at Fay. “Anything else you can tell us?” she asked.

“No other signs of trauma. No sign of sexual assault.” Jacobs answered.

Fay Findlay had move over to Ellison’s desk to hear the call better. “Was she dead when she went in the water or just unconscious?” She asked.

“No, death occurred prior to her being placed in the water… no water was inhaled. Well, not like would have been present if she were breathing when she went in,” Jacobs answered.

Fay leaned in closer to the phone, "So you put time of death at midnight to 2 AM, can you tell how long she was in the water?"

"That is a bit more difficult to say precisely but she was in there no more than 4 hours but at least an hour... that's really the best we can do," Jacob responded. "The water temp keeps us from being more precise. Full report should be ready in about 3-4 hours but it won't tell you much more. Concentration of the chloroform in the liver and if anything else was in her system, but prelims didn't show anything."

Fay stood up straight and ran her fingers through her hair. "Thanks for rushing this through, Dan. We owe you one."

"No worries, I wish I had more help. I will have my report done in a few hours and I have put a rush on all the forensics, but you know how the lab is," Jacob responded, almost apologetic.

Walt left his seat and went the whiteboard. He wrote ***T.O.D. MN-0200 12/4/17***. He erased the ***~1900~*** following the Body in Water. In it's place he wrote ***~0100-0400***

12/4/17. He turned to see Fay staring at the board. "Still not much here," he said.

"Well, at least we have a much more narrow time frame now," Fay said. "Maybe someone saw something. Maybe we can catch a break. Not much time from death to her being in the water, so maybe he killed her there and dumped the body immediately."

Walt went his desk and pulled up his case note file. "I'm going to follow up with the Public Works guys that called it in. If time-of-death was closer to 0200 maybe they heard or saw something that didn't click as unusual. They were there at 0430, so if they saw anything – a car or heard anything that time of morning, it's a long shot but worth a revisit."

"They were pretty shaken about it," Fay answered. "Their supervisor was there when I arrived. After their statements, he sent them home. Give them a call to see if they have anything new to add while it is fresh on their minds."

Nate Parker came into the office talking on his cell. Moments later Boyd and Clarke returned to the office. Ellison caught them up on the autopsy report. "Did you guys turn up anything?" Walt asked.

With the team reassembled in the office now, Amy took her seat as Nate finished his call, "Nate, what did you find at the scene?"

"Divers spent about 3 hours in the water and got absolutely nothing," Nate answered. "Lt. Guyer has been going through everything they collected at the scene and the only thing that is suspicious is the lack of any evidence. They noted that one of the canoes in the pavilion was still wet when they photographed and inventoried the scene. There was a stack of sixteen of them in the pavilion. They rent them out. Only one was wet… they went all over it. Not a single fingerprint, stray hair… nothing, Nate explained. "Just in case the workers there were that diligent, they checked them all. The wet one - #13 – was pristine compared to others. It obviously had been wiped. Guyer thinks some sort of bleach or chlorine product used to wipe the interior surfaces down, as there was absolutely nothing on it. They actually ended up bringing it in and are trying to get chemical compound analysis and doing some other things in the lab with it to see what they can find."

"With the way the body was floating and the short duration she was in the water, she had to be dead when she went in. The air in her lungs kept her afloat rather than bacterial gases that we normally see that cause bodies to rise to the surface after a time," Walt added explaining what he had learned from the ME. "Since the lake is really not moving, she had to be placed very near where she was found. Of course, the likely scenario is that canoe was used to take the body out."

"The lake is about 16 feet deep where the body was and at that end it is pretty consistent. Right at the waters edge it is about 11 feet, so the canoe makes sense for dumping the body," Nate added. "On the west end of the lake it tapers out more to just inches but not on this end so you would need to be on a boat or something to get out there" he explained using a laser pointer on the crime scene photos of the lake now showing on the overhead screens. "She was about 17 feet from the edge of the lake and about

25 feet from the dock when found. We won't know anything else until they finish with the lab work which will probably be late tomorrow, although Guyer assures me it is there top priority and he has 3 people working on it." Nate made a gesture indicating that Amy had the floor.

Amy began her report, "No positive ID of the photo, but we did get one lady who said it could be a kid that came through last week or so, but she could not be sure. This was from one of the tenants at the Y shelter. She said a young white woman with 2 kids was there last weekend, she thinks. Kids were both girls with light brown wavy hair. She guessed ages about 10 and 6... She said that they sat at her table for dinner... kids seemed well behaved and the Mom seemed stressed and didn't talk much... She said they were from Mississippi and got stranded in Birmingham for some reason or another and were waiting on family to send some help... that's all she knows."

Amy explained further, "The Y gets a photo of everyone that checks in so they are going to send those over and we can have the CSI folks compare the photos to the victim." Amy looked at Jerome who seemed a bit tense. She took a deep breath before continuing, "Okay, here is the crazy part since we are going down this rabbit hole....

According to the sign in sheet at the shelter, the Mom's name is Emma and the kids are Irene and Maylena." A definite shudder went through the room.

Nate leaned back in his chair, "Holy Shit! What are the chances?"

Jerome chimed in, "Yeah, right? It freaked me out when I saw that. When I showed Amy I think the lady at the desk thought we were going to croak or something... we both stood there staring at the paper for like 3 minutes."

Amy continued, "It is definitely freaky and scary... they don't really collect much information because most people coming through the shelter are pretty private and most don't want to do that and they are really there to try and help... She said Emma looked to be around 30 or 35 maybe and Maylena was listed as 9 years old and Irene as seven. They do ask for children's ages as they report general stats to the One Roof organization. She didn't notice anything really unusual about the family. Said they were fairly clean. The Mom had a medium size red duffle bag and the kids were wearing light jackets when they checked in. She tried referring them to a longer term shelter, but Emma said she had someone coming to pick them up the next morning."

As Amy concluded, Fay stood from her chair and walked toward the whiteboard. "Do we have a last name or any info on where they came from or where they were going?' she asked.

"She listed her last name as Hall, but the attendant wasn't sure how legit that was," Jerome answered. "Evidently when she signed in she didn't give her last name. So, when asked she was hesitant. She was told it was only for internal record keeping and all names and other information was kept private. Only then did she come up with Hall"

"No ID was shown." Amy added, "Another tenant said the kids seemed confused when she told them her last name and seemed to question their Mom but she shushed them up. She also didn't want to be photographed either but was told that it was mandatory and was assured that the photos were kept only in case something happened and they were not shared anywhere. The kids were hungry and tired and she needed a place to stay so she reluctantly agreed."

"Other than the one reference she made about being from Mississippi, we don't have anything on where they were going or coming from," Jerome added. "At the long term shelters they try to get the kids in school or make arrangements with Social Service but the Y is usually just an overnight place until they can get them into a more stable place."

Amy interjected, "We have contacted all the shelters with the names and descriptions and will send photos to see if they have been in before. I even contacted One Roof just in case they had sought help from any other organizations for food or clothes or anything else. They were traveling light with only a duffle bag for all three."

Amy Boyd turned to the whiteboard and wrote ***POI/Possible Victim – WF ~30 Emma ~Hall~ 2 children WF – Maylena -9 and Irene -7***. POI was shorthand for Person of Interest, a term police liked to use for someone they felt may be connected to a crime but were not yet ready to deem them a suspect or a victim.

Fay Findlay stepped to the center of the room. "So far I have had no luck finding any copycat cases involving century old crimes, but this latest information, if it pans out to be our victim, seems to confirm that our theory of the correlation to the Hawes case is legitimate," Fay said.

"Amy, make sure the CSI and Forensic teams on duty gets those photos when they come in and work on facial recognition. Unlike the TV shows, we know that will take time, so let's get that process going," Fay continued.

"Nate, update homicide and missing persons too. We need to find out who Emma, Maylena and Irene are and where they came from," Fay added. "Let's call it a day and regroup fresh in the morning."

"Walt, tomorrow start doing your thing with this new information we have... if Emma is not a Hall, let's see if that is an alias she has used before or if we can dig up anything at all," Fay said with her hand on Walt's shoulder.

"Nate, did CSI make it over to the golf course?" Fay asked.

"No, Ma'am, but I am meeting Lt. Guyer and two divers from his team over there at 10 AM in the morning," Nate responded. "They said the light would be best then.

That lake is only about 10 feet deep so he feels that if there is anything there, they will find it easily."

"Sorry to wreck everyone's weekend," Fay announced. "Go home and get some rest. I have a feeling we are not going to get much of it the rest of the week. See you all in the morning."

Chapter 11

Saturday, December 8, 1888 12:30

Coroner Babbitt arrived on the scene at Lakeview along with several police officers and the reporters who had been covering the inquest. The area was filled with observers from the neighborhood and from throughout the city and the crowds were growing rapidly as the word spread of the discovery of the body.

Emma Hawes lifeless body was disfigured after having been submerged in the water. She had an extensive wound on the back of her head behind the left ear. A curtain cord was tied around her neck and another around her waist and feet. The cords secured four pieces of railroad iron to her body.

As the size of the crowd of onlookers grew, their disposition also became more intense and angry. It seemed that the sight of the body further ignited their hate for Richard Hawes and talk, and even shouts, for his lynching were rampant in the growing crowd.

Finally the undertaker's curtained wagon arrived to transport the body. The body was loaded aboard and set out for the funeral home. As the wagon neared Lockwood & Miller's, a large and angry crowd was waiting around the building. An article in the *Age-Herald* described the crowd as "swelling into the hundreds and even the thousands was there to greet it." The description of the scene indicates that people filled the streets for two blocks in every direction and a dozen police officers were stationed at the back and front of the mortuary to keep the crowds back.

Fearing mob violence, several police officers met the wagon blocks before its arrival and diverted in another direction to 8th Avenue and 22nd Street, as Coroner Babbitt had decided it best to move the inquest elsewhere. However, as the crowds continued to grow, Babbitt sent word and ordered the wagon to go directly out 19th Street to the City Cemetery (now Oak Hill). There he had the body of Mrs. Hawes secured in a stone vault.

Rumors in the crowds abounded as to whether the woman's body was actually in the hearse or if it had been some diversionary tactic by authorities. Other rumors were that the curtained wagon held Richard Hawes and the Sherriff had used it to move the prisoner to a safe location fearing the mobs and escalating rumors of lynching.

By the time the wagon had reached the cemetery the crowds in the city had grown and the largest gathering appeared near the corner of 4th Avenue and 21st Street. The jail was located on the southeast corner of this intersection. Behind the jail on the corner of 3rd Avenue and 21st Street was the large new Jefferson County Courthouse. Next to the jail on the eastern side was the new jail, currently under construction. The new jail was at least five times larger than the existing structure and reached from 4th Avenue to the alley in the middle of the block off of 21st Street. Across the alley from the new jail was the courthouse. On the western end of the block was the majestic St. Paul's Cathedral.

With the crowds growing larger and obviously angrier, Sheriff Joseph S. Smith and Police Chief O.A. Pickard strengthened the guard at the jail as quickly as possible. Men were stationed at the four corners of the block and others were sent out on patrol of adjoining streets. Each lawman was armed with a shotgun or Winchester rifle. The increased presence of armed lawmen kept the mobs moving about and somewhat orderly. When interviewed about the increased guards and the gathering crowds, Smith and Pickard told the reporters that those in the crowds were just curious and only trying to "get a glimpse of the man charged with blackest crime ever committed in Jefferson County and perhaps the most revolting in the criminal annals of Alabama." It later proved that Sheriff Smith and Chief Pickard had either misjudged the growing crowd's intentions or had overestimated the effects of their actions to quell the simmering anger of the gathered citizenry.

As dusk came, the crowd had swelled even larger, filling the sidewalks and streets surrounding the jail and courthouse. It was obvious that they meant business and that the increased number of lawmen were no longer deterring the crowd. Smith and Pickard sent out a messenger to locate the mayor.

Soon Mayor B. A. Thompson arrived, surrounded by a squad of police officers, to meet the crowd. Shouting above the fray, the mayor pleaded with the crowd to disperse and go home. He reasoned that even in the face of a horrendous crime they didn't want to take actions that they would be ashamed of later. For a short time, the crowd seemed to be listening as the shouting quieted and they respectfully listened to the pleas of the Mayor. However, the peace was short lived as those in the crowd that were too far in the back to hear became louder and began pushing forward and the intensity of the anger seemed to grow even stronger.

The streets surrounding the jail and courthouse were now packed with people of all walks of life. The crowds were now tightly bunched as they pressed from both directions on 21st Street toward the alley in the center of the block that led to the jail behind the courthouse.

Several other citizens had begun to circulate through the growing crowd trying to calm the anger and reason with the mob. Among them were former Mayor Thomas Jeffers, Judge Samuel Greene, Solicitor James E. Hawkins, Postmaster Maurice B. Throckmorton and at least twelve others. While these well-respected men had some success as people listened to their pleas for calm and order, the crowds had grown too large for their efforts to matter. As darkness settled in, the crowd size and intensity continued to grow. Later estimates of the crowd size ranged from 3,000 to more than 10,000. By eleven o'clock the shouts from the crowd could be heard for several blocks drawing even more people into the streets.

Sheriff Smith had positioned himself at the doorway to the jail and had fortified the place as much as possible with his deputies and Pickard's policemen. About fifty lawmen lined the building in two lines. The first line began at the corner of 3rd Avenue and 21st Street and another at the entrance into the alley from 21st Street. In the alley and at the jail entrance the protection was even tighter. Lawmen were even stationed on the roof of the jail and adjacent courthouse. The jail door was well guarded and barricaded. Each of the Deputies, policemen and guards were heavily armed with shotguns, rifles or both and each carried extra ammunition.

Smith had continually shouted to the imposing crowd to not enter the alley lest they be shot. The lawmen had been instructed to only fire on the Sheriff's command and each man stood tense and eyeing the burgeoning crowd before them. So far, the crowd had heeded the Sheriff's continual warnings and had remained just out of the alley, but now 21st Street was so packed with angry citizens of every description, that it was difficult to move independently.

In the darkness of the night, suddenly the mass pushed into the alley and into the line of lawmen that could no longer hold them back though they tried.

"Stop or we will shoot," Sheriff Smith shouted more intensely, but the crowd continued to move forward. When the bodies began pouring into the alley toward the jail, Smith gave the signal and the lawmen opened fire into the crowd.

The roar of gunfire lit up the night and was quickly followed with another round of firing. Some in the crowd fired guns back at the lawmen as bullets ricocheted off the stone walls and bullets zipped through the walls and windows into the jail.

For a brief but terrifying moment, buckshot and bullets seared into the crowd and chaos ensued as bodies began to fall and screams of agony echoed through the darkness. In the pandemonium the assault had stopped as those not wounded or killed retreated. The Sheriff commanded the firing cease. It had only lasted a moment, but to most, it seemed like an eternity.

The crowd seemed to be stunned at the events. Most had thought the Sheriff had been bluffing and would never open fire on his own citizens. As most of the crowd retreated, some remained tending to the wounded and dead strewn about the street and sidewalks.

Sheriff Smith, not wanting to chance another assault sent couriers to the headquarters of the four local companies of the Alabama State Troops - The Birmingham Rifles, The Jefferson Volunteers, The Guards and The Light Artillery. All four units had been placed on standby earlier in the day and the soldiers had been assembled in their armories. Three of the units immediately responded to the scene.

The fourth unit, The Light Artillery, did not respond. Their Commander, Captain Maurice B. Throckmorton, who also served as the local Postmaster, had been fatally wounded in the chaos as he tried to reason with the crowds. In the aftermath, Throckmorton was quoted in a local newspaper with his last words, "Oh! That I should be killed in such an affair as this." Throckmorton died moments later from his wound as lay on the corner of 4th Avenue and 21st Street as several men tried to tend his wound.

Upon arrival, the troops organized and cleared the streets, helped administer to the wounded and cleared the dead. Newspaper reports the following day touted the heroic job that had been done by several physicians and the Charity Hospital during and after the melee.

The reports following the riots varied greatly but by most accounts more than a dozen died and more than twenty-five were wounded in the uprising. The total could never be clear because many were treated in private homes so those with minor wounds were never recorded. Some of the wounded died days, or even weeks, later from their injuries and later accounts spoke of many African-Americans that were killed and wounded that were never listed on the initial reports.

As the troops restored order, word spread of the riot and assault on the jail. As a result, additional troops were deployed on orders of Governor Seay from throughout the state and within days more than five hundred soldiers were encamped around the courthouse in downtown Birmingham.

Emotions ran high and opinions divided in the aftermath of the riot. Many thought those in charge, the mayor, sheriff and police chief, had no other choice than to act as they had done, stating that they were simply doing their job and keeping the peace. On the other side, many felt that opening fire on citizens, even an angry mob, went too far. As a result, in the days following the riot, several citizens swore out warrants for the two top lawmen for deaths or injury to loved ones. When served, the lawmen were removed from office and taken into custody. A number of prominent citizens were quick to post their bonds. However, more citizens came forward obtaining additional warrants for other deaths and injuries resulting in the pair being arrested again. More than a year later, the two were finally tried in court but the jury failed to convict either man of wrongdoing.

Jefferson County Courthouse

3rd Avenue and 21st Street

Chapter 12

Sunday December 9, 1888

As troops patrolled downtown Birmingham, soldiers padlocked all the gun shops, kept a close eye on all saloons, although they remained open. They guarded the jail and dispersed even the smallest gatherings on the streets.

Peace had returned to the Magic City but there was a definite uneasiness hung in the air. The riot and its aftermath had briefly replaced the murders as the top news story. Though related, the debate over the handling of the riot seemed to put the murders aside for a brief time.

In the early afternoon of an overcast and rainy day, the curtained funeral wagon loaded with the pure white casket, purchased through the charity of the citizens of Birmingham carried the body of little May Hawes from Lockwood & Miller to her final resting place on a grassy knoll in the City Cemetery. Just a short distance away, May's mother lay temporarily interred in a stone vault. May's funeral was simple and without fanfare. The grave was unmarked.

Soon afterward, Coroner Babbitt accompanied by Dr. Cunningham Wilson and the jurors returned to the cemetery to reexamine the body of Emma Hawes. Examining the head wound, Dr. Wilson said, "The wound was likely caused by a heavy stick or other blunt object." He stated that the injury might have caused death "by concussion of the brain." But, he could not be certain that the injury was indeed the cause of death.

While these events were taking place rumors of how the murders occurred continued to spread through the city. With soldiers keeping the peace, and the dead buried, life was returning to normal as much as possible. Newspaper headlines and stories in the next few days seem to support this: **Blood and Death,** followed by **Peace Has Come Again** and **The**

Excitement is Slowly Passing Away. These headlines were followed by an editorial in the *Age-Herald* entitled **The Hawes Horrors**. The editorial read, in part: ***"The evidence is now as strong and complete as a chain of circumstances can make it that Richard R. Hawes murdered his wife and children... Circumstantial evidence is never infallible, but nothing short of the positive testimony of substantial witnesses could furnish stronger proof of Hawes guilt than now exists... Taking all the evidence --- The facts of the murder, Hawes trip to East Lake on the dummy with May and his return without her on the very night her body must have been deposited in that sheet of water, his second marriage, and the fact that he was never divorced from the first wife and the falsehoods imposed on the second --- there is no escaping the conclusion that he is the man that murdered Emma Hawes and the two children... There should be no delay in justice... Let the Grand Jury be impaneled, the indictment found and the trial had at the earliest possible moment."***

Later that afternoon, Marion Cann, City Editor of the *Age-Herald* and E. C. Bruffey of the *Atlanta Constitution* were granted a unique opportunity and accompanied Sheriff Smith to interview Richard Hawes and Fannie Bryant through the bars in their cells.

Hawes personally knew Bruffey from his time in Atlanta and after exchanging pleasantries, Hawes asked, “Is there much talk of my affairs in Atlanta?”

“Everyone is talking about it. Some think you are innocent. Others are satisfied that you are guilty,” Bruffey replied.

“And there are more who think me guilty?” Hawes asked.

“No Dick, you are wrong,” He answered. “The general impression is that your wife jumped in the lake to drown herself and carried May and Irene with her.”

“Before God, I believe that was the way it was,” Hawes solemnly replied.

"But that could not have been, for they were found in lakes a mile apart," Bruffey told him, shaking his head in disbelief.

Hawes was silent for a moment before replying, "That's so? I cannot, of course, think that now... I did think that."

Hawes looked distraught and then raised his hands above his head and bellowed, "Oh God! This is terrible. Here I am confined in this cell charged with murdering my wife and daughters. Why should I kill them? I loved those two children and once loved their mother. The children I could not of killed for my heart was too full of love for them. The mother I could not have killed because we were apart."

Hawes paced in the small cell lamenting that his incarceration was keeping him from attending to his dead child and then turned his attention to Irene. "What may be her fate? Was she dead too? Oh, who could injure that innocent, loving child? She may be dead, and I almost pray that she is!" Hawes said despondently.

Hawes grabbed the bars before him and cried, “Oh that I could rend these bars apart... I would have one wish: To see my boy dead and then to die too. That would remove us all from earth and we could all be laid in one grave. Wouldn't that be a pleasure?”

No one responded.

Hawes then mourned his loneliness, “Last Sunday morning I was a free man and now I am in jail with officers protecting me,” he moaned as he paced in his tiny cell. “Then I was happy and now I am miserable. Then I was a happy father of two bright girls and now one is dead and the other...Oh God! Where is my Irene, my darling little girl?” he asked as he placed his hands over his face.

The reporters asked Hawes about his recent behaviors --- his plans to place the children in a convent, his relationships with his wife and children and his recent living arrangements.

He replied cautiously to each question choosing every word carefully and slowly. He told them that he sometimes stayed at the house. He said he personally paid the rent and grocery bills, explaining, “I never gave Emma any money because you know how she was. If I gave her a dollar for provisions, she would buy liquor with it and get drunk.”

He was then asked about Saturday night when the riot threatened his protection, he answered, “Not easy, of course. I was not at all nervous, but was cool. I was sure that I would be protected.”

He went on to explain that when the gunfire began all that changed. “I was ready to go with the crowd to the most ignominious death a man could ever endure,” he told the reporters.

Cann’s interview with Fannie Bryant, who had been held in jail since the body of May Hawes had been discovered, only further confused her possible involvement or knowledge of the crimes. She was in jail because she had provided several conflicting stories since the investigation had begun. Her answers to the reporter's questions followed that same pattern. In Cann's article on the interview, he concluded with the statement that he felt Fannie Bryant "could be made to tell more about the affair than anyone." His opinion was shared by many, including police, and was echoed in many newspaper articles.

The *Age-Herald* article lamented the unfortunate death of those in the riot and focused on the death of Throckmorton. *"His death is most sad because his presence at the jail was not as a rioter but to persuade the crowd against violence."* The article went on to defend the action taken by the Sheriff and Chief in opposing the rioters.

Chapter 13

1888: Birmingham, Alabama

In the coming days things in the Magic City were returning to as normal as was possible under the circumstances. The Coroner continued the inquest after the discovery of Emma Hawes body. Police continued to investigate the crimes and continued looking for Irene. Slowly the troops began to leave downtown, returning the job of guarding the jail to the sheriff.

Despite the apparent iron clad circumstantial case against Richard Hawes, detectives continued to follow leads in the investigation taking nothing for granted. Several leads that seemed to have merit at first, turned out to be dead ends, and others turned out to be pure fabrication by witnesses that were apparently seeking publicity for themselves or for some other unknown reason.

On Saturday December 15, 1888, Deputy Truss, Detective Kernan and Officer Robinson recovered the body of Irene Hawes from the lake at Lakeview approximately thirty feet from where her mother had been discovered days ago. In the preceding days, the lake had been partially drained as police continued to drag the lake. The lake bottom was very uneven with some spots being thirty or more feet in depth from the reduced lake. The child's body was retrieved from a small crevice in the lake floor.

Like her sister May, Irene wore black stockings and button shoes, but was otherwise not clothed. A brown woolen sack covered the upper part of her body, but the lower half was uncovered. Like her mother, her body had been weighted down with three short pieces of railroad iron tied around body with cords. Her body was in remarkable condition considering the amount of time it had been in the water. There were no signs of visible injury other than it appeared the girl had bitten through her bottom lip before or during her death.

When Coroner Babbitt arrived at Lakeview a large crowd was already gathering at the scene. Under orders from Babbitt, soon the curtained black wagon from Lockwood & Miller arrived and the child's body was placed in a casket and transported directly to the City Cemetery. Babbitt was determined to prevent repeating the occurrences of the past spectacles. The wagon was met at the cemetery by the jurors, where they and Coroner Babbitt examined the body. The casket was then buried alongside May.

When Hawes was notified that his youngest daughter's body had been recovered, he sat in cell and showed no emotion.

Chapter 14

Saturday December 5, 2017

Fay Findlay awoke Saturday morning without the aid of an alarm. She decided not to set an alarm and hoped she could get a good night's sleep. She had slept, but not well. She could not get her mind to turn off. All night, her mind raced as she thought, "Who was this lunatic that had caused the death of a child? Had he already killed others?" If their lead panned out, had he killed her sister and mom? If so, where were their bodies? If they were found in the golf course lake, she knew they were dealing with a seriously disturbed individual if that was not already evident. "Why the Hawes case?" Fay asked herself.

Fay's mind continued to race as she made coffee. The case was somewhat famous in certain circles, but likely 99.9% of Birmingham citizens had never heard of Richard Hawes or his murdered family. It came up sometimes in presentations about the city history but usually only ones related to police activity or on the Ghost Tours that one of the city historians offered around Halloween every year. So, what would motivate a deranged person to go to such an extreme of recreating a crime from over a century ago?

As Fay sat in her comfortable Eames recliner looking out at the city skyline as the sunrise began to reflect off the tall buildings, she tried to convince herself that she was getting ahead of herself. She only had ONE body, not an entire family. Maybe it ***was*** a coincidence. As much as she wanted to believe that, her gut told her it was not, and that the child's body was not going to be the end of this.

In more than thirty years of as a cop, Fay had run into her share difficult cases. Difficult for one reason or another, but most were what she considered typical. Cases over domestic abuse or results of a disagreement in a club. She had even had a few murders for hire cases. She had never had a case that she usually labeled in her classes as 'Movie or Novel Murders.' Serial killers who are sociopaths preying on victims they don't know. Mad men carrying out some bizarre ritual while watching their victim's lives slip away. Things that made for interesting reading or movies. If not interesting, at least they would make the hair on your neck stand up. She knew that they happened in real life too, but she had never encountered it on her turf... and she didn't want to start now.

She had studied the cases of them in both her Criminal Justice and Psychology courses. Bundy, Dahmer, Gacy made headlines and still were well known decades after their capture or deaths. These were before her career began but were still fresh enough to have been the subjects in many under-graduate courses. The closest she had come to actual involvement in such cases was as a young detective, helping FBI agents investigating the 'Railroad Killer,' Angel Maturino Resendiz, who was convicted of fifteen murders in Illinois, Florida, Georgia, Kentucky and Texas. His path, no doubt led him through Birmingham on the rails, but no deaths there were attributed to him. He confessed to fifteen murders but was suspected to have committed many more. He was executed by lethal injection.

She also consulted on a similar case, known as the 'The Boxcar Killer', Robert Joseph Silveria, Jr., who was convicted in 1996 of nine murders of fellow transients along the railways of the Southern U.S. Although convicted of nine murders, he confessed to many more and most of the bodies were never recovered.

Fay had studied even more, but rarely did one see a villainous killer that was calculating and went to the trouble of staging the victim's body as it seems this case had. What would today bring, she thought as she finished her coffee and rose to get dressed. It was 7:45 AM and she knew most of team was already on their way to the office, if not already there.

For the last few years, Fay had made a concerted effort to let the team do their work, even if it was difficult for her. She liked working alone. She liked doing things at her pace and following her gut instincts without being second-guessed. Her overzealous work ethic and high conviction rate had kept superiors from insisting that she play by their rules or do things their way. She made them look good and that was enough for them to leave her alone. When she was asked to form the SCU, she was hands-on with every single aspect of every investigation. She knew no other way. But with time, she learned to trust that her protégés had the same work ethic she demanded and she could coach, guide and encourage them and that was enough. They all knew her expectations and strived to never disappoint.

The current SCU team had been in place for more than three years now, with Ellison being the newest member. Amy Boyd had been on the squad the longest, 8 years. They were a great team and Fay often contemplated what retirement might look like, but feared she would soon be bored. She had more than 30 years in so she could retire at anytime and that made it easier to stay. "I'll know when it's time," she often said when the subject came up as many of her colleagues pulled the pin. "I'm good for now."

Her team was top notch. Amy Boyd was the de facto leader whenever Fay was absent and was more than capable. A ten-year veteran of BPD, she had served in the Marine Corp. for four years right out of high school and used her veteran's benefits to pay for college. After her discharge she joined BPD and finished her Criminal Justice degree at UAB while working as a Patrol Officer in the West Precinct. She was promoted to Detective after 5 years and Detective Sergeant 2 years later. The next year she was tapped for SCU. As a detective she had worked in Family Services, and then Property Crimes and Homicide. Two years ago, she married her partner of 11 years, Ellen, when Alabama law finally made gay marriage legal.

Nate Parker had been with BPD for 13 years and had been in SCU for the last 6. As a young African-American man that grew up in the northern section of Birmingham he had always wanted to be a cop. Officers who ran the Police Athletic Leagues in his Norwood neighborhood had made an impression on him at an early age. His mom was a schoolteacher and his dad was an HVAC technician. His parents had instilled a strong work ethic and stressed the importance of a good education. He attended the HBCU, Alabama State University, in Montgomery. While in college, Nate volunteered with the Equal Justice Initiative (EJI) founded by Bryan Stevenson. EJI works mainly on death row cases that had lost all other hope and keeping children from being tried as adults. There, Nate saw the side of the criminal justice system that seemed to be slanted in favor of those who had money and privilege. Even though many of the clients they represented were indeed criminals in the truest sense of the word, Nate saw that the circumstances were often greater than their crimes. He saw too many who had been incarcerated for years by an unjust system freed. He saw others at least gain an even playing field as they met their fate in the courtroom.

After graduating with honors, Nate headed back home to Birmingham, where enrolled in the Cumberland

Law School at Samford University. During his second semester he came home after class on a Friday afternoon to find his parent's slain in the kitchen of the home he grew up in. Victims of a home invasion robbery, they had been killed during the night.

Nate dropped out of school and two weeks later applied to the Birmingham Police Department. He started to Rookie School three weeks later. His parent's killers were soon arrested -- Four young men from the Kingston community of Birmingham, less than 6 miles from Nate's home. All four were younger than he was and all were dropouts and gang members. Nate used that horrible experience along with his three years of work at EJI to dedicate himself to making a difference. Although he thought becoming a lawyer and activist like his mentor, Bryan Stevenson, was his destiny, the event of his parent's murders changed his focused.

In dealing with his parent's murders, he sensed that he could make an impact as a police officer. While his anger raged against the senseless taking of his parent's lives, he also felt for their murderers and their families. He wanted to change the system. He wanted to make sure that justice was served but he also wanted to make a difference to keep such heinous crimes from happening.

Nate was making a difference. He started several programs working with disadvantaged youths in various parts of the city. In his third year on the force, he was promoted to Detective and worked four years in Juvenile before being tapped for SCU.

Jerome Clarke has been a team member of SCU for five years and an officer with BPD for nine. He worked as an officer with the Memphis PD for three years before moving to Birmingham when his wife graduated from medical school and came to UAB Medical Center for her residency. Following her residency, she accepted a position with a pediatric group in town and Jerome joined BPD working patrol in the South Precinct and then as an Evidence Technician in the Crime Scene Investigation unit for two years before being promoted to Detective assigned to the Homicide Unit. Two years later he was assigned to the SCU.

Walt Ellison was the newest member of the SCU and the youngest member of the team. He was assigned to SCU after only 2 years on the job. Although he never completed his college degree, Walt is what most of his teammates call a computer geek. Walt grew up in rural Chilton County about an hour south of Birmingham. His parents and most of his family are farmers. As a child, Walt showed a keen intelligence and interest for computers after he received a hand-me-down laptop from his Uncle John, who worked for the Sherriff's Department.

By the time Walt graduated from high school he was earning money doing computer repairs and special projects for businesses and churches in the community. His uncle encouraged him to consider a career in law enforcement indicating that his computer skills were in desperate need at any agency as cyber crimes were only going to get more complicated and widespread.

Walt joined BPD a year later and worked patrol for only ten months before his skill set was discovered and he was assigned to the cyber unit where he quickly excelled. After doing work for the SCU on three different cases, Fay finally convinced the powers that be, to reassign him to her team on a permanent basis. While he learned a lot in Cyber, Walt felt that he wasn't really a Police Officer there. Being a member of the SCU team had broaden his views of the work and made his skills behind the keyboard even better.

Dressed in dark jeans and a cotton sweater, Fay grabbed her keys and weapon from the drawer where she kept it by the door, punched in the code to set the alarm and locked the door to her loft. She met a neighbor and his dachshund, Rufus, in the hall heading for the elevator.

"Good Morning, Sam and Rufus," Fay said as they arrived at the elevator.

Rufus ignored her. Sam replied, "Good Morning. I can never sleep in. He is more reliable than an alarm!"

The trio rode down the three floors together in silence. When the doors parted, Rufus lunged out heading for the outside door. "Have a nice walk," Fay shouted as the pair disappeared out the door. She headed down the hall to the right for the garage and drove the seven blocks to Police Headquarters.

When she arrived at the office, as expected, the team was all at their desks working.

"Amy brought muffins over there," Walt announced, pointing toward the table that held the Kuerig and had a mini-fridge with water and soda underneath.

Fay reached in the bag for a muffin and grabbed a Coke Zero from the fridge.
"Anything new while I slept?" she asked.

"Too early yet," Nate replied. "I am going to meet Guyer and his guys at the golf course about 9:30. Okay if Jerome comes too, in case we turn up something?"

Fay looked at Amy with a look that said 'it is your call'.

"Definitely," Amy was quick to respond. "As a matter fact make sure the South Precinct commander knows what you are doing because it is Saturday and the golf course will be steady. If you find a body, it will get crazy really quick and he needs to be ready to respond."

Jerome looked up from his laptop, "Good call. I will handle that, Nate. My old precinct." He picked up the phone to make the call.

Fay took a sip of her soda and then addressed what everyone was thinking. "So, it seems we all expect to find more bodies today?" The room grew quite.

"Yeah, boss, that is the consensus opinion," Nate said.

The sighs from the rest of the team were audible. "We hope we are wrong," added Amy, "but it appears that we are dealing with a real sicko that is latched onto the Hawes murder case for whatever reason. Walt hooked us up and we are all reading *Birmingham Horrors* to refresh us."

The Birmingham Horrors is a book written in 1980 by a local historian, William Stanley Hoole, about the case. The author used public records from court documents and newspaper accounts of the crime, trial, riot and subsequent execution of Richard Hawes, to record the crime and investigation in great detail. Fay always recommended the book for her investigation courses as supplemental reading.

"I am impressed," Fay said with a smile. "You guys continue to amaze me. So what do think... what's the profile?"

"We had that discussion just before you arrived," Amy answered. "The Perp is meticulous. The total lack of evidence at the East Lake scene tells us that. We need to get more info before we can really profile him. *HIM*, simply because the odds highly indicate the perp being a white male. But, we should be getting a lot more information soon. We should have Emma identified and that will help us to know how she may have become his victim."

"Yes, that time when we are forced into a holding pattern," Fay concluded. "Let's gather up as much of the missing info as we can and reconvene this afternoon. I know you guys have given up most of your Saturday and I appreciate it. I have a feeling this one is going to consume all of our time for a bit."

Nate and Jerome stood. "We'll be in touch as soon as we know anything," Nate said as the two headed out the door for what they both figured to be long day.

"We'll be waiting anxiously," Amy replied. "Of course, we will continue digging while we wait."

As the pair left, Amy turned to Walt and asked, "Have you found anything on your deep search of the world wide interwebs?"

Walt stopped typing and spun around in his chair to face his two female colleagues. "You already know that I found nothing on missing persons and all the normal lines, so I have been on a deep dive to the dark recesses. There are quite a few chat rooms and such where those obsessed with the macabre socialize and swap ideas... I've been looking for anything related to old murder cases and in particular, the Hawes case... but so far, I am batting ZERO."

Walt stood and walked to the whiteboard. "I have also done an extensive search online for the anything about the Hawes murder case and there isn't much. You probably already know that, boss. There is a book that a newspaper reporter wrote right after the murders in 1889. Long out of print but I got a PDF copy from the Library of Congress... Don't you love the advancements of the technology age?" he mused. "There's the more recent book that the guy wrote back in the seventies. Also out of print, but I got a copy at the library downtown and did some PDF magic to get a copy to the team as it covers the case in a pretty detailed fashion. Then there is fiction novel from a local writer a few years ago that used the Hawes case as a backdrop. That one is a little creepy for me... I downloaded it from Amazon. The ghost of the little girl, May Hawes, has a recurring role... that should tell you all you need to know about why it creeped me out. Other than that, there are some short stories of Birmingham Crimes and Ghosts of Alabama books and other stories that mention it. A few articles over the years in various historical societies newsletters and such."

"As for the books, the first two are pretty straightforward accounts of the events surrounding the case. The 1889 one was a bit hard to read because of the writing, which I assume is the way they talked back then. The more recent one seems to follow the same line detailing the case... The lady at the library actually remembers helping the author with his research back in the day. She said she thought he was a History professor or something at the University of Alabama. She's read both and said the latest was easier to follow and provided a good bit more detail and I agree. The third, as I said, was just creepy and it is fiction. Newsletters were basically just excerpts from the factual stories and the ghost stories used the facts to set up some kind of BS ghost sighting or such. Again, creeping me out."

"Yes, I'm familiar with the books. I have a copy of each," Fay said. "It sounds like you've already read them?"

Walt stammered a bit, "Yes Ma'am. I read them last night."

Fay and Amy traded looks of astonishment. "Wow! That's a lot of research," Fay told him. "I am still learning things about you Mr. Ellison. Computer guru and speed reader too, who knew?"

Walt appeared both embarrassed and little proud of the attention and kind words of the boss. "I do read fast. It helped me get through school and freed up more time for computers and video games," he said with a smile. "Anyway, all three books are out of print and I checked a national database for libraries and they are not a lot of the books out there, but those that are out there haven't seen a lot of readers. Of course, as you might expect, the downtown library here has two copies of the *Hawes Horror*– the 1889 book in the research library... you can read it there but you can't check them out, but they will provide a PDF for a fee. The 1980 book, *The Horror of Birmingham*, they have three paperback copies. In the last year the old book was only checked out two times. You still have to check it out even though you cannot remove it. Once, by a housewife from Crestwood and then by a UAB Professor. The other one, the paperback, was checked out by the same two folks, plus a student from Birmingham Southern and a lady that works for Wells Fargo downtown and lives in Hoover. The spooky book is collecting dust... no one has checked it out in almost three years. My plan was to talk to everyone that had checked out the books to see if there might be a connection. I know it's a long shot and my background check does not raise any red flags so far but I haven't gotten very deep."

Amy put a hand on Walt's shoulder and said, "I am very impressed Walt. That is good groundwork."

Fay interjected, "I'm curious, who was the professor?"

Walt went back to his computer and with a few keystrokes turned and said, "John Norwood... he teaches Sociology... been there for four years. Prior to that he was at Wake Forrest as an Associate Professor for three years. He was a grad assistant there prior to that. I got that from his Facebook page and the University website. That's all I have so far... Do you know him?" he asked.

Fay hesitated for a moment, "We've met. A couple of faculty meetings and functions and he actually sat in on a couple of my classes a while ago."

Amy looked quizzically at Fay, "I don't suppose either of those times included your lecture about the Hawes murders?"

"I can't be sure," she answered as she thought. "I know the last time he sat in was last semester and I talked about considering all the pieces of the investigations – interviews, forensics, etc. from all angles when piecing your investigation together. He approached me afterward and introduced himself. He indicated he had sat in on my class once before but I don't remember him. He's fairly young and, as you know, those classes usually run all demographics and usually have 90 or more students." Fay leaned on the edge of her desk as she tried to recall the classes.

Amy was now even more curious, "Is that normal? A professor sitting in on a class like that?"

Fay thought for a second, "I don't really know. I'm just part-time, you know... He indicated he was researching a book he was planning about violence in society and thought my lecture might help."

Amy turned to Walt, "I know you have started backgrounds on these folks. Anything more on this guy yet?"

Walt looked up, "Nothing more than I reported, but I'll move him to the top of the list for the deeper dive."

Just then Amy's desk phone rang. "Boyd, SCU," she answered. "Okay.... Thanks." Amy dropped into her seat and clicked her computer to life. "That was Janice in forensics. They have identified our body... she sent me the files." Amy opened the email attachment and began reading. "Her name is Maylena Leigh Walcroft, not Hall. Age nine. Mother is Emma Jane Walcroft. Father James Daniel Walcroft, deceased 2014. Sibling Lisa Irene, age seven. Last known address 1412 Piper Lane, Jackson, Mississippi. Their lease ended there eight months ago."

"How the hell do they have all this info all of a sudden? When did they ID her?" Fay interrupted,

Amy spun in her chair to face her, "Evidently once the DNA match came through, they immediately got hits on the missing person database."

Walt chimed in, "My searches have been run on the last name Hall. I did a broad search on that database for a woman and two girls and approximate ages but I got over two hundred possible hits and I am only 15% in on that."

Fay began to pace, "Okay, so now we know who she was… where are Mom and sister?" Holding up her hand before anyone could answer, she continued, "I know we all think we know that one… but where have they been for last eight months?"

Walt was fiercely typing in his computer and answered over his shoulder, "I'm on it, Boss. Isolated their file and the reports from Jackson P.D. Looks like a relative filed the Missing Person report on October 11. I will follow up and get details from Jackson P.D."

Amy's cell phone began vibrating on her desk. She glanced down and saw Nate Parker on the screen as she snatched it up, "Nate?"

"Put me on speaker," Nate Parker said. Amy did and held her phone out as Walt and Fay stepped closer, "Well, first, we were right… they found two bodies. They have not recovered them yet. CSI has reinforcements coming. South

Precinct is setting up a perimeter… not too many gawkers now but that will likely change soon. M.E. is en route. Divers say the bodies are about 18 feet apart and both are bound and weighted to keep them down. They need help to get them up and preserve evidence so they should be recovered within the hour."

Amy spoke up, "I assume females? Adult and child?"

"Definitely one adult and one child, going strictly on size," Nate answered. "Gender not confirmed. Diver says both bodies are mired in the muck at the bottom so hard to say anything else… that's why they are waiting on reinforcements. Water is only about 10 feet deep but the bottom is muddy and visibility is less than perfect even with their big lights. Evidently they have some sort of gizmo that they put around the body and the muck to preserve everything and bring it all up at once."

Fay looked at Amy with a slight nod and Amy knew exactly what she meant. "Nate, we are headed your way. Can we bring anything or do anything?"

"No, we're good. See you in a minute," Nate answered.

"Want me to come too?" Walt asked

"No, keep digging on their background. We are going to need that. We will keep you posted on what we have out there." Amy answered.

"Will do. Be careful," Walt said as he returned to his computer.

Highland Park Golf Course was the centerpiece of the Highland Park neighborhood southeast of downtown, located at the intersection of Highland Avenue and Clairmont Avenue. Across Clairmont lay the trendy Lakeview district that is home to bars, restaurants and entertainment venues. It was also seeing several high-rise condo and apartment complexes rising on the edges of the historic district.

The golf course is also located on the edges of the Forrest Park and South Avondale Neighborhoods. A century ago these were the premiere suburban neighborhoods of the young city. Located just 2 miles from the city center, the large stately houses were home to Birmingham's early industrial movers and shakers. The neighborhoods surrounding the park are now nestled into the city but unlike the grid of straight and perpendicular streets downtown, the streets wind and curve up and down hills as they meander through the neighborhoods lined with stately homes and apartment complexes. Highland Avenue winds east to west from the park through the Southside and is lined with large mansions and manicured lawns with plenty of mini-parks and ample green-space throughout the neighborhoods.

Highland Park was home to a top tier golf course and tennis complex. It had once been the home of the Birmingham Country Club and is the oldest golf course in Alabama and was the site of many of famed golfer, Bobby Jones, early victories. The club was built in 1903 on the former site of Lakeview Park. As the city rapidly grew, the club moved further out to the suburb of Mountain Brook in 1927 and sold the clubhouse and property to the city. The city now leases both the golf course and tennis complex operations to outside contractors under the supervision of the Park and Recreation Board. The golf course lake was a large kidney shaped pond about seventy-five yards wide and a hundred or so yards long, situated at the intersection of Highland and Clairmont. It was the remnant of the much larger lake that had been the centerpiece of Lakeview Park.

When Fay and Amy approached the scene they saw a group of golfers and others watching the goings-on from the edge of the lake on the golf course side. Another group of onlookers stood along the fence at Highland Avenue. South Precinct officers were present and were maintaining a barrier keeping those behind the fence that separated the golf course from both Highland and Clairmont Avenues. They saw Nate Parker and Lt. Dan Guyer, head of the CSI unit, standing at lake's edge with about a half dozen other CSI officers. Guyer had positioned the large CSI Mobile Command Center vehicle along Clairmont to block the view from those passing by.

As the two women approached the fence, Nate walked over to meet them. "You'll have to walk up Highland about a hundred or so yards to get in," Nate said pointing up the winding, tree-lined street. "There is a maintenance gate there and an officer is manning it to keep the gawkers out."

“No press?” Amy asked.

“Not yet but I am sure they are coming.” Nate responded.

“I called the PI team and they are headed out to handle it.” Amy said.

Fay and Amy made there way up Highland past the thirty or so people standing along the fence that had come from the surrounding neighborhood or the restaurants and businesses across Clairmont from the scene. They both carefully looked at each person without being obvious. One of Fay’s investigational tactics that was practiced by all SCU officers was to ‘always watch the watchers.’ Perps have an uncanny knack of returning to the scene. Sometime to observe their handiwork but more often to see what the police do or do not do or discover that might incriminate them. As they approached the others at the lake’s edge they saw three CSI officers in full scuba gear enter the water. Two of them were carrying what looked like a blue tarp rolled up on poles.

"Welcome!" Nate greeted them. "There are already three divers down there so they should bring up the bodies soon."

Lt. Guyer shook each of their hands with a nod as greeting. His eyes were trained on the water. Without looking at them, he explained, "They basically will capture each body and the surrounding sediment in the body bags to bring them up. The bags are specifically designed for this sort of thing. Once they get topside the fabric of the bags allows the water to drain out but nothing else. That way we loose no evidence." He gave the trio a quick glance and continued as his gaze returned to the water, "Two of my guys will remain below and once the bottom resettles, and they will comb the bottom for anything that may be evidence that remains."

Within a few minutes four heads popped up from the surface of the water about fifteen feet from the bank of the lake where they were standing. One of the divers looked at Guyer and gave the thumbs up signal. Each man had the end of what looked like a fence post on his shoulder. Each pair moved with the synchronization of a marching band as they supported the pole with one hand and paddled with the other toward dry ground. As they got about six feet from the bank the two front divers stood up in waist deep water and continued walking. Soon the back two were also standing in the water. The quartet of divers walked slowly forward to within about a couple of feet of the bank. The water was hip deep on the front divers, as the back divers moved outward until they were all lined up along the bank.

One diver asked, "Ready?" And within seconds, again with practiced synchronization of a polished team, they lifted the bags from the water and held them at shoulder height as the water came cascading through blue fabric and back into the lake.

As the drainage slowed to a drip a crew of CSI officers clad in their coveralls stood along the lake edge and were handed the poles supporting the bags. They walked them over to the pop-up tent-like canopies that had been placed along the inside of the fence lining Highland Avenue. Clean plastic tarps covered the ground underneath. Each bag was carefully lowered to the ground. The two bags came to rest on the plastic about eight feet apart. The officers carefully slipped the support poles from the sheaths along the bags.

Even though the sun was out, the temperature was dropping and it was cold. Medical Examiner Dan Jacobs had joined the group. Guyer and Jacobs, followed by the detectives, moved in for a closer look. A CSI Officer pulled the sides of the canopies closed obstructing any view from the onlookers or anyone on the outside of the tent structure.

Guyer knelt down between the bags and unzipped the one on his left about halfway, as the others stood close by. Jacobs knelt on the other side. The body was pale and bloated and was surrounded by mud. The mud was not the normal red clay found throughout Alabama but was much more sandy and almost black in color. Guyer and the others watched as Jacobs zipped the bag full open.

The lifeless woman had on a blue knit top. She was nude from the waist down. Ropes were tied around her ankles, waist and neck. They were embedded into her pale wet skin. The men carefully scanned her body with experienced eyes looking for anything that may provide them information. The body lay face up and her eyes were partially opened revealing blue-green eyes that hauntingly matched those of the little girl found yesterday. Jacobs carefully used his gloved right hand to slip under the thigh of the victim just above the knee. With a simple nod to Guyer, he gently lifted and rolled the body ever so slightly as

Guyer shined his flash light underneath. Something metallic seemed to reflect the light from underneath.

"What's that?" Fay asked.

"Something metal," Guyer answered. "Rusty and flat iron... It was used to weight the body."

Guyer raised his gloved hand at the waiting CSI Officers standing by the detectives. Both jumped into action. One held a bright led light panel about eighteen inches square and the other a camera affixed with a hooded lens. Jacobs and Guyer each held back a side of the bag to fully expose the victims body while the two snapped photos starting with a general over view and then carefully zooming in for close ups, starting at the feet and methodically working their way up. Water has a way of distorting the body when submerged. Fay estimated her to be about 5'7" and about 130 pounds. This matched the description of their missing woman, Emma Walcroft.

Once the photos stopped the CSI officers stepped back without a single word. Jacobs gloved hand slowly probed around the neck before he gently took his other hand to support the head and turned it slightly to the right.

Guyer shined his light exposing a gash in the woman's head just behind her left ear. "Okay," Guyer simply said and the two officers went back into action snapping well-lit photos. "Got it?" asked Guyer.

The female officer taking the photos was scanning through the photos on her camera responded, "Yes, sir. I'm good."

Guyer looked at Jacobs as both men repositioned themselves slightly.

"Let's roll her," Jacobs said.

"To you," was Guyer's simple reply as his hands carefully slipped underneath the body and lifted as the body tilted toward Jacobs until he said, "That's good." A thick, flat piece of rusty metal secured by the ropes ran from the shoulders to just above the waist. When the officer hit his lights, Fay could not contain it, "Shit!"

The others were a bit startled.

"Railroad iron," she said.

The other SCU detectives sighed loudly. Jacobs and Guyer both looked at the group,

"Significant?" Guyer asked.

"Hawes," Amy Boyd answered simply.

"Holy Shit! Guyer said. "Nate mentioned that yesterday but I thought he was reaching... two bodies in a hundred years did not make a connection but this kind of brings it home."

"You don't know the half of it," Amy responded. "When we identify her, you'll find that her name is Emma and her daughter, *MAY*-lena, is who you fished out yesterday."

The men let the body back down.

"You're fucking kidding me, right?" Guyer asked as he rolled back into a seated position between the bodies. "We are dealing with a sick-fuck then," he said matter-of-factly.

Guyer glanced over his shoulder at the bag behind him, "Don't tell me this is the other daughter?"

"That is very likely her daughter Irene," Fay said.

Guyer removed his gloves and then his glasses and rubbed his eyes, "I couldn't remember her name from the Hawes story but that is it, isn't it?" he asked.

"Yes, indeed," Amy answered.

"What the hell are the chances of finding a family with all the right names, much less replicating the murders?" Guyer asked dumbfounded.

"Pretty damn slim," said Fay, "but that looks exactly like what we have. The details are not exact, but for 129 years later, it is too damn close."

Jacobs stood up, "I'm going to state the obvious... that is fucking creepy as shit. Have we had anything like this anywhere around here, ever?"

"Not in my 31 years, for sure." Guyer answered.

"No and I have been searching nationally for a connection anywhere to copycats of really old cases and I have found nothing," Fay said.

Jacobs zipped up the bag and pointed to the other one. "Let's take a preliminary look and get the photos and I'll get them back to the table and we will see what we can find." With that, he and Guyer turned their attention to the second bag. It was obvious that the bag contained a much smaller corpse than the other. Nothing was more distressing for cops than a child victim. No matter how long you were on the job, or how many bodies you had encountered, seeing a child hurt or killed touches something deep within you that was hard for even the most cynical or seasoned veteran.

Both men donned new gloves. Jacobs slowly unzipped the bag revealing first the small feet of the little girl. Patent shoes with white lace socks, now dingy from being submersed in the lake. Although her body was slightly bloated, it was obvious that she was a good bit smaller than Maylena, although her hair was almost identical in color and length. She was nude except for the shoes and socks. Her upper body was wrapped in a burlap cloth. Like the adult, a blue nylon rope bound her ankles together and then traveled to her waist where it made several rounds and then up and around her neck. Guyer carefully shined the light over the body. The same dark mud surrounded the child. There were no visible signs of trauma other than some abrasions around the rope on her neck and ankles.

Jacobs nodded to Guyer as he slipped his hands under the child's body, "To you," he said, and with that he rolled the body toward Guyer and he held her while Jacobs shined his light along the back of the child. She too had about an 18-inch length of a rusty railroad flat iron secured by the ropes to her back. Jacobs reached under her light brown hair and shined the light.

"No visible trauma," he said. The CSI officers stepped in and took photos. The men gently released their grips allowing the body to lie back again. They pulled the body bag open more and the CSI Officer took more photos.

"Got them," she said.

"Okay, we will help you load them in the van," said Guyer. The bags were then hoisted onto rolling tables from the Medical Examiner's van and loaded for transport back to his facility for autopsy.

Guyer turned to the SCU group and said, "As soon as we have everything cataloged and processed, we'll send them over to you."

Nate shook his hand, "Thanks."

Guyer walked toward the van and then stopped and turned back to them, "I hope the hell you get this bastard quickly.... Please let me know if we can help in any way."

The CSI team was already packing up the tents when the last two divers emerged from the water. As they made their way to dry land the first one said, "Nothing else down there, L.T. We combed the entire bottom and found nothing but nasty golf balls and one pitching wedge... we left it buried."

Guyer smiled and helped them out of their gear. "Great job, guys," he said.

Fay was relieved to see that the Public Information Team had arrived and were handling the press that had arrived and other observers that were gathered. Several shouted out to her and the others as they walked back to their vehicles. Fay simply pointed to the PI officers and left the scene.

Chapter 15

December 5, 2017, 16:47

The SCU team arrived back at headquarters to find Walt still hovered over his computer. After greeting them, he pointed up to the large monitors above and kept typing. On the screen were photos. The first screen was the driver's license photo of Emma Jane Emerson Walcroft, White Female, Date of Birth: 08/12/1989, Height: 5'6" Weight: 125 lbs. Address: 1412 Piper Lane Jackson, Mississippi. Date Issued: 08/04/2014. On the screen with the license was a finger print card with her name and date of birth, dated August 28, 2013.

On the next monitor was a Highland School ID photo of Maylena Leigh Walcroft, Date of Birth: 10/17/2008 along with a fingerprint card with her name and DOB.

On the next monitor was a photo ID from the same school of Lisa Irene Walcroft, Date of Birth: 3/22/2010 along with her fingerprints.

"Wow I wasn't expecting to see fingerprints of the kids," said Jerome.

"Yeah, I ran across those from a file at their school. The local Lions club did a volunteer awareness campaign at their school every year and offered fingerprints in case of abductions or such," Walt answered.

"The school would keep them in the file with parent's permission. Evidently the Walcrofts were not concerned with Big Brother... The school ID photos are from last year. The Mom also got fingerprinted with them, but I'm not sure why. Maybe to show the girls how or something," Walt continued.

"Damn, they look like your normal suburban family, don't they?" Amy mused staring at the monitors.

"They are just so cute and innocent looking," said Nate sadly.

Amy was definitely rattled by the case and seeing the photos of their carefree happy faces brought the anger to a boil. "They ARE fucking innocent," she said loudly. "They didn't deserve whatever the sick bastard did to them for some bizarre fantasy or something." She lowered her head a bit embarrassed by her outburst, "They had their whole life in front of them."

Nate put his arm around her shoulder and with teary eyes gave her a look that said we are all in this together and we will get justice for them. Words were not necessary. Everyone in the room knew exactly how hard it was to deal with crimes against children and everyone knew that this case was going to be a tough one for many reasons.

"Not sure this is pertinent, but just in case.... Maybe good for background if nothing else," said Walt trying to break the somber mood of the room. He pointed to the 4th screen. "This is the husband/father..." With that another driver's license appeared on the screen... James Daniel Walcroft, White Male, Date of Birth: 03/22/1987. Same address as Emma. Stamped in red on the bottom of the license was DECEASED: 08/26/2014. "He was killed in a car wreck with a drunk driver on his way home from work," Walt said. "I just got the report and file, but the drunk was a high school drop-out with 2 prior DUI's... blew a .23 and wasn't hurt in the wreck.... He's serving 10-12 for vehicular manslaughter."

"That just completes the tragedy of all this... loosing your father at that age and then encountering whatever the hell this is..." Amy said trying to maintain her composure.

Walt hesitated for a moment but then stood up and stretched his arms as if he hadn't moved since the group left earlier. "Not to be too melodramatic, but from what I uncovered so far, they appear to be a happy little family until his death. I mean, they were not living the high life... if there is high-life in Jackson, but they rented a house in what appears to be a nice neighborhood in the suburbs. The dad worked at a furniture factory just west of town and the wife worked as a hairdresser part-time. Girls made good grades and had no problems in school."

"Walt, it looks like you are well into background on them but keep digging," Fay said. "We need to know how they got here. How they ended up from suburbia to a homeless shelter and any and everything you can find out about them."

"I am on it, boss. I have emails and calls into a detective at Jackson P.D. that is somewhat familiar with the family… not sure the exact connection, but the State Trooper that worked the husband's wreck case referred me to him. Hoping to hear from him soon. I also have contact information for all the book readers from the libraries… I sent them to the drop box," Walt sat back down.

"Jerome and I will divide those up and contact them," Nate said.

"I'll take the UAB Professor. Since we know he sat in on the lectures, he may have more to contribute," Amy said.

"Sounds good," said Nate as he rolled his chair over to confer with Jerome and divide the list up between them.

"I'm going to head over to the M.E. office. He is starting the autopsy. I'll let you know what he finds," Fay said. "Once everybody wraps up what they're doing, go home and rest. We really can't do much until we get the forensics in so let's take the time while we can. Once we see what we get, then we can decide on tomorrow but you all know the drill… we have to stay on this until we exhaust every avenue so there won't be much downtime for a while."

As she walked to the door Nate said, "We got this Boss!" He returned to his desk and began the arduous task of cold calling people who had checked out a book about a murder case from more than a hundred years ago, hoping it would lead to something that would prove useful in solving the current murder case.

Four hours later, Fay sent out a group text to the team: ***Autopsy done. Nothing yet... waiting on forensics. Unless anyone has something that needs immediate attention, let's gather at 0800... Get some rest! ~FF*** Each member responded affirmatively, knowing that tomorrow would begin a string of tireless days until this case was done. They had all been involved in cases that were complex but they all knew that this case was going to take all their skills and resources. This was a once in a lifetime case that both thrilled an investigator and at the same time made them sick. There was a killer out there. Not just someone who acted in the heat of anger or passion, but someone depraved and calculating. One that had no qualms about killing children to make some bizarre statement or satisfy some sick urge.

As Fay made the short drive home from the Medical Examiner's Facilities on 6th Avenue South, she was consumed in thoughts about this case. As veteran detective she had investigated a wide variety of murder cases in her career and as a lecturer and teacher, she had studied numerous others. Most cases fit into a mold of some sort. Domestic dispute, business transaction gone awry, or some other set of circumstances that compelled someone to take another's life or at least be so consumed by emotion that reasoning was beset by rage and when all was said and done there were dead bodies and someone that caused it. Fay saw her job as an investigator as pretty straightforward, to bring justice. But she knew that every single case was far from straightforward, and this one in particular, was not going to be routine. Murder cases were always difficult. Murder not only affects the victim with their life cut short. It also affects the perpetrator. Those are a given, but it also affects the families of both. It affects the friends and acquaintances of both. It can even affect an entire community or city.

Simply identifying the bad guy and making an arrest is never enough. A detective is consumed by bringing justice by arresting the accused, but also must be constantly aware of the entirety of the case and how the case is made. One misstep along the way can mean a guilty defendant walking away, but it could also mean bringing the wrong person to trial, so care and diligence must be taken at every step along the way. Fay had studied murder cases of all types and knew that this was one that others would likely be studying in the future. Birmingham was not immune to big cases or those that garnered attention and scrutiny but they were "few and far between," as Fay's Dad would say.

Starting with the 1888 Hawes murders that this case seemed to be closely mimicking. Following Hawes arrest, a mob of thousands rushed the jailhouse hell-bent on lynching Hawes, only to have the sheriff command deputies to open fire on the advancing crowd. Dozens died and many more were injured. This had a larger affect on the city's population than the crime itself, in many ways. There were also the infamous Birmingham Axe Murder spree in the 1920's that claimed the lives of 18 victims and injured countless others over a four year period.

The first notorious case that Fay had any remote involvement with was the kidnapping and murder of an out of town businessman named Nigel Harlan. As a college intern, she was working as a file clerk/go-fer in the Homicide Division of BPD. Although the case was solved rather routinely, it garnered a lot of notoriety. Harlan, a steel company executive from Chicago, was the victim of a robbery-murder while unwinding at the Showboat Lounge in the new entertainment district marketed as "Old Town-Uptown", along Morris Avenue. The cobblestone street in the city center was the home to dozens of restaurants, bars and music entertainment venues housed in old warehouses and storefronts. The city had rezoned the district and added historic street lamps and an ample parking lot along the railroad tracks. The development was becoming a staple attraction to an otherwise dying downtown area when the murder occurred. Although the area was relatively crime free, the news of the kidnapping garnered national attention as detectives worked to locate the victim. Three weeks later his body was discovered dumped off a rural road in northern Shelby County about thirty miles south of the city. Soon afterward, a Florida couple was charged and later convicted of the crime. They worked as a team to rob unsuspecting patrons and Harlan was an unfortunate recipient of their evil on that particular evening.

That one incident brought on the demise of the entertainment district as over the next year, one by one the venues closed as attendance drastically dwindled. The murder not only derailed the entertainment district, it was vital in holding off any new development in the downtown area for decades. The area is now home to professional offices and residential lofts. Only a couple of bars remain and they are actually new, having come into existence with the latest renaissance to serve their neighboring loft dwellers and others in the revitalized loft district.. Although she was just pushing papers in the office, Fay saw firsthand what implications a murder case could bring. She realized how public perception and the media could play a vital role in a case, sometimes good and sometimes bad.

Chapter 16

1888 Birmingham, Alabama

In the days that following the discovery of Irene's body in Lakeview, the case seemed to once again fade from the front pages. Another jury was being impaneled for what would be termed the "Jail Killings." The top law enforcement officers were still under investigation as the warrants for murder and assault continued to be filed. Other citizens were just as certain the men were simply during their jobs and upholding the law. The debate would continue for months, even years.

Meanwhile, as trial preparations were going on and motions were heard, detectives continued to follow leads and gather evidence in the Hawes murder case. Many of those leads ended in dead ends but one rather lengthy and convoluted path turned out to be very fruitful. Of the many rumors that detectives had investigated, all turned out to be either bogus or of no real value except for one. Someone had reported overhearing a conversation on train discussing a young Negro man that had stated he had witnessed the Hawes crime and had to get out town to avoid testifying.

Detective E. H. Kernan, who had been doggedly investigating the case from the beginning while avoiding any publicity, was working on a theory that Hawes would likely had to have had help in disposing of his wife's body. Two men from Atlanta had been reported being in Birmingham the day of the murders. John Wylie, a locomotive engineer and longtime friend of Hawes, was seen talking to Hawes on that day. Wylie's brother, Jules, was also reported to have been in Birmingham during the same time.

Kernan was suspicious of the brothers as they fit the description that Mr. Connelly, the caretaker of the boathouse at Lakeview, had given as testimony in the inquest, as being seen at the lake. Kernan had also confirmed that Wylie had boarded a train from

Birmingham to Atlanta on the very day that May Hawes body was discovered.

With this information confirmed, the detective traveled to Atlanta and obtained a warrant for the brothers and traced them to John's house where he arrested them and brought them back to Birmingham. On their way back to Birmingham, the detective was alerted that a large crowd of spectators had gathered at the Birmingham Station. Kernan had managed to stay out of the limelight and circus that surrounded this case, and he wasn't going to join in now. He arranged with the conductor to disembark the train with the prisoners at the crossing of Twentieth Street and spirited his prisoners straight to the jail avoiding the spectacle of the waiting crowd.

Once back at the jail, the Wylie brothers were in good spirits and John freely talked to Kernan. When asked about being seen in Birmingham with lots of cash in early December, John Wylie denied that. He then told Kernan he was in town on December 1st and had dinner with Dick Hawes at the Hochstadter's Restaurant. He said Dick had cashed a $25.00 check he had received from selling his furniture. Wylie claimed that after dinner they went to Weil's store where Dick brought clothes and then went to Fuller's Boarding House where Dick showed him the room he had secured to bring his new wife. John said he asked Dick about Emma and he was told that he had given her $500 and she had left Birmingham.

John Wylie told Kernan that he didn't see Hawes again until Monday, December 3rd when they met at the Florence Hotel. Wylie said he asked Hawes to share his room that night but Dick refused, saying he may entertain a woman that night. He said when the men parted that night it was the last time he saw Dick Hawes. Unlike his jovial brother, Jules Wylie was less talkative. The brooding Jules was a known gambler and was described as a rough individual. He only complained of being arrested for no reason and refused to answer any questions.

On February 6, 1889, a few days after they were arrested, the brothers were indicted by the Grand Jury as accomplices in the murder of Emma and Irene Hawes. The theory was that Hawes would have to had help in disposing of the bodies in Lakeview Lake and the circumstantial evidence was mounting that the Wylies were likely involved. Just hours after the indictment, Attorneys Frank Haralson and Hinton Wright arrived in Birmingham from Atlanta, to represent the brothers. The lawyers immediately filed a writ of habeas corpus, which was granted. The brothers were released from custody and returned to Atlanta with the understanding that they would both return to Birmingham upon demand.

Two days later, on February 8th, the Grand Jury issued indictments for Fannie Bryant and Albert Patterson for the murder of Emma Hawes *"by choking her or strangling her or by smothering her or by throwing her in the water, whereby she drowned, or by striking her with some stick or other substance unknown to the Grand Jury or by some means of violence to the person of Emma Hawes, the character of which is unknown to the Grand Jury."* The pair had been jailed for two months and was now officially charged as accomplices of Richard Hawes. While the indictment of Patterson and Bryant did bring the case back to the front page of the newspapers, and even bigger story quickly overshadowed it.

Chapter 17

February 1889 Birmingham, Alabama

The story bore the headline of "The Silent Eye," and told of an exhaustive investigation by the *Age-Herald* reporter, Michael Cann and Phillip Givhan, a detective hired by the newspaper. The men had been chasing the rumor of the young Negro man fleeing Birmingham because he had witnessed the Hawes murders. The rumor was that a woman passing through Birmingham had overheard the young man's declaration that he was fleeing so he would not be forced to testify against his aunt, Fannie Bryant.

In the beginning, the pair assumed that Albert Patterson might have made the declaration, since Bryant had testified that he was her nephew, but Patterson had been in jail all this time and so they decided to flush out the rumor. In one of her rambling accounts during testimony Fannie Bryant had also said she had kept the nephew of her dead husband for some years. They decided to pursue the lead to see if the nephew was a real person and if so, did he indeed witness the murders.

On the knowledge that the conversation occurred on a northbound train, the pair traveled north and posed as insurance agents seeking the kin of Fannie Bryant to pay a $2,500 sum of an insurance policy, declaring that since Fannie was in jail, the sum was to be awarded to the next of kin. The pair traveled north from Birmingham through a variety of towns in Alabama spreading their story and chased various leads to locate the young man, eventually ending in New Middleton, Tennessee, east of Nashville, where a young Negro man was brought to them. The young man, Sam Patterson, claimed no knowledge of the events and did not come close to fitting the description the pair had received. Along the way, the pair had discovered that the individual they were seeking went by the name Willie Johnson, and so that also didn't match up with the man before them.

Again following more hearsay, the next morning the pair traveled six miles north through rough terrain to meet a road contractor that was said to employ Willie Johnson. Upon arrival the young man was brought to them, but vehemently denied that he was their man, although he did fit the description. Finally, the man revealed that he knew who they were looking for and he was in Middleton in Hardeman County, east of Memphis, and not New Middleton, as they had been told.

The pair then made the nine-hour trip in a cold rain, through mud to Middleton. Upon arrival, the pair enlisted the help of the local Sheriff and Postmaster and identified the young man they were seeking and was told that he was staying in a cabin with another man outside of town. The pair deftly approached the cabin and was able to capture the young man. Initially, the captive man denied everything --- his identity, being in Birmingham, knowledge of Fannie Bryant or the Hawes murders. But the men were convinced that he was their "Silent Eye" witness and continued to question him and bit-by-bit he revealed the following story.

His name was Willie Johnson but he was not the man they sought. He told them that they were looking for his twin brother, Robert. He said they were the nephews of Fannie Bryant and on the night of December 1st, they were both in Birmingham "on a frolic." He told them that Robert begged him to go to Memphis with him because he had to leave town because he did not want to be forced to testify against their aunt whom he had seen help kill a white woman and help take her body through the woods to the lake.

Willie repeatedly told the pair that his twin brother Robert was who they wanted, not him. He said that Robert was living in Memphis and he agreed to show the men where he was. When pressed for details of the murder, Willie said that Robert told him, "A white man hit her with a club, and she broke and run from him. He hollered to Aunt Fannie to hit her and she did with a brick, and then the white man came out and finished her. Then they took her off through the woods." Willie continued his brother's story saying, "That night I was going home and as I got near the ball park, two white men stopped me and put pistols on each side of my head and asked me where I was going. They cursed me and said if I didn't go I would get killed. I couldn't tell you who it was in the ball park then."

Although Willie's story matched up with other information and accounts along with the evidence, they were not convinced that there was a twin brother and thought that likely Willie was the witness but was still reluctant to testify against his aunt. As they continued to question him, he revealed that he had seen Fannie Bryant with a large roll of cash and she had told him that Hawes had given it to her. When asked about the details of the killings he told the story again but added that Robert had witnessed three white men and one colored man dragging a body through the ballpark.

Although Willie had given exacting details about the scene and was, no doubt, familiar with the Hawes house and surroundings, the men were still not convinced his detailed story and his accounts of his twin brother held any validity. They decided that since this journey had taken them weeks and more than two thousand miles already, that they should go to Memphis to either verify the story or disprove it. When the trio arrived in Memphis, Willie was housed in the jail and local detectives aided in the search to find his brother, Robert Johnson. More than thirty Negros were rounded up and arrested on suspicion and brought in but not one turned out to be Robert.

The detective and reporter provided every opportunity for Willie to locate his brother but he could not produce him. Finally, they resolved that the brother didn't exist, or at least was not in Memphis, and they returned to Birmingham with Willie.

Chapter 18

February 1889 Birmingham, Alabama

The trio arrived in Birmingham on February 3, 1889 and the *Age-Herald* proudly wrote about the escapades of their employees under the headline: **The Silent Eye**. The story touted that the pair had spent two months, traveled thousands of miles and the newspaper had spent more than two thousand dollars to locate the "Silent Eye" witness.

On February 4th, Willie Johnson testified before the Grand Jury and denied any knowledge of the Hawes murders. He said he was the twin son of Henry and Amanda Johnson of Opelika, Alabama and that he had lived with Fannie Bryant in Birmingham for several years. He went on to testify that in the summer of 1888 his father had made him and his brother Robert return home to Opelika but that later in the year they had both returned to Birmingham to look for work. He said that he did not visit Fannie and therefore was not involved with her or the crimes she is accused of. He also stated that he last saw Robert sometime in November.

Even though it completely contradicted what he had told the reporter and detective, Willie's testimony was consistent and his demeanor calm during his appearance before the Grand Jury. Meanwhile, detectives had located his twin brother working in the mines at Pratt City, only the brother claimed that ***he was Willie*** and his brother they had in custody was Robert!

When detectives interviewed the miner he said, "I am not the witness you want - that is my brother, Robert. All I can tell you is what he told me. He told me that he had seen Fannie Bryant and a white man strike a white woman in the head with a stick and after they killed her, they carried her off through some woods... Soon after that we both left town going separate ways. Around Christmas I read in the papers about the Hawes murders in Birmingham and Robert told me that was the murder he witnessed."

When the first Willie (Robert) was confronted face to face with his brother, he dropped the charade and admitted that he was, indeed, Robert and had witnessed the crime. Willie was then released and returned to his job in at the mines.

When interviewed by Sheriff Smith, Robert "told a dozen different versions of the story, proving a most fertile liar." He admitted being near the Hawes house on that Saturday night and had heard "all the fuss" and heard the blows struck and saw the bodies of Emma and Irene Hawes placed in a hack hitched near the house. He again told of being questioned later by two white men with guns about whether he had seen anything. When he told them he hadn't, they then threatened, "You had better leave town, damn quick." He said that two days later he hopped a freight train and went to Decatur, Alabama and then on to Corinth, Mississippi and finally to Middleton, Tennessee.

The *Age-Herald* not only ran the entire story that they had uncovered, they created a special edition of the paper and printed thousands of extra copies. Bundles of the special edition were distributed in Atlanta, Nashville, Chattanooga, Montgomery and other cities across Alabama and the South. The widespread distribution of the story prompted a former Sheriff of Elmore County, Alabama to contact detectives in Birmingham. Mr. N. W. Greene was now a conductor on the Ensley Railroad dummy line. He said that an old Negro woman had told him that she had heard a Negro boy from Wetumpka, named Sam Bryant say that he was the son of Fannie Bryant and that he had seen Fannie hit Emma Hawes in the head with a rock near the fence as she ran away from Mr. Hawes. Hawes and Fannie then took the body to her house and the next night some other men came and they moved the body but he didn't know where.

When interviewed in jail about this new revelation, Fannie Bryant denied having a son and any knowledge of the story.

Meanwhile, the Wylie brothers were returned to Birmingham and Robert Johnson immediately picked out Jules as one of the two men that had threatened him. He also picked out John, but stated that he could not be sure about the identity of John, as he had since changed his hairstyle.

As the trial date approached for Richard Hawes, there were now six people jailed in connection with the crime - Hawes, the Wylie brothers, Robert Johnson, Albert Patterson and Fannie Bryant. Detectives continued to piece the story together and follow leads to make the case.

Sheriff Smith decided to take Robert Johnson out to the Hawes house to see if he could extract any new information from the supposed witness. When they arrived, Johnson pointed out several landmarks at the scene including a large tree about fifty yards from the house, saying that was where he hid on the fateful night as he watched things unfold. Johnson said, " I heard a noise like somebody fighting. Then I saw two men come out of the house. They were carrying something that looked like the body of a woman. There was another man and a woman following them. They all went toward the hack and then after a while it drove off toward the lake. I waited about fifteen minutes and nobody returned. I thought I heard something behind me but didn't see anyone so I headed back toward town."

Later in the day, the most experienced interrogator from the Sheriff's staff questioned Johnson again. Captain J. H. Sharp reported that Robert had "broke down" and said, "Captain, I done shook all the lies. I got my brother in a hole trying to keep myself out, but now I am going to tell you all I know." Johnson then recounted the same story he had been telling about hiding behind the tree, hearing the fighting noise and seeing two men carry out a body followed closely by another man and a woman. "I was very much frightened at what I saw that night and I hugged that tree close so I didn't see everything I might. It was after it was all over and I started back to town, that two white men stopped me in the grove at Beeler's Station on the dummy line. They had pistols in their hands and I thought I was dead for sure. They asked where I had been so late at night and I told them I had been to visit my aunt. They asked me if I had seen anything going on in that part of town that night and I told them no. They cursed at me and told me to make myself scarce and I hurried off to my boarding house on Avenue F at Eighteenth Street."

Johnson told Sharp that said the next day he was going to see his aunt and was confronted by the same two men in the same vicinity as the night before. They again questioned him and told him if he wanted to live he should leave town in a hurry. He said he left town a couple of days later but in the meantime he avoided the neighborhood around the Hawes house.

Detectives continued to follow leads and gather information, most of which turned out to be useless. However, one turned out to be very vital in the case. An elderly Negro woman, Emaline Croom, lived near the ballpark. When the detectives interviewed her she was bed-ridden and sat in her bed propped on pillows.

“I want to tell all I know, beginning at the first. Mrs. Hawes was a nice woman. About two weeks before all this killing I went to her house and found her in bed. Her arm was all crippled,” Croom said holding up her right arm, “and she said that she could not use it to cook and had nothing to eat. Irene got me some coffee and I made it. Mrs. Hawes had her right eye and side of face badly bruised,” she said motioning to her face. “She didn’t say how she got hurt, but I saw her bruised many times. Fannie Bryant was usually with her there.”

Emaline took a deep breath and continued, “On Saturday before the killing, I went down on the dummy tracks about three hundred yards picking up wood,” she said gesturing to her left. “As I got near the place I saw Fannie Bryant with a sack picking up something on the tracks. I asked her if she was looking for wood too and she said she was but she closed up that sack and put it under her arm. There was nothing there where she was except a lot of irons off the railroad; there was no wood there at all. I watched her and she went off right home. I thought it was strange that she would come so far."

Emaline told the men that the next day she went back up to the Hawes house and knocked on the door several times, but nobody came to the door. She said that she could definitely hear someone inside, "as clear as you can hear me now. I got scared and went out the gate," she said. She told them that every shutter on the house was closed and she also noticed that the small pile of coal that was usually in the corner of the yard was all gone, although a small spade was still there. She said she then walked up to Fannie Bryant's house and Fannie told her that there had been a big "flare up" and Mrs. Hawes had taken the children and gone away.

"Then I looked in the house and I felt queer when I saw Mrs. Hawes dresses hanging up on the wall, and a lot of her carpets and stuff rolled up and pushed under the bed as if they was trying to hide it. Her dishes were all on the table too," she added. Emaline went on to explain that Fannie told her that she was taking care of Mrs. Hawes stuff and that she was coming back as soon as things quieted down. “I was uncomfortable for two or three days, then I heard about the killing and the finding of the bodies,” Emaline told the detectives leaning forward in the bed. “I was there at Lakeview, up by the pavilion, when they found little Irene’s body,” she continued. “I went up and looked at that poor child and then I saw those irons... Two on one side and one on the other and it just burst right over me. My God! That’s the irons that woman was picking up that day when she was pretending to pick up wood. I know they was the same as them when she had that sack.”

Chapter 19

March 4, 1889: Birmingham, Alabama

Signs of spring were beginning to show as the weather warmed. The long awaited day had come. The scheduled day for the trial of Richard R. Hawes was to begin. The courtroom of Judge Greene was packed, but after weeks of anticipation they all soon left disappointed. Citing recent changes in Alabama law regarding jury selection and numerous other technical issues and a very crowded docket, Judge Greene announced to the gathered crowd a postponement of the proceedings.

The trial was finally resumed on April 22, 1889. It was a beautiful spring day and the courthouse was packed. The morning session dealt with a number of motions and it wasn't until the afternoon session that they finally started empaneling the jury for the special trial of Richard R. Hawes.

After more than two days of motions and technical moves by both sides, finally on April 24th, Richard Hawes was escorted from his jail cell and into the courtroom. He was fatter and paler than his last appearance months earlier when he was jailed. His beard was now full and getting longer. Hawes was escorted by several deputies to the front of the large courtroom and took his seat at the table in front next to his lawyer. Throughout the proceedings to follow, several accounts said that Hawes seemed stoic and paid close attention to the proceedings but when the court was in recess or just prior to court convening, he seemed most relaxed and jovial, conversing with friends and acquaintances. He seemed to never be bothered by the ever-present curiosity seekers gawking and pointing at him. Even those that crowded the bar, he seemed to ignore their presence and always acted like a gentleman.

As the trial progressed, a parade of testimony was presented. Most testifying were the same that testified during the inquests and told their same story as then with no new revelations.

Chapter 20

Monday, April 29, 1889 Birmingham, Alabama

As the trial entered the second week, the proceedings moved through each day methodically. The courtroom was packed each day as people watched and listened, waiting for some new turn or revelation in the case.

The defense had presented a parade of character witnesses. All had spoke of Richard Hawes as a fine citizen and good worker. In the afternoon, he took the stand himself. He identified himself as Richard Hawes, a native of Russell County, thirty-two years old. As he his lawyer led him through a series of question to validate and establish his history and standing in the community, the onlookers watched intently for any new information. Hawes said he lived in Atlanta for a long time before moving to

Montgomery and then to Birmingham. He has been employed as a railroad engineer with Georgia Pacific Railroad since July 1888. He and Emma had been married about ten years and they had four children, one of which died in 1886.

Responding to his lawyer's questions in a calm and courteous manner, Hawes testimony entailed the reasons he could not be responsible for the death of his daughter on December 3rd for the simple reason he was elsewhere at the time he is alleged to have been seen on the train with her in Eastlake. His testimony went on uninterrupted for well over an hour as he told the jury that on the night of Saturday December 1st, he brought his daughter, May, to town on the Eastlake dummy line and bought her stockings at Reese's store and then took her home, all in an hour or less. "At 9 o'clock in the evening, I left the house with my son, Willie, leaving Emma, May and Irene at the house," Hawes explained. "I took Willie to the railway station so that he could go with his Uncle James to Atlanta. I then returned home but they were all gone. The next morning, Fannie Bryant told me that they had gone to Mrs. C. F. Carrodine's boarding house."

“Where were you on Sunday of that week?” the lawyer asked.

“On Sunday afternoon, I went over to Lakeview Park and spent the afternoon there and returned home around dusk,” Hawes answered.

“And then on Monday?” the lawyer continued.

“On Monday I visited the Georgia Pacific shops for a while and then went over to Mrs. Fuller’s Boarding House to check on my room,” he answered. “I then went to Cline’s mattress place and to the Weil Brother’s Store, where I purchased underwear and an overcoat.”

“And this was Monday morning?” the lawyer inquired.

“Yes,” Hawes answered.

“Where did go after that?” the lawyer continued.

"I then walked up First Avenue where I met and talked with Phillip Dunlap" Hawes answered without hesitation. "I then ate lunch at the Bank Restaurant and then went to Caheen's Dry Goods, then Nabors & Morrow's Drug Store on Twentieth Street between First and Second Avenues and then back to the restaurant. There I met my brother, James, and we walked to the depot from there."

"At eleven thirty, he registered at the Florence Hotel where Ie spent the night," Hawes continued. "At six o'clock the following morning I left the hotel and walked to the station where I boarded the seven o'clock train to Columbus, Mississippi to my wedding."

When asked about his attire from the various testimonies about his presence on the dummy line to Eastlake, Hawes answered, "On Monday, I wore a pair of light pants, a blue coat and vest and a soft hat. I wore the same Saturday, Sunday and Monday and I wore them to Columbus. I wore no other clothes on those days. The suit I am wearing now was given to me by my friend, Dag Gordon, in Columbus on Wednesday."

"You were said to have been seen with an umbrella. Did you carry an umbrella on those days?" the lawyer asked.

"I have never owned a gold-headed umbrella, nor was I carrying one," Hawes testified.

Hawes demeanor on the stand was impeccable and showed no sign of a mad man that could have possible killed his entire family. He answered each question directly and without hesitation.

"Were you on the Eastlake dummy car with your daughter on December 3rd?" the lawyer asked.

"I was not on the dummy train with my daughter May on December 3rd" Hawes said allowing his voice to rise with a hint of indignation at the accusation.

"When did you last see your daughter, May?" The lawyer asked.

"I have never seen her alive since Saturday, December 1st." Hawes answered in a quitter tone as his eyes diverted downward.

"So, you were not with her at East Lake on Monday the 3rd of December?" the lawyer continued.

"I was not at East Lake on Monday or Monday night, December 3rd. I was at East Lake for the balloon ascension last summer, but have not been there since," Hawes answered emphatically, but controlled.

Hawes testimony was direct and thorough. His demeanor remained calm and sincere. Nothing about him hinted that he could be capable of the heinous acts that he was accused as his lawyer continued.

"It has been the testimony in this court from others that you had given your wife, Emma a sum of $500 in the days just prior to her death. Is this a fact?" the lawyer asked.

"Emma was going away and I agreed to give her $500. I paid her the money on Saturday. The children and Fannie Bryant were present when I handed her the money," Hawes answered.

"And where did you get this money that you gave to your wife?" the lawyer asked.

"The money I gave her, I had saved from my wages, Hawes answered.

"And what are your wages from the railroad, Sir?" the lawyer asked.

"I made from $125 to $150 each month," Hawes answered solemnly.

"There has been testimony in this court regarding your divorce from your wife, Emma. Was she aware of the divorce?" the lawyer asked.

"Emma had known of my divorce for several months," Hawes answered.

"The divorce it seems cannot be verified. Can you explain that, Sir?" the lawyer asked.

"I believed I was divorced from her," Hawes explained. "I had sued for divorce in Atlanta and had employed one of the best lawyers there. I had heard nothing from him up to September, when I got another lawyer to write him. He answered that he had filed the suit and that everything was all right."

"Did you feel that this was adequate and you were indeed, divorced?" the lawyer pushed on.

"Soon afterward, I went to Atlanta and my lawyer told me that he would get the divorce as soon as the court met and that I would not need to come back and see him again," Hawes answered.

"So, you believed that you were divorced from Emma?" the lawyer asked.

"I believed I was divorced from Emma. We did not live together as man and wife after that. I never went to the house except to see the children," Hawes stated.

"Was Emma aware of the divorce?" the lawyer asked.

“She told me had been served with a summons and knew that we were divorced.”

“Can you explain to the court why you divorced your wife?” the lawyer asked.

“She was a habitual drunkard. Her character was well known to my brother and other railroad men. She had been in a scandal in Atlanta and was arrested,” Hawes answered.

“Sir, there has been testimony in this court that you have told others that you either planned to place your children in a school or convent or had already done so. Can you speak to this?” the lawyer asked.

“I did not say to several people on Sunday and Monday that Irene and May were in a convent. I had an understanding with Emma that I would support her if she would behave herself,” Hawes answered refuting the numerous testimonies.

“We have heard testimony about your character in this court, Sir. What do you have to say about your own character?” the lawyer asked.

“I was never arrested but once before. I was arrested in Atlanta for beating a man about my wife, but the Captain of Police turned me loose as soon as I reached the station house,” Hawes said.

Hawes had now been on the stand for more than two hours straight and Judge Greene adjourned the court for lunch. When the afternoon session convened, Hawes resumed his testimony. He told of selling his furniture to Jake Bandmann and that he had been told that Fannie Bryant was the wife of Albert Patterson. He said that Fannie had helped him move the furniture. “When Fannie came to the house on Sunday, she asked me where Miss Emma was,” Hawes testified.

Hawes then refuted Fannie Bryant’s earlier testimony saying, “I did not tell her that she had gone where she’d never bother me anymore. I don’t think I ever told Fannie that Emma had gone to her aunt’s in

Lockport, New York, though that was where she was going."

"Did you tell Fannie Bryant of your divorce?" the lawyer asked.

"I did not tell Fannie that Emma had found out about the divorce," Hawes said.

The questioning then returned back to Hawes' marital status. "You left here to be married. Did you get married?" the lawyer asked.

"I was married at Columbus on December 5th to Miss Mayes Storey." Hawes answered.

"How long had you courted Miss Storey before the marriage?" the lawyer asked.

"We had been engaged for four months," Hawes answered.

"Did you show her father your divorce decree?" the lawyer asked.

"I did not show her father a decree of divorce," he answered.

The lawyers then returned to the sum of money that Hawes claimed to have paid his wife.

"You have testified that you gave your wife, Emma, a sum of $500. Can you tell us when this money was given to her?" the lawyer asked.

"It was the Saturday morning before she left," he stated.

"Were there any witnesses present when you gave her this money?" the lawyer asked.

"My children and Fannie Bryant were all there and saw me give her the money," Hawes said.

"Testimony in this court, including your own, have pointed to your wife's drinking. You have said that she drank to excess. Have you ever struck her in response to her drunkenness or for any other reason?" the lawyer asked.

"My wife was a habitual drunkard and we had trouble when she got drunk. I don't believe I ever struck her in my life," Hawes said.

Dick Hawes' testimony was concluded and the rest of the session was filled with witnesses recalled to punch holes or outright refute the testimony given by Hawes. One by one each witness refuted his testimony point by point.

On Thursday May 2nd 1889, Judge Green called for closing arguments. The state recounted the facts of the case with all pointing to Richard Hawes killing his family. In his closing statement, Prosecutor Hawkins implored the jury to "be honest and do your duty to God and to the society of brave men. There is no middle ground. If you find the defendant guilty of the crimes charged, you must return a verdict in accordance, and that verdict must fix the penalty of death. The protection of society and the claims of eternal justice demand it and it will be satisfied with nothing less." The prosecutor's long oration went on for the rest of the afternoon and when completed, Judge Greene adjourned the proceedings for the day.

On Friday morning, the defense gave their final arguments for more than two hours, pointing to all the disparities in the State's case of only circumstantial evidence. Each side had now fully presented their case to the jurors, emphasizing their strong points and ignoring the weak ones. After a fifteen-minute recess, Judge Greene gave instruction to the jurors. He read the explicit laws and instructed the jury on their duty before they filed into the jury room.

As the jury left the room and the courtroom emptied, the courthouse doors were locked and a half dozen deputies stationed in inside. No one was admitted inside the courthouse other than officers, attorneys and reporters. Although the crowds left the courthouse, they all remained in the area of 3rd Avenue. Reports showed hundreds of people milling around the courthouse for hours after the court adjourned.

Chapter 21

Saturday, 12/5/2017 :19:50

As Fay pulled her vehicle into the garage, she tried to think of anything other than the case as she made her way into the elevator to head up to her loft. She made a conscious effort to do this everyday -- Don't bring the work home. It will consume you if you let it. The practice was always more difficult when she had an active case open, but this one was going to multiply that difficulty exponentially.

She unlocked her door and stepped inside and coded out the alarm. She dropped her keys in the bowl on the mid-century modern buffet just inside the door and placed her Glock and holster in the top drawer. She stepped over to the shelving unit that lined the brick wall and thumbed through the album covers looking for something to help her with the task of NOT thinking about work. Something I can sing along to, she thought. *Elton John Greatest Hits*... always a winner. She clicked on the vintage Marantz receiver and put the vinyl record on the turntable. As it began to spin she picked up the small brush beside the turntable and held it just above the spinning record to let the bristles lightly glide along removing any dust or particles from the vinyl. She closed the brush and laid it back on the edge of the table and slowly lowered the needle cartridge to the edge of the record, before heading to the closet.

As she reached the closet she removed her top and tossed it in the hamper and just as she unzipped her slacks she heard EJ belt out the track one, side one... *Your Song*. She sank to the bench in the center of the closet as emotions flooded her entire being. "With more than 500 records, I pick that one," she thought as tears began to stream down her cheeks.

Bill had insisted on the band playing the song at their wedding reception and dedicating it to her as he lip-synched and danced her across the floor. Anytime he was practicing his guitar when she came home, he would automatically switch to the song and sing, ever so slightly off key. She loved that about him. She loved everything about him. His impromptu concerts were one of the many things she missed about him. "He has been gone for over five years now, and I still miss him so much," she said quietly as she slipped off her slacks and tried to dry the tears. She flipped on the lights in the bathroom and looked in the magnifying mirror at her swollen eyes, dabbing them with a tissue and powdered her nose and under-eyes and ran a brush through her hair. She stood looking in the mirror at herself. She tried to compose herself, while another part of her wanted to let it out and have a good cry, get drunk and go to bed. "I am passed that," she thought. "I am not going to go back down that road." With that the decision was made. She grabbed a pair of jeans from the closet and her favorite red sweater from the shelf and pulled them on. She grabbed the red suede loafers off the shelf and dropped them and slipped them on. She paused for another quick look in the full-length mirror before exiting the closet.

The final verse of the 5th track of side one was nearing the end. "*Saturday Night's Alright For Fighting* is more appropriate," she thought smiling at the irony of emotions bought about by music. She clicked the player off and grabbed her bag and headed out the door. Downstairs she encountered some neighbors waiting to board the elevator, backed up and greeted them with a smile and a nod. Once out the door she headed west down 2nd Avenue. The Wine Loft on the corner of 1st Avenue and 22nd Street just around the corner from her building. It was the favorite gathering spot for the Downtowners. Fay knew that there was a high percentage of likelihood that she would run into to one or more of her downtown friends there and be spared having to eat and drink alone. It was Saturday night and the streets were crowded with downtown dwellers and those who had driven in from the suburbs for a taste of the fine food and nightlife that was ever-present in downtown.

As Fay entered the doors, she immediately heard greetings from friends at a large table near the bar. She knew she would have a relaxing night of good food and good drink with her friends. With a little effort she could forget about her heartbreak and forget about work, at least for tonight.

Chapter 22

Sunday, 12/6/2017

Fay awoke Sunday morning feeling refreshed and rested. She had slept well and was thankful for great friends that kept her focused on things other than work... and other than Bill. She turned on the shower and checked her phone... no messages. That was a good sign. It was 7:05 AM and she knew that most, if not all, of the team were already at the office working. She stepped into the shower and let the hot water run over her body. Last night had been a little scary. She had not allowed thoughts of Bill that close to the surface in months and yet they came flooding in quickly. As she shampooed her hair she tried to concentrate on the day ahead, on the case, but she could not stay focused. It was as if her subconscious wouldn't let her. She had been sure she had finished grieving and was ready to move on but last night had caused that certainty to be doubtful, at best. She *had* moved on. She had dated a few times in the last two years or so but never allowed anything to go beyond a couple of dates. She had resolved that at her age, there would simply not be another love. How could anyone possibly stand up to what she and Bill had for more than twenty years? Comparing new relationships to one so perfect was an exercise in futility. She knew that *IF* someone else came along, that it wouldn't be a replacement... it had to be new and different. There was no room for comparison. She had to move on. She knew that her grief was unhealthy and had sought counseling to get through it and it had helped immensely. She thought she was through it, but last night made her seriously doubt that. She reasoned that it was a normal reaction and she was probably making more of it than it was, but something deep within her knew that she didn't dare go back to the deep recess that she found herself in following Bill's death.

The thought actually frightened her and not much could do that. "I'll call Sarah tomorrow," she thought. "She's the professional and will tell me if I should make an appointment or not." She already knew the answer. Her therapist, Sarah, had advised against stopping their weekly sessions last year, but Fay decided she was in a good place and didn't need it any longer and it had been good for over a year, but last night made her realize that maybe this had been building for a while. As she emerged from the shower and dried off, she thought, "When was the last time I dated? It has been months."

She looked at her naked body in the mirror as she wrapped the towel around her hair. She loved the way Bill looked at her and the way his hands caressed her body when they made love. She felt chills run through her body that had not surfaced in years. "Damn, I am too old to be horny," she said out loud to herself. "Girl, you have got to fix this!" She tried to laugh and made a mental note to call the therapist first thing Monday morning.

Fay entered the office and her earlier assumptions were correct. 08:12 AM and the entire team were all at their desks except for Amy who was at the board filling in the details acquired the night before and this morning.

"Good morning, boss," Nate said being the first to greet her as others joined in as they swapped pleasantries.

"Krispie-Kremes are fresh," said Amy as she turned from the board.

"Thanks," said Fay reaching into the box. "My Coke Zero should mitigate all the sugar, right?"

"It's God's most perfect food," Nate said with a coy smile.

"Alright, catch me up," said Fay pulling her chair from the desk and facing the room as she sat down.

"Walt, you're first. We waited for you before we started," Amy said taking her seat.

Walt took his keyboard in his lap and the large screens above came to life. "Okay, I'll start with the victims… Just as it appeared, by all accounts this was a normal lower-middle class family until the dad was killed in the wreck. They were typical hard working parents and pretty much lived from paycheck to paycheck. Dad only made about $25,000 a year. Mom's part-time work brought in another $4,000-$5,000 according to their tax records. Their credit was decent. Rented the house on Piper Lane for the last 4 years. One car, a 1989 Corolla, was paid off, and a 2013 Ford

F-150 was being paid monthly when it was totaled when he was killed in the crash,"

Walt paused for a breath and a bite from his doughnut before continuing. "I spoke with Sergeant James White with Jackson P.D. He actually knew the family. His son, Mike and Jimmy, that's what the deceased dad went by, were best friends. When the wreck happened, Sergeant White went to the scene when he heard the identity of the driver on the radio. He went with the troopers to the house to notify the wife. He says they were a normal family but both came from poor families and were not prepared for the death. They had no savings or insurance. The community tried to help and raised some money but most of them are in the same boat. The wife sued the driver but, as my Granddaddy would say, he didn't have a pot to piss in or a window to through it out of."

Walt continued, "Within a few months she was behind on the rent and other bills. The family moved out of the house in April when the eviction notice was served, and best anyone can tell they lived with various friends and in their car afterwards. She continued to work at the salon a couple of days a week when the girls were in school but didn't make much money. Her last day to work was October 7. Last day the girls were in school too. "

The SCU team listened as Walt told of the rather ordinary family that they all knew no longer lived. Their photos were emblazoned on the screens above them as Walt continued his briefing.

"After that, no one seems to know what happened. The next week, an elderly aunt called police after she didn't get an answer from Emma's phone and then she called every friend she knew and couldn't find them. White finally got wind of the report and had detectives follow up to see what they could find. Two of her friends said that she had an old friend in Meridian, Mississippi that thought she could get full time work there and she took the kids and left for Meridian," Walt continued. "Jackson PD contacted the friend, Mary Andrews, who reported that she did arrive with the kids and spent two nights with them but then left for Alabama. Said that she had a good job prospect... that was all they knew." Walt explained, "They kind of dropped off the grid until they showed up at the shelter... no record of school enrollment for the girls, no social security or any other indications from the mom. That is it for now, but I am still digging... her credit and debit cards were long cancelled so there isn't a good paper trail of their travels. I have a BOLO out on the Corolla, but nothing so far. She was driving it when last seen in Meridian, but no one in Birmingham seems to think they had a car," Walt concluded.

Fay stood and went for a coffee. "That's great work, Walt. Surely, the car will turn up," Fay said.

"What did you guys turn up on the books? I'll go last," Amy said.

Nate insisted that Jerome go first. Jerome turned to his keyboard and with a few keystrokes and mouse clicks, pointed to the screens. "This is Marsha Wellington," Jerome stated as her driver license appeared on the screen. "As you can see, she lives in Hoover. Works in the payroll department at Wells Fargo downtown. In October, she and three of her co-workers stayed after work and had dinner at John's and then went on the walking ghost tour downtown. She was intrigued by the Hawes story and went to the library the next week for the books. She actually just got back from a ski trip with her family, so she has a solid alibi, although nothing points to her being involved anyway."

Jerome turned back to the computer briefly and another license appeared on the screen. "This is Keith Warren from Huntsville. He is a junior at Birmingham-Southern. He was doing research on the old courthouse for a history paper on Birmingham and ran across an old article about the riot following Hawes arrest and was intrigued and dug a bit deeper. His reason for checking out the book... no other connection or any reason to flag." Jerome gestured to Nate.

"Well, I checked out the other two from the library," Nate said, "First is Lisa Harrell, a Real Estate agent from Crestwood, NOT a housewife as previously reported," Nate said looking at Walt with a grin. As Harrell's Alabama Drivers License appeared on the overhead screen. "Although in Walt's defense, she has had her real estate license less than a year and by all accounts works very sparingly, but her husband is a Doc at Saint Vincent's. She checked out the book, also after being with a group of friends on the Ghost Tour. Nothing really points to involvement. She has a pretty solid alibi for the night of December 3, as she was attending a birthday party for a co-worker at Highland's Bar and Grill until just after midnight. Amy do you want me to keep going or do you want to take this?"

"Nate and I have both been working on the final book reader since he seems a bit more interesting than the others. As Walt dug up in the preliminaries," Amy said as she gestured to the screens as his Alabama driver's license and UAB ID filled two of the screens. "Doctor John Norman Norwood is a Sociology Professor at UAB. Did his undergrad work at UNC and grad work at Wake Forrest, where he also worked as faculty for a couple of years before coming to UAB. As the boss pointed out he had attended at least two of her lectures, although she didn't remember the first. He introduced himself on the last occurrence of sitting in on her lecture and told her he had attended in the past," Amy reported as she stood under the screens above. "In our interview he indicated that he had sat in on at least four lectures, maybe as many as six.... He can't really remember," Amy continued. "As he told Fay, he is researching a book he is writing regarding criminality in American Society. He told me that in the last 2 years he has sat in on her and other Criminal Justice Professor lectures whenever he had time and could. His best guess was 4-7 times of sitting in on Fay's lectures. He does admit to being in one where the main topic was based on the Hawes case and how timing and circumstantial evidence are used to corroborate physical evidence, etc. His alibi for Friday evening was that he was driving to visit family in Montgomery. He says he left Birmingham about 6 PM and arrived there around 7:45 or so. Spent the night with his Aunt and went to his nephew's football game on Saturday before driving back home. Nate has more," Amy concluded.

Nate stood and stretched. "Yes, Norwood is married to Michael Joseph Clarkson," Nate said pointing to the screens as his driver's license and work ID popped up. "They have been together for 6 years and married two years ago. Mike is an Administrative Assistant at the School of Business at UAB. John checked out the books after hearing Fay's lecturers and Mike admits that he too read them. I would describe both men as a bit uneasy during the interviews and Amy picked up on that too. They were interviewed separately and both seemed tense, even on the initial phone calls. We went to see each one and they both seemed very nervous. I mean more than most people when being interviewed by cops."

"Yeah, when I called Norwood and explained who I was," Amy chimed back in, "he immediately was edgy and when I told him I would rather do it face to face. He was really nervous and made excuses to not do it and kept insisting that I ask whatever I needed to know on the phone.

I was cordial at first but finally had to threaten to show up at his classes to get him to set up a time. I didn't give him much but told him that we were investigating a murder and were interviewing everyone that had checked out the Hawes murder books. As I said, he was way more nervous than you would expect. I did my best to calm him and reassure him that it was just routine. I thought maybe it was just his nature, but then we interviewed the husband and was he was maybe even more nervous... Obviously Norwood had called him and he was pretty worked up when we got there. Unlike Norwood, Clarkson has no alibi," Amy added. "Says he came home from work and since John was gone, he ate dinner at home and watched TV all night."

"Yeah and he had a bit of a hard time remembering just what he watched even though it was just 2 days ago," Nate added.

Amy walked to the whiteboards and said, "I have both of them listed as Person of Interest. We don't really have anything except their uneasiness. No motive or even a tie-in to the victims. Walt is doing a deeper dive to see if either of them have had a bad interaction with police at some point or something that may explain their behavior."

"Yes I have a call into a the college police department at Wake Forrest but I haven't heard back yet. Neither have anything but traffic tickets and that isn't much. John has 2 speeding tickets... one in Georgia from 7 years ago and one in Alabama last year. Mike got a stop sign ticket in Homewood 2 years ago. Everything else is clean," Walt said.

"Do we have forensics yet?" Fay asked.

"Not yet, but all labs are being rushed. We do have the preliminary autopsy reports, but you knew that... you were there," Walt answered.

"I haven't seen the written report. Jacobs was going to finish last night. I left when he finished the autopsies. Bottom line is both were dead when they entered the water just like Maylena." Fay said.

Fay returned to her seat and took a deep breath. "As you already know, both were weighted down with a length of railroad flat iron tied to the bodies with heavy blue nylon rope. They are doing forensics on both the rope and iron to see what they can find. According to Guyer, there is not much hope in finding anything on the metal. It is very likely that if there were any trace evidence, it would have not survived the water. The rope however may yield something, but it is a long shot. We will have to wait on the lab results for a targeted time of death, but the general time frame is close to the same as Maylena... hopefully they will be able to pinpoint more. While we are waiting on the lab reports, let's back trace everything we have," Fay continued. "We need to fill in that gap from when they were last seen in Mississippi until they showed up here at the shelter... If we can find that out, along with where the car is, I think that may point us to something that leads us somewhere."

Fay stood again and walked to the center of the room, "We also need to follow the obvious obsession, or whatever you want to call it, with the Hawes murders... it is way more than obvious now that this cannot be a coincidence. Whoever did this is familiar with the case and is making an attempt to replicate the crime in many ways, but they are not fastidious about the details... one hundred and twenty years later, it would extremely hard to do that, I guess.... For instance, the nylon rope used was not available in 1888. The Hawes victims were tied with cords from a window. While Maylena was dressed up, she was not wearing the same sort of garments as May Hawes was... but the perp is going to a lot of trouble to mimic the Hawes case.... Dumping the bodies in two locations... the railroad iron to weight the bodies… I don't think that is available at the Home Depot, so we need to determine where one could obtain that. Where is it stored in the area?"

Fay was now pacing as her mind raced. "So, as I see it we have two avenues to pursue… the gap in the timeline of the victim's whereabouts and what we do know about the physical evidence… Eastlake is fairly secluded, especially at night, so I can see someone getting a body in there and not being seen… but the lake at the golf course is fairly visible from Highland and somewhat so from Clairmont Avenue. That area is pretty busy even late at night with all the bars and restaurants in Lakeview… So tell me your thoughts," Fay concluded, taking her seat again.

"That is the same conclusion we came to," Amy said. "Perhaps the trace evidence will shed some light, but from what we have now, the more we can find out about the victims, especially their last days, could reveal a lot about who they were with and what they were doing… Jerome and I are going to canvas the shelters again and see if we can turn up any more information. Walt, can you interview the friend in Meridian to see what you can find out from her?"

"Most definitely, I have her contact information already," Walt responded.

Nate spoke up, "I'm working more information about Norwood and Clarkson... I have reached out to Albert Ransom, Investigator at UAB PD and we are going to dig a little deeper on both and may call them in for another interview and see if their demeanor is better or worse than when we first talked to them. According to Al, Norwood had a sexual harassment complaint a few months back but it didn't go anywhere... maybe he is just nervous about that. We will see."

Amy stood and grabbed her jacket off of the back of her chair, "Great! Boss do you want us to meet up again this afternoon to debrief?"

Fay stood also, "No, I don't think that is necessary unless someone gets a big break... ya'll do your thing and keep the team informed by text and let's meet at 0800 in the morning... I hoping we will have some, if not most of the lab results in by then."

Amy and Jerome headed for the door while Walt was surfing through his computer and Nate was talking on the phone. Fay sat back in her chair and took a deep breath. She always had trouble coping with her lack of patience in the early days of a case... it always moved much too slowly for her and there was absolutely nothing she could do to speed it up... it was a process, but even after three decades on the job she knew she would never like it. She decided to spend the day immersed in paperwork and answering emails and other office busywork... she hoped that the doldrums would soon be done and the case would require full attention and the cleaner her plate was at the beginning, the smaller the pile of work at the end would be... PLUS it would keep her from going home and the inherent risks of not being fully engaged in work. She typed in a reminder in her calendar to call for a therapy appointment first thing Monday morning.

Chapter 23

Monday December 7, 2017

Fay Findlay arose early knowing that a full day and busy week lay ahead of her. She had put extra effort into relaxing Sunday afternoon after leaving the office. She walked to Railroad Park and strolled through the park at least three times trying to clear work from her head and relax. From the park, her view of the city skyline offered a slightly different perspective than the one from her loft windows, but one she loved to take advantage of as often as possible. Both views had a similar effect of relaxation.

Railroad Park was an expansive green space on the south side of the tracks that divided Birmingham's north and south sides. As its name implies, the space was once a rail yard and had been abandoned for decades until a dedicated group of visionaries raised the funds to turn the space into rolling meadows, a small lake and landscaped trails. The transformation was completed within the last decade and many point to the park as the catalyst for the recent development all over the city. Once the park was complete, the surrounding real estate turned from desolate vacant industrial properties into vibrant buildings converted into lofts, retail and office space. The Birmingham Barons, the city's minor league franchise, relocated from the suburbs into a new stadium adjacent to Railroad Park, expanding the redevelopment even more.

Fay came here often to walk and clear her mind or to get away from distractions in order think more clearly. She never enjoyed running, but loved to walk through the city and the park had become her favorite place. The great thing about the south was the ability to take a leisurely afternoon stroll in December. While cold weather was not uncommon, it generally came in short spans as fronts moved through from the north. One week ago the temperatures struggled to get above freezing for three days, but for the last four days it had been more normal with highs in the low sixties. Great weather for a brisk walk.

As Fay walked along the edge of the lake looking at the city skyline ahead, she thought of her grief and further resolved that she was ready to finally really deal with it. It was time. She thought about the case and wondered where it would take her and the team. She was proud of the way they stepped up and were handling everything and reminded herself to stand back and let them continue, but she was finding that more difficult with this case. Although it was early, this was no doubt, not a typical case in every sense. There was no denying that whoever had committed the heinous acts was going out of their way to align the crime to the Hawes case and Fay had a gut feeling that she was somehow the link between the past and present.

The Hawes case was not that well known and the only real links to it were the Ghost Walk Tours and her lectures. The more she thought of possible motives and profiles of potential suspects, the more personal it felt. When she thought about the Hawes case, she automatically thought about her reference to the case in various lectures. She knew that it was too early to make that jump and knew she had to keep an open mind in order to allow the case and the evidence develop, but she was finding that more difficult with this case. After her walk at the park she walked down 14th Street to 1st Avenue North and down to the Police building and picked up her car. She ordered take out as she drove home. She parked the car in the basement garage of her building and walked the three blocks to Paramount to pick up her dinner. Paramount was one of the few restaurants or bars on the north side of town open on Sunday and the burger was a favorite indulgence for Fay, along with the fried onion rings.

Back at her loft, Fay listened to music, being careful to avoid the *Elton John Love Songs,* and enjoyed her meal in solitude. With *St. Paul and The Broken Bones* playing on the turntable, Fay tried to read, but finally gave up and just listened to the music and tried to completely relax. She thought of the first time she heard *St. Paul and The Broken Bones* play. It was only three years ago. The band was comprised of local college students playing in a local bar. Fay was struck by their sound as the covered old R & B tunes popular before any of them were born. They also played some original music that was obviously rooted in the old school soul, but also had a mix of blues, gospel and even big band and funk. She really liked their sound and tried to catch them anytime they played. She was listening to their second album and thinking of that first night in a small bar, knowing that the band was now touring the world and although most of them still lived in the city, their days of playing dive bars was behind them. Something about that soulful sound and the view of the Birmingham Skyline at night made her finally relax. She slept well, determined that the morning would be the beginning of getting to the bottom of this crazy case, or least a good start.

Even though Fay arrived at the office an hour ahead of the scheduled meeting at 0800, her team was already there working, "Damn, I cannot get ahead of you guys! Good Morning!"

The response was almost in unison "Good morning, boss!"

"Do we have anything yet?" Fay asked as she took her seat,

Amy glanced up from computer, "The preliminary lab results from the autopsies just landed, I am opening them now." With a few clicks of her mouse, the plasma screens came to life.

Cause of death: Blunt force trauma was the first thing visible to Fay as she read the Medical Examiner's autopsy report on Emma. This was certainly no surprise since they had all seen the gash behind Emma's right ear, but somehow Fay felt relieved that there was not a bizarre turn pointing in another direction. This case was already too weird. She was relieved to have something turn out as expected.

"I hate to leave now, but I've got an interview set-up with the professor between his first two classes," said Nate. "Trying to play nice cop by meeting him on his turf and terms to see if we can get anything new. Ransom is going to join me... I'll let you know if anything new comes up."

As Nate left, the others turned back to reading the reports. The report was several pages long and each person was reading at their own pace on their computer screens even though the document was displayed on the big screen. Each skimmed through the medical techno-jumble for the highlights. This practice was something one got used to and only occasionally would you run into a phrase or description that could not be easily translated into common layman terms. Walt finished first and looked at the others without being too obvious awaiting them to finish before discussing.

The report for Emma included abundant descriptions of the head wound and measurements and descriptive narratives about organs. Samples were removed from the wound for analysis. Indications of lung examination indicate victim was deceased prior to entering the water. Skin abrasions around her neck, abdomen and ankles from the rope are indicated as post-mortem injuries. Trauma to the vagina and vaginal area indicates bruising and abrasions as pre-mortem injuries. Left shoulder was dislocated although evidence indicates that this was very likely a post-mortem injury. Swabs had been taken and forwarded with other samples collected to the forensic lab.

The report for Irene contained the same descriptions and measurements of organs. The only trauma noted were the post-mortem skin abrasions around the neck and ankles from the rope. Indications are the victim was deceased prior to being bound and prior to entering the water. No signs of sexual assault or other injuries are noted.

After Fay finished reading she glanced up and caught Walt watching her and the others just as he tried to look away. She smiled at him in a way that relieved the awkwardness he felt. Amy looked up and saw that the others had finished reading, "Well that doesn't tell us a lot we didn't already know until we get the labs back, but if the vaginal swabs turn up anything we could have the perp's DNA."

"The preliminary lab results should be here within the hour. I checked with them when I got in this morning," Walt said.

Fay rocked back in her chair as she faced the others, "Well we now know she was raped before being killed, so that is new and could be a big piece of the puzzle."

"With the whole Hawes tie-in, I was not expecting that, I am correct – There was no rape of the Hawes wife?" Amy said looking at Fay.

"No, there was no indication," Fay responded. "One doctor opined that May Hawes was sexually assaulted but the coroner sought two other doctor's opinions and both concluded there was no sign of sexual assault. Of course, remember this was 1888 and they didn't have the resources or knowledge we do now. The wife was rumored to be a loose woman who drank to excess but there was no mention of her being raped, but we don't know if they even considered that at that time. So, we once again have a divergence from the Hawes case, however so slight."

"Preliminary labs just landed," Walt announced. "Irene was chloroformed like her sister." Walt was quickly scanning the report as he spoke. "On Emma… semen was present in the vagina along with traces of what appears to be latex. Samples are undergoing further analysis. Debris from the head wound appears to be wood and paint and are undergoing further analysis… I don't see anything else that jumps out to me."

Fay stood and stretched as she reached for a bottled water in the fridge, "Hopefully, the lab results will give us something… Jacobs warned that much of the trace evidence would be lost or degraded with the bodies submerged, so this is really good news that they do have something."

"With traces of latex and semen, maybe the perp was wearing a condom that broke and now he is compromised." Amy said.

Walt turned in his chair to face his two female bosses with a hesitant look, "Generally, when traces of condom use are present, it is the lubricants or spermicides that are detected. These are generally water-soluble so in cases like ours where time has passed they are less detectable and especially since the body was submerged, a lot of trace evidence would have been washed away or degraded... But this indicates that the perp did wear a condom and it likely broke during the act because according to the report, they actually removed two pieces of what is believed to be latex from the vagina... not just lubricants. Hopefully they can get DNA from that and the semen."

Fay stood looking at Walt's screen over his shoulder, "That is a first for me," she said. "I've worked many rape cases but I have never known of actual condom fragments being recovered... this is definitely a break, no pun intended," she said with a slight smile, trying to lighten the mood in the room. They laughed. "Of course, we will have to get the full results and hopefully a match, but at least we have something."

"I am expanding my dig to rape cases." Walt announced as he typed.

"Good," Amy answered. "We need to try to figure this psycho out... murderer, rapist, kidnapper... so far he is looking like a real gem! I am going to go down and talk to Julie Willis in Family Services...I've been trying to connect with her since this case started and she just texted that she is in her office. She's been working with the National task force on sex trafficking, but she is quite the expert in perverts, so I want to read her in on this to see if the chloroform pushes any buttons for her."

Amy headed for the door, Fay sat down at her desk, "Great idea! I am going to add in the rape info to my research and see what I can find. Walt is still digging and Nate should be done with their interviews soon, so let's reconvene after lunch to see where we are. Hopefully, we will all get more info and we an start putting the pieces together."

Chapter 24

Monday, 12/7/2017: 09:30

Professor Norwood was visibly unnerved as he invited the Detectives into his office. "Thanks for taking time for us, Dr. Norwood, this shouldn't take too long," Nate said has he entered the tiny office and sat in one of the two seats in front of the small cluttered desk.

"This is Detective Albert Ransom with UAB Police, I think you have met before."

Norwood managed a nervous smile as he extended his hand to ransom, "Yes, nice to see you." The professor took his seat behind the desk and nervously shuffled some papers.

"We just wanted to follow up, since I know we caught you off guard the first time we talked," said Nate. "Is there anything that you have thought of since then that we haven't heard yet?"

Norwood adjusted his glasses and never looked up, "No, as I said, I really have no information. I read the books simply as research for my book."

"Yeah, how is that coming… your book?" Nate asked.

Norwood glanced up at him briefly, slightly surprised, "Well, you know, it's a text book, so lots and lots of research… but I am progressing."

Nate shifted forward in his chair a bit, "I'm curious, did you and John discuss the Hawes book at all?"

"Uh, no, I don't think so. Why would we?" Norwood answered.

"I don't know, maybe like a book club? Since you both read it, I thought maybe you guys discussed it," Nate said.

Again, not looking up, Norwood responded hesitantly, "I don't think we ever did."

"Okay. Now this may be a bit uncomfortable, but I need your honest answer," said Nate leaning all the way in to the edge of the front of the desk. "Tell me about the complaint last year from your student, Ashley Manning."

Norwood was visibly surprised and just stared for several seconds as he thought of how to respond. "Uh… that was just a huge misunderstanding, that's all. Just a misunderstanding."

Nate tilted his head slightly and he locked eyes with the professor, "So, you're saying that you didn't come on to her?"

Norwood broke the stare, diverting his eyes down, "No, I didn't… I am gay! And Married!"

Nate leaned back ever so slightly, "Well why would this young lady file a complaint like that? Did you piss her off or something?"

Norwood looked as though he wanted the floor he was staring at to swallow him up and take him from this misery. "No! I didn't do anything. She was… or is, a good student and I just took an interest in helping her," he said glancing up for just a second. "That is all. She totally misconstrued my intentions completely!"

Ransom broke his silence, "I know we covered this last year, but for the record, you didn't touch her as she claimed in the complaint?"

Never looking up, Norwood responded in an almost monotone voice, "No, never."

"My understanding is this whole thing was a 'he said – she said thing', so you kept your job and reputation, but I am trying to understand why this girl would single you out to make a false accusation. I mean a gay man, of all people. She didn't resent a bad grade or anything... just out of the blue files a complaint that you tried to force yourself on her... kissing her and grabbing her tits... I mean that seems far fetched," Nate said as he rocked back in his chair and stared at Norwood.

Norwood was still shaken but seemed to recover some stability, "Yes there was no basis. What does this all have to do with your investigation... the book and all? I thought this was all settled... Am I being accused again of something?"

Nate stood up, "No sir, if we accuse you of something you will know it... we are just investigating a murder and I am trying to cover all the bases. So, just between us, you are gay and never fool around with girls or women at all?" Nate let the bombshell question just hang in the air as Norwood stammered from the surprise again.

"No, not since high school... I am gay... no women... no girls," Norwood said.

As Ransom stood he added the final blow, "So is your husband aware of the allegations Ms. Manning made against you?"

Norwood returned his gaze to the floor, "No, I never told him... I didn't want him to be upset and it ended so there was never a reason to tell him... it's over... or at least I thought it was."

As the detectives left the office, Nate said, "You have my card. Give me a call if you think of anything you feel may be pertinent." Norwood looked both rattled and relieved as he closed the door behind them.

Once outside in the parking lot, Ransom turned to Nate, "So what did you think?"

Nate paused, "Something is still not quite right with that guy... not sure what he is hiding, but something is up with him."

"He did seem super uptight," Ransom agreed. "Even more than he was when I interviewed him last year about the student... which by the way, I think he is guilty as hell on that... gay or not... the girl had absolutely no motive but we couldn't get anything to back her up."

"Yeah, I am not sure he had anything to do with my case, but he is guilty of something," Nate said. "Hey, thanks for this... I will keep you posted on our progress. Amy or I will interview the husband again and see if he acts the same way... they both are hiding something, I am just not sure what that is."

Chapter 25

Monday, December 7, 2017: 11:40

Amy Boyd exited the elevator on the 3rd Floor of the Police Headquarters Building and made her way to a cluster of offices in the front of the building. The Family Services Division handled a wide variety of cases involving domestic situations crimes against or committed by juveniles. Within the division were three squads -- Juvenile, Gang Intervention and Domestic Abuse.

Along with the detectives, there were professional counselors to cope with the wide variety of cases that fit the category. In some cases, it was a little bit of everything, but since juveniles had to be handled differently than adults, these officers were specially trained and were use to dealing with both the juveniles and the juvenile court system. The offices also provided space for several intervention programs such as D.A.R.E. (Drug Abuse Resistance

Education) and P.A.L (Police Athletic League) to hopefully keep some out of the system and on the right path.

Julie Willis, a strikingly beautiful African-American woman, was Amy's roommate in the Police Academy. Like Amy, Julie rose quickly through the ranks and found her calling as an investigator in the Family Services Division, where she had been a Detective Sergeant for ten years. During the last six years she specialized in human trafficking crimes and has been part of a national task force for the last three years.

Birmingham is at the crossroads for modern human trafficking with four interstate highways intersecting in the city center. I-65 runs from the gulf coast to Chicago. I-20/59 is the corridor from New Orleans to Atlanta and the east coast and the recently completed I-22 runs to Memphis. With this convergence of traffic thoroughfares, the Magic City has experienced a significant increase in criminal activity from drug traffickers and pimps and perverts passing through and choosing the city as a meeting place to do business. The national task force was comprised of Julie and two other BPD detectives, two FBI agents, two DEA agents and an Investigator from the Federal Prosecutors office. The team had made significant progress making several key arrests, but the crimes of forced prostitution and drugs seem to grow at a rate that would always out pace their efforts.

When Amy entered Julie's office, she was on the phone and gestured for her to wait. She finished the call and greeted Amy with a hug, "Good Morning, Sunshine! I never see you since I am out of the office so much... I miss our lunches... we have to make a point to get together more often."

"I miss you too! How have you been? How are Corey and the girls?" Amy responded.

Julie's smile was one that could compete with Amy's. "Oh, they are all good. The girls are playing tennis and are just being kids! I hear you guys caught a real sicko case, huh?"

Amy's smile faded quickly, "Indeed... three victims – a mom and two daughters not much older than your twins."

Julie's smile turned serious as well, "I heard it was a copy cat of some case from a hundred years ago? What's up with that?"

"Yeah, the Hawes murders... you know, Fay uses the case in her lectures at the Academy and UAB... from 1888. Guy kills his family and dumps one girl in the lake at Eastlake and the wife and other daughter in Lakeview... well that is exactly where we found our victims," Amy explained.

"That is some sick shit. Same M.O.?" Julie asked.

"Well kinda... it is like he is trying to copy cat but not every detailed... what I wanted to ask you about is he used chloroform on the girls... have you guys seen this in any cases?" Amy asked.

"Most of the freaks are using drugs to get women, but you know, we did have a case last year where we thought the guy used chloroform... A hooker out at a truck stop on Highway 78 said a pimp was trying to recruit her to go to Memphis and work for him and she refused... later that night, somebody comes up behind her and puts a rag or something over her mouth and that was the last thing she remembered. She woke up at a flea-bag motel down the road naked and sore, but alive... she had been raped and left there." Julie said.

"Did you get the guy?" Amy asked.

"No, she wanted nothing to do with prosecuting... as a matter of fact, she didn't even report it. We heard of it from an informant who said several of the girls had experienced something similar going back a few months... we interviewed several girls but no one was willing to step up. We only got vague descriptions and they were kinda all over the place... White male, bald shaved head and that is about it.... Some put him in his thirties and others said he was older... some said beard and others said clean face... they all did agree that he was all cool and lovey-dovey until they refused him and then he went off and went bad-ass... we worked it for a few weeks but it kinda fell to the back burner as we have a lot of other things going on, you know," Julie explained.

Amy was curious to know more, "Was he always at the same place?"

"No, we had reports from all over but mostly here in the metro area," Julie said. "One report in Slidell, Louisiana and I followed up on that one with the local cops but they had no reports. There were others in Tuscaloosa and one in

Anniston, but like I said, we could never put anything together to do anything or even ID the guy."

"One girl said he ran a crew and was a dealer and pimp but she really had just heard that and had no evidence or anything," Julie continued.

"Well, at least that's something... we know someone is still using the stuff... we got very few hits on searching the national databases... but nothing usually goes in unless a case is made, so that's why I came to you," Amy said.

"Yeah, you know with us the line between perp and victim gets a bit blurry sometimes, and it seems to be getting worse," Julie said.

"Yeah I don't know how you do it... especially the young ones," Amy said.

"The older the twins get, the harder it is... I see them when I look into the faces of some of these girls, but if I can save just one it is worth it," Julie said.

"Hey let's get together soon, Okay?" Amy said as she turned for the door.

"Yes, I would love that. Hey, keep me posted on your case and let me know if I can help in any way," Julie said as she returned to her desk.

"Will do," Amy said as she headed back for the elevator.

As the elevator doors opened, she saw Nate scanning his phone as she stepped in. "Did you get a confession from the Professor?" Amy asked.

"Hey, Sunshine! Nate said as he looked up. "No, but he is still not telling us everything... not sure if he has anything to do with this or not but he is definitely hiding something."

The doors opened to the 4th floor and Nate held the door as Amy stepped out and he followed, "Did I miss any new developments?" He asked.

"Not really. I was just down talking to Julie and she tells me they had a string of vague reports of a guy possibly using chloroform on hookers in and around town but never could pin anything or even ID him." Amy said.

“That’s interesting, since the database didn’t really give us anything,” Nick mused.

“Yeah, since they never made a case, their info was never entered either… I am going to follow up with other departments to see if anyone has anything,” Amy said as they reached the SCU office.

As the two entered the office, the others seemed engrossed in their computers. Amy announced their arrival, “Please, somebody tell me you have a solid lead!”

“Nothing earth shattering that I am aware of.” Fay answered. Jerome and Walt agreed with a quick nod. Jerome was on the phone and Walt was doing his thing with two screens full of information in front of him.

“What about either of you? Fay asked. “Anything that can’t wait until after lunch?”

Amy and Nate glanced at each other and Amy said, “Mine can wait.”

“Mine too.” Nate agreed.

Fay smiled and said, "I ordered lunch for us all from O'Carrs… I hope that was okay. I'll run over and pick it up."

Nate was excited, "Oh hell yeah! I love that place." Jerome still had the phone to his ear but had not missed the news as he grinned and gave the thumbs up.

"That is the good thing about all of us working together for so long, I don't have to take orders," said Fay. "I know what everyone eats."

Walt stood up, "I've got to run down to cyber and pick something up from Cheryl, so I can run out and pick it up if you want."

"Thanks, Walt… that is perfect… it is all paid… I figure I owe ya'll for all the pastries I have eaten this weekend!" Fay said.

Chapter 26

December 7, 2017: 13:53

After a delicious lunch of world famous chicken salad and soup, it was back to business. "Walt, you go first," said Amy as everyone cleared their desks of lunch remnants.

Walt stood and clicked his keyboard to reveal his notes. "I followed up on a deeper dig of our Persons of Interest, but I know that Nate just finished another interview with the Professor so I will wait to provide that after Nate... Don't want to be the spoiler!" he said with smirkish grin. Nate smiled and gave him a thumbs up.

"I also followed up and talked to Sergeant White in Jackson," Walt continued. "He didn't have much to add. I also spoke with the friend in Meridian that the family stayed with on October 8th and 9th. Mary Andrews is an old high school friend of Emma and they have remained in touch although Mary moved to Meridian when she got married right after high school. She said that she knew that Emma and the children were in trouble and she wanted to help but didn't know how... evidently, as you might imagine, Emma was not advertising that they were homeless. Mary said that when she learned that, she invited them to come and stay at her place. She and her husband have one kid – a boy 4 years old. She told Emma that she had a guest room and they were welcome as long as they needed a place. Mary had arranged for work for Emma at a local salon that a friend of hers owns. Emma met with the owner when she got to town and filled out the paperwork for her to work... it was a percentage thing so she wouldn't make anything until she built up her business but Mary said she was eager to start over. She was going to start work on that following Tuesday."

Walt opened a bottle of water and took a long drink before continuing his report, "She said they were settling in and Emma went out pick up some things for the kids at the store the next morning and when she came back she said she had met some folks that were friends of friends and that they had a fantastic job opportunity for her in Birmingham, but she had to be there the next day, so they had dinner and she loaded up the Toyota with the girls and left about 7 PM on the 9th," Walt continued.

"Did she Mary try to convince her stay?" Fay asked.

"Mary said that Emma's entire demeanor changed when she came home that day… it was like she was excited about the new job but she was also short on details… Mary asked her if it was a salon job and she replied yes, but didn't provide any details… She said it seemed she didn't know a lot of details. She asked her what part of town the salon was in but she didn't know. She said that she seemed happy but uneasy," Walt said. "Mary said that she knew she didn't have any money, so they lent her $120, which was all the cash they had. Emma promised to pay them within two weeks," he added.

"So far, still no hits on the car. I checked with the beat car around the shelters to see if they had noticed it parked in an alley or anything… no one remembers seeing it and no one at the shelters were aware of a car. That's it for me for now," Walt concluded his report and returned to his seat.

"Well, Nate," Amy said looking in Nate's direction, "since Walt set us up with the tease, let's hear from you."

"Well if you think I have a big breakthrough or something, Walt oversold it!" Nate smiled, "I did interview the Professor again this morning in his office between his classes. Al Ransom, detective at UAB, came and sat in. It seems that late last year, Al investigated our professor after receiving a sexual harassment complaint from a student of his – a female student. Victim said that Norwood and she were in a discussion after class and he leaned in and tried to kiss her and she backed away before contact and according to her, he grabbed her and pulled her in close and held her kissing her neck and fondling her breast... she pulled out of his grasp and ran out... about an hour later she calmed down and told her roommate about it who insisted she report it... from there it got reported to various people and departments until... long story short... UAB police got the notice the following morning," Nate said.

Nate stood and was thumbing through his notes, "Ransom followed up and interviewed the professor who was shocked at the allegation and provided full denial... said that he did talk to the girl but never made any advance or physical contact," Nate continued. "As he did again today when the subject came up, he reminded us that he was a gay man... a married gay man and would never ever do such a thing. Ransom thinks he is lying about it, but has no other evidence so it is a he said, she said thing... He is on some kind of double secret probation, but nothing official happened... the girl was pissed but not interested in pushing it. She dropped his class and has avoided him. This could explain the professor's aversion to our interviews or police presence, but it doesn't explain the husbands, because according to Norwood, his husband was never told of the incident and he was pretty adamant that he wanted it to remain that way... and this is where Walt's dig comes into play," Nate said motioning to Walt. "Walt discovered that during his last semester at Wake Forrest, a very similar complaint was filed by a young co-ed," Nate continued. "If you read the report it could almost be the same report as the UAB one. In this case, the investigation ended when the professor took another job and left Wake Forrest... for UAB. In that case, hubby was interviewed and by all accounts went ballistic."

"The cops at Wake said he was furious," Walt said. "First at the husband, but then he turned on them and threatened to sue and file discrimination charges... they said the University kept the whole thing quiet until the husband got involved and then it became very public and got a lot bigger, which was likely the reason the exit was hastened."

"Now that I know that, it makes me know why Norwood was so anxious to leave hubby out of the loop on this one," Nate offered. "Seems he is the over-the-top jealous type. Ransom agreed with my observation that he may not be our guy... but he is holding something. Hopefully when the labs start coming in, I will have a reason to give him another visit. That's it for me."

Amy stood, "That is very interesting... definitely holds them both as staying on the board as Person of Interest. Jerome, you are on..."

"Amy and I canvased the shelters again, to see if anybody had anything new," Jerome began. "As shelters go, there were some new folks and some of the folks that were there two days ago were gone. I spoke with the lady that had sat at the table with the family at dinner the last night anyone remembers seeing them. She didn't really have any more details to add, but she was pretty certain that Emma was hiding from someone. She said it was fairly common in women's shelter that women are hiding from an abusive partner so she thought nothing about it, but she said she was real protective of the girls and was very quiet. Of course, we knew that already as she was reluctant to provide her identity and then when she did, she gave a false name. No one there is sure how they arrived but was fairly certain it wasn't in a car, as they have to be listed and registered to use the gated lot behind the building."

Jerome stood a grabbed his note pad and flipped through it. "I also canvased the businesses along Clairmont to see if anyone saw anything suspicious around the golf course," Jerome continued. "I completely struck out there. I also talked to some of the residents that live across the street going up the hill toward the clubhouse... no one saw anything out of the ordinary, but I may have caught a break... as I am walking back to my car from one of the houses a lady is jogging down the hill so I stopped and talked to her... she lives around the corner up on Highland. She said that when she walked her dog around midnight on Thursday, there was a car pulled off the road next to the golf course fence right off Clairmont... she could not give a color other than dark... she said when she came around the curve the trunk was open but she didn't she anyone, but then someone came from the fence side of the car and shut the trunk and got in and drove away... she was too far away to get any kind of description. Person had on dark clothes."

"She said that when you guys were fishing out the bodies, she stopped to see what was going on and when her neighbors told her, she approached the officer at the gate and told him what she saw and he said he would report it, so she assumed we already had the info. It's not much, but I called Lt. Guyer to see if they had, by chance, gotten any tire marks or anything in the area. He said there were tons of marks where people turn around at that spot so they couldn't get anything... I am going to find out who was on that gate and see why we didn't get this earlier. It could be nothing but it could be our killer dumping the bodies. Guyer is sending a tech out to see if they can find any prints on the chain-link fence or any other evidence in that spot that may have been overlooked. I will let you know what they find, if anything. That's all I have to report...I'm done!"

Amy stood back up, "I guess it's my turn... Jerome covered the shelter but I want to add that more than one person pointed to the fact that Emma seemed extremely nervous and seemed to be hiding from someone, which isn't that unusual in a women's shelter, but most said she seemed over the top nervous and paranoid... so that is definitely something we need to consider. We need to figure out what was the big job opportunity she had here when she didn't really have any contacts that we know of... and what happened when she got here that she ended up with no car in a shelter hiding?" Amy paced as she continued, "I feel that is the key to our puzzle... or at least it could lead us somewhere if we can figure that out. I have reached out to a friend of mine in Meridian P.D. She is going to check with the two stores that Mary knows that Emma went to before coming in and telling her they were leaving for Birmingham... hopefully she can turn up something."

Amy was now pacing in circles as the team took notes. "I also had a good conversation with Julie Willis this morning to see if she knew of any cases similar to any aspect of ours... mainly, did her task force know of any use of chloroform on victims... And, she told me an interesting story of this phantom guy that is said to use chloroform on prostitutes mainly here in the metro area but also as far away as Slidell, Louisiana and Gadsden... nothing shows up in the databases really because no case has ever been made and most of the victims are reluctant to file a report or even talk... but someone is out there... I put my full report on this in the dropbox so you can read all the details, but this guy is a rapist and he has beaten at least two women pretty severely. Of course, it may have nothing to do with our case but it seems like the best thing we have with a physical tie-in so let's keep following it," Amy said. "I am going to follow up with Vice… I know they have been working with the Task Force out at the truck stops on Finley Avenue and out Highway 78… I will let you know if they have any more info." Amy returned to her seat, "Boss, what do you have?"

Fay leaned forward in her chair, "I am just taking all this in. We seem to have some morsels and hopefully we will get some forensics that help shed some light on at least one of these leads… I think Amy is right… If we can fill in that missing time and find out what seems to be a sudden change from 'I am staying with my friend in Meridian until I get back on my feet' to 'I am heading to Birmingham'… where, as far as we know, she knew no one… has some mystery job… and then ends up scared and paranoid in a homeless shelter with no car and no money. If we can find out what the job was or who she was coming here to work for, and why the urgency… and what happened on the way here or when she arrived… that is our key to figuring out who may have done this to her."

Fay stood and paced as she shared her thoughts with the team, "She and her kids were murdered, so obviously her fear or paranoia was justified… we just need a break and hopefully the forensics will give us the break we need… we should have some things back soon… even though the rush is on it will be a few more days on any DNA evidence but that is better than the normal 6 weeks, so I am not complaining."

Fay paced across the floor in silent contemplation as the team watched and listened. "What can we do to shake the tree?" Fay asked. "Amy is working with Julie and vice to see what we can uncover on our mystery guy that likes to use chloroform," she said as she walked over the whiteboard. "Our professor and husband have done little to eliminate their role as suspects, although their only connection seems to be reading the Hawes books, attending my lectures and the professor's apparent straying from his marriage vows and his gayness… Let's push hard with Meridian to see what we can find out about her sudden change of plans… we can go down there if we need to… what is it, a two or three hour drive?" Fay asked before continuing. "Walt, get the description and info on the car out to all the precinct shift commanders… ask them to put this on the roll call list so that every cop in the city is looking for that car. Everyone, just keep digging… surely we will catch a break soon."

Fay pointed to the whiteboard. "We need to know what happened between October 9th and November 29th," she said as she drew a big circle in the timeline. "Where were they and what were they doing? If we can answer that, we can start to unravel this," Fay concluded and took her seat again.

Amy stood and added the new notes to the whiteboard and turned back to face the room. "Jerome and Walt, you guys head to Meridian early tomorrow. Meredith McRae, is my contact their and has been working this already. She is a Lieutenant with Meridian P.D. I will call her to let them know ya'll are coming. See what you can find out from the stores she visited… talk to clerks, see if any of them have video surveillance… just she what you can turn up… I have the feeling that whoever she met with is key to this since her friend said that her whole demeanor changed while she was on that shopping trip."

"Hopefully, we will get some forensics in today or tomorrow that may point us somewhere," Amy continued taking her seat. "Nate and I are going to canvas some of the truck stops with the task force and vice to see what other information we can garner on our mystery rapist."

Fay stood, "It is almost 4 so we probably won't get anything more today, but I am going downstairs and lean on the lab and talk to Guyer and see what I can find out and we will reconvene in the morning.... Except for you two," nodding at Jerome and Walt. "Be careful and report in with anything you find. I'll see everyone in the morning. Try to get some rest tonight."

Chapter 27

Friday, May 3, 1889: 14:30

The handcuffed Richard Hawes, under heavy guard was escorted back in to the courtroom and took his usual seat at the table.

As word circulated that court was about to resume, the courtroom filled quickly as people rushed to their seats. Almost an hour later, Judge Greene came to the bench and ordered the crowd to quiet down and called the court in session. Once order was restored, the judge turned to the jury and asked if a verdict had been reached. Foreman N.F. Thompson stood and answered, “We have, your Honor.”

The judge struck the gavel and ordered the crowd quiet again, then said, “Pass it to the clerk.”

Clerk Burgin received the slip of paper and read it aloud, “We, the jury, find the defendant guilty of murder in the first degree, as charged in the indictment, and say he shall suffer death.”

A brief moment of utter silence filled the courtroom with all eyes focused on the prisoner. Richard Hawes sat with his elbows on the table in front of him staring ahead and showed no emotion at hearing the verdict. A murmur began to rise in the audience and Judge Greene quickly restored order. He then ordered the jury to be polled. Each man stood and answered firmly his agreement with the verdict as read.

Mr. Talliaferro, Hawes attorney, began assuring his client that an appeal could be won and would be filed immediately. As the men stood in close conversation, Deputy Thompson walked up and placed the handcuffs on Hawes and led him to the rear of the courtroom where nine other deputies surrounded the condemned man as they left the courtroom and silently marched up 3rd Avenue and down 21st Street, back to the jail. The group marched in almost complete silence and Hawes, with his head high and looking straight ahead, showed no emotion still. Small groups of men and boys followed, pointing and talking.

As they reached the jail and went inside, the crowds lingered outside. Thompson escorted Hawes to his cell where he laid down on his cot but still said nothing. His supper soon came but he didn't eat. He lay on the cot in silence.

In the following days, all the newspapers led with headlines of the guilty verdict and recounts of the trial. Richard Hawes lay in his cell, silent and brooding. The verdict was not unexpected, but knowing that his life was now officially doomed weighed heavily.

Chapter 28

Tuesday, December 8, 2017 --- Meridian, MS

Walt and Jerome left Birmingham early for the two and half hour drive southwest on I-20/59 to Meridian. They were meeting Detective Lt. Meredith McRae who headed the department's Crimes Against Persons squad. McRae was a friend of Amy Boyd, who had set up the meeting. McRae and Boyd attended the same session of the prestigious FBI National Academy 5 years ago and had remained close friends.

Walt steered the black Chevrolet SUV into the parking lot at Meridian PD headquarters at 0817, thirteen minutes ahead of schedule. Inside they introduced themselves to the receptionist. In less than a minute, McRae emerged from the frosted glass door labeled **Detective Division**. After exchanging greetings, she invited the duo back to her office. McRae explained that she had assigned a detective to do some preliminary work on the case, Mike Turner, who had been retracing Emma tracks on the day before she left Meridian for Birmingham.

Moments later, Turner came into the office, "Sorry, I'm late."

Jerome and Walt stood to greet him. "Actually we arrived early... who knew there would be no wrecks on I-20... that never happens!" Walt said.

After an exchange of greetings, Turner pulled out his iPad and reported his progress. "I spoke to Mary Andrews a few times and I told her that we may want to pay her a visit when you guys were here. Based on info from her, I have tried to track Emma's movements on that last day. She went to at least three stores, and two have video surveillance so she may have gone to more, as there are some time gaps that I haven't accounted for," Turner continued. "I haven't found anyone that spoke to her, or really remembers her, for that matter. Video didn't provide anything other than times."

Reading his notes, Turner continued, "She entered the Wal-Mart at 11:56 AM and exited at 12:17. I have the video clips on this thumb drive for you guys, by the way," he said producing a thumb drive from his pocket. "She appears to be alone when she came in and when she left. Next appearance was at the Dollar General store about a half-mile down the highway… she enters there at 13:49 and exits at 14:02. According to Mary, Emma got back home around 14:30 or so," he continued. "She went to her room for minute. The kids were outside playing. She then came into the kitchen and helped Mary with supper preparations. She didn't announce her plans to leave for Birmingham until they were cleaning up after dinner and then left almost immediately and that was a little after 19:00."

Turner closed his iPad and looked the detectives, "So, there is an hour and a half or so unaccounted for even though the two stores are a half-mile apart… Mary only remembers seeing bags from Wal-Mart and Dollar General but says she also had a small plain white plastic bag with no logo… there could have been others, but she is pretty sure those were the only ones."

"There are few stores nowadays without video but without knowing where she went it would be impossible to know… there are at least 30 stores in that immediate area and about a half dozen gas stations. Unfortunately, Meridian doesn't have many traffic cameras. However, I did pull the video for that day from the BP station on the corner. It is about halfway between the two stores and has a great new video system that not only covers the store and pumps but also both roads and the intersection… we've gotten stuff from them several times for nearby robberies and even wrecks. Our folks are looking through the tape now to see if they can spot her car. Even if she didn't stop there, I figured if we can get the time she passed through the intersection, we could determine what side she was on for the unaccounted time and that would help narrow things down."

"Wow! That is great work… We don't have much to go on so we are here to try and see if we can find anything that will tell us why she had such a sudden change of plans and why she decided to come to Birmingham," Jerome said.

"We feel like that if we can answer that or get any indication, it may help us determine where she went once she arrived in Birmingham or who she may have been with," Walt added. "We have a missing gap from October 9th to November 29th and since it started here, anything that we can find out to point us somewhere will be crucial. We don't have much in the way of forensics yet so we are just filling in the time line."

Meredith stood, "Mike will take you guys out to the stores and anywhere else you need to go. I hope you can uncover something that helps." Jerome and Walt thanked her for her hospitality and help.

"Let's go see if the Evidence Techs have found anything on the BP videos yet and then we can head out," Mike said guiding the detectives down the hallway and entered a door with a simple label, **Evidence Technicians**. The two followed Mike as they entered. The room was not very large. On the right was a long built in desk that ran about fifteen feet long and had five computer workstations. On the other side were shelves holding various cases and duffle bags. About halfway back, the room was divided by a metal fence that was locked with a large pad lock and a clipboard hung next to the gate entrance. Inside was an array of shelves and in the right hand corner were two large refrigerators. The detectives immediately recognized that this was the evidence locker. The two Birmingham officers gave each other a glance, impressed with the efficient use of space.

The CSI Division in Birmingham occupied an entire floor of their building and the Evidence Room occupied the entire basement, plus a large garage behind the building for vehicles and large items. Although this was much smaller, it seemed to be well maintained and organized. The trio headed towards two officers occupying the back two workstations. Mike made the introductions, "Gentlemen, this is Officers Ashley Gaines and Jason Meadows. They are our two best Evidence Techs and they are looking for your car. This is Walt and Jerome, Detectives from Birmingham."

The group exchanged handshakes and pleasantries. Ashley returned to her keyboard and said, "You guys have perfect timing, we think we just spotted the car and if it is the one, she stopped at the station, so we may have some good video of her. Jason is looking through the other cameras to locate her now."

"That is awesome!" Walt was almost giddy.

Ashley's screen filled with a shot of the intersection as the dark blue Toyota turned into the station. The frame froze and she zoomed in to the driver through the windshield. "As you can see, there is too much glare to make an ID but now that we have a time frame Jason is bringing all the cameras to that time," she said. "The station is equipped with 34 cameras outside and 8 inside, so it will take a minute."

Jason was busily working the mouse and keypad as his two monitors divided into eight smaller screens and the cameras fast-forwarded and stopped at 12:22 to match the image on Ashley's monitor. Then, her second monitor flickered to life with 8 smaller screens and video screaming by until each one froze at 12:22.

"The video is incredible," said Walt. "Anytime we pull video it looks like a bad movie from 1950."

Ashley laughed, "Yeah, we get that a lot too, but this is a really state of the art system." Jason was now advancing the video screens frame by frame.

"There she is at the pump!" he exclaimed looking at a frame showing the video of pump number 7. He quickly switched to another camera feed that showed the Toyota pulling up to the pump viewed from the rear. He zoomed in on the plate, "That is her tag." Jerome and Walt took a step in closer as the camera widened backed out to show Emma exit the driver door and walk around the rear of the car. She was wearing a simple red tank top and jeans. Her hair was pulled back in a short ponytail and she wore sunglasses.

"She had no cards so she has to go in to pay," Walt said.

Jason switched the feed again to focus on the door as Emma entered the door and stood in a short line to pay for her gas. He switched the feed again for a view from behind the cashier as Emma stepped up and handed the clerk a twenty.

"Is there any audio?" Walt asked.

"No audio," Ashley answered. Emma took her receipt and appeared to ask the clerk something as he gestured to his left, Emma left in that direction. Jason was already scanning other feeds and quickly another feed appeared showing Emma heading through the store toward the restroom at the rear.

"That bald dude is really checking her out," said Mike. As Emma made her way across the store a man standing near the cashier stepped into the frame and seemed to be laser locked on her. He stood watching until she entered the restroom. It was hard to tell much about him from the back. He was white with a shaved head and wore a sleeveless white tee shirt and faded jeans.

"She looks 10 or 15 years younger here than the other video and photos," he said. Walt said noting the difference in Emma's appearance from the video and photos from the shelter about from about seven weeks earlier. As Emma disappeared into the restroom, the bald man disappeared from the frame heading back toward the entrance.

"No cameras in the restrooms, of course," stated Jason. "The guy did seem to take a long hard stare at her." Others nodded in agreement.

Almost three minutes later, Emma emerged from the restroom door, sunglasses on top of her head as she walked toward the camera. "Not meaning to be creepy, but she is a nice looking woman," said Jerome. "Can't really blame the guy for looking. She did age and loose a lot of weight in the next few weeks."

As Emma walked out the frame, Jason was ready and switched the feed to a camera over the door as the group watched her as she approached the exit. As she reached for the door, the feed switched to a camera outside. "I am getting the hang of this now," said Jason.

"Damn good, I would say," offered Walt. As the door opened and Emma emerged, a man engrossed in his smart phone was entering and walked right into her. As both regained their balance the man seemed to apologize and gently placed his hand on Emma's upper arm.

"Son of a bitch!" Jerome exclaimed. The man was bald and wore a white sleeveless tee shirt and jeans. From this angle the group could see his salt and pepper facial hair, neatly trimmed into a moustache and goatee.

"Damn, I wish we did have audio now," said Ashley. After a brief moment the pair turned and both headed toward her car.

"Can you believe that?" asked Walt. "You know that had to be intentional, right?" All nodded and expressed agreement as Jason switched to another feed as the two made their way to pump #7. As Emma began to open the gas cap the man politely intervened and took the pump and began to pump the gas into the Toyota. After a brief protest,

Emma leaned on the car as the two talked as the pump filled the car.

"This guy is working it hard," said Mike as they watched the two continuing their silent dialogue.

"I wish to hell we could hear what they are saying," Jerome said.

"It looks like he is doing most of the talking." Jason looked back at the others for a brief second as he continued monitoring the video.

"She appears to be a good listener though," Jerome agreed. As the bald man hung up the pump, the silent conversation continued. The man turned slightly and pointed to something behind them and then returned to face Emma. She was saying something and shaking her head slightly back and forth as if to say no.

"No to what," Walt wondered aloud.

"Exactly," Ashley responded.

After the exchange, Emma got back into her car as the bald man walked out of the frame. Immediately Jason switched the feed on the right monitor to a camera with the man walking away from the pumps and back toward the store. The left monitor showed Emma close the door and crank the car as a white puff exited the tail pipe of the Toyota, but the car remained at the pump for several seconds. On the other screen, the bald man reached for the handle of a Lexus SUV parked near the store entrance and entered the driver's seat.

"I didn't have him pegged for a Lexus guy," said Walt.

"Yeah, more like a Ford pick-up type," said Ashley.

Jason switched the feed on a third monitor to see the back of the Lexus backing out. "Alabama plate," he said zooming in on the Heart of Dixie plate affixed to the rear of the luxury SUV.

"From Birmingham," Jerome added.

"How can you tell that?" Ashley asked.

"The first digits of the plate indicate county," Walt said. "The 1 indicates Jefferson County."

The Lexus backed out and then pulled along side the Toyota waiting at the pump. As the Lexus pulled forward, Emma fell in behind. Jason switched the feed again as the screen showed the two vehicles turn right out of the gas station and head west down the highway.

"Damn, we need to know where they are going. She is obviously following him," Jerome said.

"The Dollar General store is that direction, but we know she didn't get there for another hour," Mike informed them.

"So it looks like she followed this guy somewhere, so we just need to figure out where. And we need to know who this guy is... did he know her? It certainly didn't appear that way from the staged bump meeting at the door," Jerome offered.

"The car is registered to BluLine Enterprises on Finley Avenue West," Ashley stated peering into her computer screen. “Ever heard of this company or know where the address is?” she asked.

“Finley Avenue, yes… but not familiar with company,” Jerome said.

Walt voiced agreement and then asked, “Did you Google the company?”

Ashley looked up, “Yep... no website and no social media… a couple of listings describes it as a security and/or consultant business, but that is all I get on the initial search.”

Jerome sighed, “Yeah, that is kind of vague.”

Walt had his smartphone in hand and was doing double-time with his thumbs, “Company is registered as an LLC with the state and as a security consultant and guard service. No principals are listed here… LLC is owned by another corporation… JC Enterprises, Inc. out of Louisiana. I will do a deep dive later when I get my laptop.”

“Can we get freeze frames of the Lexus and the guy’s face? I will send them back to the office to circulate,” Jerome asked.

Ashley located the frames, "How about these?" she asked.

"Perfect!" Walt interjected, "Capture one of Emma too, since she looks so different… it might come in handy."

With a few clicks, she said, "I have printed off some for you and sent copies to your email so you can forward them to whomever." Walt and Jerome expressed their thanks, each checking their smartphones.

"I am sending them to the office now. Amy or Nate can distribute them and see if anyone recognizes either the car or the guy. They can also initiate facial recognition to see if we get any hits," Walt said.

Ashley retrieved the prints from the printer and handed them to Walt. "Yeah, too bad it is not like on TV. We could have a full package on the guy from our magic facial recognition program in 30 seconds."

"Wouldn't that make things easy!" Walt laughed.

"Let's go canvas the businesses between that gas station and the Dollar General and see what we can find," Jerome said.

Mike nodded in agreement, "You guys follow me and we will head out there. There are a lot of businesses... let's go out there and take a look and decide how we want to approach it."

"Sounds good... we are on your six!" Jerome answered.

Turning back to the Evidence Techs, Walt offered his sincere thanks for all the help. "If either of you are ever in Birmingham, let us know... we owe you a big one, for sure.... Let us know if we can ever help!"

Chapter 29

Tuesday, December 8, 2017 --- Birmingham, AL -- SCU HQ

When Fay arrived at the office at 0823, Amy was standing at the white board rearranging items to the timeline for the case. She turned and greeted Fay, "Good morning! I am just updating although there isn't much… we got back some of the forensics… no DNA yet, so we already knew most of this stuff… it is just now official."

Faye dropped her bag at her desk and walked over for a closer look. "Have you heard from Jerome and Walt?"

"Yep, they arrived there a few minutes ago. They called me to let me know they had arrived. I also spoke to Meredith and she assigned a detective to do some preliminary work. He has pulled video from both the Wal-Mart and the Dollar General, as well as a service station on the same road that has a high tech camera system that covers some of the highway... they were hoping that they may get a shot of her car as it passed through the intersection to pinpoint a time.... It is a long shot and will take some digging, but hopefully they will find something."

Fay retrieved a Coke Zero from the fridge, "That is great. Have we turned up anything here?"

Amy turned from the board, "Nothing that I have heard. Nate is out with the Vice Unit this morning... The phantom guy that Julie told us about is pretty well known to vice although they haven't been able to identify him either... Nate is meeting with Rodriguez and Harrison to talk to some folks to try to pin him down."

Fay cocked her head to one side with a puzzled look, "So they are familiar with him but don't know who he is? Does that make any sense?"

Amy chuckled, "My question exactly! Evidently, this guy is like a ghost... for the last two or three years they have had vague references to him pop up in various places all relating to drugs and prostitution. However, he remains a mystery... the few that have described him have varied so much they are not sure all the stories relate to the same guy… the descriptions run from white to Hispanic… late 30's to late 50's in age… tall and muscular to average with a belly… The commonalities point to him being pretty savvy since after several reports over three years and this is all they have. He is said to be some type of pimp or boss though, that is fairly common with all the stories and he is not someone anyone wants to mess with… he is evidently a bad-ass or at least has convinced all those who have encountered him that he is."

Fay sat at her desk and spun around to face Amy, "I still can't believe with all the shit he has been associated with, they haven't identified him."

Amy took her seat too, "Yeah, it is hard to believe. Nate talked to Rodriguez last night. According to him, the guy is always on the periphery and the few times he has been a suspect, the victim and witnesses scatter or refuse to cooperate. He is not convinced it is one guy and thinks this whole persona has kind of been blown up… BUT… he does think there is a guy or guys operating a ring of some kind and that is what the task force has been targeted on for the last six months or so."

"It is still sketchy but they are thinking that whoever or whatever it is... they are likely doing a little of everything from running drugs and guns to pimping... The territory seems to run from New Orleans to Atlanta and Memphis and maybe Nashville with Birmingham as the cross roads... Also some reports indicate that it may extend south to Florida. They are classifying it as highly professional since they have accumulated very little evidence or information. Seems like every operation – drugs, prostitution and guns is very compartmentalized. The few arrests they have made are low rungs on the ladder and they have been unable to point to anyone in charge," Amy said.

Fay rocked back in her chair and allowed the information to sink in. "Any hints of child trafficking?" She asked.

Amy leaned forward, "I thought the same thing... They have busted a couple of prostitutes – one thirteen and another fifteen, they think they were associated with this guy... but neither had any good info... Both were evidently aware of him but neither had much info... he was not their direct pimp but was involved in luring them into the life... so it seems he or they have no boundaries!"

Both Amy and Fay were alerted as their phones began to buzz. Amy answered, "What's up Walt?" She listened intently for several seconds, "Thanks... we will get these out to everyone. Keep me posted on any other developments and ya'll be careful."

She turned to her computer, "You have an email too," she said over her shoulder to Fay, "but I am putting them up on the big screen." The overhead screens flickered to life with a photo of the Lexus from the side and then a close up of the rear license plate. Next, an image of the bald white male walking toward the Lexus and then a close up of the man's face.

"They pulled these from the gas station on the corner I told you about... Emma stopped for gas after leaving Wal-Mart. This guy eyed her in the store as she went to the bathroom and then waited outside and..." Amy gestured quotation marks in the air, "bumped into her as she left. They struck up a conversation and he returned to her car with her and pumped her gas as they talked... she then seemed to wait for him to get in his car and followed him out of the lot and they both headed west on the highway... the guys are heading out there to see if they can get more or figure out where they may of gone... She appears at the

Dollar General about an hour afterward so they must have gone somewhere nearby."

Fay stood staring into the mystery man's face. "I assume we have the car registration?"

Amy clicked her mouse a few times, and answered, "Yes... Lexus is registered to BluLiine Enterprises, LLC of 337 Finley Avenue West, Birmingham... According to Walt, that LLC was registered by a Louisiana Corporation called JC Enterprises, Inc. in Slidell... Ring any bells?"

Fay was still staring at the face on the screen. "Not at all... but we can dig deeper and find who the principals are... This guy... something about him seems familiar but I can't tell you what... The big sunglasses make it harder if I did know him, but my gut is telling me something about him is familiar... I just don't know why."

Amy spun around in her chair and stood beside Fay. "I just texted Nate to check his inbox. Maybe the car or face will ring some bells with him or the vice squad."

Fay broke her stare, "That would be too much to hope for… It may be an innocent flirtation and a quick lunch, but it is the best lead we have."

Amy agreed. "Walt and Jerome have the full video but they said these are the best shots for identification. I will get to work on distributing these and trying to unravel the company that the car is registered to."

Now Fay was staring at the screen of Emma. "Oh my God... she looks twenty years younger than her photo from here. What the hell happened in those six weeks?"

Amy stood by her, "It is an incredible difference."

Chapter 30

Tuesday, December 8, 2017   Birmingham, AL

Detectives Nate Parker and Rick Rodriguez exited the vehicle and headed into the Blue Bird Motel on Highway 78 on the northwestern edge of the city. It was their fifth motel visit this morning looking for any information that may lead them somewhere or assist in some way of gaining an identity of the mystery man that had managed to stay off the police radar for months now. So far, they had struck out. They spoke to a woman earlier at the Super 8 who obviously knew just who they were talking about but was reluctant to provide much in the way of a description or anything else. Her name was Jenny Holsomback and it was obvious she was a "working woman" in her early twenties and was most uncomfortable talking to two cops. After several attempts to get more detail, Nate decided to leave it for now and part on friendly terms in hopes that he may get more information later on. Jenny appeared to be a bit high on something and was, at first, a bit more talkative. But once she understood what the Detectives were looking for, whatever drugs she had on board were not enough to overcome the fear that surfaced and she clammed up quickly. Rodriguez began to press for more information with threats of arrest but Nate intervened in the role of "good cop" and simply asked her to give him a call if she thought of anything else as he handed her his card.

The Blue Bird was a motel straight out of 1960 when Highway 78 was the direct route between Memphis and Birmingham. The old one-story motel was still operational but was now surrounded by an expansive truck stop. The twenty-eight rooms were available to weary travelers but the seedy appearance only attracted the most desperate truck drivers and travelers since more modern hotels lined the highway in either direction.

The Blue Bird was a gathering place for trouble and had the constant attention of both the Vice Squad and the West Precinct beat car that covered the area. Drug deals and prostitution seemed a constant even with a beefed up police presence. Arrests were made on a regular basis but it seemed to have little affect. The two detectives were looking for a girl named Jasmine who was reported to be staying here. Jenny had mentioned Jasmine as having been victimized by the mystery man a while back but as soon as the information came from her mouth and she heard what she was saying, she wanted to unsay it all. It was as if her drug induced loose lips had been quelled by her own fear of hearing her own voice. All they had learned was that Jasmine had been on the receiving end of the guy's wrath about five or six weeks ago.

The desk clerk was only as cooperative as he felt he needed to be and pointed the pair to Room 18. "I'm pretty sure, she ain't there, though," he warned.

The detectives exited the office and headed toward the north end of the complex to Room 18. Rodriguez thumbed his smart phone and then held the screen out, "This is her," he said showing Nate the most recent mug shot of one Jasmine Elaine Fornoy. We busted her last October... the name didn't click at first but she went ballistic on a truck driver that didn't pay her or something... not sure if we ever got the full story but we arrested her and the driver who was so wasted he couldn't stand up. He evidently crossed some line and the girl beat the shit out of him in the sleeper of his truck. If we hadn't been close, she might have killed the dude."

As the pair made their way down the sidewalk, a tall African-American woman emerged from the door ahead. She was dressed in a light blue tank top and cut off jeans that barely covered her curvaceous rear-end despite the chilly day. Nate and Rick immediately recognized her and she made them as well. She quickly stepped back in and pulled the door but before she could get it closed, Rick grabbed the door and yanked hard to reopen it. The move startled Jasmine as both men showed their badges.

"Can we talk to you a minute, Jasmine?" Nate politely asked as he stepped closer.

Jasmine, wearing wedge sandals, looked the 6' 2" detective in the eye. Her eyes scanned him trying to process if their paths had ever crossed.

Rick broke the tension, "Do you remember me?"

Jasmine's gaze refocused on Rodriquez. Although almost six feet tall, Rodriguez's chiseled muscular body seemed dwarfed by the tall slender woman whose Afro hairdo added at least six more inches to her already imposing height.

"Yeah, you busted me for beating the shit out of that motherfucker in the truck.... He deserved what he got, ya know!"

Rick gave a wry smile, "There is no doubt in my mind that he did... but you kind of owe me because if I hadn't been there you would of killed that dude and you would be serving time now. We are not here to hassle you. We just need some information on another asshole that we think you may know."

Jasmine didn't say anything. She stood her ground looking into Rodriguez's face and then purposefully returned her stare to Nate and then back to Rodriguez. Rick took the clue, "This is Detective Nate Parker, and he works in the Special Crimes Unit."

Jasmine returned her gaze back to Nate. She slowly looked him up and down before returning her eyes to his and leaning in close to his face, "What exactly can I do for you, detective?" she asked in a sultry voice as a coy smile appeared on her face.

Nate tried to remain stone-faced but found it very difficult. "Can we come in and talk for a minute?"

Jasmine stepped back and waved her arm, "Sorry, gentlemen but I don't have anything to offer you but make yourselves comfortable."

"We are looking for man that is said to run in this area,' Nate began. "We don't even have a good description other than he treats women like shit... White guy, may be balding... we heard that you may have had a nasty encounter a few weeks ago with a man and we want to know if your offender and the guy we are looking for may be the same one."

Jasmine's flirtatious and playful demeanor disappeared. Her eyes fixed downward as she slowly took a seat on the edge of the bed. Nate could see that he had struck a chord with the woman and left her some time. He reached behind him and grabbed the wooden chair from the desk and sat down leaning forward toward Jasmine who seemed to be contemplating her next move.

After a few long seconds, Nate asked, "I'm right... Someone hurt you a few weeks ago?"

Jasmine's face slowly rose as her eyes met Nate's. "Occupational hazard," she said matter-of-factly in a quiet voice.

"Can you tell us who?" Nate responded with no demand in his voice. "Nobody deserves to be beaten."

Jasmine shook her head, "It happens. This ain't the life I want but it's what I got for now. I don't do drugs no more. Been clean for almost two years. I am just trying to make enough money to get out this life, that's all," she said looking back at the floor. "I know you can't understand that, but that is all I want. I just want to get out and get a real job and maybe one day get my babies back."

Nate stayed close, his voice soft and patient. "You have kids?"

Her eyes rose again to meet his, "Yeah, a little girl, four and a boy that will be two next month. They're in foster care but I see them as often as I can. The Foster Mom is really good, she's taken good care of them cause I sure can't right now." After a long hesitation, she finished her thought, "but I want to... I want to so bad... but it's hard." Her voice was emotional.

Nate reached out and put his hand on Jasmine's shoulder, "I know you are trying and I want to help you any way I can. The guy I am looking for... he is a bad dude... I know that he has beat up several women... many of them just like you ... stuck in a bad situation... But he also might be responsible for killing... two children and their mother."

That news registered shock on Jasmine's face as she processed the information. "Here in Birmingham?" she asked.

"Yes," Nate responded. "We are just trying to figure out who this guy is so we can learn more about him... he may not be our guy but I want to talk to him and I want to get him off the street if he is our guy... Can you help me find him?"

Jasmine took a deep breath, "I can't," she finally whispered.

"Can't or won't?" Rick chimed in.

Jasmine looked up at Rick in disgust, "You have no fucking idea what he is capable of… I want to get outta here… I want my babies back... but I also want to be alive."

Nate looked at Rick and then back to Jasmine, "Jasmine, we can protect you."

Jasmine stood and forced a fake chuckle, "Yeah, I believe that shit. You don't even know who he is but you gonna protect me."

Nate rose and tried to keep his voice calm, "What is he to you? Boyfriend? Pimp? … Give us a name or something so we can at least look into him."

Jasmine flashed a sarcastic smile at Nate and said, "You ain't gonna find shit… he can't be touched. Name is Jay... that's is all I know and all I am gonna say… He stays clean because he don't let nobody get close… and if you cross him you end up dead or worse… and I ain't interested in being either one. I got to go," she said heading for the door.

"Wait just a damn minute," Nate said, finally raising his voice. "Can you give me a last name or tell me where he lives... anything else?"

Jasmine continued to the door, "I have said too much already." As she reached for the doorknob, she turned to face Nate. "I am sorry but I can't... I do hope you get the son of a bitch, though." With that she was out the door.

Rick started after her but Nate grabbed is arm... "Let her go. She will help us more, but not now."

Rick looked at him like he had fallen from another planet and shrugged. "What you want to do now?" he asked.

"Keep on going. Don't we have four more places yet?" nate answered.

Rick grinned, "Yes we do but we are going to need to stop for lunch at some point."

Nate was checking his email and messages on his smart phone as they headed across the lot to the car when he stopped in his tracks and spun to look around. "Did you see where Jasmine went," he asked excitedly.

"She went around the end of the building. Why?" Rick answered.

Nate didn't answer but instead sprinted off in that direction.

"What the hell?" Rodriguez shouted after him before running behind him.

As Nate rounded the corner he could see Jasmine striding sexily across the lot behind the motel heading toward the large parking area behind the truck stop where fifty or more big rigs sat lined up as truckers logged their mandatory rest time.

"Jasmine, wait!" Nate shouted.

She turned and gave him a laser stare. "Leave me the hell alone… I ain't gonna say nothing else," she said.

"Look at this for me, please, and I won't bother you again," Nate said trying to catch his breath and extending his smartphone towards her. Jasmine placed her hand next to the screen to shade the glare and leaned in for a closer look.

"You know this guy?" Nate asked.

Jasmine could not hide the surprise on her face and she stared at the photo Nate had just received of the man at the gas station in Meridian. Jasmine looked at Nate almost pleading, "No... I don't know him... please leave me alone."

"At least tell me if this is Jay," Nate asked trying to reason with her as she walked away.

She stopped and looked back over her shoulder, "You figure it out," she said and began to walk away but turned after only two steps. She looked at Nate and simply said, "But you be careful with him," as she turned and continued toward the trucks.

Rick had caught up but remained a few feet behind Nate during the exchange. "What the hell was that?" he asked as Nate turned and started back to the car. He showed Rick the photo.

"Taken at a gas station in Meridian. This guy struck up a conversation with our victim and she followed him somewhere... Walt and Jerome are following up on it there....

But this son of a bitch is, no doubt, Jay.... We just have to figure out who he really is and why everyone is afraid of even mentioning his name. Does he look familiar to you?"

Rick took the phone for a closer look. "Hard to say with those big sunglasses, but something about him is familiar," Rick said handing the phone back to Nate.

"Here is the car he was driving," Nate said showing him the Lexus SUV photo. "Registered to a business on Finley Avenue, BluLine Enterprises. Does that ring any bells?"

Rick looked at the photo. "No, nothing remarkable about it. Where on Finley is the business?" he asked as they both got back into the car.

Nate thumbed through the his phone and answered, "337 Finley Avenue."

Rick cranked the car. "That is like five minutes from here, just past Arkadelphia Road."

Nate was still scanning his phone reading messages. "Let's do a drive by, but the boss doesn't want to spook anyone until we know more about the business and who owns it. Amy is working through the state office in Louisiana to see if she can unravel the corporations to see who the principals are... so far she is about five layers into it and has three different law firms listed on all the documents – one in Birmingham, one in Baton Rouge and one in Memphis... the fact that there are that many layers of ownership and no real people revealed speaks volumes."

"You thinking it some kind of Mafia thing or something?" Rick asked.

Nate looked up from his phone, "Not Mafia, per se, but it definitely speaks to a more sophisticated organization than your average thug, pimp or dealer, wouldn't you say?"

"Yeah, no doubt... the address should be ahead on the right," Rick said.

Finley Avenue is a major thoroughfare through the western part of the city and is most known for the large Farmer's Market where farmers from across the state come to sell their goods to stores, restaurants and individuals. The street is lined with related businesses along with several trucking companies and truck repair businesses. Its close proximity to I-20/59 makes it a good location that is close to the city center but with much lower rent or real estate costs. Rick slowed the black SUV as they passed by the address. The stand-alone building was fairly unremarkable. It was a one-story brick building that looked as though it may have been a neighborhood grocery store or some other store in an earlier life. The storefront windows were tinted black and no signs or markings were visible other than the required 337 by the front double doors that were also tinted black. A small parking lot to the right of the building was empty. The property appeared to be maintained but otherwise unoccupied.

"Well it doesn't look like a hub of activity, does it," Nate remarked as they drove passed.

"For sure. I drive by here fairly often since the Task Force has been active but I have never really paid attention other than it is one of the older buildings remaining in this area… most are big metal buildings from the 1970's… there are only of few of these older buildings left in this area," Rick said.

"Hey, since we are here, let's go to lunch at Niki's West before we finish canvasing the truck stops and motels," Nate said.

"Man, you read my mind!" Rick answered.

Chapter 31

Wednesday, December 9, 2017 --- SCU

When Amy arrived to the office at 6:50 AM she was planning on a quiet hour of working alone assimilating and compiling all the various information from the previous day. She had left her wife, Ellen, in bed since she was working the late shift at the hospital this week. She was arriving early to update the whiteboards and make plans for follow-up assignments, but when she entered the darkened office she was surprised to find Fay at her desks surrounded by piles of case folders neatly stacked in a semi circle on the floor behind her as well as several stacks on her desk. Her desk lamp and computer screen were the only illumination in the office.

"Well, good morning," Amy announced. "What are you doing here so early."

Fay looked up from the folder she was holding, "Oh, good morning... what time is it?"

Amy dropped her bag on her desk and clicked her computer to life. "It's almost 7. Don't tell me you have been here all night."

Fay laid down the folder on top of a stack of others, "Not exactly. I couldn't sleep, so I finally gave up about two and just came in."

Amy made her way to the whiteboard and started updating it with the new information.

"So, you want to tell me what all this is?" she asked pointing to all the folders.

"Well, I couldn't sleep because there is something about our mystery man that is familiar to me but I cannot, for the life of me, figure out what. So I spent the first couple of hours backing through cases and then I moved on to those that predated the computer system. I am hoping that I will read or see something that will unlock something in this old brain that I can't seem to get to. So, far I have nothing," Fay answered picking up the folder again.

"Do you think you have arrested him before?" Amy asked.

"Not sure, but something about him is so familiar somewhere in the dark recesses of my mind and it seems the more I think about it, the further away it gets. I can't even tell you what is familiar. Between the sunglasses and the beard, you can't really tell much about his features but there is definitely something setting off alarms in my brain. I just wish I could make the connection."

Nate Parker entered the office and was surprised to see his two colleagues working in the darkened office. "Did we forget to pay the light bill or what?" he joked as he dropped his bag at his desk.

Amy smiled and walked over to flip on the lights. "Sorry, I walked in on the boss working in the dark so I guess I joined her and never thought about it."

Moments later, Jerome and Walt entered the office. Walt was carrying a large flat box. "The new Hero Doughnut shop opened on the ground floor of my building," he announced holding up the box. "This is not going to be a good thing. I am weak so I may be forced to move. I found it impossible to walk past it this morning, so enjoy!"

Nate reached in for a doughnut, "So how was Mississippi? You guys have fun on the road trip?"

Walt laughed, "I don't know that I would call it fun. Jerome is quite an entertaining travel partner, though. And, we did get some good information I think. I am queuing up the video I edited last night when we got back. I condensed all the footage to the pertinent stuff."

Jerome joined in, "We can't really take any credit. The Meridian PD folks really knocked it out of the park. Mike Turner, the detective there had done a lot of legwork before we arrived.... And we lucked out that she stopped for gas at a station with the most kick-ass surveillance system I have ever seen."

Nate stood in the center of the office looking at the stacks of folders and asked, "Boss, I cannot help it... I have to ask what you have going on here."

Fay looked up as she began stacking the folders from her desk onto a cart. "Frustration, Nate... What you see here is frustration! Something about our mystery man struck a chord with me, but I cannot figure out exactly what or why. So, for the last several hours I have been combing through old case files hoping to read or see something that may help me make a connection. It did not."

Amy had finished updating the whiteboard and turned to face the group. "Let's take a quick review and see where we are and let me know if I am missing anything. Then we will hear details and observations from Nate and from Jerome and Walt and talk about where we go from here."

Amy reviewed the updated timeline on the board. She also went through the addition of the mysterious white male in the Lexus and his encounter with the victim. "Jerome or Walt, do want to kick us off with more details from Mississippi?"

"Sure," Jerome answered looking at his iPad for notes. "Walt edited the surveillance videos we collected last night to highlight the scenes we feel are pertinent and we will roll that for ya'll to see in a minute. As you know, Emma stopped for gas and to use the restroom while she was out shopping. Our mystery man seemed to stage a a meeting by bumping into her and then befriended her, chatting while he pumped her gas for her… unfortunately we don't have any audio, but he did most of the talking. She seemed to be at ease and he made her smile. She then followed him down the street to a Wendy's where he bought her lunch and they chatted more… for about 40 minutes. During lunch he wrote something on a small piece of paper and handed it to her and she seemed to read it and fold it up and put it in her purse. They then parted ways. Walt, you want to fill in the gaps?"

Walt spun his chair around to face the group. "You can watch the video and see what we are talking about. I have my friends in forensics working on cutting through the layers to see who owns the company that owns the Lexus… Since they are registered in 3 states, Amy and I made it through several layers before turning it over to them. My opinion is that anytime you deal with that sort of corporate layering, you are up to no good…. You are either covering your ass for some potential liability down the road… shady contracting or development firms use this tactic…. But, it is also used by organized crime syndicates to insulate the main players from prosecution. Let's run the video and let me know if you have questions."

The video began with the Toyota Corolla pulling into the station and up to the pump. The screen zoomed in on the license plate and then jumped to Emma exiting the car and walking into the store and paying for gas. Walt paused the video.

"You have to look carefully in the upper right hand corner, but this is the first appearance of our mystery man," Walt commented. The video resumed as the screen showed Emma leaving the counter and head toward the restrooms as the bald man seemed to stop and watch.

"Wow, he is not being very subtle," Nate commented. "He is staring a hole in her, stepping out to get a better view."

"Just wait, it gets creepier," Jerome said.

The screen flips and Emma emerges from the restroom door and walks through the store. The screen flips again as Emma walks toward the door. As she passes through the exit, a bald man staring at his smartphone walks right into her. As they both regain their balance, the camera zooms in to reveal that the encounter was with the bald man who was staring at her just minutes earlier.

"That was so damn obvious!" Amy said. On the screen, the man picked up Emma's purse and returned it to her and then did a 180 and walked beside her as she headed out to the gas pumps.

"He is turning it on, isn't he," said Amy. Emma seems to be trying to brush him off on the short walk but the mystery man is not cooperating. As they reach the car he is insistent on pumping the gas and Emma finally relents and leans on the back door of the car has he pumps the gas. The conversation continues and Emma smiles, seeming a bit more at ease with each passing moment. As the mystery man replaces the pump and the gas cap on the car the dialogue continues. The final exchange ends with Emma nodding yes as she gets in the driver's seat. The screen flips to another camera as we see the man walk back toward the store and enter a dark Lexus SUV. Another camera zooms in on the rear plate. The screen then switches back to the previous position as we see Emma's Toyota still sitting at the pump as the Lexus pulls along side. The bald man is driving with the side window down and gives a wave toward Emma as he pulls off and she pulls out to follow. The screen then switches to a much grainier black and white shot of a parking lot as we see the pair of vehicles enter and park.

"As you can see the video here at Wendy's is much lower quality," Walt said. The screen feed then shows Emma and the mystery man exit their cars and enter the Wendy's. Once their orders are placed and they gather their food and take a seat across from one another at a small table near the front of the store. They have a relaxed conversation as they both eat sandwiches and smile and even laugh at times.

"She seems pretty comfortable with this guy," Amy remarked. The group watched in silence as the muted conversation continued for almost 40 minutes. Before they they stand up and discard their trash, the mystery man takes a card and pen from his pocket and writes something on the card and hands it to Emma. She looks briefly at the card and then places it in her purse. The pair then exit the building as they head to their respective cars. Emma extends her hand for a handshake. The mystery man takes her hand and then leans in for a hug. Emma reluctantly embraces the men carefully. They both enter their vehicles and depart.

"We noticed our mystery man removed his big sunglasses while thye ate but his back is always to the camera and he puts them back on before he turns around. That may be coincidence, but I think he knew exactly where the cameras were," Jerome said.

"Yeah, it is a bit creepy," Walt stated mater-of-factly. "Nate checked out the address on Finley that is listed on the Lexus registration, so I will let him take it from there."

Nate stood and recounted his activities yesterday with Detective Rick Rodriguez of the Vice Squad, including their interviews with prostitutes, Jenny and later Jasmine. "We rode by the address… No signage and no cars in the lot," Nate began. With a nod to Walt, the old grocery store building popped up on the screen.

"This is the building. We snapped this photo yesterday as we drove by. This second photo is from Google maps street view from about 14 months ago… as you can see, nothing seems to have changed except this one has two cars in the lot. The Ford is easy to detect but the one parked behind it that you can't really see from the street view, the forensic team has used comparative analysis and identified it as the same model Lexus that our mystery man was driving… Of course, we can't see the tag or make a positive ID but the likelihood is very good that this is the same vehicle... So, we know that he does go there or at least did." Nate then clicked his computer and a mug shot of Jasmine Elaine Fornoy appeared on the screen.

"Jasmine is a working girl that is currently living out at the Blue Bird on 78 just past Finley Avenue. She is an interesting character to say the least. I got the video and photos from Jerome and Walt while we were talking to her. She let me know... without letting me know, if you get my drift... that this guy was definitely the one who had beaten her up about 6 weeks ago. I haven't gone through the channels to get a warrant yet and wouldn't probably get much past the HIPAA laws, but a source tells me that Jasmine was brought to the ER at Princeton in pretty bad shape about a month or so ago. Broken ribs and concussion among other things. Spent 4 days in the hospital and then left AMA." Nate then clicked the computer again and the mystery man appeared in a close up facial front view from the video and then a full body view on the next screen.

"Jasmine identified this guy as Jay... she would not give us anything more and what she did give was cryptic. She is obviously scared of him, and I have a feeling that not much scares her. She told us that folks who cross him either end up dead or worse... and she said we could not protect her or touch him because he was careful and clean. Rodríguez is circulating his photo and the info with Vice and the Task Force to see if anyone knows him or has heard that name. We need to ID this guy and then see what he knows about Emma and the kids. Did she come to Birmingham to meet up with him again? Did he promise her work? We need to fill in the gap. That is all I have for now."

Amy stood again. "We have a lot more information today than we had two days ago but we do need to fill in these gaps. I have been peeling the corporate layers back on this corporation but so far all I have are names of lawyers in three states. Even if we get a warrant, I doubt we will ever get to the actual principals of the company or what it is that they really do. Since the Task Force has Feds imbedded and they are much more familiar with this sort of thing, they have agreed to assist. Julie Willis is working on this with me along with others on the task force. We all are in agreement that this could very easily be tied to human trafficking and so it fits with their guidelines, although they say they have never encountered a sophisticated organized presence here... usually local thugs or a gang but not corporations."

Amy continued, "Julie and Rick Rodriguez have now both been personally involved and they are making this a top priority and think that it could parallel with the ring that they have been targeting for the last several months."

Amy paced as she talked, "If Emma did get lured into something she wouldn't be the first. She is certainly older than your typical teenager that is usually the target of these type thugs, but seeing her in the videos from Mississippi, she could have easily passed for a teenager and is certainly attractive. That makes her a potential target and given her desperate financial situation, she would certainly be vulnerable. But we still need to know what happened when she got to Birmingham… Did she meet this Jay guy again or someone else? What did she do and where did she live for those weeks? And where were the kids? We need to keep turning over rocks but we need to find this Jay too. The West Precinct is aware of the car and if spotted, they are to observe and call the Task Force and us immediately. If this guy is around we will find him, and if nothing else, we can get a positive ID on him and, at least, find out his real name."

Nate stood and declared, "I am going to follow up on these new developments with Jasmine. I think I can get her to cooperate if I can convince her that we can protect her. She knows this guy well it seems. Remember that she said he was untouchable and that gives me great concern… not because of what she said but by the fact that this guy is obviously deep into something and he wasn't even really on the task force's radar and the fact that we still don't even have him identified." Nate walked over and looked at the whiteboard and then return his focus to the mystery man on the overhead screen. "We know that a lot of things take more work and time than they do on the movies, but getting an ID on someone is usually pretty quick and simple these days.... but not this guy," he said pointing to the screen. "I think Jasmine's assessment is spot on... this guy is not only dangerous, but he is not our typical thug either. He is careful and likely, connected... and that makes him dangerous. I am also afraid that since he is obviously good at avoiding the law, that when we turn up the heat and start showing his picture around that he may just disappear on us, so we need to get this done quickly and that means all of us working as we do – as a team and everyone doing their job until we find this guy."

"Before you head out, Nate, let's review what we have and who is doing what to make sure we cover everything and aren't stepping on each other," Amy cautioned. "Boss, you have been awfully quiet. Do you want to add anything?"

Fay had a pensive look on her face. "Walt can you send me those video clips? I want to watch them again, but I don't want to hold everyone up… I still feel like there is something about the guy that is so familiar but I don't know what… maybe watching the videos will trip something in my brain. I think the human trafficking angle is the best avenue but don't overlook other things that may creep up. We still need to uncover what Emma did once she arrived here – where did she stay? What happened to her car? These are things we need along with the identity of our mystery man."

"Jerome can you follow up at the shelters and see if anyone recognizes the man?" Fay asked.

"Walt, I want you to coordinate with the Feds and the Task Force… not that I don't trust them, but I know you will keep them on point and get the info to us in a timely manner," she said.

"Amy and Nate, you guys keep working your sources to overturn any additional leads you can. I will keep pressuring forensics for information. Yesterday was a good day and we have a lot of new information but we still need so much more, so keep digging!" Fay said.

Fay sat her desk watching the video clips on her computer screen. She had now watched it four times. The first time through she looked for anything that might help identify the mystery man. The second and third times she looked beyond the obvious to see if there may clues in plain sight in the background of the video. Often the best clues were in a decal on the car or a reflection in the window, but so far she saw nothing of use. She was still convinced that something about the mystery man was familiar to her and she was determined to figure it out. As she watched the fourth time she concentrated on the man... his gait, his mannerisms, his facial expressions. There was something about him that was so familiar, she felt as though she should know exactly what it was and know who he was or, at least, why he seemed familiar but it just would not come. Then has she watched him laughing and reaching for the gas pump, she saw the ring -- a pinky ring. Who wears a pinky ring, she thought. She continue watching as the jovial banter ensued between Emma and the mystery man and she could not help but wonder how this beautiful young woman's appearance changed so much in the following weeks. She seemed to age drastically. Even though Fay had seen a lot, the change in Emma's physical appearance was startling.

She watched again as the man replaced the pump nozzle and walked away from the camera and toward his vehicle. The camera view switched to a view of him walking toward his vehicle and into the camera. He had a swagger in his walk. Fay felt a wave of nausea deep in her gut. Her head was spinning as she clicked the pause button and looked at the figure on her computer screen. She took a deep breath and ran the video back to the beginning of the walk and hit play. She replayed the segment several times.

"Walt, can you access personnel files?" she asked without looking up.

"For what company?" Walt asked.

"Here... Birmingham PD," Fay answered looking over her shoulder.

"Sure, with your permission, I can," Walt answered, somewhat curious of what his boss was looking for. Fay walked over to Walt's desk and dropped a piece of paper with a name on his desk.

"Just between us for right now... I need his entire jacket including any photos we have," Fay instructed. Walt read the name on the paper but didn't recognize it.

"I am on it, boss... shouldn't take too long," he said.

Chapter 32

Wednesday, December 9, 2017: 11:30

As Jerome made is way off the interstate and onto Arkadelphia Road, he called Rick Rodriguez to tell him that he was headed to find Jasmine for another interview. He explained that while he wanted to handle it alone and thought Jasmine might be more forthcoming to just him, he also wanted the task force to be aware of his presence. His experience had taught him to always expect the unexpected. Encounters with informants and witnesses outside of the police building could go sideways in a hurry. He pulled into the motel parking lot and parked. No matter what you drove, there was no concealment in an area like this, but the black Chevy SUV announced the presence of a cop on the premises. He saw eyes peering from around the curtains on more than one window, but it was a fairly quiet scene in the middle of the day. Nate got out of the car and scanned the area as he headed toward Room 18.

Nate stood beside the wooden door and knocked lightly as he listened. He could hear shuffling inside but no answer came. He knocked again. "Jasmine, it is Nate Parker. I know you are in there. I just want to talk for a moment," Nate said in a soft voice loud enough to penetrate the cheap motel door. The room became quiet but still no answer. Nate glanced at the window behind him and saw the curtains move slightly. He waited and heard light footsteps. He pushed his jacket back and placed his hand on his weapon just in case. As he reached out to knock again, he heard the deadbolt slide open. The door opened slightly to reveal the security chain latched as Jasmine peered through the opening.

"I told you, I ain't got nothing to say so leave me alone," Jasmine said.

Nate stepped in close and peered back through the small opening. "Jasmine," he said quietly. "I need to talk and I am not going away until we do." The door closed and the sound of the chain being removed was clear as the door opened.

"Get in here before everybody sees you... not that they ain't already," Jasmine said with a sarcastic tone.

"Thank you," Nate said as he entered the darkened room, scanning to make sure they were alone. The bathroom door was open and he could see in without having to be obvious. He removed his hand from his gun and relaxed a bit.

Jasmine was wearing a yellow top with spaghetti straps. The cotton garment was more than a bit too tight as it stretched across her braless breasts and left little to the imagination. Her jeans were almost as tight. She wore the same wedge shoes as she did on his last visit putting her at eye level with the detective. Her natural hair stood tall adding to her height. Nate tried to consciously look at anything other than her breasts but found that almost impossible to do.

"Jasmine, I know you are scared of this guy, but I promise you that I can protect you. I really need to know more about him. I know you have no reason to trust me, but you can. We need to get this guy and I need your help before he hurts someone else or disappears so we can't get him," Nate said, his voice almost pleading. Jasmine sat on the edge of the bed and took a deep breath as she listened to Nate's plea but said nothing. Nate pulled out the chair and sat down to face her. "I know it is hard and scary, but I want to help you and I can if you will help me find this monster," Nate said staring at Jasmine.

After a long pause, Jasmine stood up. "Give me your card," she stated matter-of-factly. "I can't talk now. They may be watching. I will call you tonight and tell you where to meet me, but you have got to promise to help me get away from here and make sure that my babies will be safe too."

Nate stood and handed her his card. "My cell number is on the back. I'll be waiting to hear from you and I promise you I will take care of you and your kids. Bit time is short so call me." With that he left and headed to his car. After Nate got in the car, he scanned the premises to see if anyone was watching, wondering if Jasmine's concerns were valid. He noticed the same clerk from yesterday standing out front of the lobby smoking a cigarette and trying unsuccessfully to look like he was not watching Nate. The man was talking on his cell phone. This concerned him enough to take action. He pulled the shifter into drive and rolled through the parking lot stopping few feet from the man. Nate exited the car and flashed his badge. "You remember me?" he asked the nervous man who promptly ended his call and stomped out his smoke.

"Uh, yeah ... you was here yesterday looking for Jasmine," the man answered with a somewhat confused look on his face.

Nate nodded and put away his badge. "Yeah, I just came from there again. How well do you know her?" He asked.

The man became even more nervous with the question. "Who me?" he asked.

"Who the hell else am I talking to? Yes you! Do you know her?" Nate asked inflecting irritation with the young man.

The man's nervousness level intensified, "Not really, man.... I just collect her rent, you know." Finally looking up at Nate for the briefest glance. Nate continued his stare at the man. "I, uh I really don't know her at all, man," The man stammered.

Nate stepped in close to the man, purposely invading his personal space to further escalate his discomfort. "Well, I think she stole an expensive watch from a truck driver last week, but she won't admit to it. Did you happen to see her go to a truck at the truck stop last Tuesday evening?" The man seemed to relax just a bit feeling he was no longer the target of investigation.

"Naw, man… I mean unless I am out here smoking or something I don't know what goes on, you know." Nate took a step back and handed him his card.

"Let me know if you remember anything or if you see anything suspicious out of her, okay? Or, if you hear anything about someone selling a nice watch, okay?"

The man reached out and took the card. "Yeah, I will."

Nate returned to his car and drove away. He watched the man in his mirror as he waited to pull back into the highway traffic. The man quickly pulled his phone and dialed a number as he walked back toward the motel office door. As Nate accelerated into traffic, he saw the man turn to watch him drive away as he spoke into the phone. Nate assumed that he was likely paid to keep tabs on Jasmine and the other residents of the motel and would certainly report the presence of detectives. He hoped that that his ruse would dissipate any heat that might indicate that Jasmine was cooperating or providing information.

Chapter 33

Wednesday, December 9, 2017

Within three minutes after receiving Fay's cryptic request Walt had the personnel file of one Vincent Thomas Tyler pulled up on his screen. The computerized personnel files are usually accurate and to the point. Any significant occurrences are noted – awards, disciplinary actions, promotions, etc. The highlights are there but if you want to see detail, you are going to have to obtain the paper files and dig through the paperwork to see actual documentation. In recent years, more information is available digitally, but BPD was far from a paperless organization. There was still a lot trees dying for the cause and personnel records, like most files in the department, anything more than ten years old were almost all on paper only. The highlights are all you get until you dig.

Tyler was a Birmingham Police Officer for 16 years and 4 months. He began his career in 1988 and was promoted to Patrol Sergeant in 1996 and was assigned to Vice in 1999. He was dismissed for "conduct unbecoming an officer" with criminal charges pending in 2004. Walt had this information quickly as part of the personnel database file, but he was going to have to dig a bit deeper to find any details. The summary indicated that Tyler was a good officer with only minor disciplinary actions for the first ten years of his career. He took the Sergeant's exam three times before scoring high enough to be eligible for promotion and was promoted and served as a Patrol Sergeant in the West Precinct on night shift for three and a half years before being assigned to the Vice Squad. Within six months of his new assignment he was disciplined for using excessive force on a suspect. He was suspended four days without pay. Two years later there was an Internal Affairs investigation launched involving Tyler and he was fired for Conduct Unbecoming An Officer.

Walt was curious and so he went to the Internet to see what he could find. He found articles outlining the investigation and subsequent firing of Tyler and 3 other officers. The men were investigated for the burglary of a pharmacy warehouse while on duty but no formal criminal charges were filed due to a lack of evidence. All four men were fired despite the lack of evidence to proceed with criminal charges against them. All four went through the grievance process to get reinstated, but only one was able to get their badge back. According to the articles, Patrolman Jerry Ryan had served as a lookout and driver for the quartet as did his partner, Richard Samson. The investigation determined that the pair had limited knowledge of the crime but were paid and took part willingly. Samson was unable to get reinstated because of prior indiscretions in his jacket. Ryan's exemplary record managed to be enough for him to keep his badge. After serving a 20-day suspension he was reassigned to another precinct.

Walt and Fay were now alone in the SCU office. Fay was still engrossed in watching the video on her computer. "Boss, I just sent you the computer file on Tyler. It is quiet intriguing but short on details. You will have to get the hard copy file, that is above my pay grade," Walt mused.

"Thanks, Walt," Fay answered as she pulled up her email.

"You think this is our mystery guy or he is somehow involved? Hard to tell from his ID photo from fourteen years ago."

Fay was scanning the file on her screen. "I am not sure, but I knew this guy and something about the way our mystery man walks reminded me of him. That is why I wanted to keep this between us until we get more info. Can you do your thing and see if he still lives in the area... where he works, or anything else you can find. I am going to call HR and request the hard copy to see the details... he had a rocky career, especially in the end."

Walt was already typing away, "Yeah, looks like he was alright for the first ten years or so and then kind of went off the rails. I have his social so I should be able to locate him fairly easily."

Chapter 34

Wednesday, December 9, 2017

Jerome entered the office and dropped his bag at his desk. "Have I missed anything?"

Walt stopped his computer search and turned to answer, "Not really. You are the first one back. The boss just ran downstairs to pick up some files. I haven't heard from Nate or Amy yet. How did your canvassing go?"

Jerome rocked back in his chair and exhaled deeply. "Man, I struck out. Went to every shelter and showed these photos around... no one recognizes the guy or the car. I should be used to it, but I really hate to spend all that time and energy and get absolutely nothing... not even a *'Hey, he kinda looks familiar, you know'*. I even went out to the West Precinct in Ensley to see if anyone in patrol may recognize anything since the car is registered out there."

"So, you get anything there?" Walt responded.

"Not much, but more than I did at the shelters," Jerome chuckled. "Demsky just made Sergeant and was orienting in the station with the Lieutenant and he said the car and the guy looked familiar. He worked evening shift in that area for the last 4 years before he got his stripes. Says if this is the guy he's thinking of, he was rumored to be a pimp but was very careful and anytime any shit went down, he was not around but rumor was he was the guy in charge. He said that vice and narcotics were aware of him too. He had several different rides -- A Harley, and old Chevy pick up and an old van. He had seen him in all of them at various places in Ensley, 5 Points West and all over the west side but mostly out Highway 78."

Walt stood and stretched, "Well, at least that is something... did he ever engage him? Like questioning him or anything?"

Jerome shook his head, "No, he was very evasive he said. Laid low and was never near any kind of fray or problems, but he said you could tell the guy was bad news but never even came close to giving them a reason to confront him. He said as far as he knew, no cops ever even knew his name… it was like anytime the subject came up during an investigation, the perp and witnesses would clam up tight… Kinda goes along with the story Nate got from the hooker."

The phone on Walt's desk rang and he answered, " Ellison, SCU." As he listened and he jotted down notes and then gave a look to Jerome that made him know it was something of importance. "Hey, we are own our way and I will roll a CSI unit to meet us. Tell them to hold tight and don't mess with anything until we get there. Thanks!" Walt hung up the phone. "Bessemer PD just stopped our car and have the driver and a passenger in custody. Let's roll."

Jerome grabbed his bag as they headed to the door, "The Lexus?"

Walt stopped as they got to the elevator, "Oh, No… sorry I should have said… it's the Toyota… The victim's car. Two teenagers saying they bought it a couple of weeks ago from a guy. Can you drive? I'll call Fay and CSI."

Chapter 35

Wednesday, December 9, 2017

Bessemer is a city about 15 miles Southwest of Birmingham. It was developed in the same time frame as Birmingham in the late 1800's and early 1900's. Like Birmingham, it was founded on the making of steel and iron. Henry DeBardeleben and other industrialists played a vital role in the development of both cities. Unlike Birmingham, The Marvel City, as Bessemer is known, never reached the size of its northern sister. Population today is about 28,000. The downtown area consists of about 30 city blocks and unfortunately now about half the buildings are unoccupied, as most businesses moved from downtown closer the interstate highway, although there has been some resurgence in recent years of businesses.

Jerome pulled up behind the Bessemer PD patrol car on Carolina Avenue near the downtown. The Toyota was in front of the patrol vehicle and a dark blue SUV was parked in front of the Toyota. The Birmingham Detectives soon learned that the SUV was Bessemer PD Detectives who had come to the scene to assist. Detective Max Garrett met the duo as they exited the car and introduced himself and Patrolman John Phillips. Garrett was a giant of a man standing at least 6'8" tall and weighing well over 300 pounds. He was wearing a pale blue golf shirt and khaki pants. He was white and had the look of a warrior that had been on the job for decades. His face and eyes showed the signs that the job can bring after a long career. Patrolman Phillips was a young African American in his late twenties and was impeccably dressed in his uniform. After introductions and pleasantries were exchanged, Garrett said, "John, tell them how you happened upon these two citizens in the car."

Phillips smiled uncomfortably and began his report, "Well, I fell in behind the car on 18th street and I noticed that the tag was very clean compared to the dirty car so I ran it… registration came back on a 1998 Ford Taurus, so I hit the lights and they turned on Carolina here and I thought they were going to rabbit but then they stopped. I instructed them to remain in the car with their hands visible… standard protocol and within a minute I had two backup cars and we got them out, patted them down and did a quick visual search of the car. While I was interviewing the driver, Sgt. Robinson put the passenger in his car and the other patrolmen called in the VIN on the car. When it came back flagged in a homicide with you guys, we called you."

"Have ya'll gone through the car?" Jerome asked.

"No Sir, we did a quick look for weapons in plain view but we have not been in the car," Phillips answered.

Walt asked nodding at the car, "Did you get anything out of either one of them?"

Phillips shifted his rigid stance slightly and continued, "No sir, not really. The passenger, James Witherspoon, is 13, so Sarge took him to the station and called Juvenile. He is supposedly the cousin of the driver, Marquis Johnston. Both live here in Bessemer, not too far from here." Phillips was looking at his notebook as he continued his report, "Johnston has a sheet but mostly petty stuff... one burglary as a juvie and 2 theft of property 3rd degree. He hasn't done any time. He is on probation for the theft back about a year ago... shoplifting at Wal-Mart and the second charge, a theft at an auto parts store hasn't come up yet... he says he has a court date next week. Claims he bought the car from a friend of his cousin, not the juvie, in Ensley about 5 or 6 weeks ago. Paid him $600 cash but didn't get any paperwork. He claims no knowledge of the switched tag or the car being stolen. Says he doesn't even know the guy he bought it from's name... only knows him as Slick and has only met him twice. His cousin is Jamal Hooks and lives in Ensley."

"Do you guys mind if we get him out and talk to him?" Jerome asked. With that, Garrett reached his massive hand and opened the back door of the patrol car and motioned for the prisoner to step out. Marquis Johnston was a slender black male with his hair in tight cornrows and facial hair that struggled to be considered a beard. The hair on the chin was decent but the whiskers from there to the sideburns were sparse. He wore faded jeans, a red Alabama sweatshirt and Nike sneakers. His hands were cuffed behind him and after a brief look at the Birmingham Detectives his gaze returned to the ground.

"Marquis, my name is Jerome Clark and this is Walt Ellison, we are detectives with Birmingham Police. I know you have already told these officers, but tell me about your car here. When did you get it and how?"

Johnston shifted his stance and took a deep breath. "I bought it from a friend of my cousin. I didn't know it was stolen, I swear," he said in a quiet voice without ever looking up.

"Did you get a bill of sale or a title to the car?" Walt asked.

Johnston finally looked up, almost apologetically, "Naw, man I just gave him $600 cash and he gave me the keys."

"So what is this guys name?" Jerome asked.

Again, Johnston's stared at the ground and said, "All I know is he go by Slick. He hangs with my cousin Jamal out in Ensley."

Jerome stepped in a bit closer. "So you are telling us that you gave $600 to man you don't know for a car with no title or even a bill of sale? How were you planning on getting the tag renewed?"

Johnston began to fidget a bit, "I dunno, man... I just need some wheels to get to work... I didn't really think about it."

Jerome reached out and lifted Johnston's chin to force him to look at him. "You do understand how bad this looks for you, right? Where do you work?" Johnston bristled but didn't draw away from the detective. His fear and angst showed heavy in his face.

"I'm working at the Burger King right now," he said trying not to look away but obviously discomforted by the detective in his face. "I swear I did'nt steal the car and I didn't know it was stolen."

Jerome positioned his own nose just inches from Johnston's to make sure he had his full attention. "Oh, Marquis, it so much worse... more than you can imagine." He paused to let his words sink in. "This car belongs to woman that was murdered," Jerome said. The muscles in Johnston's jaw visibly tightened. "Her kids were murdered too.... What do you know about that?" Jerome asked

Johnston slumped back against the patrol car as his emotions came to the surface. "Aw, man.... I swear I don't know nuthin' bout that... oh shit.... You gotta believe me, I don't know nuthin."

Jerome turned to the Bessemer officers. "Ya'll okay if he comes with us? You need to process him on anything?"

Garrett spoke up first, "He is all yours... you got a tow coming?"

"Our CSI unit is about 5 minutes out and they'll photograph and do their thing and then tow it back to process it fully. We will really appreciate it, gentlemen," Walt said.

Jerome turned Johnston around and leaned him over the trunk of the patrol car. "I've got to swap out the cuffs, Marquis... don't give me any trouble, okay?"

Johnston complied readily, "No, sir. I ain't gonna do nuthin." Jerome removed the cuffs and handed them over to Officer Phillips and then pulled his own from his holder in the small of his back and placed them on Johnston's wrists.

The Birmingham PD CSI Van arrived and pulled in behind the detective's SUV. Officer Janice Perez got out of the driver's seat and walked toward the group and Lt. Dan Guyer exited from the passenger side.

"Janice, what the hell did you do? Having the big boss shadow you?" Walt asked smiling at the CSI Officer.

Perez flashed a smile, "He was in the office when I got your call and insisted on coming... I literally could not say no!"

"Damn right! Guyer smirked, "I don't want anything screwed up on this one."

Perez looked back over her shoulder, "Was that directed at me?"

Guyer placed his hand on her shoulder, "No, they know you are the best... I just came along to hand you shit!"

"Truth is he can't stay away from a big case... he is just that nosey!" Perez smiled.

Walt informed the pair that no one had been in the car so it was just as found. "Juvenile passenger and the driver here," he said nodding at the handcuffed man Jerome was walking back to their car. "Do your thing and let us know if you find anything we need to know... we are taking him back to the jail... we will probably drop by Ensley on the way to ride through where he says he bought the car just to see," Walt told the CSI team. Walt then turned to the Bessemer cops, "Thanks again... I will be in touch to set up an interview with the juvenile."

"Anytime!" Garrett said and turned heading for his car.

Walt paused and extended his hand to Phillips, "Great work, John! It was great to meet you and thanks again for everything."

Chapter 36

Wednesday, December 9, 2017

Jerome helped the handcuffed man into the back of the SUV and advised him of his Miranda rights as he buckled the seat belt around him. Walt drove the SUV with Jerome sitting in the backseat with the silent, but visibly shaken, Marquis Johnston. They pulled up onto I-20/59 headed back toward downtown.

"Marquis, you think you could direct us to Slick's house if we just drive by?" Walt asked.
Johnston raised his head where he had been staring at the floor since their journey started. He looked at Jerome but could not say anything.

"We are not going to stop or anything, we just need to know where you got the car, OK?" Jerome informed him.

Johnston's jaw tightened and his gaze darted about the car as they sped down the interstate. "I don't know... Slick hangs with some bad dudes... if they see me cruise with cops..." His voice trailed off and his eyes went back to the floor.

Jerome leaned over closer and tried to reason with him, "Look man, you're ass deep in a mass murder so any help you can give us will go a long way from keeping you from of spending the rest of your life in prison or worse. The windows are tinted... we are not going to stop or even slow down... we just need you to show us where he lives and your cousin too. Can you do that?"

Johnston took a deep breath, "I didn't do no murders, man."

"Then help us prove that," Jerome said placing his hand on Johnston's knee.

Johnston finally looked him the eye. "Get off at this exit and go left up to Avenue C and turn left," he said. Walt steered the SUV off the interstate and onto 19th street in Ensley through the area known as Tuxedo Junction, made famous by the 1939 song written by jazz great Erskine

Hawkins and arranged by Glenn Miller. Hawkins grew up in this neighborhood.

Ensley began life as a separate city much like Birmingham filled with steel mills and related industries. Like Bessemer, it had its own thriving downtown known for fraternal clubs and dance halls in the early twentieth century. The city was annexed and became part of the City of Birmingham in 1910. By the turn of the next century most of the steel mills were shuttered, the middle class neighborhoods had succumbed to white-flight and decay. The once thriving downtown now housed more abandoned buildings than businesses. Although the resurgence of downtown Birmingham was spurring some resurgence in the Ensley neighborhoods and downtown, it still had a way to go. As Walt turned onto Avenue C, Johnston instructed the pair that Slick's house was ahead on the left.

"This one here with the metal roof?" Walt asked.

"Yeah that's it," Johnston answered as they drove by. The house was a post World War 2 bungalow, much like others that lined the street. Over the decades many of the houses had been replaced as nearby industry expanded. Others had simply disappeared with deterioration leaving the empty lot behind. Slick's residence seemed to be well cared for. The shingle roof on the brick house had been replaced by a metal one that did nothing to add to its charm but one could assume kept the home dry. In the driveway was a 1964 Chevrolet Impala tricked out with 24 inch rims and a navy blue-almost purple custom paint job and shiny chrome. On the right of the house, a large fenced lot stretched out for several hundred feet to the next cross street. To the left were more of the cookie cutter bungalows in various stages of condition but they all looked lived in and some were well maintained like Slick's. All along Avenue C the industry, commercial and residential seemed to intermingle as if zoning had long since been abandoned.

"Is that Slick's Impala?" Jerome asked as they passed the house.

"Yeah but he don't drive it much... his regular car is a Silver Lexus," Marquis answered.

"What kind of Lexus? SUV or car?" Jerome asked.

"ES 350," Johnston answered.

Walt chuckled slightly from the front, "So what does Slick do for a living that he can afford a show car like that Impala and a $50,000 Lexus?"

Johnston shook his ahead, "I don't know, man... like I said he usually has a posse of some bad dudes... I only talked to him twice in my life."

"Is your cousin Jamal in his posse? Does he work for Slick?" Jerome asked.

Again Johnston shook his head, "Naw man, they grew up together... right here, you know. That's all."

"Where is your cousin's place?" Walt asked. Johnston was a little more relaxed after the drive by and instructed Walt to the house about 4 blocks away. The homes on Avenue F were in the same various stages of condition as those on Avenue C but these appeared to be several decades older with wooden siding, steep roof lines and large porches that in days gone by had welcomed visitors and passers-by with shade from the Alabama sun.

"Up there on the right with the Cadillac," Johnston said as they approached the house on the right. Walt recorded the address and snapped a photo as they passed just as he had done at Slick's.

"That your cousin's Caddy?" Jerome asked noting the battleship sized 1980's car parked out front that was fully stock like it drove off the showroom floor. The paint was faded a bit but otherwise it looked like it did in 1985.

"Naw, that's my Uncle's. Jamal ain't got a ride," Marquis answered.

Walt picked up speed and headed back to the interstate and asked, "Jamal live with your Uncle?"

Johnston seemed to relax even more now that they were leaving the neighborhood. "Yes, his daddy.... Uncle Raymond," he said.

"Who else lives there?" Jerome asked.

"Just them. My Aunt passed last year and Jamal came back to stay. He's got three sisters but they all live up north," Marquis said.

Jerome sensed Johnston relaxing a bit and decided to keep the conversation going. "How old is Jamal?" he asked.

"Umm… about 35, I think," he answered promptly.

"Has he been in any trouble?" Jerome asked.

Johnston hesitated for a moment before answering, "Yeah, he just got out of prison about two years ago."

Jerome tried to keep the conversation casual as if he just wanted to get to know the family. He had a knack for doing that and had learned early in his career that he could get a lot of information with patience and a friendly tone rather than playing the bad cop role.

"What was he in for?" Jerome asked.

Johnston shifted trying to find a comfortable position while strapped in the seat with his hands bound behind him. "A bunch of stuff… drugs, robbery… he went off when he was younger than me… he was about 16, I think… I didn't really meet him till last year… I was little when he went off."

The downtown skyline came into view as Walt steered the SUV through the interchange of I-20, I-59 and I-65 know to locals as Malfunction Junction, just west of downtown. He exited the interstate headed through downtown toward the Birmingham Jail on 6th Avenue South.

Chapter 37

Wednesday, December 9, 2017

Nate came into the office in the afternoon to find Fay and Amy busily working at their desks. "I heard we found the Toyota. Any news from the boys yet?" He asked.

Both women turned in their chairs to greet him. "I just got off the phone with Walt. They are at the jail with the driver and wrapping up his statement on tape," Amy informed him. "Claims to have bought the car –with no paperwork to validate that – from a guy only known only as Slick in Ensley," she continued. "On the way back from Bessemer they drove through Ensley and the perp showed them Slick's house and his cousin who introduced him to Slick... cousin lives with his elderly Dad. Cousin got out of prison a year or so ago. Perez and Guyer photographed the car and sealed it up and transported back to the lab."

Nate dropped his bag and thumbed through his messages on his desk. "Well, Perez is the best and Guyer is a legend… so if the car has anything to show us they will find it.," Nate said. He picked up his phone, and punched in a number. "Hey, Neal... it's Nate… You have a minute? Know anybody in Ensley that goes by Slick?" Nate listened, laughed and scribbled notes. "Hey, what can I say.... We are thorough! Thanks, man! How is the new gig going? You have your assignment yet? Hey man, I owe you!" Nate hung up the phone still laughing. "That was Neal Demsky… he worked the evening shift out in Ensley for 4 or 5 years and he knows all the players, so I figured he would know who this Slick character is… He said he was just hanging up from Jerome who had called to ask the same thing!"

Nate clicked his computer to life. "Alfonso Gregory Hightower, also known as Slick" Nate said as a mug shot of Slick appeared on one of the overhead screens. "On parole for Armed Robbery for a carjacking… served a little more than 8 years and as been out since November two years ago… parole ends July 2019," Nate said as the others looked at the screen. Nate then pulled his full record up on his computer and began to scan… "According to parole, he is employed at L & L Enterprises as a janitor… No doubt, Walt will be calling us with this info too."

"L & L is one of the companies owned by the same corporation that owns BluLine and the others tagged with our mystery man," Amy said as her computer dinged and she opened the message. After reading it she shared with the others, "Okay, I have the recording of the statement of Marquis Johnston, the Toyota driver... should be enough for us to get a warrant for Slick to bring him in.... Walt and Jerome think he is being honest and has told them all he knows. He has been booked on the possession of stolen property, so unless someone posts his bail he will be with us for a while. Bessemer also sent the transcript of the interview with Juvenile passenger... straight A student with no priors or history... seems he just took a ride with the wrong cousin at the wrong time."

Chapter 38

Wednesday, December 9, 2017

Walt and Jerome entered the office and noticed immediately that Slick's mug shot and history were emblazoned on the screens... Jerome laughed and headed to Nate's desk. "Yeah, Demsky called me back to tell me you called at almost the same time I did... great minds, think alike," he said giving Nate a fist bump.

"Yep, Amy is already working on a warrant... learn anything else?" Nate asked.

Jerome took his seat at his desk, "Not really... we both think Johnston is shooting straight... he is scared shitless but we got him on the possession until we get more into this... plus we will need him as a witness. He said Slick was known as a badass and hung with a posse of badasses that he heard were into all kinds of shit but he had no details... only met him twice.... The cousin that introduced them... he grew up with him, but according to Johnson, he was not part of Slick's crew... and not a badass... described him as just a crack head... we are going to find him to see what he has to say, though."

Amy stood and walked to the center of the room. "We have made good progress today and caught a break with finding the car," she announced. "Warrant for Hightower is working and we should have it signed off later today. I spoke to Guyer just a few minutes ago. They are pulling a lot of prints from the Toyota so it will take them a while to go through them. He has a team working it though and they are processing as others are still collecting because he knows how critical this is. He says, they didn't find anything obvious... nothing that could be tied to the victims, but he said there is a lot of prints and trace evidence in the car and they will analyze it all... they already have pulled prints from all three victims from the car, so he knows that it wasn't cleaned, so hopefully they will be able to lift something from the bad guys too."

"Great job guys... perfect interview with Johnston," Amy said and gestured toward Walt and Jerome. "It appears he doesn't know much but as we get deeper into this he may know something that will help us and he is in a mood to cooperate." She turned to Nate, "You want fill everyone in on your progress?"

"I don't have much," Nate said, "I went to see Jasmine today and she agreed to talk but was fearful that she was being watched and she promised to call me tonight to arrange a meeting... she is scared, and as I have said before, I don't think she is one that scares easily... I was only in her place for a minute, but when I came out the sleazy motel clerk was standing out front smoking and watching me... I approached him with a story of how I was trying to pin a theft on Jasmine and asked about her going and coming. He, of course, had no information... but I think he bought it... as I drove off he made a call, no doubt to his handlers, to report... My feeling is he watches all the girls staying there and keeps our mystery guy informed about anything going on. I didn't mention anything about our case or the mystery man... don't want to spook him. I am looking for a call from Jasmine tonight. I think she will come through."

"Thanks, Nate," Amy said. "Make sure you have one of us with you when you take that meeting... even if we have to hang back... I don't trust any of the players... and the more I talk with Julie and the task force, I think our guy may be ass deep in the things they have been chasing for two plus years. The Feds are now very interested in what we are doing but so far Julie is keeping them at bay," Amy continued as she continued to pace. "The last thing we need is for them to screw up our case by overstepping... we all know how they work... they want all we have but only want to give us what they want us to know. According to Julie, they have been chasing a king pin in their case they call Mister X... Julie and I think from the vague descriptions and his elusiveness, that their Mister X and our Mystery Man may be one and the same... The rest of the task force isn't so sure... they have Mister X profiled as a Foreigner and maybe affiliated with a Mexican or South American Cartel... Time will tell but be careful with your distribution of information on this case... even more so than usual." Amy stood solemnly for a moment and then turned to Fay, "Boss, do you have anything to add?"

Fay grabbed the TV remote from her desk and rose. "Walt, will you get the blinds?" She said as she walked toward the overhead screens. Walt was caught off guard by the request but scrambled from his desk and pushed the button on the wall near the coffee pot. The mini-blinds in the glass partition separating the SCU from the rest of the floor spun to a vertical position isolating them in their office. With that, Fay clicked the overhead screens and Slick's photo and information disappeared and was replaced by the video images of the mystery man at the service station in Mississippi. One screen showed a full body shot the man as he walked toward the camera. The next showed an enhanced, yet slightly blurry, close up of his face from that same shot.

"What I am about to show you stays with us here and is not for dissemination," Fay said sternly. "For now, this is all unconfirmed speculation on my part, but my feelings are strong on this and my research has done nothing to sway me away from that feeling." She clicked the remote and the headshot of Vincent Thomas Tyler filled the screen adjacent to the blurry photo. "This is Vince Tyler... he was a cop here for about 16 years... he was fired in 2004 after he and some other cops were implicated in a burglary of a pharmacy warehouse... the DA never brought charges, but he was fired along with 3 others. Something about his walk in the video led me to believe that Vince and our Mystery Man could be one and the same... Forensic enhanced the surveillance video shot on the left as best they could but you can see it is still pretty blurry, plus the big sunglasses... When he was a cop he had a head full of hair, as you can see, but the facial shape is similar... they tried the facial recognition software but could not get enough on the video to get a match... they did confirm that plus or minus one centimeter, both subjects are the same height - about 6 feet even. We have been trying to locate Mr. Tyler, but it seems somewhere around 2011, he disappeared off the grid. His social has not been used for employment, no tax returns... it is like he vanished.... From the time he left the department until then, he had a least five address changes - two here in Birmingham, then a move to Memphis and then to New Orleans and his last address was in Slidell, Louisiana in May of 2011. At that time his bank accounts were closed and credit cards cancelled... he virtually vanished. No family that we can find... he was brought up through the foster system here in Jefferson County... never married. In 2005, he applied to Memphis PD for a job but was black balled because of his jacket here. After that, he listed several employers over the next couple of years from working at a Home Depot to driving a truck.... It seems that stuck and he listed a company headquartered in New Orleans as his employer from 2007 until late 2010... he was listed as a truck driver and then as a Supervisor with the company on his tax returns... left the company in September 2010. We have no employment records after that... 2010 was his last year to file taxes and then he completely vanishes in May of 2011."

Fay was more tense than usual as she continued to pace with the entire team at full attention. “So as you can see, this history and his disappearance do nothing to convince me that these two are not the same person... Having said that, I don’t want us to assume that they are the same either... as always - follow the evidence... see where it leads us. I wanted you all to be aware just in case. Tyler is not only a former police officer with training and knowledge of how we work. He is a former Army Ranger and is very skilled and if he is our guy, that makes him both cunning and dangerous. That seems to parallel with what we have heard about the Mystery Man, so be careful! I am going to keep digging. I have requested his Army jacket and we will see if that provides any clues. I am digging from this end, so you guys keep following your leads and keep each other looped in on your progress. Let’s meet here at 0800 tomorrow and review what we all have... we should have preliminary forensics on the car and maybe Nate will have more information from his informant. Try to get some rest and let’s hit again in the morning.”

Chapter 39

Wednesday, December 9, 2017

It was just after 8 PM and Nate was leaving the Druid Hills Community Center where his 12-year-old basketball team had just notched their fifth consecutive win of the season. He had given up on Jasmine and was headed home when his phone buzzed. He glanced at the screen, which displayed an unfamiliar number from Iowa. He answered, "Parker."

Following a brief silence with background noise, he recognized Jasmine voice, "Detective? It's me... Jasmine... I am on a borrowed phone just in case... McDonald's in 5 Points West... just drive through... I'll come out the back and meet you."

"It will take me about 15 to get there," Nate said.

"Okay," Jasmine answered and then the phone clicked dead.

Nate dialed Amy as he headed west on 4th Avenue to make the meet. "What's up, Nate?" She asked.

"Hey, sorry to bother you but I just got the call from Jasmine... headed to meet her at the McDonald's in 5 Points West... She is being safe... called from a borrowed phone... I assume a trucker from Iowa... Just wanted someone to know where I was just in case... I am about 5 minutes out... I will let you know when I am done."

"Thanks for calling... Be safe!" Amy said.

Nate pulled his black SUV into the McDonald's. It was fairly empty with one family coming out and a couple of teens heading in. He slowly rolled through the lot and was heading toward the rear of the building when he saw Jasmine come out of the side rear door. She was wearing the familiar tight jeans but everything else was different. She wore sneakers and a black sweater. Her hair was subdued underneath a knit ski cap. Her stature and caramel skin were unmistakable though. She walked out and around to the passenger side and hopped in beside Nate.

"Let's drive," she commanded.

"Thanks for meeting me," Nate said. "Where to?"

Jasmine's apparel was not the only thing that was different. Nate had seen her serious side before, but tonight she seemed even more vulnerable, almost as if the façade had been removed and he was seeing the real Jasmine for the first time.

"Just drive... I figure if we are moving no one can see us or know about this," she said.

Nate was curious, "You think somebody is watching you that close?"

As they stopped for a red light at Lomb Avenue, she shot him a look that said – you don't really get it, do you? "Yeah, they always watch... but more so lately... that's why I am so scared... I am only doing this because I think they are watching me even closer and probably think I already talked to you or something... so you gotta protect me..." Her words trailed off, "...and my babies."

Nate headed east back into downtown. "I told you that I will keep you safe. Is this Jay you are afraid of?" He asked.

Jasmine was staring straight ahead and speaking in a soft voice. Her usual flirtatious manners were non-existent tonight. "Yes, Jay and his goons. They usually just watch me go and come… collect once a week and some of them hassle me for freebies…. But lately, I have noticed them following me places… they are trying to hide, but they're not very good at it."

"Has this been just since my last visit or earlier?" Nate asked.

Jasmine looked into his eyes, "More like your first visit…. I've been on the radar for a while 'cause I don't take a lot of shit other girls do… I ain't using so they watch me close, but I am still paying them and they like that."

Nate steered the SUV into an empty parking lot near the Regions Field Stadium, home of the Birmingham Barons minor League baseball team, just a few blocks away from police headquarters. He killed the engine and lights. "We can talk here and not be bothered," he said. "So tell me about Jay."

Jasmine turned in her seat to face Nate. "Ain't much to tell... I don't know him well... Nobody does. He is a badass, I know that... that bastard will kill you or fuck you up so bad you wish you was dead."

"Has he ever hurt you?" Nate asked.

"No, not really... but he scares the shit outa me... and everybody else... That's kind of his thing... intimidation and fear... you can tell that even his goons that work for him are scared shitless of that motherfucker," she said.

"So, what is Jay into, besides prostitution?" Nate asked.

Jasmine smirked and rolled her eyes, "Anything and everything that makes him money and power... drugs, guns, cars... you name it."

Nate unbuckled his seat belt and shifted to face Jasmine as much as he could. "So where does he live? Does he run all this from home or does he have a business or what?" He asked.

Jasmine gestured with palms up, "I don't know... I heard he had an office or something over on Arkadelphia, but I ain't never been there... every time I see him he's in a car... he's always in different rides, you know... he shows up here and there... but he don't get close to anybody."

"Does he have a special girl or anything?" Nate asked.

"Nope... he fucks all the girls but never more than once or twice... he don't let nobody get close... Even his goons rotate in and out... like every time I see him he has a different goon or two with him," she said.

Nate leaned back and gathered his thoughts, "So do you even know his name or anything that may help me track him?"

For the first time since she began talking tonight, Jasmine seemed to tense up and hesitated before answering, "His name is Jose Hernandez... that's all I know."

"So, he's Hispanic?" Nate asked.

"Yeah, I guess... he's a little dark... but he don't have an accent.... He speaks perfect English," Jasmine said.

"So, does he sound like he is from here in South or up North? Tell me anything you can about him," Nate said.

Jasmine relaxed a bit and leaned back in the seat. "I'd say he sounds southern... not like country, but like most white folks... certainly not a real Yankee." She hesitated and shifted. "I met him a couple of years ago when I started working, you know... I was getting drugs from one his guys for a while then he introduced me to Jay at this place and he made me feel real good and said that he could help me make a lot of money and keep me safe... a couple of weeks before that a truck driver had got a little rough and bruised me up some." Jasmine paused, as she seemed to be thinking back. "He was real nice that night. We had sex... he gave me cash and some dope and told me I didn't have anything to worry about... he'd take care of me.... Never seen him like that since... I don't know if it is an act or if he is just that fucked up... you know split personality kinda thing or something, you know? All I know is I have seen folks he has really fucked up and I have known people that disappeared after crossing him and nobody ever seen 'em again. That is why I am so scared… the police are always sniffing around and they have busted some his guys from time to time, but they never touch him."

Nate leaned in and asked, "Have you ever seen him or his crew with kids or anything? You said he was into all sorts of shit… trafficking kids one of them?"

Jasmine tilted her head, "That is sick shit… I don't know of any kids, but I wouldn't put it past him… I have seen him bring in girls… you know, like 13 or 14 year olds… they don't usually stay long… I think he moves 'em around, you know… or gets rid of them… I don't know… a few months ago he had a couple of girls in the place I stay, but they were only there for about a week or so… I heard he moved them to New Orleans… but I don't know… they had two rooms down from me… Goons would bring in tricks and stay outside till they were done and then take them back wherever they came from, I guess."

Nate asked again, "What else can tell me about him… Do you know where he's from or anything that might help me locate him or identify him?"

Jasmine was tiring, "I don't know… It is like he knows when the po-po is coming or is around… he is never there when any shit goes down… Some say he is a cop but most say he's like a Mafia guy or something… he is into stuff all over… down to New Orleans and up to Nashville and Memphis but he seems to stay here most of the time."

"How often do you see him?" Nate asked.

"It depends… sometimes 2 or 3 times a week and then it may be 3 or 4 weeks before I see him again," she said.

"So, when was the last time you saw him?" Nate asked.

"Yesterday," she answered. "He picked up the new girl 2 doors down… he was dressed up all nice and she was too. His goon was driving a big black Escalade… Picked her up around 8 but I never saw them come back."

"So, does he come around to visit you… you know…" Jasmine cut him off, "No, just that one time… like I said, he don't let nobody get close."

"Anything else I need to know?" Nate asked.

"Just know he is a bad motherfucker... like I said I don't know about killing kids or anything like that, but I know he has killed folks and he can be so cold and heartless, I would not put that passed him if they somehow got in his way or something," Jasmine said.

Nate cranked up the SUV and buckled his seat belt. "Where do you want me take you?" Nate asked.

"Take me over to the bus station and I will call a taxi," Jasmine answered as she sat up and buckled her seat belt.

"You sure? I can drive you back," Nate said.

"I can't chance that," she said.

Nate drove three blocks east to the Intermodal Station. "Take this for your fare," he said handing her two twenties. She took the money as she slid out of the seat.

"Thanks," she said as she got out and closed the door. She leaned back in the vehicle and said, "I hope you get the bastard." With that she turned and walked toward the station. Nate waited until she made inside and saw her get into a taxi before he drove away.

As Nate he headed home he dialed his phone. "Hi Walt, sorry to bother you tonight... just wrapped up with Jasmine... First thing tomorrow can you do your thing on a Jose Hernandez? That is all I have... that is the name that she knows as Jay, our Mystery Man... Thinks he lives in Birmingham but that is all she knows... says he has no accent so he is either American or he has been here for a while."

"I'll hit it first thing so maybe we'll have something before eight," Walt said.

"Thanks, man... I owe you!" Nate said as he ended the call and then called Amy to fill her in and let her know he was safe and heading in. He then clicked the phone off and headed home although he doubted he would be able to sleep much.

Chapter 40

Wednesday, Evening December 9, 2017

Fay sipped her Pinot Noir while *B.B. King Live at the Regal* played on the turntable as she looked at the city lights from her loft window. She had enjoyed a quick dinner with friends at Bamboo on 2nd, a great sushi restaurant, less than a block from her loft. The case occupied her mind and she knew she'd be less than ideal company so she excused herself right after the meal. She found that getting away from the job was good on several fronts and she tried to do that even when she didn't really feel like going out or socializing but this case was making turning it off even more difficult than usual. She could not get Vince Tyler out of her mind. Was that really him on the video? Her gut told her it was and the more she watched the video, the more convinced she became.

She didn't really know Vince in the early years. She was a Patrol Sergeant working the South Precinct day shift in 1988 when Vince came out of the academy where he was assigned to the night shift in the West Precinct. Later that year she was promoted to Detective and assigned to Property Crimes. After two years as a Detective she was assigned to Internal Affairs. It is said that all cops who climb the ladder must take their turn in IA and Fay was no different, although she had to take two turns. The IA Unit of BPD is a small unit consisting of a lieutenant, heading the unit, and three Detective Sergeants. Most served for at least two years but rarely anyone stayed more than four before moving on. Investigating other cops was stressful and isolating and most moved on as soon as they could and Fay did too. After 26 months in IA, Fay transferred to Homicide where she began to really hone her skills as a detective. During her time in IA, she also completed her PhD degree and began teaching under-graduate Criminal Justice courses part-time at UAB and continued lecturing at the BPD Police Academy.

In 1997, Fay was promoted to Lieutenant. After serving in Patrol for a year, she returned to the Detective Division as Commander of the Homicide Unit. In 2003, she was reassigned as Commander of IA, where she served for two and a half years before returning to Homicide. In 2006, the Special Crimes Unit was created and she was tapped as Commander.

The paths of Vincent Tyler and Fay Findlay did cross twice during the arc of their careers. The first remembrance Fay had of Tyler was in the early 1990's at the Police Academy where she would come in to teach a two-day course on basic investigation techniques and interviewing. Tyler served as a Training Officer in the West Precinct and regularly attended the latter stages of the academy where he would be assigned a rookie officer.

For three months after an Officer graduated from the academy, they were assigned to a Field Training Officer (FTO). The FTO and Rookie would be assigned to ride together to make sure that the rookie was capable of handling the life as a cop on the streets. Although their interaction was minimal, she remembered Tyler as a nice guy. He was always respectful and helpful at the academy. His demeanor exuded his military service. From what she could see, he always appeared as a put-together officer with a bright future ahead of him.

Fay's second encounter with Tyler was much different. In late 2003, while serving her second stint in IA, this time as the Commander, Tyler surfaced in an investigation that was begun by the Property Crimes detectives investigating a burglary at a large pharmaceutical warehouse in the western edge of the city. Because the burglary involved a very large quantity of narcotic drugs, BPD Vice and the Federal Drug Enforcement Agency (DEA) joined the effort to solve the crime. Not long after the DEA became involved the entire investigation went sideways. It was a fairly routine burglary other than the sophisticated alarm system had been disabled and little trace evidence was left behind. It was apparent this was not your typical crowbar burglary and the perpetrators were very professional. Security cameras in the warehouse captured at least 2 people dressed all in black with faces covered enter the building. Each camera was immediately sprayed with black paint, so no useful images of the theft were captured. The fact that the estimated street value of the drugs taken exceeded well over a million dollars also escalated the crime up the list of priorities. After investigating the case for weeks, the DEA received a tip from a Confidential Informant that one or more Birmingham Police Officers were involved in the theft. Because of this, the BPD IA Unit became involved in the case but otherwise the circle of those investigating tightened. The investigation took several months but finally four BPD officers were implicated. Tyler and his partner from the vice unit and two patrol officers from the west precinct who were on their off days when the burglary occurred. Although the quartet was, no doubt guilty according to everyone involved in the investigation, there was not enough evidence to bring anyone to trial. Through a web of lies and missteps by those accused along with circumstantial evidence, the investigators knew they had done it but needed one of them to confess and roll on the others to have a solid case that would hold up in court. After weeks of trying, none confessed or ratted on others. Because of other violations uncovered during the investigation and past misconducts, the circumstantial evidence was enough to fire them from the job for conduct unbecoming an officer. All four filed a Civil Service grievance to be reinstated. Tyler and his partner had too much circumstantial evidence to overcome and their firing was upheld. One of the patrol officers was also upheld on technical reports and past infractions. The remaining suspect, Officer Jerry Ryan, served a 20-day suspension but his 6-year perfectly clean record enabled him to keep his badge. He was reinstated reassigned to the South Precinct. He was now approaching his 20th anniversary with the department and still working as a patrol officer on the evening shift out of the East Precinct.

Fay thought about that investigation and of Tyler. The man she had met at the academy as a top-flight FTO was not the man she encountered as burglary suspect a few years later. She wondered then as she did tonight, what had changed in his life to cause such a dramatic transformation. Had his earlier appearance been a façade or did he change? What would make a man sworn to uphold the law commit an organized crime like the burglary? Money was the obvious answer, but was it just that? And, if Tyler was the mystery man, was he also capable of murder? The murder of innocent children? In her years on the job she had experienced and seen a lot of evil in the people she investigated, but this case was raising evil to another level. She tried to remember, was Tyler ever there when she lectured about the Hawes case? She could not specifically remember but he was there a lot during rookie schools, although she barely mentioned the case in the Basic Investigation course. She did use it extensively in the weeklong course she taught for new Detectives, but he was never a Detective... did he sit in on one or more of those lectures? She couldn't be sure but he did have opportunity.

If he saw Fay as the reason for being fired from the force, that would certainly provide a motive for the staging of the bodies… it would make it personal, she thought. Would someone really take the life of three people, two of them kids, just to make a point about being fired over a decade earlier? The more she ran through the possibilities, the more her mind raced. She finished her wine, took the record off the turntable and headed to bed although she knew there would not be much sleep tonight.

Chapter 41

1889: Birmingham, Alabama

With Hawes now convicted, there was no delay in continuing with the other trials. On May 4th the Wylie brothers were returned to Birmingham from Atlanta and within two days were arraigned and set for trial.

Hawes remained isolated in his jail cell as his lawyers tried every avenue to get his case heard by the Alabama Supreme Court on appeal. On May 23rd the public saw Hawes for the first time since his condemnation as he was brought back into court for his official sentencing. Less than a hundred people, mostly lawyers and reporters, were in Judge Greene's large courtroom as Hawes was led in. The judge had purposely left this off his docket until earlier in the day and had made no announcement, hoping to keep the gawkers away. Once he brought the court to order, Greene called Hawes to come forward. As Hawes neared the bench, he asked if he had anything to say before sentence was pronounced.

"Yes, your honor," Hawes replied softly. "There is much I would like to say why this sentence should not be passed upon me. I won't attempt to say it however, for I do not believe it would do me any good. I do not believe I had a fair and impartial trial. The jury was not unbiased. I am an innocent man, but I had a biased jury. I hope that I may yet get a trial by a jury that is fair and impartial, and then I will prove my innocence."

Judge Greene replied that his trial "had been tried and convicted fairly and impartially." He further noted that his lawyers had already filed motions of appeal to the State Supreme Court and if the conviction were reversed he would stand trial again. The judge then added, "In the meantime, it is better for you to make such preparation as you think ought to be made for the infliction of the death penalty. It is the sentence of the jury that you suffer death, and of this court, that on Friday, the 12th of

July next, you be hanged by the neck until you are dead."

As Hawes stepped back to his seat, the gravity of the announcement seemed to settle on him and emotions finally came to the surface as he trembled and tears filled his eyes. He sat back down and placed his elbows on the table with his face in his hands. Without comment, Deputy Thomas came over and handcuffed Hawes and led him out of the courtroom. Reports of the day described the stoic man as emotional. As tears streamed down his face, he raised his handcuffed hands to brush them away but they flowed too heavily to keep them at bay.

The prisoner said nothing as onlookers watched as deputies escorted him from the courthouse and along 3rd Avenue and then down 21st Street. As they entered the alley off 21st Street and out of sight of the crowds, Hawes head bowed as the gravity of his situation settled in.

Hawes remained in the solitude of his cell for weeks until June 19th when he granted an interview with a reporter from the *Age-Herald*. Hawes relayed to the reporter that he spent of his days reading and pacing in the small cell. The reporter stated that Hawes was very interested in his appeal process and the transcripts of his trial and was hopeful of a reversal from the Supreme Court of Alabama.

Richard Hawes and the case seemed to once again fade from the news throughout the summer, but once again came to the forefront on September 6th when Fannie Bryant was finally brought to trial. Bryant, after more than nine months of incarceration was finally seeing her day in court. In the days following, witness after witness accounted the story again as they had done in the Hawes trial and the Coroner's Inquest. The turning point of the proceedings came toward the end when Emaline Croom was called to the stand. Her testimony would prove to be the undoing of Bryant.

"I knew Fannie Well," Croom testified. "I saw her picking up railroad irons on the dummy track near the baseball park, next to the woods. I asked her what she was doing and she told me she was picking up wood. She put the irons in an oat sack. I recognized the irons as soon as I saw them when they were taken out of the water on the dead people."

On the following Monday, with less than two hours of deliberations, the jury foreman announced that had found Fannie Bryant "Guilty of aiding and abetting Richard R. Hawes in the murder of his wife and two daughters." Bryant was said to show little emotion at the verdict.

Two weeks later, September 24th, 1889, Bryant was once again brought before Judge Green. Greene imposed the sentence of life in prison for the murder of Emma Hawes. Bryant was returned to the jail where she resumed her duties as a cook. Reports stated, "She appeared as unconcerned as though nothing had happened at all."

Chapter 42

1890: Birmingham, Alabama

Alabama Supreme Court Justice McClellen wrote the following:

"We find no error in the record, and the judgment of the Criminal Court is affirmed. The day fixed for execution of the sentence of death pronounced against the defendant having passed, it becomes our duty to specify another day for the execution. It is accordingly ordered and adjudged that on Friday the 28th day of February, 1890, the Sheriff of Jefferson County execute the sentence of the law by hanging the defendant, the said Dick Hawes, by the neck until he is dead, in obedience to the judgment and the sentence of the Criminal Court of Jefferson County, as herein affirmed."

Sheriff Joe Smith received a telegram announcing the action just after noon on Tuesday. Smith soon relayed the news to Hawes in his cell.

Sheriff Smith then reported to the newspapers, "The doomed man, whose iron nerves have stood every test, did not falter. He simply said that the certainty was better than the suspense, and asked that no one, especially newspaper reporters, be allowed to come and see him. He didn't wish to talk or be disturbed."

As news spread throughout the city, it seemed that finally Dick Hawes saga would soon come to an end. In the days following, Hawes tried to make peace with his impending doom. Hawes brother James and Sheriff Smith met with the condemned man several times. They both implored that Dick "come clean" with the details to clear his conscious.

Dick assured them that he had nothing else to tell and insisted that he was completely innocent in the fray. His brother appealed that his various accounts of the events didn't show that and once again appealed for his brother to tell them what happened. He explained that because he had taken Willie before just before the murders that rumors were swirling of his knowledge and involvement in the crime.

Richard Hawes was surprised by this revelation, "Why, Jim, you had nothing to do with it."

"Yes, but lots of people think I did, Dick," James replied.

"Why don't you tell us all about it, Dick, and clear your brother of any suspicion?" Sheriff Smith implored.

As the conversation continued, both brothers began to weep. James said, "Dick, suppose when little Willie is grown, he should come to me and say, 'Uncle Jim, on the night my mother and sisters were put out of the world, you brought me from Birmingham to Atlanta. People say you know who killed them. My father was hanged for the crime. Who did it, Uncle Jim?' Then what am I to say to him?"

Through the tears, Dick Hawes continued to swear his innocence. As his brother and the Sheriff continued to beg, Hawes seemed to grow tired or weaken and finally asked, "Give me twenty-four hours... until tomorrow."

As the visit came to an end and the brothers embraced, both still weeping, Sheriff Smith admonished the prisoner, "Remember, that woman in Mississippi doesn't care any more about you. You can't help her by making your brother suffer. It is now 12 o'clock and we will return at 4 o'clock for you to tell us everything."

The men returned to Hawes cell promptly at 4 o'clock and the Sheriff announced, "We have come on business this time, Dick. There is no use in wasting anytime. Just open your mouth and tell us all."

Hawes was still defiant saying, "I don't have a damn thing to tell. I have told you all I know!"

Seeing that Hawes was adamant, James broke down and again began weeping. The brothers hugged and both wept openly. Finally in a low voice, Dick said, "Oh, I can't tell it... I just can't." James was now sobbing uncontrollably as he sensed the truth was finally about to be told.

"I don't know where to start," Dick continued.

The sheriff interjected, "Dick, are you going to die and not tell how your children and wife came to their death?"

With tears still flowing, Hawes said, "Before God, I never put hands on those little children. You know that I would not harm a hair on their heads. I loved them too much!"

"Who did it, then, Dick? For God's sake don't keep us in suspense," exclaimed James.

"You both know the man as well as I do!" Dick answered solemnly.

"Who did it, Dick? James responded. "We may know him but we can't tell from that fact unless you tell his name."

Hawes hesitated for a long moment and then announced, "John Wylie did it. You know... John Wylie did it!"

"Thank, God," said James. "You have said that much... Now go ahead and tell us the rest."

Hawes stared at the floor, "Oh, I can't... I can't..."

James encouraged him, "What made John Wylie do it? Tell us."

Finally, without looking up, Hawes replied, "I paid him $200 to do it."

James could not hide his astonishment at this revelation. "My God, Dick, how did you come to that?"

As Dick Hawes continued to stare at the floor and shuffle his feet, he rambled on, sometimes incoherently telling them that several days before he was to marry Mayes Storey, his wife, Emma had agreed to leave the three children with him and go to live with family elsewhere, but that two days before the day of the wedding, Emma got drunk and refused to leave or give up the children.

"I had lived in hell for four years and I was looking forward to the time when I would be married to a sweet woman and have my children in a convent and Emma would be in New York where she would never bother me again." Hawes continue, still without looking at the men, "I was desperate. I had gone down the street and I met John Wylie, whom I had known all my life and I told him of my troubles. He said he would get them out of my way if I would pay him enough money. He knew I had some money and I agreed to pay him $200."

Hawes continued to explain that the next Saturday night he met Wylie at the Florence Hotel and "that the work had been done." Hawes said he asked where they were and Wylie responded, "They are out of your way where they will never give you trouble." Hawes explained that he didn't fully trust Wylie "because he was tricky" and so he refused to pay him the money. He made Wylie wait while he went to the house and then to Fannie Bryant's place to see for himself. "There was nobody at either place and I came back to the hotel and paid Wylie the $200."

When Hawes finally stopped talking, Sheriff Smith urged him for more details, but he insisted that was all he knew. Smith asked, "Dick, who helped John Wylie?"

"I don't know. Jules Wylie was in town that night, but I didn't see him. I made my trade with only John," Hawes replied.

Hawes continued to pace about the cell as he insisted that was the whole story and he knew no other details. He then added, "I don't particularly want to see John Wylie punished, for that would do me no good. I am ready to meet my God and I suppose he will meet his some time. As I stand in the presence of those dead folks, Jim, what I have told you is the truth."

It was almost dark as the men left the jail. Smith sent a telegraph and relayed the news he had learned to Chief Connelly of the Atlanta Police, and took the next train to Atlanta and brought the Wylies back to Birmingham under arrest. On the train back to Birmingham, John Wylie continued to deny any knowledge of the crimes.

As news of the jailhouse confession circulated, a reporter arranged to interview Fannie Bryant, now housed at the State Penitentiary in Wetumpka, Alabama. Upon hearing of Hawes confession and implication of John Wylie, Bryant responded that it was all a lie, saying she had never seen Wylie. "Why don't he tell the real truth and stop this worrying of innocent people?" she asked. She continued to state her own innocence in the affair and added, "If Mr. Hawes would only tell the truth I'd be released."

Chapter 43

Thursday, December 10, 2017

When Fay arrived at the office at 0725, she found Amy and Nate updating the whiteboard. Jerome was on the phone and Walt, as usual, had both of his computer monitors full and was furiously typing away.

"Good Morning, everyone!" she greeted them. "I brought muffins from Urban Standard. I see you are all busy, so let me know when everyone is ready to start."

Each one greeted Fay and returned to finish up their tasks before returning to their desks and turned facing out. Walt was still typing and swiping. Amy announced, "When Walt gets to a stopping place, we can start." Walt turn to see that everyone was waiting on him.

"Sorry, I am just digging away... go ahead," he said turning to face the others.

"Who wants to go first?" Amy asked.

Nate gestured and put his muffin on his desk behind him, "I met with Jasmine last night. She is being super careful, or paranoid, depending on how you look at it. She called me from a borrowed phone and asked me to pick her up at the McDonald's out in 5 Points West. She got in the car but she didn't want to be seen with me anywhere so we drove back downtown and I parked in the Baron's lot down the street and we talked. She really didn't provide any earthshattering info other than his name – Jose Hernandez, which we think is an alias, but I will leave that part of the story to Walt."

"She did reconfirm over and over what a badass this guy is," Nate continued as he stood and began to pace slowly. "She said that he has several girls working at various motels and that he is into everything from guns to drugs and is wide spread all over the south... she knows specifically of operations in New Orleans and Memphis and maybe Nashville. She said he is paranoid to the point that even his close crew rotates often... she rarely sees him with the same goons, as she calls them. Although they do must of the dirty work, she said that he does his own when the situation calls for it or to make a point... like we have been hearing, he operates by intimidation and fear. She has heard that he has killed several people that have crossed him... she says numerous others have disappeared since she has known him."

Nate took another bite of his muffin and continued, "I specifically asked her if she had ever heard of or known him to traffic kids. She said no, but then tells me that from time to time he will have girls that look to be 12 or 13 years old, so yes he does traffic in kids. She said that usually they only stay in one place for a week and then he moves them or gets rid of them, she couldn't be sure what happens to them. She said that not long ago there were two young girls in her motel just down from her. The goons would bring in tricks and wait outside for a couple of hours and then take them back to wherever they came from. The girls were there less than a week and she heard that they were taken to New Orleans."

"She also told me that she thought they were following her more closely since my first visit to her place... she said they always are watching her come and go but she had noticed people following her everywhere. Said they were trying to be discreet but weren't very good at it. She said she had garnered more attention anyway since she got clean… since she does not use and doesn't rely on them for dope, they have less control and have always kept a closer eye but that lately it is more… she is afraid that they think she is talking to us… even before she was talking to us. I want to wrap this us for her sake if nothing else. She is also afraid that he might go after her kids in foster care, although they should be safe, she thinks he has the reach to find them. One interesting thing she did say kind of supports the boss's angle… She said some of the girls think he may be a cop since he seems to always seem to know when the police are going to show up and he is always conveniently not around… she said most just think he is in the mafia or cartel or something… either way, he does seem to have a knack for staying out of the light. I called Walt last night and asked him to dig into the name José Hernandez… she thinks that although he works the southeast that he is here in the Birmingham area so often that he has a place here. She heard about an office on Arkadelphia but had never been there. Walt, you want share what you have?"

"I am not nearly finished, but I do have a good bit already," Walt said looking at his notes. He turned to his desk and grabbed the TV remote and flashed the blurry image from the video. "First I called in a favor from a tech at the FBI and got her to use their software to enhance the video close up…" The image of the Mystery Man on the screen became much clearer. "As you can see this is a great improvement but because of the big sunglasses it is still not positive… running it through facial recognition software gets a score of 62% that this guy and this one." He clicked the second TV on to show the headshot of Vince Tyler, "are the same person." Walt continued, "That is not enough for a warrant or anything but it does go a long way with the my other discoveries. I have found two Jose Hernandez." He clicked the other two TV's to life. The first showed a Commercial Driver's License from Louisiana. The second showed an Alabama Driver's License, both with a photo that appeared to match the others.

"Now Facial recognition of both of the DL's are 96% plus match to each other… You can see the Louisiana one he has facial hair and a buzz cut and the Alabama he has the shaved head that more matches the video image. The Louisiana DL was issued a little over three years ago and the Alabama one just last year. So here is where it gets interesting… like I said, I am not done yet, but as we know, Vince Tyler dropped off the grid in 2011. Well, Jose doesn't appear on the grid until February 2013… He has a social that is that of a man born in Laredo, Texas in 1973." Walt clicked the remote and the two driver's license merged into one split screen and a Texas Driver's License for Jose Hernandez appeared on the screen. "This was issued in 2010 and has not been renewed in Texas. As you can see there is only a very slight resemblance to the others and note the height here is 5'8" instead of the 6'1" on the newer ones."

"Facial recognition says that this Jose is not the same as the others although records show they all have the same social. This Jose worked as a truck driver doing deliveries in east Texas and Louisiana," Walt explained. "I spoke to the owner of the small trucking company in Houston. He says that Jose was making deliveries in November 2011 and failed to return home. His last delivery was in New Orleans and he had seven more stops that he never made. They filed a missing persons report and his truck was found between New Orleans and Baton Rouge two days later abandoned at a truck stop. No sign of Jose. He just disappeared. The owner said he didn't have any family here in the states… his mom was undocumented and died when Jose was a teen."

"The question is why hasn't this missing person report been flagged when the social security number began being used again? So far it looks like a case of Federal Bureaucracy and you're not really missing if no one is looking for you. I am still digging through the background, which will take time, but I am going out on a limb saying that this Jose, or whatever his real name is, stole the identity of this Jose. I am also convinced that Vince Tyler is this Jose but we need more evidence to get that to stand up in court but I am working on it."

As Walt finished the others looked back and forth to see who would go next. Finally, Fay stood and walked over gazing up at the faces on the screen. "This is great work folks, I am impressed with this. Last night, I was trying to convince myself that my fixation on Tyler was unfounded, but you guys have shot holes in that. I also tried to reason as to why... if it is Tyler, why he would risk staging the bodies and all... As we have heard, there is good evidence that he is ruthless and has made people disappear before... so for whatever reason that he killed these three... why go to the risk of staging the bodies? Why didn't they disappear? They would likely have fit that same profile of missing but no one really looking for them."

Fay returned to her seat and seemed to be searching her mind for the next words. "The only conclusion that I can come up with is that it was personal... aimed at me. I hope I am wrong... Although it still seems bizarre to me, it is the only scenario that makes any sense," she said. Fay leaned forward in her chair as she recounted her experience with Tyler. "He was an FTO and was around the Academy and so he likely heard me lecturing on the Hawes case, but I don't know that for sure... we need to wrap that up by putting him there on the days I lectured... I have no idea if they track stuff like that or how long they keep it if they do. It doesn't make sense really for two reasons – one, it seems that he has been very careful to avoid any detection for years although he was obviously into all sorts of criminal activity.

Second, I was the Commander of IA when he went down, but I was not directly involved as far as interviewing him or anything... to my recollection, during the final stages of the investigation when we knew we had them but we needed the case to stick we interviewed all four several times and quickly determined that he was not going to crack... most of the pressure was applied on the patrolmen involved... as far as we could tell they served as look out and drivers and were not involved in the planning or execution of the burglary, so they didn't have any information to share, really. No one ever caved. Even though the DA wouldn't prosecute, there was enough stink and infractions that came out during the investigation that all were terminated."

Fay stood and began to pace again as she continued, “Everyone appealed the firings. One of the patrolmen, who basically were the driver, was reinstated with a suspension, while the others were all upheld.” Fay looked down at a file on her desk, “The guy that got his job back is Jerry Ryan... still working Patrol in Eastlake... his 20 year anniversary is next month. I would like to get his take on all this,” she said turning to Nate and handing him the folder. “Does anyone know him?”

All shook their heads, no.

“Maybe he can give us some insight... perhaps he has been in contact with Tyler or maybe after all this time he has changed his ways. I pulled his personnel records and it seems he has been a model officer since then, so maybe he will talk. Use your interview skills, Nate,” Fay said.

Fay paced in front of the group as she thought and then finally spoke again. “I know this goes without saying, but you all know that I am going to say it anyway. We need to move quickly on this information because we know he has the resources and skill to disappear if he knows we are coming. We also know that he is capable and dangerous, so be careful and don't do anything stupid. The questions is..." she paused as she began to pace again, "who can we trust to help us find this guy? If anyone says something in the wrong place or makes a stupid move, we could loose him... we obviously have to locate him but we can't scare him off either. Any suggestions of how to proceed?"

Again, they all traded glances before Nate and Amy spoke at the same time.

"Go ahead, Amy," Nate said.

Amy nodded, "I trust Julie and her partners but I'm not sure about sharing this with the entire Task Force... there are some cowboys there and they have been working this for over two years and haven't gotten very far... plus I am afraid the feds will pull something hoping to get an even bigger fish, especially if he is involved with a cartel or something... so you never know... I say we keep it tight... bring in those we trust and sit on places we know he has girls and his office, although they think that may strictly be a physical address for the shell company... since we brought it to the Task Force's attention, they installed a camera somewhere near there on a pole and have had zero activity according to Julie."

"Amy is right," Nate agreed. "It will take more work on our part but I don't want to this scum to get away and if he does, all of us and people like Jasmine will have to watch their six for the rest of their lives... he obviously holds a grudge and is vindictive, so we have to get him. I need to make a call... Jerome or Amy can you take the interview with Ryan and I will join you?"

They both agreed. "According to the roster he is off today but he is scheduled for municipal court in an hour," Jerome said. "That would be a great place to catch him and see what he knows."

Amy stood, "If you can handle that, I'll call Julie and meet with her to fill her in. Everyone let's meet back at one and make our plan... does that give everyone enough time?"

"I think we have enough to get warrants on Tyler and search warrants for the places we know," Fay said. "I'll go down to legal and make the case and see if the judge will sign off on it."

All agreed and went about their ways... Walt returned to his computer, while Nate grabbed his jacket and headed out and Amy and Jerome followed behind. Fay took a deep breath and stared at the faces on the screen above. She still could not wrap her head around Tyler being this sadistic, even though she never really knew him. It was hard to think that anyone who ever wore the badge could be capable of something like this.

Chapter 44

Thursday, December 10, 2017

Walt was continuing to try to unravel the identities of Jose Hernandez. The more he uncovered, the more convinced he was that Tyler, or someone, had taken over the life of the truck driver from Texas who disappeared in 2011. He was reading the files of the missing person report filed by the Louisiana State Police. Hernandez truck was parked in an overnight space at the Love Truck Stop at the Gonzales exit on I-10. Video surveillance showed the driver pumping fuel and then moving the truck to the parking space. The driver exited the building with another person but video could not identify either person as Hernandez due to the poor video quality. There was no video available for the parking area. The manager of the truck stop reported the vehicle abandoned and the Highway Patrol found the connection to the missing person report from Texas. There was not much else in the report. No forensics or other investigation was performed on the vehicle. The trucking company sent a driver to retrieve the vehicle and the missing person report was filed on Jose Hernandez, although it appears that no real investigation was ever done to locate him.

The phone on Walt's desk jolted him from his concentration, "Ellison, SCU." The call was from the forensics lab. Walt listened intently, "Thanks... I see the email... Let me know if you find anything else." He opened the email and the attached report. "Hey Boss, we have the results from forensics on the Toyota... it appears all 3 bodies were transported in the trunk at some point."

Fay joined Walt at his desk pulling her chair alongside his as they both scanned the report.

Blood and other fibers and hair had confirmed that all three victims had been in the trunk of the Toyota. Fingerprint's lifted from the car were numerous. Positive matches had been made for both occupants of the vehicle when arrests were made – James Witherspoon, the Juvenile and Marquis Johnston. Neither had prints found in the trunk area. Lifts of prints belonging to Alfonso Greggory (Slick) Hightower were also found in numerous places outside and inside the passenger compartment but not in the trunk. Three lifts were found in the trunk including a bloody, full palm print on a spare tire but it was smeared and not useful. The blood on the print was identified as that of Emma with traces of the other victims. There were also numerous lifts from the trunk consistent with a person wearing latex or similar type of gloves. Blood samples from all three victims were found in the trunk along with hair and fibers consistent to each victim and the clothing of the two children. Touch DNA reports were not back yet and should be available within the next 48 hours according to the report. Fay rocked back in the chair.

"Have they picked up Hightower yet?" She asked.

"No Ma'am... warrant was issued and they have been to his house but no sign yet... he may be in the wind," Walt answered. "BOLO is out on him though, so he if he is still around, we should get him soon."

"This should help with the warrants I asked for so make sure the clerk in legal gets that report," Fay said.

Fay stood and began to pace behind Walt and began to think out loud, "This doesn't make sense.... He is so careful... careful is not leaving the victim's bloody car intact and selling it or giving it some kids... The fact that his prints were not found makes sense, but the rest of this makes no sense."

Walt spun his chair to face Fay. "I agree... it does not fit the profile at all," he said. "I forwarded the report to legal marked as urgent. I also just sent a text to the guys at Bessemer that found the car and to the beat car in Ensley that covers the area where Slick lives... if he shows up, they are aware to arrest him immediately and contact us."

Chapter 45

Thursday, December 10, 2017

Jerome and Nate made their way to Jerome's SUV and Nate dialed the number of the burner phone he had given Jasmine the night before and hoped that she would be in a place where she could answer.

"Hey," she answered on the second ring, "You miss me already?" she teased.

"Jasmine, we have enough to bring him in so if you spot him or hear anything, you call me immediately... do you understand?"

There was no response.

"Jasmine, did you hear me?" Nate asked.

Finally she responded, “Uh... yeah... I heard... are you sure you got enough to take him down?” She asked sounding less confident than Nate’s declaration. “I mean you know how he is...”

Nate cut her off, “Yes, we have enough and once he is in custody, I can get you to a safe place... you lay low and just call me the second you see him or if you hear anything, okay?”

Jasmine sounded somewhat bewildered by the news, “I will.... You be careful,” she added as she hung up the phone.

Jerome steered the SUV into an empty space designated for police in front of the municipal court building. As the pair got out, Nate asked, “Do you know what he looks like?” Jerome flashed Ryan’s ID Headshot photo he was carrying. “Thanks, man... I didn’t even think about it,” Nate said.

The detectives walked down the marble hallway toward the courtroom and saw several people milling around outside the courtroom. Many were seated along the long benches that lined either side. Jerry Ryan was talking to two other officers just outside the doorway. Jerome recognized one of the officers as Sergeant Nick Downs, someone he worked with in Patrol.

"Hi Nick, how's it going?" Jerome announced.

Nick was surprised to see the pair, "What brings the suits from SCU down to city court?"

Jerome laughed, "We try to keep in touch… you never know when you might get reassigned!" he said jokingly.

Downs introduced the other two officers and Jerome introduced Nate to the trio of uniforms. Jerome acted as though his introduction to Ryan had triggered a thought, "Ryan… you work Eastlake, right?"

Ryan nodded yes as a bit of apprehension came to his face.

"Mind if I pick your brain about something we are working on? It will only take a minute," Jerome asked.

Ryan was hesitant at the request but wasn't sure how to react with his Sergeant standing there. "Sure… these guys can call me if my case gets called," he said nodding to the other two. Ryan followed the detectives into one of the many privacy rooms on the opposite side of the hallway. These small rooms were places attorneys could meet privately with their clients or witnesses.

As Nate closed the door, he slid the "occupied" sign in the door.

"Man thanks for taking a moment for us," Jerome said. "We didn't really have time to call you and we saw you were on the roster for court... I know this is kind of unusual and I hope we haven't freaked you out."

"No... No, not at all... how can I help?" Ryan said trying to keep his cool.

Jerome pulled one of the chairs away from the small table situated in the center of the room. "Mind if we sit?" Jerome asked as he and Nate both took a seat. Ryan looked even more perplexed but pulled out the chair and sank into it.

Nate spoke for the first time, "I don't want to freak you out but I know that if I were you this would probably freak me out, so I am just going to throw it out... Please know that you are in no way in trouble or anything but we need to ask about the burglary case back in Ensley..." Ryan stood at those words.

"You have got to be fucking kidding me! I am 6 months from my pension... that is ancient history," Ryan said expressing his anger but trying to not shout. Both detectives rose slightly from their chairs and each one gave him their most compassionate face.

"Your pension is secure, man. Jerome assured him. "It is not like that at all, I promise. It is just that one of the guys in that incident has appeared on our radar and we are just covering all of our bases." Ryan sank back into the chair but his neatly pressed uniform was even more rigid now as his entire body showed the angst of even discussing the subject at hand.

"Do you have any contact with any of those guys?" Nate asked.

Ryan stared at the wooden table and seemed to be carefully considering the question.

"Not really. I have done my best to put all that behind me. It's been a long time, man... I was just a kid..." his voiced trailed off as the painful memories of the time flooded his consciousness.

Jerome leaned across the table. "Jerry, we don't want to know anything about that really, we just need to know if you have had any contact with any of those guys since then."

Ryan looked at both detectives and seemed to analyze their intent. Finally, he looked at Jerome. "I talk to Rick Samson sometimes. He is married to my cousin. He was fired back then with me, but he didn't get his job back... I was the only one that survived... but I guess you guys know the whole story."

Jerome was jotting notes down. "What's Rick doing these days? He still lives here in town?"

Ryan seemed to relax, ever so slightly, "Yes, he works at Edward's Chevy on 3rd Avenue... he was always a car guy... went to work there right after all that shit went down... been there ever since."

"What about the others?" Nate asked.

Ryan shook his head, "No, I really never knew the others… they worked vice and offered us some money to help them on a case… or so we thought… I told all this a million times… nobody believed us but that don't matter now… I have put all that behind me." He looked up and stared at Nate, "I moved on… I am a good cop."

Nate gave him his most assuring look, "Jerry, I have no doubt about that. You have had a superior record for 20 years, man. Vince Tyler's name has come up in an investigation and we are just chasing down every possible connection and lead. As we told you, you are not involved, we are just hoping that you could help us in some way. Maybe something from the past or if you had been contacted by him or anything."

Ryan sat back in his chair, "No… as I said, I never really knew him at all and I haven't talked to him in twenty years… what is he into?"

"Let's just say some bad shit has gone down and he seems to be around it." Jerome quipped.

Ryan relaxed even more, "Man, I didn't know he was even still around."

"Do you know if Rick has had any contact with him since back then?" Nate asked.

"If he has, he hadn't mentioned it to me," Rick said. "And I think he would... we don't talk that much, you know... but all that shit that went down, we were both young and stupid and got caught up in it... Rick lost his family when all that went down but he got the job and has kept his nose clean ever since. Our family ain't that close, you know, but I see Rick every couple of years or so at weddings and funerals and such."

"When was the last time you spoke?" Jerome asked.

Ryan answered quickly, "He called me about two or three weeks ago... he was worried about his nephew Earl... he is like a son to him... he thought he might be mixed up in a drug gang or something out in Ensley and called to see if I knew anything... he was trying to keep the kid out of trouble."

Nate leaned in, "So, did you help?"

Ryan gestured with his hands in the air. "What the hell can I do? I called some friends out in the West Precinct to see if him or any the guys he was running with were known... you know tried to get the scoop if Rick needed to worry or not."

"Anything to it?" Jerome asked as he leaned into the table. Ryan seemed to tighten back up a bit as the detectives seemed to be interested in his loose conversation about low life thugs in Ensley.

"Well, some of the names that Rick gave me turned out to be some pretty badass dudes... some maybe mixed up in a Mexican Drug Cartel or something... I mean Earl is just kid... maybe twenty and stupid... he has had some scrapes but nothing really and Rick wanted to make sure he was okay... so I told him that he was not keeping good company and Rick thanked me. I assume he handled it."

"Do you remember any of the names?" Nate asked.

Ryan thought and pulled a small note pad from his pocket and flipped through pages. "Just street names is all I have," Ryan offered. "Buzzy, Big John, Bones, Chancey, Slick and Cooper... what he gave me... Guys in the West said that they all ran with the same crowd... all into drugs, whores and maybe guns and cars.. Had rumors that they may be ganged up with a cartel as their supplier but nothing has gone down on that and so, you know, that may be some street talk bullshit... Mexican Cartels is the new street cred to be a ultimate badass... so I don't necessarily buy that."

Nate stood and reached out to shake Ryan's hand, "I cannot thank you enough for your time, man... this has been very helpful."

Jerome shook his hand and also thanked him. Each detective gave him their card. "Our cell numbers are on the back... don't hesitate to call us if you need anything," Jerome said as they opened the door and returned to the hallway. As the detectives headed back to the car, Jerome asked, "Do we have time to run by Edward's for a chat with Rick?"

Nate looked at his watch as he got into the SUV. "Yes, we may have to eat our lunch in the office, but let's head over there," he said. "I know the service manager, so I will give him a call and get him to pull Richard somewhere we can chat in private."

Chapter 46

Thursday, December 10, 2017

The detectives entered the Chevrolet dealership and walked past the antique Chevy in the front window. The 1916 Model 490 was juxtaposed against the new Corvette sitting next to it and perfectly told the history of the dealership that was almost as old as the Chevrolet brand itself. The dealership was now entering the fourth generation of ownership of the Edward's family. Founded in 1916, the Dealership had survived The Great Depression, World Wars, Civil Rights era, the downtown decline and resurgence and now thrived in downtown Birmingham. Most dealerships had long fled to the suburbs, and most had gone through dozens of changes in ownership, but this icon remained. The pair were led to a private office in the rear where a nervous Richard "Rick" Samson was sitting and waiting. The detectives introduced themselves and took a seat on small sofa adjacent to the chair Samson occupied.

"Rick, I really appreciate your taking time to talk to us," Nate began. "We will be as brief as we possibly can. We spoke with Jerry Ryan earlier today about a case we are working on and he said your nephew, Earl, might know some of the people we are looking into. We were hoping you may provide us with a little more information."

Samson shifted nervously in the chair. "I am not sure how I can help... I don't talk to Earl very often, but I do try to look out for him. His Dad was killed in a wreck when he was young and my Sister has done her best but he pushed her patience during his teen years... but he is a good kid... is he in trouble?"

"No, Rick... we don't think he is, but some of his friends might be involved with some things we are investigating... do you know any of his friends?" Jerome asked.

Rick grimaced and bit his lip as he contemplated his answer. He let out a big breath. "You're probably talking about Slick and that group, right?"

"Do you know Slick?" Nate asked.

Rick let out another audible sigh, "Not really... met him once or twice... I told Earl he was bad news and he needed to find new friends, but you know how that is..." His words trailed off and his gaze went to the floor as he leaned forward in the chair, his elbows planted on his knees.

"What makes you say that Slick is bad news?" Nate inquired.

Rick looked up and answered, "Well, I wasn't a cop for very long... only 3 years... and that was almost twenty years ago, but it was pretty easy to see this guy had way too much money for a thirty-something high school dropout living in Ensley... I have been trying to keep Earl straight, you know... he has had some scrapes but nothing too bad... but I told him he was asking for trouble hanging with those dudes... he don't listen, though."

Jerome leaned in close, "Do you know what they are into?" He asked.

Rick rubbed his brow with his hand. "I am not sure but I figure it is not good... they are always taking these trips... two or three days at time... always got cash. Always shady… I avoid them, but I have picked up Earl over there a few times."

"Does Earl go on these trips?" Jerome asked.

Rick nodded, "Yeah sometimes… but not often… it's like they are still feeling him out… can you tell me what they are into?"

Nate spoke up, "Well, we are early in the investigation, but as you say… it looks like they may be into several things and none are good."

Rick's look of grimace turned to one of almost pain as he asked, "Is Earl involved? I need to know."

Jerome reached out and put his left hand on Rick's knee. "We don't know… that is what we are trying to find out… Can you tell us where to find Earl or Slick? We haven't been able to find either one."

Rick stood and ran his greasy nails through his graying hair as he paced in a small circle behind the chair. After a few rotations, he sat back down with his face in his hands staring at the floor.

Nate broke the silence, "Rick, if you know something that can help us, we will do everything we can to protect Earl, but we need to know what these guys are into."

Rick leaned back into the chair and his face looked anguished as he pondered the detective's words. With another big sigh, Rick leaned forward and looked the detectives in the eye. "I don't know much, but I am going to shoot straight with you and I hope to God you can help Earl... He is hiding... been hiding since yesterday and I can take you to him."

This news got the full attention of the detectives as both leaned in to hear more.

"Here is the deal," Rick continued. "These guys he got mixed up with are some badass motherfuckers... sorry about my language, but that is just what they are... some kind of Mexican cartel or something and Earl got swept up with them some how before he realized all the shit they were into... I didn't know anything about this until he called me yesterday, scared shitless and said they were gonna kill him. I knew these guys were no-goods but I had no idea how bad. I mean, they just seemed like some local thugs...

not anything like he said... they are all black except for him and one other dude... none are Mexican but evidently the guys they work for are... Anyway, he calls me and he is like crazy scared... I ain't never seen him like that... he said that they killed Slick and they were coming for him and he didn't know what to do."

Rick stands up and begins to pace in the small room as the detectives give him time to get the story out. "He tells me that a few weeks back him and Slick were delivering some cars to New Orleans and on their way back, Slick gets a call from the boss to meet in Ensley. They meet this Mexican dude somewhere out on Arkadelphia and he gives them a car and tells Slick to get rid of it... he wants it burned completely, he says... so, Slick puts Earl to driving it and he follows in his car... now they are supposed to be going somewhere out in the woods of Walker County to dump the car but Slick calls Earl on the way tells him to drive it back to Slick's house in Ensley... when they get to Slick's his cousin or somebody is there and he sells them the car for cash."

Rick takes a deep breath and takes his seat again as he continues the saga, "Everything is cool until yesterday when Slick calls Earl and asks if he has talked to the boss or anybody else about the Toyota... that is the car they were supposed to get rid of... Earl says Slick is all crazy and says they're gonna kill him... he says they killed somebody and used the car to dump the bodies... he did not know that and now they were gonna kill him cause the cops had the car... he told Earl he was leaving town and told him to do the same.... Except another friend called him later that day and said that they killed Slick and word was that Earl was next... Earl called me and was going ape shit, you know.... I left work and went and picked him up and took him up to a friends place up on Logan Martin Lake... I told him not to leave the trailer... he is there now... but my sister said some thugs had been to the house several times looking for Earl and she is sure somebody's is sitting outside in a car watching her." Rick returned to his pacing, "Shit, I am afraid they are gonna come after her... I told her to stay put there and not leave for nothing. I've went by last night to check on her."

Rick then took his seat again and looked at Nate and asked, "Can you help us? I swear he had no idea what he was getting mixed up with..." Rick looked at both detectives with a look of pleading hopelessness. "I swear, he is too stupid to know what he was into."

“Did he describe this boss guy that told them to dump the car?” Nate asked.

Rick nodded, “Said he had met him a couple of times… Mexican dude about 45 or 50 but he spoke perfect English – no accent. Shaved head… I think his name was Jay. I know that ain’t much, but maybe Earl can tell you more.”

Nate looked at Rick and tried to be as comforting as possible. “Is Earl armed?” he asked.

Rick looked disheartened, “Yeah, he’s got a shotgun… but he won’t hurt anyone.”

“Okay, here is what I need for you to do,” Nate said. “I am going to call a friend of mine at the St. Clair County Sherriff’s Department. He is a detective and he will go and pick up Earl. I need you to call Earl when he gets there so he isn’t spooked. He will bring Earl back to Birmingham and we will place him in protective custody. We already have a line on this boss so we will get him but we need to talk to Earl once he gets here and get his statement and we will probably need him to testify. Can you get him to agree to that?” Nate asked.

Rick still had a worried look on his face. "Can he get a deal so he doesn't do time for the car thing?"

Nate nodded reassuringly, "If he cooperates, that should be no problem."

"He really is a good kid... stupid, but he is a good kid." Rick said.

Nate and Jerome stood and each shook Rick's hand before heading for the door. "Now, don't call him until the Sheriff's Department is there, okay? I will call you... do you have a cell?" Nate asked.

Rick nodded and pulled his phone from the back pocket of his work uniform. "Good, I will call you when they arrive and you call him and tell him to step out with his hands visible... they'll pat him down and transport him to Birmingham and we will meet him there. Write the address and your phone here, please," Nate instructed, handing him a small piece of paper. They all shook hands again and the detectives headed back through the showroom and thanked the manager on their way out.

As they got back in the car, Nate called and made arrangements for the pick up. "That was definitely worth that stop, huh?" Jerome joked as he pulled out of the dealership and into traffic.

"And we will make the meeting at the office in time!" Nate added, checking his phone for messages. "Just got a text from Amy to make sure we were going to make it... she is picking up lunch at Ted's."

Jerome let out a yell, "Home cooked vegetables! This day just keeps getting better!"

Chapter 47

Thursday, December 10, 2017: 12:19

Nate and Jerome entered the CSU Office to find their colleagues gathered around the "campfire" table in the center of the office. The table was a large round folding table that only came out when the team was working on a group project involving a lot of paper files that had to be shared or for a shared group meal, such as today.

"Just in time!" Amy announced as they arrived. "I got a variety of vegetables, fish and chicken... extra mac and cheese since everybody loves the mac and cheese. Tasos hooked us up and there is baklava for desert! We are going to work while we eat, so fill us in on this development."

After everyone had filled their plates with southern goodness, Nate related the events of the morning -- first interviewing Officer Jerry Ryan and then former officer Rick

Samson and the revelation of his nephew, Earl Kendricks. He told of how Earl had gotten involved with Slick and others doing odd jobs and errands for a guy that was supposedly with a Mexican Cartel. He related how Slick did not get rid of the victim's car as he was instructed and instead sold it and how, when it was discovered the police had taken possession of the car, that Slick Hightower had disappeared and was rumored to have been killed and that Earl was targeted to be killed also but his Uncle stowed him away in a friend's lake house and was now being transported to Birmingham for questioning. As he was wrapping up the details, Nate's phone buzzed.

"Earl is in custody and they are rolling this way... no resistance," Nate announced to the group. "My buddy Jim says he is scared shitless and ready to talk. They should be here in 45 minutes or so... Delk has a room ready for us downstairs. Jerome, do you want to add your observations?" Nate asked.

Jerome put his cornbread down, "I think you covered it... we had a busy morning, but a very productive morning... hopefully Earl will give us enough to make things stick when we find Tyler... we are pretty sure he is the Mexican Cartel guy... Rick said the guy had no accent... so we assume this

Mexican Cartel persona is some kind rouse he runs to add to the intimidation."

Walt interrupted looking at his tablet screen, "They just found Slick's tricked out Impala… I put out a BOLO on both cars when you called me… Impala just found on Birmingport Road… burned with a body in the trunk… it will be a while before they can get a positive ID, but I think we can assume we know who it is."

"Well, this means he is very aware that we are at least looking his way and he is tying up loose ends… maybe he is still around" Fay said. "Amy, where are we on locating him?"

"Julie and her partners are sitting on his most frequent stops… as we already know, he is very careful and doesn't have a routine and now is probably suspicious of his entourage and more likely to be going it alone," Amy said. "Nate, do think this Earl guy knows how to contact him?" Amy asked.

"I'm not sure," Nate responded. "Rick seemed to think that contact was always initiated from Slick to Earl…

but maybe he knows how to contact him or knows someone else that does... that will be the first thing we ask."

"Yeah, our assessment was that Earl was just beginning to earn the trust of this group but he may know more than we think," Jerome added.

Everyone was finished eating and began clearing the table. "Walt, how is your research coming?" Fay asked. "Any new locations on Tyler or the shell companies?"

Walt walked over to his desk and brought the computer back to life. "Not really anything to share but I am getting closer... There are about six companies that look to be shells for this organization or whatever we want to call it and there are properties that are either owned or rented in four states... There are three more addresses here in Birmingham other than the one on Arkadelphia we already knew about. All commercial... one downtown on Southside, one in Ensley and another out near Gate City... from simple drive-by's they all seem to be unoccupied and not in daily use but the task force has eyes on all four as of last night... I am still digging."

"Thanks, Walt," Fay said. "Nate, you and Jerome interview Earl and we will watch from here and then we can decide what our next move will be."

Jerome looked at his watch. "They should be here soon, I am going to head downstairs. I will have my Bluetooth in if you need to communicate during the interview," he said. Nate and Jerome both grabbed their jackets and headed downstairs while Walt folded the table away. Amy was busy updating the white board, while Fay stared at the image of Tyler on her computer monitor as she tried to wrap her head around all the new information. She needed to figure out his next move, but she didn't have a lot to go on. So far, every thing he had done followed no pattern, yet every move seemed cold and calculated.

Nate stuck his head back in the door. "Boss can we get Jasmine picked up and brought in? If he is tying up loose ends, he might be crazy enough to..."

Fay stopped his words with a motion of her hands, "Sure, we will take care of it... will she be okay with someone showing up unannounced? Will she cooperate?"

Nate shook his head, "Call the burner and tell her they are bringing her in to see me and that it is all over... she will come."

Amy spoke up, "I'll call Julie and get her to do it... she is out near there." Nate gave them a thumbs up and was back out the door.

On the first floor of the Police Administration Building were six interview rooms used by all the Detective Division. The rooms were set up with video and audio for taking statements and conducting interviews. They were almost identical to those at the Jail, but were a little less intimidating since they were *NOT* at the jail. There were two holding cells at either end of the hallway adjacent to the rooms. These were usually used as house suspects under arrest between interviews or before being transported to booking at the jail.

Jerome and Walt checked in at the desk. Sergeant Delk instructed them that their perp had just arrived and was placed in Room 112. They entered the room and found Detectives Randy Marsh and Jim South from the St. Clair Sherriff's Department and a very anxious looking Earl Kendricks.

“Thanks so much for your help on this, we owe you a big one,” Nate said shaking each of their hands.

“No problem… I like having you in my debt! We’ll talk to you soon!” Marsh said as they exited.

“Earl, my name is Jerome Clark and this Nate Parker… can we get you anything? A coke or water?” Jerome asked.

Earl looked at both Detectives and shook his head, “Naw, I’m good… I just want to get this over with.”

Nate and Jerome sat down on the opposite side of the table and clicked on the camera mounted in the corner of the room near the ceiling. “Earl, we are going to be recording our talk so that we have a record, do you understand?” Jerome asked.

Earl nodded, “I’m good… I am glad to be here… I know the drill so you don’t have to read me my rights or nothing.”

Nate smiled, "You are not under arrest, so reading you the Miranda warning isn't required. We are just going to talk, okay?"

Earl nodded again, still staring at the table. Nate looked at Jerome who nodded to him that they were ready to start.

Jerome began, "Earl we have the video rolling now so we want to get everything on the record. I am Detective Jerome Clark with the Birmingham Police Department and this is my partner, Detective Sergeant, Nate Parker. Today is December 12, 2017 and it is now 1310 hours. Will you state your full name for the record?" Earl straightened up in the chair and leaned in toward the table.

"My name is Earl Kendricks," he said confidently.

"Earl, tell us about your relationship with Alfonso Gregory Hightower, also known as Slick," Nate said.

Earl hesitated for a moment as he gathered his thoughts, "Me and Slick are friends... His little brother, Jimmy and me was best friends growing up... Slick was older but was around, you know... Then he went off to prison for bit... right before he got out, Jimmy got killed in a drive-by in Fairfield... so stupid... they wasn't even after him, you know... wrong place at the wrong time, man... Anyway after all that went down and Slick came home, he kinda looked after me... got me jobs and stuff, you know."

Nate had a folder on the table in front of him and he shuffled through some of the contents.

"Earl, tell us about how you and Slick came into possession of the Toyota," Jerome asked.

That question made Earl fidget a little and the anguish returned to his face. "Man, I told Slick that it was a bad idea to sell that car, but he told me he was doing a solid for his cuz, you know... he didn't know what had gone down or he never would've done that, you know."

"So tell us about the meeting where you got the car." Nate asked.

Earl leaned into the table and placed both elbows on the table, "Well, we were on our way back from delivering a car to New Orleans and was almost back in town when Slick got a call from the boss to meet out at this tire place on Finley Avenue."

"Sorry to interrupt, but before you continue, can you tell us about this boss? Nate asked. "He got a name?"

Earl cocked his head slightly, "I really can't tell you much. I met him three times. His name is Jay or Jose, I think... but we just called him boss." Earl's nervousness was exposed with his rampant description of the boss. His voice growing higher with every word and struggling to get a breath as the words came fast. "They say he's a Mexican dude, but he don't seem like it," he continued. "I mean he is tanned but he speaks perfect English, no accent or nothing like that... anyway, he is older... probably 45 or 50... bald... shaved head... good shape for an old man, you know. Also, from the moment I started hanging with Slick and those guys, I was warned... you don't EVER cross the boss... he would as soon kill you as look at you... that's what they told me and I believe 'em... Like I said, I only saw him three times, but I knew that he was a badass... I saw him cold-cock a guy that just said the wrong thing... first time I saw him... one punch and he messed up that dude's face, man. I don't really know anything else... Slick told me he didn't take no shit from no one and to never cross him... which is exactly why he should have never kept that car, man… he knew better, you know. Like I said, only saw him three times and I stayed outa his way, you know… I did whatever Slick asked and kept my mouth shut."

"So back to the car," Jerome interjected. "You were with Slick when he went to the meet and got the car… what was said?" he asked.

Earl leaned back in the chair and took a deep breath, "Not much really… Boss was there with another dude named Big John… they were waiting behind the shop… Toyota was sitting there and the Boss's Lexus was beside it…"

Nate interrupted again, "What kind of Lexus?"

"Black SUV… one of those new fancy ones… custom wheels," Earl answered.

Nate pulled a photo taken of the Lexus from the service station video and laid it in front of Earl. "Is this the Lexus?"

Earl leaned in and looked at the photo, "Yeah man, that looks like his… probably don't see to many with those wheels, you know… it's a fine ride." Nate told him to continue.

"Well, he just told Slick to take the car to Walker County and make sure nothing is left… we got this place up off I-22, way out in the woods where we have dumped cars before a couple of times… pull 'em off the dirt road and put a couple of gas cans in the back seat… slosh some gas on the front seat and light a rag or something and throw it in and run like hell… usually takes a minute or two for them to really get going but you never know… Slick said he saw a guy get blowed up doing it, so I was careful… but I only done that twice…" His voice trailed off as the realization that he had just described his involvement in a crime to two detectives while being recorded.

"We don't care about the past," Nate assured him. "We need information on the things we are asking about and if you can help us, we can make sure you get out of this with as little trouble as possible, okay?"

Earl nodded but didn't seem completely convinced.

"So what happened next," Jerome asked.

"Well, Slick told me to drive the Toyota and he followed in his car. The Boss and Big John got in the Lexus and drove out same as us. I was heading for I-22 when Slick called me and said take the car to his house. I thought the boss changed his mind or something. Then we got to Slick's place and his cousin Marquis is there. We shoot the shit for a little bit and then Slick hands him the keys and Marquis hands him a roll of cash. I was kind of shocked, you know. But, I didn't say nothing till he drove off. I asked Slick what's up and he told me don't worry about it. I'm thinking this ain't good but it ain't my business really. I never really thought no more about it, but then last night, Slick calls me and he is bent out of shape… like crazy, you know… asking me if I told anybody about the Toyota and if the boss had asked me about it… he was like crazy, man… I ain't never seen him like that… I told him I ain't said nothing to nobody… especially the boss… how the fuck am I gonna tell the boss… he don't even know me really… Then Slick tells me that the police has got the Toyota and his cuz… and then he finds out that there was some murders involved and bodies and shit… which is why the boss wanted us to torch it…. Slick didn't know that when we got it… I swear! I certainly didn't!"

Earl's discomfort became more obvious as he continued to relate the story, "Then Slick tells me he is a dead man and he is leaving town and tells me to do the same... I start screaming at him on the phone but he hangs up and won't answer... I ain't even got a car, man... how the fuck am I supposed to get outa town... where the hell am I going to go? I tried to call Slick for like an hour... I didn't know what to do... I was at my Mama's house... she was at work and all I could think about was the boss coming in and blowing my brains out... I finally called my Uncle Rick... I didn't know what else to do.... He picked me up in like twenty minutes and took me up to the place at the lake... told me not to come out until he called... he was going to figure something out..."

"What do you know about Big John?" Jerome asked.

Earl shook his head, "I seen him around... him and Slick were kinda like the bosses... you know under THE Boss... He's a big black dude like Slick... but much bigger... he played football I think... I mean he's like 6'6" or something and strong as an ox... nice guy but I wouldn't want to mess with him, you know?"

"Do you know where either one of them lives?" Nate asked. Earl shook his head, "Naw, man... I just saw them places when Slick would meet or something to pick up a car or packages… sometimes we would take girls from one place to another… but I don't know where they live, man."

Nate turned in his chair slightly and nodded at the camera as a signal he was ready to wrap up if anyone had additional questions from the office. Jerome got a question from Fay in his ear.

"Earl, tell us about some of the meeting places," Jerome asked. "Were they always public places or did you ever go to house or a business or office?"

Earl seemed to think for moment. "We never went to no house… mostly the hotels where they got girls, you know… We met at the tire place there at Finley and Arkadelphia a couple of times… like I told you, that's where we got the Toyota… There was a place out past the old steel mills in Ensley… abandoned place but Slick had a key to the gate…. We met there sometimes… it is big so all the cars could pull inside, you know… that's the place I first saw the Boss and the only time he talked to me… asked me my name and asked me could I do what I was told and asked me if I could keep my mouth shut… I said yes sir and he told me to do whatever Slick told me and that was it…. Saw him one other time about month or so ago at the same place... about ten or twelve guys that night and a truck... we all unloaded boxes off the truck and into the cars... I didn't ask no questions... Slick paid me like five hundred dollars that night and said I had done good and more would be coming."

Nate stood up, "could you take us to this steel mill place? You know where it is?"

Earl answered quickly, "Oh yeah, I know right where it is... gate has a chain and lock though... but I can take you there."

Jerome explained to Earl that they were going to hold him in one of the holding cells at the end of the hall for his protection and that someone would get him some food. They may be back in a bit to go out to the warehouse.

"Thanks, Earl," Nate said. "You have been a big help and we are going to keep you safe. We will be back in a couple of hours or less, okay?"

"Okay," Earl answered as they escorted him down the hall and into the holding cell. Jerome explained their intentions to the desk sergeant and then headed for the elevators to rejoin the team in SCU.

Chapter 48

1890 Birmingham, Alabama

As the execution day drew nearer it seemed that Richard Hawes became more despondent and depressed. Sheriff Smith was concerned that Hawes may try to take his own life and had him closely watched. When he was handed a bulky letter from Hawes to mail to his bride in Mississippi, the sheriff decided to read it.

In the letter, Hawes continued to express his unending love for the young woman and apologized for the troubled he had caused her. He told her that "by the time you get this, I will no longer be on this earth," confirming the sheriff's suspicions of a suicide attempt. He went on to tell her that his story of John Wylie's involvement in the crime had all been fabricated to punish Wylie who had reported to the

Sheriff a planned escape by Hawes and two other prisoners during Wylie's first incarceration. "John Wylie never saw one of my children in his life, or was even in my house after I was married. I hope they hang him as they think they will me, but he is innocent of knowing anything about it," Hawes wrote.

Even in as a condemned man, Dick Hawes continued to not be able to stick to one story. Four days after the letter exposed his lies, he told Sheriff Smith's brother, who was a deputy, that he had hired John Wylie and Fannie Bryant to kill his wife and Irene, insinuating that Irene was not his daughter but the result of his wife's affair. He continued with another different account, saying that when he went to pick up May at Fannie Bryant's house that Fannie was drunk and May told him that a strange white man had killed Irene and her mother. He said, "I didn't want to take May's life, but she was talking about it all the time." He then told of taking her to Eastlake on the dummy line and giving her whiskey. When she was drunk he took some twine from his pocket and tied some irons around her body but then heard a horse nearby and fearing discovery threw her into the lake. "The weights must have rolled off, else she would have sunk," he said.

The trial of the Wylie brothers was to begin the very day that the letter from Hawes was intercepted by the sheriff. Because of the notoriety of the whole affair, the trial had been quietly transferred to the Circuit Court and the brothers were brought before Justice of the Peace, William T. Poe. All eyes were fixed as Richard Hawes was led into the court to testify. The condemned man looked to be some twenty pounds heavier. His thick black beard was now long and full and his face appeared more aged.

In his testimony he told of paying John Wylie $200. When asked about his subsequent confession to Deputy Smith, Hawes denied that it ever occurred, saying that he had never made such a declaration. He denied having any involvement in his daughter May's death. When confronted with his letter recanting Wylie's involvement, he said that it was not true. His testimony was full of contradiction and twisting of the various stories that he had produced.

Once both sides had made final arguments, a brief argument was heard from Solicitor Hawkins, and then Justice Poe announced that he was discharging all charges against the Wylie brothers.

During the final days of Dick Hawes life, his brother continued to care for him despite Hawes request that all desert him and leave him.

Rumors abounded that Hawes was writing a book length confession, which he planned to be released following his death, in hopes that it would be sold to aid in the rearing of his son Willie.

In his last days he took counsel from Birmingham clergy and was visited often by Methodist minister, Dr. W. C. McCoy, as well as other ministers, Dr. T.G. Slaughter, Dr. D. I. Purser and

Rabbi Eisenberg and Father Daly and several other priests from St. Paul's Cathedral.

On March 1, 1890, Richard Hawes was marched from his cell and out into a cold, light rain. The small gallows had been built in the alley just off 21st Street behind the jail. Richard Hawes was impeccably dressed in a black suit provided by a local tailor. He wore a red geranium in lapel. At 12:59, the sheriff gave the signal and Hawes was hanged for his crimes before a large crowd.

Fannie Bryant died in a prison riot at the prison in Wetumpka.

Albert Patterson received a reduced sentence after testifying for the state.

As far as anyone knows, Willie Hawes was raised by his Uncle Jim in Atlanta and no records of him have surfaced. Speculation is that he changed his name to avoid the publicity of his family tragedy.

Emma, May and Irene Hawes are buried side-by-side in an unmarked plot at Oak Hill Cemetery in Birmingham, Alabama.

Chapter 49

Thursday, December 10, 2017: 14:40

Jerome and Nate came into the SCU office to find both Amy and Fay talking on their phones and Walt, as usual, burning up his keyboard. Walt paused to acknowledge the pair and Jerome asked, "What's up?"

Walt stopped typing and gestured to his female colleagues, "Amy is coordinating things with the task force and the Tactical Team and Fay is trying to expedite warrants… While Earl was providing details to you guys, it seems that Slick had the last word… Guyer called to say they found a small fireproof safe hidden in the trunk of the burned out car… they are still going through it… but it had photos, thumb drives with recordings, handwritten notes and such… not sure whether it was his insurance or if was he working for the Feds… if it was insurance, it didn't work." Walt's report was cut off as Fay wrapped her called up.

"We have arrest warrants for Tyler and search warrants for all the properties we are aware of... Guyer found addresses for three other places in the metro as well as the one on Finley we have been watching... one seems to match the description Earl gave you of the old steel mill in Ensley... it is an abandoned fabrication facility that closed almost twenty years ago... purchased 3 years ago by one of the shell corporations related to Tyler. Amy is trying to confirm if Slick was a CI or just covering his ass... and putting everyone on alert... if Tyler is still in town and he is spotted, we want to move quickly before he disappears, if he hasn't already."

Amy hung up the phone. "Tact team is on stand-by at the West Precinct... they are ready to roll on our command. All Task Force personnel are on duty and covering the various places... no good way to watch the steel plant or warehouse or whatever you want to call it, since it is secluded with one way in and out... Julie and Rick did a drive by and reported that the gate was locked. They are stationed at a gas station on Avenue J that leads in there so they can see if anyone goes or comes. Now we watch and wait," she said.

"Slick was not working for the Feds," Amy continued. "Evidently, that was his insurance policy if he ever got busted. Guyer said it was hard to be certain with the condition of the body, but looked as though it was a quick professional hit. Small caliber double tap to the head, likely 9mm. No sign of torture. Appears to have happened in the car," she informed the team and then asked, "Walt how is it going?"

Walt spun around from his desk, "Everyone has been notified... TSA has his photo so if tries to get on a plan anywhere, he is flagged... alerted all LEO's as well and Media Relations... they are running it on all the local stations for the 5 o'clock news... so his face will be plastered everywhere... along with a list of all his vehicles. Fugitive Detail is helping identify all the other players from the photos Guyer recovered... between them and Gang Detail we should be able to put names to the faces and get additional warrants and start shaking their trees too," Walt said.

"I already have one," Walt continued as he clicked the overhead screens to life. "Big John is John Cameron Mason," he said as photos appeared on the screens. "Grew up in Kingston. Played football at Ole Miss. Got kicked out of school before his freshman season was up for drug violations. Worked as a Correction Officer for DOC at Tutwiler Prison for 3 years before he got booted in the last Federal probe for supplying drugs for sex to inmates and a laundry list of other despicable things. Feds did not prosecute so he didn't serve time. Various employment records as security at a number of bars and such. Latest employment is with BluLine Enterprises… one of Tyler's shell companies. According to the notes Guyer sent me… he and Slick were the closest to Tyler."

Fay stood and said, "Let's all go home and do whatever you need to do and then we will need to relieve the task force at some of their posts. Amy is going to pick up the warrants and she will text everyone their assignments of where to be at 1900 hours. Jerome, unfortunately, you drew me," she said as she gathered her bag. "We are relieving Julie and Rick. Shall I pick you up about 6:40?"

Jerome smiled, "I have my go-bag with me… pick me outside the ER at Children's… I will take my wife out for quick dinner if she has time."

"You got it," Fay answered. "Everyone, let's be careful. He may be long gone but if he is around, remember that he is trained and dangerous. We have plenty of help nearby so don't be stupid! If we don't find him by midnight, we will start executing the search warrants."

With that the team parted ways for a couple of hours of downtime before resuming watch. Surveillance is a tedious and boring part of the job but necessary on almost every case. No one really liked it but everyone had developed their own way to deal with the monotony. All hoped that tonight would bring an end to this. They would either capture Tyler or discover he had fled. Either way, hopefully they could all get back to a normal routine soon.

Chapter 50

Thursday, December 10, 2017: 15:18

Fay pulled her black city SUV into the garage for the alley of 2nd Avenue. She usually left her city car at the office but since she would be going back out in a few hours she drove it home. The basement garage of the loft was tight but thankfully most of her neighbors drove small cars. Each loft was assigned one parking space so those with more than one car were forced to find space in a nearby rental lot or park on the street.

At the far end of the garage were storage units for each loft. The units were simply chain-link fences providing a space for each resident that was six feet wide and ten feet deep. Most were stuffed with holiday decorations and plastic tubs on shelves. Fay kept Christmas and Halloween decorations in hers along with the bicycle she rarely rode anymore. She also had several bins that contained family heirlooms that she kept, knowing that most likely they would be discarded when she was gone. Since she never had children of her own and she was an only child, the branch of her family tree ended with her. She had long ago acknowledged this and knew her conscious decision to not have kids would have some ramifications in later life, but she was satisfied with her place and had no regrets.

Fay made her way past the storage units and determined that as soon this case was over she would go through it and perform a thorough clean out. There were holiday decorations in there that hadn't seen the light of day in years, not to mention her Mom's stuff and the bike.

She entered the elevator lobby and rode the lift up to her floor. She unlocked the door and coded out the alarm dropping her bag on the chair near the door. She stopped at the fridge and looked at the bottle of Chardonnay that she opened the night before, and then she reached for a beer -- her new local favorite, Muchacho from Good People Brewery. The Mexican style lager had become her favorite at summer cookouts but it also proved satisfying as winter edged in. She was not a prolific beer drinker, especially local beers since she found most too harsh and bitter, but this one was great with both burgers and nachos – her two favorite food indulgences.

She stopped and put the beer back and grabbed a bottle of water. If anything were to go down tonight and she had to make an arrest or even speak to the press, the last thing she wanted was beer on her breath. She decided to just chill until it was time to leave for the stake out. She had time for a nap but she knew that would never happen. She was having enough trouble sleeping at night these days. A nap would never happen. She moved her bag from the chair and sat down in the 1960's era chair made of formed plywood and leather. Even though it was probably older than she was, it was the most comfortable chair she had ever sat in. She found it in a local vintage furniture store soon after moving into her loft. The chair and its matching ottoman proved to be the launching point for the entire décor of the loft -- a mixture of mid-century modern vintage furniture, industrial upcycled pieces and some modern accents thrown in for good measure. She settled into the chair and clicked the remote to start the music. At times like this, the digital music supplanted the vinyl merely for convenience. No flipping and attending needed, just streaming through the speakers. She picked up some magazines and flipped through trying to think about anything but work.

She flipped through the latest *Garden & Gun* but she had already read every article. Next in the queue was *Southern Living*, a magazine based in Birmingham. Fay still subscribed but rarely read it anymore. She no longer had a garden and she rarely cooked and since *Time* bought the magazine a decade or so ago, it had lost its charm for her. What did Yankees know about southern living anyhow, she thought. Next in the stack was Esquire. Bill had been dead now for over six years but she kept the magazine coming. Bill's only two vices were music and clothes. He was definitely the best-dressed DEA Agent, or any kind of agent, for that matter. She smiled as she flipped through the pages looking at the ads and thinking of Bill. He would usually make fun of the outrageous looks promoted by the fashion houses. He always said that good fashion was timeless and he was always dressed to impress. Nothing flashy or outrageous, but classically styled. Even if he wore jeans and a tee shirt, it was always perfect, she thought. She always fought back her memories because they were just too painful. She tried to think about the good times like his laugh and his enormous collection of shoes that over ran the closet when he moved in, but eventually her thoughts turned to that day she got the call and it was like it was happening all over again.

She was teaching an evening class at UAB. Her lecture had just barely begun when she looked up and saw Amy and Nate come in the door. She knew immediately that they were not bringing good news, but she couldn't have imagined that it was the worst news. Bill's car was found off a county road less than a mile from I-59 in Sumter County, just south of Tuscaloosa. When the deputy arrived, the car was engulfed in flames. Bill had been shot --Twice in the chest and twice in the face. It was so shocking. He had been a cop all of his life. Twelve years with Nashville P.D. and then more than ten years as a DEA Agent. Danger is always present in the life of a cop. Bill had been in several scary situations in his first years with the DEA working undercover assignments with the most ruthless criminals. When he and Fay got serious he took an assignment as the Chief of the Birmingham Metro office of DEA. The job not only took him off the street, it provided more normal hours and they were both ready for that.

Bill had been headed to a meeting with agents from the DEA and FBI in Tuscaloosa and failed to show. They traced his car and found it burning with his body in the front seat. The case was still active and no substantial leads had ever been established. It was as though it was a random act, though everyone knew that it wasn't. The meeting involved a sting operation that was ongoing on the campus of the University of Alabama. The Perps were mostly local thugs and frat boys so no link was established to Bill's murder. He had been off the street for more than three years so there seemed to be no reason for his removal. It remained a mystery that haunted several agencies and all that knew or worked with Bill.

The usually stoic Fay Findlay was devastated. The news hit her hard and despite her best efforts she had spiraled into a deep depression. She tried to manage the grief like she did everything. She analyzed it and met it head on, but she was no match for it. She soon realized how much her life had become intertwined with his. They met at a conference and Bill was immediately smitten. Fay staved of his charms for a while but finally succumbed and agreed to go out to dinner. Although she had convinced herself she would never get that serious, within a few weeks she realized she was hopelessly in love with this man who was unlike any other man she had ever known. He was so confident and yet so humble. He was compassionate about life and made her feel that the world revolved around her.

Once he was gone she realized just how her entire being was tied to him. Every thought or action was about Bill or something they had done together or planned to do together. His absence left her adrift in a life that she was no longer accustomed to and was sure she didn't want to experience life without him.

After almost a year, her friends finally convinced her that she needed professional help and over the next several months she had pulled a life back together, although it was a life much different than she planned. At the advice of her therapist, she had explored new things but found her only comfort in those things most familiar – music, friends and her work. She not only spent more time at the PD, she took more teaching assignments and until recently was virtually working two full time jobs. Only in the last year had she taken a more administrative role at work and cut her teaching hours in half. Most days she felt that she was emerging from the grief but then something would trigger a thought or an emotion and it would all come flooding back.

She had dated a few times just to get her friends to quit pestering her. None had gone past two dates. Part of it was she subconsciously guarded and didn't want to experience the pain again but mostly no matter how hard she tried not to, every man was compared to Bill and all failed miserably. She was content socializing with her downtowner friends. There were married couples and some singles that were widowed or divorced but mostly women. The few single men in the group were single for a reason they all soon deduced. She still missed Bill everyday. She missed the physical intimacy. She missed his charm and intelligence. He kept her grounded. He kept her from taking work or life in general too seriously. There was no doubt that her years with Bill were the best. Just recently she had come to appreciate that having him in her life had made her a better person. Even though they met later in life, he was a big influence on who she was. She never fully realized that until he was gone.

Even though the chair was comfy, Fay realized she was not relaxing and she tried to change her thoughts... anything but Bill. She looked out across the city. It was now getting dark and the lights began to illuminate all across the horizon. She stood looking out the window. She saw the illuminated windows on the mirrored Regions Tower decorated for Christmas and suddenly remembered that the Downtowner's Pot Luck Holiday Dinner was Saturday night. She would probably still be immersed in this case so she didn't have to think about what she'd bring. She checked the time. It was now almost five thirty. She headed into the closet and grabbed a pair of jeans and black tee shirt and a lightweight black hoodie. Stakeout clothes had to be comfortable. Sitting in a car for hours on end was never fun but tight or otherwise uncomfortable clothes would make that time unbearable. She reached in and turned the shower on. She removed her clothes and tossed them in the hamper. She removed her bra and panties and glanced back to see if the water was hot yet. Puffs of steam were beginning to rise above the glass wall. She reached in the drawer and removed a shower cap and started to put it on and looked in the mirror and laughed out loud. Bill used to give her grief when she showered and didn't wash her hair. She always used a shower cap. He said all he could see was a smoking hot lunchroom lady standing naked before him. God how she missed his quips and jokes. She missed the caress of his big hands exploring her body. She missed his embrace and their communal showers. When Bill moved in they had renovated the loft and created a larger shower and doubled the size of the walk in closet. The guest bedroom had never been used so the space was perfect for their spa like bathroom. She snapped the elastic cap over her hair. "So much for changing my course of thought," she said out loud as she stepped into the steaming shower.

The only thing that could disrupt her thoughts of Bill was the case. Although she hadn't relaxed very much in her down time, she had managed to put the case aside for a few hours. As the water streamed over her she felt her muscles relaxing. Her thoughts turned back to the case. Would they find Tyler tonight or was he long gone? He had avoided detection for so long and had been so careful. The analyst in her said that disappearing was the most likely scenario. But, his actions had been so contradictory... cold and calculated on one hand and sinister and vindictive on the other hand. What changed? What made him stage the bodies? If it was meant for her... why? She barely knew him... was only administratively involved in his firing years ago. It just didn't make sense... Could she be wrong? Obviously, Tyler was a criminal but could someone else be involved? There just didn't seem to be another answer... perhaps he may talk when arrested... perhaps more forensic evidence would make more sense of it all.

Fay dried off and brushed out her thick blonde hair. She looked at her own reflection and could imagine Bill coming up behind her and caressing her before carrying her off to bed. She grabbed her clothes and tried to think about the case -- *Anything* but Bill.

She threw on her jeans and tee and slipped on her favorite gray Nike running shoes. Grabbed her hoodie and iWatch checking the time. One last look in the mirror and she was ready. She stopped by the kitchen and grabbed two bottles of water from the fridge and a box of granola bars from the cabinet. Her go-bag was in the car but one can never have enough water or snacks. She stuffed them in her bag and retrieved her Glock from the drawer and slipped it into the holster in her belt. She coded her alarm and slipped out the door.

Chapter 51

Thursday, December 10, 2017: 18:31

The building was quiet and Fay looked out the window onto Second Avenue while she waited on the elevator. The city was also quite. The restaurants and bars were busy but it was Thursday night. Tomorrow night the streets would be packed as the weekend kicked off. Especially this time of year, Holiday parties and gatherings made the wait for tables at restaurants even longer. The bell dinged as the elevator arrived and the doors slid open. Fay stepped into the elevator and pushed G. She grabbed her car keys from her bag and stepped out of the elevator and down the short hall to the garage.

As she approached the police SUV she heard a slight sound but before she could look around she felt the cold steel against her neck.

"Don't even think of making a sudden move," She heard the distinct voice from behind her.

Fay held her hands out instinctively as she tried to turn toward the voice.

"Do not move," the voiced warned. She felt a hand remove her weapon from her waist and then remove her bag from her shoulder.

"Do exactly what I say and you won't be harmed... I just want us to have a conversation... finally," the male voice said.

Fay remained frozen and started to speak, "Look..." He cut her off as he grabbed her left wrist.

"Don't talk! There will be time later... we have to move. I would hate for anything to happen to your neighbors if they came in on us now," he said. He grabbed the other wrist and pulled the zip tie tight around both wrists behind her back and then fed another one through her belt and belt loop and secured it to the one around her wrist. He patted her down, feeling around her waistband and then down each leg. He then reached up and ran his hand under her tee shirt and Fay recoiled. Then she felt the cold steel embed in her neck and she stopped.

"I just want to make sure you don't have anything else that might hurt me... I know cops can be resourceful," he said. He ran his hand under her bra and around her body. "Sorry to be so forward on our first date Fay, but I have to make sure." He removed his hand and released her hair. He commanded, "Walk! My car is in the alley," still using a low voice. He gently nudged the back of her neck with what she knew was a gun and she walked toward the door at the back of the garage.

Fay's mind was racing through all the training scenarios that she had participated in, and even taught, throughout her career. This scenario was one that never ended well for the victim and even worse if the victim was a cop. She was already down one on the list of "Don't Do". She had surrendered her weapon. From day one in the academy and every bit of training since, it had been stressed --- NEVER, EVER give up your gun!

Fay emerged into the darkness of the dimly lit alley and saw the black Mercedes sitting just outside the door. The trunk popped open as they exited the building. "Sorry, but you're going to have to ride in here... I cannot drive and watch you too," the man said still suing a low calm voice.

Fay bowed her back and she felt the gun in her neck, "There is no way in hell I am getting in there..." The gun pushed back into the flesh of her neck, "You are going in one way or another... your choice." Then she felt the assailant's lips on her left ear as he whispered, "I don't want to hurt you but you know I will... I just want to talk but not here... get in the fucking car." He guided her down with a hand full of hair. Her butt hit the deck with force. She saw him for the first time as she rolled into the spacious trunk. It was indeed Vince Tyler. He was dressed in a dark gray long sleeve tee shirt and jeans. He wore a black baseball cap. "By the way, I disabled the emergency release, so don't bother. We will be where we can talk in less than thirty minutes, so just relax." The trunk lid shut and Fay was immersed in total darkness.

She felt the car lurch into motion and tried to plan her next move. She had to be ready to attack when he opened the trunk but even with her training that would be hard to do with her hands bound behind her. She had been trained in escape from zip tie handcuffs. If there were in front of her body it was a fairly simple move but not so with them bound behind her and attached to her jeans. That was going to be a difficult move... impossible actually.

Fay sensed the car accelerate and she tried to track movements – left turns, right turns, hills and declines, but the luxury car made it difficult as the ride was smooth and quiet. All she could hear was the gentle roar of the tires on the pavement. He had said the drive was less than thirty minutes. Jerome was expecting her to pick him up in ten minutes, so hopefully her strict punctuality would make him initiate a search quickly when she failed to show up. She also knew that even if he began looking immediately, it would likely take an hour or more before they figured out what had happened and then they would be looking for a needle in a haystack. During her encounter in the garage, Fay had noted that the camera in the garage had been disabled with spray paint on the lens. He had likely done the same to the other camera in the garage and the one on the back of the building and alley. Help may come, but it would not be in time. She was own her own to get out of this.

She ran through dozens of scenarios in her head and none of them seemed feasible, especially knowing that her captor was a highly trained and cautious individual. The thought occurred that this might be her last hours in the world… she tried to suppress it but that proved hard to do given her current situation. She thought of Bill again. Soon after his death she had gone there – what were his last minutes like? Had he seen it coming? Was it quick? Did it happen before he knew it? She wondered what was better, having time to get ready or boom and your gone. She took a deep breath and thought, "I am not ready to die… not tonight… I am going to fight like hell if I do."

She pushed the negative thoughts from her mind and resumed planning… What was her best course of action? Clearly, he would try to kill her but if that was his sole intention, he could have easily dropped her on the garage floor and left unnoticed. Maybe he did want to talk… but about what? Perhaps he could explain his actions and why he had done all of this. Even if he was successful maybe he could satisfy the dilemma for her before she left this world. She began an assessment of her best moves to disarm him using kicks. She was trained in several forms of martial arts but was certainly not an expert in any. Police training exposes one to various forms of the martial arts for both self-defense and subduing attackers. Even though she had practiced leg sweeps and a variety of kicks, they were all followed by some sort of move with the hands or arms to complete the move. She tried to remain calm and steady herself. She knew that what ever she did, it would not be her best if she were emotional. She needed to be razor focused. "He wants to talk," she thought. "I am a trained negotiator... I have more training in talking than all my physical skills combined. I will talk... I will reason... and when I sense he least expects it or my time is up... I will make a move... and it will end, one way or another." She felt a peace come over her and she relaxed ever so slightly.

The whining of the tires had been slower for the last few minutes. She tried to check her watch for the time but could not contort her body to even come close... then she remembered! She contorted her right hand against the zip tie as the plastic dug painfully into her wrist. She carefully positioned the middle finger of her right hand and probed for the iWatch on her left wrist. She gently tapped the face and listened as Mickey Mouse announced, "It's seven thirteen, Good Evening Pal!" She knew they would be searching by now. At least she hoped they were. She wished that she used the iWatch for more than time and fitness tracking. She could probably send a text or something, but she would have difficulty doing anything on the watch with her hands totally free, much less bound behind her. She had no idea that if she could do that, but she had no way of knowing that it would not work since Tyler had tossed her phone along with her bag into the dumpster behind her building before driving away.

The whining of the wheels turned to the crunch of gravel beneath them and then a few seconds later came to a halt. Fay listened carefully and heard the car door open. Her breath quickened as she anticipated the trunk opening. About thirty seconds later she heard the door close again and the car lurched forward. The sound of the gravel under the tires was less intense as the wheels slowed. Within a few seconds the sound disappeared even though the car was still moving slowly... no sound at all. Then the car stopped again and the sound of the door opening again. Seconds later the trunk lid opened. Fay peered out into the darkness. She could see the moonlit sky through an opening to the right. They were in some sort of building. Tyler was not visible at first having stayed at the car's side when he opened the trunk just as a precaution. He then stepped into view and reached in and grabbed her arm just above the elbow and her leg and lifted her out of the car. He held her as she steadied herself leaning against the car.

"This way," Tyler said motioning to his left, "we can talk over here." Fay walked and scanned the building and her surroundings. It was a very large building that appeared to be some sort of abandoned factory. One side had large openings where she could see the dark skies. At either end were large overhead doors. The building was at least five hundred feet in length. It was empty except for some scattered empty pallets strewn about. About a hundred feet ahead she saw a small concrete block wall with a door and a small window. She assumed that in an earlier life it was some sort of office. She saw nothing that could identify where she was and she saw nothing she could use as a weapon.

As they reached the office, Tyler reached around her an opened the door and flipped a switch. A single bare light bulb on the ceiling illuminated the small room. There was a small crudely constructed plywood table against the wall and four metal folding chairs. Tyler kicked one of the chairs around and guided Fay into it as he closed the door behind them.

Chapter 52

Thursday, December 10, 2017: 18:46

Jerome dialed Amy from the 6th Avenue South Lobby of Children's Hospital, where his wife worked as a Pediatric Oncologist. After a quick dinner at the nearby Taziki's, he had walked her back to the hospital where Fay was to pick him up.

"Hey Amy, have you heard from Fay?" He asked as Amy answered.

"No, I thought she was with you. Nate and I are almost to our spot for the stake out," Amy answered.

"Well, she was to pick me at Children's at 1840," Jerome continued, "and you know she is always five minutes early... but she hasn't showed and she's not answering her phone, which has me concerned... the boss always answers."

Amy switched her phone to speaker so Nate could hear the conversation, "Yeah, that is not like her. Walt was still at the office a minute ago, so call him and have him go by her place as he leaves.... And keep us posted!"

"Will do," Jerome answered as he hung up and dialed Walt. "Hi Walt, are you still at the office?" he asked.

"I am just pulling out of the lot, what did you forget?" Walt answered.

"Nothing, but Fay hasn't picked me up and she's not answering her phone. Can you drop by her place to see what's up?" He asked.

"Sure, I'm about three blocks away now. I will call you back in a minute." he said. Walt pulled up and in front of Fay's building and parked in the loading zone and activated his flashers. He dialed in her unit on the keypad by the front entrance but got no answer. He then dialed the phone for the buildings management company listed on the box. He listened to the recording about office hours and then hit 5 to dial the emergency number. When the person answered, he explained the situation.

"Well, it will take me about 40 minutes to get there," the attendant said. "Let me call one of the other residents. Jane is the Home Owners Association President, she can let you in but neither of us have a key to Fay's loft. Hang on and let me see if Jane's home."

Walt waited, peering through the glass storefront hoping that a resident would be going or coming through the lobby. "Walt, are you still at the front?" the attendant asked. "Jane is going to buzz you in and she will meet you in the lobby by the elevator."

Walt thanked her and heard the buzz and the lock disengage. He entered the door into the small hallway that led to a small lobby with a wall of mailboxes on one side and an elevator on the other. He had been to Fay's place a few times when she'd have everyone over for a meal but it had been a while. The elevator doors opened and an elegantly dressed lady in her fifties emerged, "Walt?".... I'm Jane. I was just about to leave for my firm's Christmas party so I am glad I was still here. I live across the hall from Fay. I knocked on her door but she didn't answer. I'm sorry but I don't have a key," she said.

"Thanks, can we see if her car is in the garage?" Walt asked.

Jane motioned to the door beside the mailboxes, "Sure... her spot is third one on the left right beside mine." They made their way down the short hall to the garage entrance and Walt pushed the door opened. He had never been in the garage and was surprised to see how big and well lit it was. Immediately he saw the black police SUV in Fay's spot. He walked over and peered through the driver's window as Jane stood just inside the door. The car doors were locked and nothing looked out of place. He walked around the car as he scanned the area. The garage had 10 spaces on one side and 12 on the other side. There was an additional double space marked for bicycles and motorcycles. At the end were the chain-link enclosed storage units.

"Does anything look out place?" Walt asked as he walked back toward Jane.

Jane seemed surprised by the question, "Huh... no... not really.... I mean, all the cars look familiar, if that's what you mean."

"I assume the doors lead out to the alley?" he asked pointing to the garage door and a walk-through door at the rear of the building. "Are the camera feeds stored here or off-site?" Walt asked.

"Yes, those lead to the alley and the video system is in the mechanical room over there." Jane answered, pointing to a door beside the storage area.

"How many cameras?" Walt asked.

Jane thought for a moment before answering, "Two here in the garage, one covers the alley and one out front, one in the lobby and one on each floor at the elevator and one on the roof deck. We just had them serviced and checked last month."

Walt walked up for a closer look at the camera. His heart accelerated as he saw the precise black dot of paint on the lens. "Can you let me in to see?" He asked pointing to the Mechanical Room door.

"Sure," said Jane as she headed to the door and fumbled through the keys on the carbineer in her hand.

Walt dialed Amy. When she answered he turned his back and stepped away from Jane.

"We have a problem," he announced when she answered. "Fay's car is here but the cameras in the garage have been sprayed. I am about to look at the footage to see what I can see, but you need to get the word out. I think he may have jumped her or something."

"Oh, shit! Amy said, trying not to hyperventilate. "Any other signs or evidence around the car?" She asked.

"Nothing... place is clean... I will call you back once I see the video feeds. Give me a couple of minutes," Walt said. He hung up the phone and turned his attention to the make shift security station. A large flat screen monitor was mounted to the wall above a simple shelf that held the hard drive. Another shelf below held the keyboard and mouse. The monitor was divided into ten screens, each showing a live feed from each camera. The room was simply a mechanical room providing access to all the various mechanics of the building. Other than the make shift video system, the room and walls were filled electrical boxes of various forms and shapes and conduit pipes of all sizes that disappeared into the ceiling above him. A box of light bulbs sat on the shelf next to the computer and two five-gallon buckets of paint sat on the floor under the shelves.

Walt sat on one of the buckets and began scrolling through the footage. He clicked on the camera in the alley and scrolled back to the time stamp of 18:15 and started the fast-forward. The image on the screen was constant except for a plastic bag on a wire across the alley that flapped in the breeze. The camera view gave a distorted fish-eye view of the alley in both directions. There were no vehicles present. Walt watched the time clock click forward rapidly, and then at 18:24 something caught his eye. He ran it back and started again at normal speed. A hand with a can of spray paint appears from the right and within two seconds the screen is blackened. Walt pulled a thumb drive from his jacket pocket and ran the tape back and transferred the footage to his drive. He switched the view to the footage to the cameras inside the garage. The image on the right was from the camera at the front of the garage showing the entire garage to the back wall. The left screen was the view from the camera mounted above the alley door. It showed the entire garage to the front wall and entrance into the lobby hallway. He ran the timestamps of both to 18:23 and started them forward. At 18:25 the right screen showed a person come through the walk in door from the alley. The person was dressed in jeans and wore a long sleeve gray tee shirt, black baseball cap and black gloves. He had a black scarf of some kind over his face and wore sunglasses. He stepped in and closed the door behind him and Walt watched as he stood still just inside the door and scanned his surroundings. He looked up and then knelt down and scanned the perimeter again. He stood back up and pulled a can from his back and sprayed the camera above the door.

Walt saw the left screen go black and he clicked the right image to go full screen. The figure walked quickly forward as his head scanned back and forth with each step. When he reached the front Nate saw the handle of a semi automatic pistol l in his waistband. His left arm extended and the screen went black. Walt clicked on the camera in the front of the forth floor elevator and ran it back. He saw Fay exit her loft and push the button. She stood looking out the window, waiting on the elevator then stepped in. He switched to the lobby and watched her exit the elevator and enter the door to the garage. The timestamp read 18:33. Walt removed the thumb drive and returned it to his pocket and picked up his phone to call Amy and Nate. He was startled to see Jane still standing there inside the door. He had completely forgotten about her.

"Oh my God!" she said, "Do you think that man took Fay?"

"It certainly appears to be the case," Walt said. "I am calling for an evidence team. Can you stay until they get here?" he asked. "They will secure the garage and likely will go through her loft. This is now a crime scene."

"Certainly... what ever you need," Jane answered.

Walt hit Amy on the speed dial. "I have the video although it doesn't show much but he definitely has her. Came in through the garage... painted out the alley camera and then each of the ones inside... Fay entered the garage at 18:33 but the cameras were already out so that is the last visual... no vehicle visible in the alley maybe we can get some other cameras that may show him entering the alley or leaving."

"There is a car in the alley and one out front," Amy advised him. "They can secure the scene... Evidence Techs are enroute.... I also called Guyer at home so he is headed that way. Get back to the office, you will be able to find a camera feed before anyone else so get working on that. I will issue the BOLO... but we have no idea what we are looking for," she said.

Walt hung up the call and instructed Jane to let the officers in at the front door and he headed to the rear. He thanked Jane as he left and promised to keep her informed. She handed him her card and thanked him. Walt gave instructions to the policemen arriving to secure the building. One was stationed at the front door and another at the rear door. Another stood in the lobby to make sure no resident wandered into the garage. Another officer was stationed outside Fay's door.

Walt walked outside. There were cameras in front of the El Barrio restaurant two doors down but he doubted the view would show much from that distance and he was pretty sure they left the same way he came in – through the alley. He pulled to the corner and looked at all the buildings for cameras. He then turned into the alley. Fay's building was in the middle of the block. He stopped in front of the police cruiser and got out and walked down the alley. The camera was mounted on the wall about seven feet up between the garage door and walk through door. The spray paint glistened in the glow of the streetlight across the alley. He walked around the dumpster and decided that it would obscure all but a large van or truck from the sight of the camera. He remembered the view from the alley camera and knew that the angle would allow someone to stay close to the wall and not be seen. Walt got back in his car and drove through the alley to the other end. Directly across the street was a bank with an ATM. He scrolled through the contacts on his phone and dialed.

"Bill, this is Walt Ellison. I hate to bother you but I have an emergency situation and need video from your ATM at the branch on the corner of 2nd and 22nd. How can I access that? Awesome! Can you text me that? I am almost back to the office and I can access it." The bank security team leader informed Walt that their new system had just gone online two months earlier. All video leads could be accessed through a secure web portal. ATM cameras maintained footage for 10 days before it was discarded. Hopefully, this would show something to identify the car, he thought as he raced back to the Police Headquarters.

Chapter 53

Thursday, December 10, 2018: 19:07

Walt pulled into the parking lot of the Police Administration Building and badged into the back door and sprinted up the stairs to the SCU Office. He sank into his desk chair and placed his phone on the desk. He monitored the texts going back and forth between his team members on the screen as he worked his computer. His first task was to ping Fay's phone although he knew that it was likely turned off or destroyed. He was surprised to find it was still live and showed a location of the alley behind her building. He called the Sergeant on the scene and asked him to check to see if had been tossed... most likely in one of the dumpsters in the alley. He could kick himself because he realized he walked all around the dumpster behind Fay's building and never looked in. "How stupid," he thought, "What if Fay's body is found..." He stopped his thought. He could not go there... not yet."

He returned his focus back to his computer and pulled up the secure bank website and followed the instructions Bill had texted. He clicked on the feed from the ATM and scrolled the footage back to 18: 15 and started the forward movement. Several vehicles passed along 22nd Street. The one-way street had three travel lanes all headed south with parallel parking on both sides. The view of the ATM camera was much higher quality than at Fay's building. Resolution was high definition color. Even though it was dark outside the cars passing through were very visible.

At 18:21 Walt sees a black Mercedes turn into the alley from 22nd street. He freezes the feed and zooms on the image. Mercedes AMG S... Alabama license 1B 34389. Walt saved the screen shot and then sent the image to the printer. At 18:27 a couple approaches the ATM. The female operates the transaction while the male is talking his phone just behind her visible over her left shoulder. She completes the transaction and they walk away to the north. Walt fast forwarded and no other vehicles or persons entered or exited the alley until 19:02 on the timestamp when Walt recognized his police car emerge.

"I need video from the other end of the alley," he thought as he picked up his phone and dialed Amy. "New Mercedes AMG S - Black... Alabama, 1Bravo 34389," Walt announced. "It entered the alley a couple minutes before the cameras went out... got to be him, but that vehicle is not on the list of his known vehicles. Tag is listed to a 2004 Buick, so it is switched... No video for 23rd street, which is where he would have exited... I have people scanning all the cameras downtown to see if we can locate it but that is a long shot.... Any movement there?"

"Nothing. We are sitting and watching," Amy answered. "I see you added the car to the BOLO so hopefully someone will spot it... I am open for suggestions."

Nate's voice came over the phone, "Walt, go downstairs and talk to the Earl guy.... See if he knows the car or knows anywhere that Tyler would likely take her."

Walt sprang from his desk, "Great idea... I'm heading down the stairs now. By the way, her phone was tossed in the dumpster behind the building... he didn't even turn it off... not sure what that is about... Techs are combing through the dumpster to see if they find anything else. "

Walt continued as he descended the stairs, "On the video he looked to be wearing black latex gloves so likely didn't leave any evidence but they are combing the place. Fay's loft was locked and they made entry but everything looks normal there. I will call you back after I talk to Earl."

Walt found Earl asleep in the bunk of the holding cell. "Hey Earl, wake up we need to talk!" He announced.

Earl jumped up, startled and took a second to get his bearings.

"I am Detective Walt Ellison, I work with Nate and Jerome." Walt said. "Have you ever seen Jay in a black Mercedes?" he asked showing him the freeze frame he had just printed.

Earl scratched his head, "Maybe… I mean that dude had a lot of cars, but no, I can't say I ever seen him with a Mercedes." Earl walked over closer to the bars in front of Walt and continued, "Now I do know for a fact that he had several Mercedes and Lexus boosted from the dealerships off 459. He had someway of getting the electronic keys and guys would just go in at night and drive them off. Me and Slick delivered a Lexus to New Orleans… I think he was sending them overseas or something.... We was coming back from there when he called us about the Toyota.... I told the other guys about that."

"How often did this happen?" Walt asked.

"Ah, man, I don't know... I just heard about it and I made that one delivery... I think he like took orders and then would get them specifically, you know... always went to New Orleans... we dropped that one at a warehouse near the port. Slick parked it and then got in the car with me and we headed back."

Walt leaned on the bars. "Earl, we think Jay may have kidnapped someone tonight... do you have any idea where he may take someone like that?"

Earl's face showed his surprise by the question. "Oh shit, man, I have no idea... I didn't get involved in anything like that, man."

Walt tried to remain calm but he knew time was running out, "I know man, just think... of all the places he had, where would he take someone... are there any other places we don't know about? What is the most secure? Anything is better than nothing!"

Earl sat on the edge of his bunk with his head in his hands. "Man, I don't know of any place... your detectives knew more places than I did, you know... The most secure is probably the warehouse where we unloaded the trucks... it's there all by itself, you know... that's where we always unloaded the trucks... I heard that once he snatched like five cars and they brought them there and loaded 'em into two trailers and took to New Orleans.... That was before my time though. I just heard about it."

"So you are talking about the warehouse out in Ensley," Walt asked. "The old steel mill?"

Earl stood back up, "Yeah, man that place is out there... especially at night it is kinda creepy, you know."

"There is only one way in and out, right... off Avenue J, I think," Walt asked.

Earl nodded, "Yep, you turn off Avenue J at the entrance and the gate is probably a couple of hundred yards back off the road. That is the way we went... Slick had a key to the lock on the gate... but it ain't the only way in."

Walt was caught off guard by this revelation. "What do you mean? I looked at the Google satellite photo and I didn't see another way in or out," Walt said.

Earl walked back over close to Walt and peered through the bars at him as if to reveal a big secret, "That's the only way I have ever been but that night we unloaded the truck, Big John and The Boss led the truck in from the back side. Later Slick told me there was a way they came through the fence from the old U.S. Steel plant... you know that place is huge... it goes on for miles and miles.... Evidently they would roll back the fence and come in that way and didn't have to come through the neighborhood... you know that plant has been shut down for years... my granddaddy used to work out there... he died not long after I was born. I ain't sure where exactly, but there is another way in."

"Thanks Earl!" Walt shouted as he turned and hurried away down the hall. He sprinted back up the steps and dialed Amy, "Who is sitting on the Avenue J warehouse site?"

"Rick and Julie are still there," Nate answered. "Fay and Jerome were supposed to relieve them, why?"

Walt was now pulling up the Google image of the site on his computer. "I assume that haven't seen a Mercedes come in, have they?" Walt asked.

Nate was a bit perturbed by the question, "No, I am sure we would have heard about that... do you think he is going there?" He asked.

Walt zoomed in on the image and moved around the perimeter of the property. "Earl just told me there is another way into that site... I am looking at the Google image and trying to figure it out... he's never been in that way but said the boss led trucks in and out from the back... thinks they came through the old U. S. Steel plant property and through the fence somehow. I am looking at it now... there is an unnamed road that runs of Valley Road between Republic Fabrication and Vulcan Materials plants... it winds back in to the old USS property along the railroad and right past the target property... it would be easy to have a gate or a hole in the fence and get in that way. Do you think it is worth a shot to check it out? I can head that way."

"No stay put for now, we may need your navigation," Nate answered. "Jerome should be here in a minute, a patrol car picked him up and he is now in his car heading this way… I will jump in and we will check it out, but we may need your guidance to get in there."

Walt was less than thrilled that everyone was in the field but him, but he understood. His phone buzzed on his desk… it was Auto Theft. "Ellison, SCU," he answered.

"Hi Walt, It's Jim… I have my whole team screening video looking for the Mercedes…. I think we found it. We picked it up on I-59/20 going west but that camera is bad and we couldn't get the tag… We picked up again at the Ensley Ave exit and tag confirms… went toward Pratt City but as you may know, not too many cameras out there. But I thought you should know… the time stamp was 19:04 at the exit if that helps."

Walt recovered from his funk and dialed Nate. "Mercedes was confirmed exiting at Ensley Avenue at 19:04 heading toward Pratt City… that lines up with our assumption. Do you want me to send the Calvary?" Walt asked.

"No! If he sees us coming there is no telling what he may do," Nate answered. "Jerome is with me now and we are heading out there. According to my phone we should be two minutes away from the unnamed road. Can you tell from the satellite image.... Can we drive that... I mean does it look passable? It's hard to tell on my phone it looks like part of the railroad tracks once you get in there."

"Yeah, it's a satellite image so I can't be sure, but if they have been driving trucks in and out it should be passable," Walt said as he zoomed in on the image.

"Can you activate the tracker on Jerome's car and see us? Nate asked. "How accurate are those things?"

Walt was clicking the program open. "Okay, I have you on my screen... supposed to be accurate to within 3 meters... okay, the road is coming up on your right," Walt said.

"Okay, there is a pig trail between the fences here... is this the road?" Nate asked.

Walt watched the blinking dot on his computer screen. "Yep, that should be it… it will follow the Vulcan Materials fence for about a half mile and then it runs beside the railroad tracks for about three miles to the back of the target. "How is the surface?"

Nate and Jerome were now off the grid on the unnamed road. Nate viewed the complete blackness that surrounded them. "Not too bad actually. I mean it is an old gravel road. There's weeds everywhere… you can tell it isn't traveled much… would likely be hell in the summertime. It is dark as pitch out here… there is certainly no light pollution here. We are going slow because you only see where your headlights are… can you conference Amy in with us, Walt?" Nate asked. "She is with Julie and Rick at the service station near the front entrance. I want them to know what is going on in case we do encounter him."

Walt dialed in Amy. "Amy, Walt here… I am conferencing us all in together… Nate, do you have us?" He asked.

Nate signaled for Jerome to stop the car. "Walt, Jerome and I are now on our Bluetooth… we don't want to spook anyone with your voice! Amy I hear you, do you have us?" He asked.

Amy answered putting her phone on speaker so that Julie and Rick could hear. "Gotcha!" she replied.

"Walt we've stopped," Nate informed them. "I don't want to get too close... how far out are we?" He asked.

Walt zoomed in on the blinking dot. "It's hard to say exactly, the fences are hard to see from the satellite image and according to my research this photo is 11 months old.... My best guess is your about 1500 meters out."

Nate nodded to Jerome and he put the car in park and killed the engine.

"Walt we are going to walk in from here... if they are there, I don't want to chance him seeing our lights and we can't drive in this darkness," Nate said.

Jerome popped the trunk and removed an AR-15 rifle and two magazines from the locker in the trunk. He handed it to Nate. He reached back in and grabbed the Remington 870 Shotgun. He slung the gun strap over his left shoulder and then retrieved a belt lined with shotgun shells and fastened it around his body.

"How's your flashlight?" Jerome asked.

Nate pulled his light out and turned it on. "New batteries... let's go," he said.

The two men took off toward their target in a fast walk. Nate whispered into his headset, "Walt, is there any kind of landmark that will tell us when we are there?"

Walt zoomed in on the satellite photo again. "There looks to be some sort of tower in the rear corner of the property... hard to tell from the overview but it's casting a shadow so if my geometry is correct it should be at least sixty feet tall. I know it's dark but you should be able to see it when you're close."

Jerome signaled Nate to stop with a raised closed fist and pointed ahead to their right. About three hundred feet in the distance stood a metal structure that appeared to be an old crane base or something similar. The men moved to a single file formation and hugged the fence line and proceeded. As they neared the tower, they could see a section of the fence rolled neatly back opening a space about ten feet wide in the chain-link.

Nate whispered in his headset. "There is an opening in the fence and tire marks leading in... you guys notify the tactical team and be ready to roll on our command. There is a large building about a hundred meters inside... no movement or lights visible. We are going in."

Nate checked his watch – 19:27. He hoped that they were not too late. He took a deep breath and nodded to Jerome. The pair slipped through the fence and ran to the base of the tower.

Chapter 54

Thursday, December 10, 2017: 19:17

Fay fidgeted in the metal chair as Tyler pulled up another chair and sat in front of her. There was about five feet of space between them. At first he said nothing and just stared at her with a slight sarcastic smile.

"Where the hell are we?" Fay said finally.

Tyler's smile broadened, "We are in a safe place... where we can talk... something you and I have never really done."

Fay tried to find a way to get comfortable but that was not possible on the small metal chair with her arms bound tightly behind her. "So, what do you want to talk about?" she asked.

"Oh, we are going to talk about you ... and me... us," Tyler sadi still smiling.

Fay stared at him as she tried to figure out what his intentions were. She knew that the longer she could keep him talking, the longer she would stay alive and have more time to figure out some way to get out of this in one piece. "If we are going to talk, you've got to help me... my arms are killing me.... Can you at least, move the cuffs to the front?" She asked.

Tyler didn't answer but looked as though he was considering the request.

"Come on, you have eyes on me and a gun in your hand, what am I going to do?" Fay pleaded.

Tyler stood up and pointed the gun at her. "Get on your knees," he commanded. "You make the slightest move and you're dead... Understand?"

Fay eased out of the chair and rested her knees on the dirty concrete floor. Tyler stepped carefully to the side and then around behind her moving the chair aside with his foot. He holstered the gun and pulled out a large knife from his belt and sliced through the zip tie freeing her hands.

"Slowly raise your hands together straight over your head," he said.

Fay did as commanded as she felt the blood returning to her fingers. Tyler pulled another tie from his back pocket and zipped it around her wrist. He then moved back around to face her.

"Is that better?" he asked smiling. Fay was on her knees below this mad man and was still not sure what her options were.

"Yes, thank you," she finally said slowly dropping her arms in front of her. Tyler reached out and helped her return to the chair.

"So, Fay, You're the cop… I know you have questions, don't you?" He asked.

Fay looked into his eyes still trying to figure it all out and then finally asked, "Why?"

Tyler chuckled lightly, "Ah, you can do better than that! That's not much of a question. Why what?" he asked.

"Why this?" Fay responded. "You've obviously been a successful criminal for a long time and gone undetected. Why risk staging bodies and now kidnapping me?"

A big smile returned to Tyler's face and he leaned back in the chair. "The simple answer is it was all for you Fay!" he said. He could see the slight surprise register on Fay's face as he continued. "It's always been about you, but you were too blind or caught up in your own ego to ever notice," he said in a firm but calm tone, still smiling. His voice gained intensity and the smile disappeared to a stern look as he spoke again, "Those days at the academy… I thought the world revolved around you… but you never even acknowledged my existence… did you?" He looked at Fay with a determined stare.

"Vince, I remember that you were an excellent training officer. I am sorry if I never expressed that… I was only at the academy part-time…"

Tyler cut her off, "Yeah you were the rising star... catching the big cases and getting promotions… never time for a guy like me, huh?"

Fay was processing the information and beginning to understand the mindset that motivated Tyler. "Vincent, I am sorry if I ever mistreated you. I promise that was not my intention. I was kind of single-minded in those days, I will admit." She could tell that her contrition and tone calmed the anger and resentment slightly.

Tyler stood and paced before stopping behind the chair he had just occupied and looked down at Fay. "Yeah, you weren't the only one with ambition, you know... mine went sideways after I got fired but that turned out to be a good thing," he said. "Turns out I was a good criminal. You know how cops always say criminals are dumb? It's mostly true! Just look at the dumb shits that work for me! But, you know, if you use your brains, the sky is the limit." Tyler's words were coming faster as he explained his history to Fay. "Over the last few years I have amassed more money than I will ever be able to spend. You see, it turns out the badass criminals these days are the Mexican and South America Cartels. They are ruthless sons of bitches and I got caught up in their shit before I knew what was up. Turns out the only thing those bastards are scared of is each other! So I used my wit and training to slowly eliminate them and point the finger at the other."

Tyler sat back in the metal chair and leaned toward Fay as he continued, "I spent over two years systematically killing off two cartel operations and blaming them for it all... and the whole time I took over the operations for myself," he said as big grin flashed on his face. "The Rinossas thought the Mendezes had taken them over and vice versa.... Took them three more years to figure it out... which is the real reason it is time for me to retire... but as I said, I got more money than I can ever spend anyway," he said as the grin faded to a more serious face and he stood again behind the chair.

"I had my retirement set already for the end of the year... I was gonna disappear into the sunset, you know... but then I that whole thing with Emma happened and I thought it would be a good way to say good-bye to you!" He said leaning down with a sadistic smile that sent a chill up Fay's spine. The evil smirk seemed to intensify as he continued, "You know I saw her and thought she was hot and recruited her to work for me... then I found out she had the kids tagging along... but I thought she may be worth the hassle... I mean I am sure you have seen her before you pulled her out... she was a fine piece of ass."

Tyler began to pace again and seemed to be thinking of how he would continue the story. "I underestimated her though. I will admit that... had her pegged as a perfect ignorant country girl that I could make some money on and have a little fun with. I mean she was so desperate and gullible when I found her... the kids they were too young, but you know in a couple of years perverts would be paying big money from them too. Anyway, when I got her here and met the kids, the irony dawned on me and immediately I thought of you... back at the academy talking about the Hawes murders and how ole Dickie offed the whole family so he could marry a new bride.... I mean what are the chances that all the names matched up and all." He sat back down and leaned into look directly into Fay's eyes to make sure she was listening. She was fixated on the explanation.

"Anyway, she turned out to be too much trouble... bitch tried to kill me you know... of course, you see how that turned out for her... so what was I supposed to do with two kids who just happen to be witness to the whole fiasco... so again, you came to mind! I thought, I am about to disappear. What better gift could I leave for you than a case you could add to your lectures?" he said as the evil smile returned with even more intensity. "Of course, then my dipshits kinda screwed up the whole quiet exit sort of thing and you guys started nosing a little too close... but I just couldn't leave without sharing with you... telling you good-bye, you know?"

Fay sat in silence trying to process all the information.

"You are being very quiet... don't you have anything to say?" He asked.

Fay sat up straight and said, "So flaunting all this and taking all these chances were for my benefit? What did I ever do to make you hate me that much?"

Tyler chuckled his evil laugh again, "Oh Fay, don't flatter yourself... it wasn't all about you... I kind of got over that years ago... let's just say it was a cosmic alignment or something... me running into this girl named Emma, who just happened to have two kids named May and Irene... I mean what are the fucking odds? And then I had to cave her skull in and get rid of the kids... so it just seemed like it was meant to be, you know? I would've been long gone by now if they had got rid of the car like they were supposed to but that gave you guys a head start and so I called an audible... you still a big football fan aren't you? Audible is right isn't it?"

Tyler looked at his watch. "Well, I hate to wrap the party up so soon, but I cannot chance your flunkies tracking us down... but I have got one more surprise before you go," he announced. Tyler reached into a small duffle bag on the floor that he had brought in with them. He pulled out a Glock pistol and racked the slide back loading a round into the chamber.

"Recognize this?" he asked holding the gun out in front Fay.

Fay did not respond.

"Of course, you don't... all these things look alike, don't they? Don't you miss the old cowboy days when everyone had a revolver and you could get your name engraved on it or put on pearly handles or something? Those were the days." He laughed that sinister laugh again. "Of course, if you had one those against one of these, you'd be deader than fried chicken, wouldn't you?" He said. Tyler was the only one laughing and his face turned immediately sincere again. He bounced the gun on his fingers in front of Fay again.

"This gun here... I took this off your boyfriend Billy before I lit his ass up!" he announced.

That news struck every nerve in Fay's body as a wave of both panic and nausea raged through her like a gulf coast rip current.

"Oh yeah, you had no idea did you?" he said seeing the shock on her face.

Fay could tell that Tyler was delighted at her surprise and whatever look her face was conveying. Her head was spinning. She had never even considered his involvement in Bill's murder. The Fed's were handling the case and she put it behind her years ago for her own sanity.

"Yep, Ole Billy figured out that the Frat Boy network that the Feds were working to bust down in Tuscaloosa was bigger than that... He was good. I will give him credit. He figured out that I had duped the cartels and was making bank on both cartels operations so I couldn't let him undo all my hard work... It was him or me, I hope you understand that," he said in a sickening sarcastic voice.

Fay doubled over in the chair and groaned loudly.

"Aww, don't get sick on me now," Tyler laughed. He placed his hand on Fay's chin and lifted her face to see tears streaming down her face. Before he could say anything else, Fay sprang forward, the crown of her head colliding with his face as her bound arms swept across his hands and the Glock went sailing across the room. He staggered back, blood flowing from his nose and mouth. He reached his right hand back to find his gun in the small of his back but the blow had slowed his reflexes. Before he could find the handle, Fay's bound hands pulled the knife from his belt on his left and with one quick motion she shoved the blade deep into front of his throat and he dropped the gun that had just cleared the holster.

Tyler's eyes bulged and he gasped for air that was not there as Fay withdrew the knife. He tried to regain his balance as she shoved the blade into his abdomen just below his ribs. He groaned loudly and blood spewed from the wound in his neck as he exhaled and dropped to his knees still looking at Fay. Their eyes locked as she raised the knife to strike again. Tyler toppled to his left, his face crashing into the metal chair before striking the concrete with a thud.

His eyes fixed and open as the blood began to puddle under him.

Chapter 55

Thursday, December 10, 2017

Fay was not sure how she was still standing. Her gaze was fixed on the lifeless figure at her feet. She kicked the gun beside Tyler away and took a deep breath. She tried to turn the knife around to cut the zip tie that bound her hands and something caught her attention outside the door. She recoiled and reached for the gun on the floor. She was relieved as she saw Jerome dart toward the office. She yelled, "Jerome! In here! I am safe!"

Fay saw his head pop up in the window beside the door. He looked horrified at her and then glanced down at the body on the floor as the door swung open and Nate came in, AR-15 in hand and ready.

"You good, boss? Nate asked. "Anyone else here?"

She sank back into the chair and her body seemed to melt. "No, I don't thinks so… it was just us." Her voice was quiet.

Nate kneeled down beside her and placed his gloved hand on hers, as he removed the knife from her hands and placed it in an evidence bag. He removed his knife from his pocket and cut the zip tie freeing her hands.

Jerome was on the phone with the others and announced, "Tact is sweeping the perimeter just to be sure. Boss, do you need the medics?" He asked.

She stared at the indentions in her wrists and rubbed them with her bloody hands. "No, I am okay. I head butted him so I have a headache, but otherwise, I am good, I think." Fay took a deep breath and leaned back in the chair. Somehow she found comfort in the hard metal that had been so unpleasant just moments ago. Her hands and arms were covered in blood that was already beginning to dry in places. She felt cold and wet as she looked down to see that her tee shirt was saturated in blood. She looked down at her jeans and shoes that were splattered and soaked also.

"He killed Bill," she said without any preface.

Jerome was standing in the door watching as the Calvary began to descend on the scene. Nate was kneeling over the body and checking for a pulse. Both turned, not sure they heard correctly.

"Your Bill?" Nate asked.

Fay nodded slowly, "Yes, it's a long story... he told me everything... but that will have to wait until the morning," she said. "I know I have to give IA a statement tonight, but then I am going home and have a very stiff drink... or three. I will deal with the paperwork tomorrow."

Within minutes the scene was crawling with cops. Evidence Technicians from the Crime Scene Unit were taking photographs and measurements. The Medical Examiner was collecting the body. Fay had discarded her bloody clothes, which were now stored in evidence bags collected by the techs along with everything else at the scene. She was dressed in a pair of police coveralls two sizes too large and had recited the story of what happened three times to Internal Affairs detectives and the FBI who had arrived on the scene. It was now just after midnight and the adrenaline had drained from her body. She was tired. She was exhausted. Finally, it was over – she could hardly remember what day it was. The entire team was there waiting. Certainly, no one was going to leave, but no one quiet knew what to do either. There had been other situations where officers had to use deadly force, but no one had been kidnapped, let alone the boss.

When Fay finally emerged from the mobile crime scene unit where she had been interviewed, they all greeted her. Even Walt had made it to the scene to join his team. She hugged them all and thanked them. Few words were spoken.

Fay tried to lighten the mood. "I am done here, who wants to take me home?" she asked. "And, by the way, I will be late tomorrow and as soon as my report is complete, I am leaving early!" They all laughed.

"We are all headed home, we can give you a ride under one condition – we get the weekend off!" Nate said.

Amy put her arm around her, "Let's go home!" Amy dropped Fay off at her loft. Fay took the elevator up and saw three post-it notes on her door:

Fay, we broke your lock getting in... nice place! New lock installed and your key should work. I took the liberty of replacing the damaged cameras and while we were at it we upgraded them all to High Definition and added some so this kind of shit will be harder next time! --- D. Guyer

Fay laughed out loud. She went in, poured a glass of Dettling's Bespoke Bourbon from the top shelf of the bar. She made her way to the bathroom and turned on the shower. She drank the whiskey and watched as the steam billowed above the glass. She stepped out of the coveralls and into the hot shower. Her mind wanted to retrace the bizarre day, but it was just too exhausted.

She watched as Vincent Tyler's blood swirled on the tile floor beneath her and disappeared down the drain. She felt empty. Why was she not more emotional? Could she really be that tired? She stepped out and dried off. She finished the whiskey and fell into bed and went to sleep immediately.

Chapter 56

Friday, December 11, 2017

Fay awoke and looked at her phone. It was 9:38. She could not remember the last time she slept past 7. She had 47 text messages, 183 emails and 17 missed phone calls. "Well I am guessing I made the morning news cycle," she thought. She still felt numb. She knew this was going to take some time. She had to go in and file her mandatory reports, but she would be on administrative leave until the department cleared her. That would take IA ruling her actions were both justified and within department policy and being cleared by the department psychiatrist as ready and fit to return to duty.

She took her time getting ready and arrived at the office just before eleven. "Did I miss lunch?" she asked as she came in. The team all laughed and got up to greet her. It was more than a bit awkward as no one seemed to know how to act.

"Okay, I am going to say this before things get even crazier... I am fine. Physically I am fine. I slept like a rock last night, hence my timely arrival. Mentally... emotionally... I don't really know how I feel... I am still kind of numb... as you all know, I had to fire my weapon years ago and I took a life. That was hard but this time was different and I am not sure why or how, but it's different. I will work through it... I will see the shrink next week... I just don't need you guys walking on eggshells, okay? I will be off until I am cleared for duty... you all have earned some time this past week, so take it... unless we catch another case, I want you all to take some time off. It's Christmas! Spend time with your families and get away for a little while. Do not worry about me... I am fine. I am going to write up my report and get out of here. I know ya'll know this but I cannot say thank you enough... I know you were doing your job, but because you did it so well, I am alive and here and I cannot thank you enough or be more proud of you as a team."

The task force had spent the night rounding up Tyler's associates. Seventeen arrests in the Birmingham area alone. Another twelve had been arrested by the feds out of state and six warrants were still outstanding. More than fourteen million dollars in assets had been seized, including a duffle bag in the rear seat of the stolen Mercedes that contained almost three million in cash.

It would take the feds weeks to untangle the network and all the holdings but Fay knew that it would fall to others to mop up. The case was making national news and would likely bring more focus, good and bad, on Fay and the unit. Fay filed her report an hour later. Her team had already filed all the related reports and paperwork and were just waiting for Fay to finish. They each agreed to take a long weekend and Fay promised to call if she needed anything. They shared a group hug and all parted ways.

Epilogue

Saturday, December 19, 2017: 18:45

Fay looked in the mirror as she brushed her hair. It had been exactly one week since the case wrapped and her world changed forever. She was looking forward to the Downtowner's Christmas Party tonight. Although she had been cleared for duty two days earlier, she made the decision to burn the weeks of vacation that she had been accumulating. The SCU was in good hands and she needed time away. She had a lot to think about – work, her personal life, her future... she resolved that her thoughts were normal for a person of her age, especially considering what had just occurred.

Reflections of a career and life in general were inevitable and they had crept into her consciousness several times in the last few years but she suppressed them to be dealt with at a later time. That time had now come. She had resumed sessions with her therapist and was trying to deal with it all. No matter how she framed it, her life was changed one week ago and it would never be the same... ***she*** would never be the same. She contemplated retirement. After all, she had her years in, but she could not picture what that would look like. She liked teaching but not enough to do only that. It had always been a diversionary thing. A way of passing on her experiences to the next generation, but she knew she could never *JUST* teach. At the same time, right now she could not imagine going back to work, but somehow that felt like she was quitting... giving up and that was definitely not her. She had the time, so she was taking it.

She knew that time would ease things, but she also knew this was different. She had experienced big cases. She had dealt with taking a life before. She had dealt with Bill's death. Maybe this was a culmination of all those things or maybe it was a natural progression. Whatever it was, she knew that things had changed and she had decisions to make, but there was time. She had almost eleven more weeks of time to burn. She was going to try and relax. Maybe she would take a trip. She determined that she would follow her therapist's advice finally and try new things, although she had no idea what.

Having come that close to death was something she had yet to deal with fully. During her mandatory therapy sessions last week, she was actually surprised when the therapist bought it up. She was dealing with killing another human. She was dealing with the revelation of the details of Bill's death, but the near-death experience was buried deep and she was forced to acknowledge the existence and the impact it had on her life. She wasn't sure what the future held but she was headed to a party with her dear friends and that was all she was going to concern herself with tonight.

Fay entered The Wine Loft dressed in the perfect little black dress. Smooth Jazz music filled the large room from the five-piece band in the corner led by Keith "Cashmere" Williams on guitar. The group was one of Fay's favorites. Her friends, Lisa and Peggy, greeted Fay immediately. They had been her best friends for years and both lived one block away on 1st Avenue. Peggy and her husband had recently retired and traveled as often as possible. Lisa was a recent widow and was looking forward to retirement next year. The trio had met for coffee or lunch everyday this week. Their friendship had been a great diversion from the police world and all that had happened. Their conversations were both deep and frivolous and never strayed into her work and Fay appreciated that.

Lisa whispered in her ear, "You have got to meet our new neighbor... he is divine!"
Lisa and Peggy escorted her over to a group gathered on two large sofas in the corner. Peggy made the introduction, "Fay, this is our brand new neighbor, Cole Hammonds, he is moving into our building next week."

Cole stood and extended a hand. "Very nice to meet you, Fay... I have heard a lot about you."

Cole was a handsome man in his late fifties or early sixties. He was tall, at least six-three or more. His smile and handshake were sincere.

"Nice to meet you Cole," Fay responded and took a seat. "So what brings you to Birmingham?" Fay asked.

"Oh I grew up here," he answered. "I've been gone for a while but I coming home," he said with a smile.

During the conversation that ensued through the evening, Fay learned that Cole was an artist and a writer. He had traveled a lot and lived in various places around the world but mostly in New York and Washington, D.C.

"Cole is such an interesting name," Fay offered.

"Well, until I was about thirty I was known to most as Bobby, but then some art agent thought that Cole could sell more than Bobby and so I began using my middle name. I haven't had a real job since, so I guess it worked!" They both laughed. The party rocked on and Fay mingled with all of her familiar Downtown friends and met many newcomers. Just after eleven, Cole found her again.

"Fay, I hope I am not out of line, but I have been back in town for three days and I have already started a tradition of having a nightcap on the roof of the Empire Building. Would you do me the honor of joining me tonight?" He asked. Fay was caught off guard with the invitation but could feel a huge smile on her face. She could not explain that smile but decided to embrace it.

"That sounds fabulous," she said. Moments later the two were heading down 1st Avenue to the "Heaviest Corner on Earth." The title was bestowed upon the corner of 1st Avenue and 20th Street when four skyscrapers were erected almost simultaneously in the early twentieth century. An article appeared in a magazine announcing the *Heaviest Corner in the South*. Over the next few months the "south" had somehow transformed into the "world" and the moniker stuck. With the recent renovations to the four buildings, large brass medallions had been incorporated into the sidewalks of each corner commemorating the title.

The Empire Building had been transformed from an office tower into a Boutique Hotel with an award-winning restaurant on the ground floor and a bar called *Moonshine* on the roof that provided panoramic views of the city.

Fay and Cole stepped off the elevator and found a cozy spot on a sofa with a view of the Southside and ordered cocktails. Fay was lost in conversation as she learned more about Cole. Their conversation covered a variety of topics of everything but her work. She could not remember the last time she was this relaxed with someone, and this was someone she had known less than six hours. She embraced it. Maybe this was the new Fay. She smile as she thought, "I think I like this Fay."

The End

www.ingramcontent.com/pod-product-compliance
Lightning Source LLC
Chambersburg PA
CBHW060606310726
48982CB00008B/1257/J

* 9 7 8 0 9 6 0 0 3 8 3 0 5 *